Harry's Game

Hell's Corner

Harry's Game

Hell's Corner

Karl Jackson

Alpaca & Goose
2020

Book design & Illustration by Karl Jackson

First published – February 2020 by Alpaca & Goose

www.alpacagoose.com

First Edition

ISBN 978-1-9162651-1-0

www.harrysgame.com

'Friends'

Dedicated to 'The Few'

The women of the Air Transport Auxiliary, whose bravery, sacrifice, and dedication to duty during history's darkest hour, paved the way for future generations of female aviators

Chapter 1

Waking

"Good morning, young lady," a soft, yet firm Scottish accent said, as Harriet opened her eyes wide with surprise and looked urgently around the room. The walls were a brilliant white, as was almost everything else, with a brightness that made Harriet squint and blink. "You've had a good sleep!"

"What?" Harriet gasped, coughing as her words tickled her dry throat. She blinked again, as the sound of pouring water was followed by a glass appearing in front of her. She wriggled up the stack of soft pillows to prop herself up, before reaching forward and pausing momentarily to look in fascination at the rainbow coloured beams of light that were dancing through the glass. She took it and looked at the owner of the hand that had offered it, a nurse, dressed in her clinically pristine blue and white uniform. She had dark hair, neatly tied back under her hat, and piercing turquoise eyes which flared with equal parts compassion and stern authority. Harriet drank the water and sighed with relief as it cooled and softened her dry, burning throat. "Thank you," she gasped after she'd sipped, then quickly gulped the entire glass. "Could I please have some more?" The nurse nodded and poured more water from a large jug, which Harriet quickly gulped down before holding the glass out again.

"That's enough for now," the nurse said as she took the glass.

"But I'm thirsty."

"I'm not surprised, you've been asleep for three days. You can have some more in a while, but for now we need to give you a check over and see how you are."

"Where am I?" Harriet asked as she looked down at herself. When she first opened her eyes, she'd thought for a moment that she'd died and gone to heaven; but when she took a minute to compose herself she realised that she was nestled comfortably between thick, clean, white sheets, and a tightly tucked royal blue blanket that matched the nurse's blouse; and she accepted that in all likelihood she wasn't in heaven. If she were dead, she wouldn't feel quite as bad, or at least she hoped she wouldn't. If she were dead, she probably wouldn't be wearing a nightshirt either, and her right arm wouldn't be neatly dressed in a bandage as white as the sheets, that crisscrossed its way from her hand to halfway between her elbow and shoulder.

"Under the tongue," the nurse instructed, then without hesitation popped a thermometer in Harriet's mouth, before putting her hand under her chin and gently, yet firmly, pushing her jaw closed. "You're in a hospital, of course. Where else would you be?" Harriet tried to open her mouth to answer, for a moment forgetting the narrow rod of warming glass under her tongue. "Careful, thermometers are expensive. We can't afford to break one, can we? Not with a war on." Harriet sat back against the pillows and looked around the room. The only other colour in the sea of white and blue came from a beautiful bunch of flowers sitting in a vase on the dresser opposite the bed. She then looked at the nurse again, as she took her wrist and felt for her pulse while looking studiously at her fob watch. Harriet watched her closely. She was young, but not too young. She had no wrinkles or signs of age, but she looked mature somehow. Harriet guessed somewhere in the mid twenties, maybe, but no older. The nurse released Harriet's wrist, and whipped the thermometer from her mouth, then shook it and slipped it into a pocket in her apron.

"Am I alive?"

"You'll do. How's your arm?" she asked, as she lifted the sleeve of Harriet's nightdress and checked the bandages.

"Tingling."

"Good!"

"Is it?"

"Isn't it?"

"Nurse Strachan, report your patient!" an older and even more stern looking nurse demanded as she entered the room, accompanied by an elderly doctor. Harriet's nurse stood smartly to attention and gave a sharp nod.

"Good morning, Sister. Good morning, Doctor Goode. My patient is female, approximately twenty years of age."

"Her presentation?"

"Currently conscious. Blood pressure one hundred and eighteen over seventy eight, pulse fifty five beats per minute, with a strong and regular beat, and respirations of fifteen breaths per minute. Temperature ninety eight point six Fahrenheit."

"And she's thirsty," Harriet added.

"Her history?" the Sister continued, totally ignoring Harriet. Something which made her frown in disgust.

"Believed to be a pilot who was rescued from the Channel suffering from acute hypothermia. She has a deep puncture to the right forearm, topical burns between the right wrist and elbow, superficial burns to the neck and right side of the face, thirteen minor puncture wounds, and superficial scratches to the right arm and hand."

"And the treatment?"

"Being ignored," Harriet replied. "I really can't be part of this pantomime!" She sat up, ready to pull off the sheets and get out of the bed. "Where are my clothes?"

11

"They'll be brought to you when the doctor decides you're leaving!" the Sister said forcefully. "Now sit still!" Harriet froze instinctively and stared at the angry little Sister. "Really, Nurse Strachan. You must learn to manage your patients!"

"Yes, Sister."

"Well, it appears our patient is at least ambulatory," the doctor said as he ignored the escalating scene. "Remove the bandage please, Nurse Strachan, and I'll have a look at the burn." He pulled his stethoscope from around his neck while looking closely in Harriet's eyes, each in turn. She raised an eyebrow in response. "OK, follow my finger," he drew a large figure of eight in the air and watched closely as her eyes tracked his finger. "Good, good. Sit forward for me!" He pushed the stethoscope cup against her back. "Deep breaths. Good. Cough. Again. Good. So, how are you feeling?" Harriet continued looking at the flowers across from the bed, while Nurse Strachan took the fresh bandage from her arm. "Miss?" The doctor tapped Harriet on the shoulder.

"Me?" Harriet asked.

"Who else?"

"I don't know. I thought I was invisible."

"Ah, you haven't stayed in a hospital that much, have you?" he asked with a smile. Harriet shook her head and shrugged. "We have lots of routines and procedures, things that may appear a little strange to an outsider. Probably a little similar to your air force, whose rules and orders I'm quite sure you'd agree would confuse the likes of the nurses and me?"

"Well they confuse me, so I suppose you're right."

"Quite. So, how are you feeling?"

"I don't know... Thirsty?"

"Yes, well, I suppose that's to be expected. You'd swallowed a lot of saltwater while bobbing around in the Channel, which can be quite dehydrating. Not to mention the damage done by that burn on your arm. Speaking of which, how did that happen? If you don't mind me asking?"

"The engine of my aeroplane caught fire after I was shot down by a German, and I was trapped in the burning cockpit when I crashed on the beach at Dunkirk." She frowned as she remembered being terrified as the cockpit filled with hot smoke and flames.

"I see... And what were you doing flying over the beaches at Dunkirk?"

"Shooting down Germans."

"Shooting down Germans? From an aeroplane?"

"Well I wasn't riding a seagull!"

"No..." he let out a laugh. "I don't suppose you were."

"I'm a girl... I know."

"Well yes, so do I. I may be old, but the basics of human anatomy haven't changed that much, and I like to think I can still tell female from male." Harriet felt herself smiling involuntarily. "It was a silly question on my part, I suppose. It's just that I've never met a female fighter pilot before. My apologies."

"It's fine," Harriet said as she relaxed a little, smiling at being called a fighter pilot. "Am I OK?" she asked as he started checking the burn on her arm.

"Surprisingly," he replied. "Considering you were swimming around in the Channel for several hours. The burn is healing remarkably well, too. You put honey on it right away?"

"The medic who found me on the beach did that."

"Well, you should track him down one day and buy him a drink. It's an old way of doing things, but his quick thinking with the honey probably saved your arm from infection. You could have lost it!" Harriet smiled and bit her tongue; the doctor probably wouldn't appreciate knowing it had been a German medic that had helped her. He continued to prod lightly at the wound. "OK, Nurse Strachan. Fresh honey and dressing, please."

"Am I OK otherwise?"

"Incredibly, yes. Aside from a little exhaustion, and some swelling in your throat; something which is explained by your story about being trapped in a confined space and breathing hot smoke. You're going to need to rest awhile, to give your body time to recover. You were quite chilled when you came in, so cold, in fact, that your body had started to shut down. If I'm honest, it was touch and go as to whether you'd pull through at all, so it's a result to have you awake and talking."

"I do feel tired..." Harriet said as she fought a yawn.

"Can you remember what happened?"

"No... Not really," she replied, after a moment searching her mind. "I remember being on a boat, and then being in the water with somebody else."

"Geoffrey Douglas."

"Excuse me?"

"Leading Seaman Geoffrey Douglas. Formerly of the HMS Magpie, I believe. He's the sailor who kept you afloat until you were picked up by a small boat heading for Dover." Harriet frowned, then smiled as she remembered the distinctly northern voice that had been ringing around her head, telling her to stay awake and kick her legs, and asking her

14

complicated maths questions. "You've been through a traumatic experience, young lady. You'll remember things, slowly, when your brain is ready." She nodded and smiled. "He's OK; you'll be happy to know. A hot meal and a night of good sleep, and more than a tipple of rum, and he was on his way back to the Navy. Another one for you to buy a drink for some time." Harriet smiled as the doctor stood back and looked at her with a warming smile. "Well, I can't stay and talk, as interesting as that might be. I have other patients to see."

"What happens next?"

"Rest... And in the meantime, I'll let our liaison officer know that you're awake. He can sort out getting you home for some sick leave. Doctor's orders."

"Home...?"

"Home, to give your body and mind time to convalesce. Don't worry; I expect there'll be plenty of war left to fight in the future. Right, must dash." He left the room with the Sister in his wake.

"You'll get me into trouble!" Nurse Strachan said with a firm look, as she finished spreading honey on the burn.

"Don't be ridiculous," Harriet replied, and received a withering look from
Strachan. "What?"

"There are rules here. You're my patient! You're supposed to lay in bed obediently, and stay quiet so that I can care for you. Sister will be furious."

"That old snapdragon?"

"That old snapdragon happens to be in charge of me, and she can make life very uncomfortable if things aren't done properly."

"Sorry..."

"You will be if you don't behave."

"You're very bossy. I thought nurses were supposed to be all compassionate."

"The two are not mutually exclusive traits. Some patients need to be managed!"

"Managed?"

"Bossed about until they behave," she said with a smirk. "So we can do our job, and be all compassionate." Harriet smiled back. "Can I ask you something?"

"I suppose?"

"What's it like? Flying, I mean?"

"Freedom," Harriet replied without hesitation.

"Freedom?"

"Yes... It's just you, alone, floating almost weightless among the clouds, and seeing the world as so few others could. The towns and the people are so small, like toys, they seem almost insignificant as you weave in and out of the clouds. It's so peaceful; you feel like you can do anything or go anywhere. When I was flying above Dunkirk I could see England, can you believe that?" Her eyes were full of passion and excitement.

"I can't begin to imagine what it's like."

"You should try it. You'd love it."

"No, thank you. Not for me."

"Why not?"

"You have to ask? You were trapped in a burning aeroplane, your burning aeroplane. That's not something I'd find particularly peaceful."

"Don't be ridiculous, that only happened because I crashed..."

"That doesn't make it sound any more appealing. Do all pilots crash? Or just the poor ones?"

"I didn't crash on purpose!"

"A careless accident?"

"A German shot me down. More than one of them, in fact!"

"Gang up on you, did they?"

"Something like that."

"They must have already met you and your winning personality."

"Thanks!"

"You're welcome. Now, how about some breakfast?"

"Yes, please, I'm starving. What's on offer?"

"I'll see what I can find... Now, sit back and relax. Remember what the doctor said, you need rest and lots of it."

Harriet did as she was told and relaxed back into the pillows that were propping her up. She looked around the room; it was starkly austere and clinically white, with not a spot of dirt or dust to be seen. The flowers in the vase opposite the bed were just about all of the colour in the room, making it a very dull place in Harriet's mind, which the longer she was awake became more active with memories, one memory in particular.

Nicole. Around and around it went, Nicole's Hurricane, burning and smoking as it disappeared into the clouds, with no response from Nicole to Harriet's desperate screams. It had been the worst battle she'd experienced in her short time flying with the RAF, and in that short time, she'd been in plenty. They must have been outnumbered by four to one, or five to one, or more. Her brain spun as she thought of it. Everywhere she turned there was a German shooting at her, gunners in bombers, fighters; everyone was having a go. The more she thought of it, the more she questioned how she'd survived, and how many more of the squadron were shot down? Did any of them make it back? Could any of them make it back through that firestorm? One memory led to another, and she felt her temperature rise as she remembered being stuck in her burning Hurricane. She could almost smell the acrid black smoke from the melting control panel, mixed with fumes from the flaming petrol leaking into the cockpit from the ruptured fuel tank.

"Hello?" Nurse Strachan said. Harriet blinked and looked up at her and smiled; she'd placed a plate of bacon and eggs on a table pulled over the bed, accompanied by some toast and a large cup of tea.

"Hello..." Harriet replied innocently, and a little confused as to how Strachan had managed to pull the table over the bed and present the breakfast without her noticing.

"Been somewhere nice?"

"I haven't left the room?"

"Your eyes suggested otherwise; you seemed miles away... Come on, sit up and I'll straighten your pillows so you can eat," Strachan ordered. Harriet did as she was asked, and Strachan straightened the pillows and piled them in a way that was very supportive and comfortable. She relaxed into them again and stared at the breakfast.

"Bacon?" Harriet asked, a little excitedly.

"Bacon."

"I haven't had bacon in a while..."

"Neither have many of us since the rationing started."

"Rationing?"

"Did you knock your head when you crashed your aeroplane, too?"

"Probably, why?"

"Because you can't remember that the bacon and eggs you're currently staring at are more than a week's rations for most of us. I haven't had bacon in months!" Strachan replied with a roll of her eyes.

"Really?" Harriet asked with a frown.

"This is going to be a difficult day, I fear," Strachan sighed. "Just eat up before it gets cold, Doctor Goode made a special order for you to have that." Harriet shrugged and chopped a piece of bacon before slipping it into her mouth, then after a couple of chews felt her eyes watering and a tear run down her cheek as the salt from the bacon burned the sores in her mouth. Not wanting to be rude, she swallowed, and the salt burned all the way down. "What is it?" Strachan asked with concern, as she noticed Harriet's distress. Harriet shook her head dismissively, then cut off another piece of bacon and started to raise it to her mouth, determined to eat the food she'd been given. She couldn't, though, it hurt too much, she put down her fork and reached for her glass of water, which Strachan quickly handed to her. "Oh gosh, it's the salt, isn't it?" Strachan asked as she realised what was happening.

"I'm sorry..." Harriet said with embarrassment as she looked away, ashamed of not being able to eat the food people had prepared specially for her.

"It's OK; I should have thought. Maybe an egg?" Harriet nodded as Strachan cleaned her fork of any residual salt before handing it back.

Harriet cut the egg and tasted it with a smile of relief. "Better?" A nod came in reply as the almost cold egg slid down her throat and soothed the burning, she quickly ate the rest of it and the second.

"Thank you," she said politely. "I'm really very sorry that I can't eat the bacon."

"Don't let it worry you."

"You have it."

"I don't think so."

"I mean it; you have it. It's my bacon, and I get to choose what happens to it."

"It goes back to the kitchen; somebody else may need it."

"They can't eat the rasher I started... They wouldn't know where it had come from, isn't there a rule that patients can't share food in a hospital? In case they have a disease or something?"

"So, you'd happily give any disease you may have to me, your nurse, but not another patient?" Strachan asked, as Harriet cut the top strip off the bacon and used the knife to push the remains across the plate towards Strachan.

"There, no disease. Take the other rasher back to the kitchen if you must, but the piece I started is yours." Strachan stared at her. "Besides, I'm an awkward patient, and if you're going to look after me, you're going to need to keep your strength up," Harriet smirked. "You know I'm right..."

"I don't..."

"I can be annoying."

"I don't doubt that."

20

"When did you last have bacon?"

"Christmas, but that's not important."

"I didn't fight Germans just so you can starve yourself!"

"I'm not starving. I had some very nice porridge this morning, thank you."

"I bet it wasn't as nice as bacon."

"It was lovely."

"Not as lovely as bacon."

"I'm sure."

"How can you be sure if you haven't tried it?"

"I know what bacon tastes like. Now, are you ready for a bath?"

"A bath?"

"Yes, I'll fetch some hot water."

"I don't want a bath!"

"You have to have a bath."

"And if I don't?"

"Then Sister will be particularly irritated."

"With you or me?"

"With both of us…"

"You'd better eat the bacon in that case."

"What?"

"You'd better eat the bacon..."

"And what's that supposed to mean, young lady?"

"It means that if you eat the bacon, I'll have my bath, and Sister doesn't need to know any different." Strachan narrowed her eyes in irritation at Harriet, then grabbed the rasher and stuffed it into her mouth. She chewed it quickly, but not so quick that she couldn't savour the taste.

"There, happy?" she asked.

"Happy," Harriet replied with a smile.

"I'd better go and prepare the hot water," Strachan said firmly as she took the plate and left the room, leaving Harriet to relax back into the pillows again with a smile of victory on her face. The smile soon faded as her mind slipped back to Nicole, and the fun they used to have bickering with each other. They argued frequently, and they teased, but they always smiled and never fell out, even when the bickering led to fighting and wrestling. They were happy memories, happy but tinged with a heavy sadness of Nicole no longer being around, and that led to the persistent image of Nicole's Hurricane spiralling into the clouds trailing black smoke and streaks of flame. Tears ran down Harriet's cheeks as she stared at the flowers on the dresser across the room. Not seeing them, just gazing into space while thinking about the battle and her friends from the squadron. Did anyone make it back? What about Cas? He'd led them into the fight of their lives, he was an ace with lines of medals on his chest, but he hadn't flown in combat for years, decades even. Would he be rusty? Would his skills be lacking? He was much older than everyone else, were his reflexes as sharp? Or was he sitting at the bottom of the Channel strapped into his Hurricane and staring at nothing? "Hello?" Strachan's voice cut through the thoughts again, eventually. Harriet quickly blinked and rubbed the tears from her face, desperate not to be seen crying.

"Hello," she replied.

"Welcome back."

"Did I go somewhere?"

"You tell me."

"I don't think so?"

"You don't?"

"I don't."

"You know if you ever want to talk..."

"About what?"

"About wherever you go to in your mind that's so upsetting and consuming for you."

"What makes you think anything is upsetting and consuming me?"

"Nursing is more than bandaging wounds and bed baths, you know. The mind is as important as the body, and if there's something bothering us, it can be as harmful as an infection; and in some cases, it can kill us just as easily."

"I'm fine."

"If you say so, but we both know that's not true. I know you were shot down and burned, and I can't begin to imagine how terrifying that was for you, but there's something else, something more than that. You're sad about something, not scared."

23

"Get out of my head!"

"Excuse me?"

"Never mind. Weren't you going to take me for a bath? Shouldn't we be going?" Harriet sat forward and pulled at the bedclothes, only for Strachan to hold them firmly in place.

"You're not going anywhere."

"I'm not?"

"You're not... You're on bed rest, which means the bath comes to you."

"I don't understand?"

"Bath time," Strachan said with a cheerful smile, as she lifted a white washcloth and a bar of soap from behind the steaming bowl of hot water.

"No!" Harriet said as her eyes opened wide.

"No?"

"No! You're not bathing me!"

"Well, you're entitled to your opinion on that, but you will be having a bath. Sister's orders."

"Don't be ridiculous!" Harriet said as she blushed, while Strachan soaked the cloth and scrubbed it with the bar of soap. "I'm perfectly able to bathe myself!"

"Oh, for goodness sake," Strachan said with a sigh. "Look, you've got nothing I haven't seen before, I'm a nurse. Besides, how do you think you got into that nightdress?" Harriet looked down and blushed more. "Now, enough of this nonsense. I have a job to do!" Harriet let out a snarl of irritation, then let go of the covers and flopped back into the pillows while Strachan started her work.

"Get it over with, then."

"For a fighter pilot, you really are such a baby."

"Because you're treating me like a baby by bathing me. No one has washed me since I was five."

"You should make the most of it; some people pay a fortune for this service in the most exclusive spas."

"I'm not in a most exclusive spa; I'm in... I don't even know where I am!"

"Kent... On the coast, about halfway between Dover and Folkeştone."

"How did I get here?"

"An army doctor brought you after you were landed at Dover. He thought it would be inappropriate to send you to one of the large hospitals where all the male casualties were being seen, so he brought you here, to our small country hospital. It makes sense, I suppose."

"Are there other female casualties?"

"A couple, but not many. Most of our patients are either locals or army officers. Apparently, it was thought they shouldn't share a hospital with the other ranks, either. Though in my mind, that makes much less sense."

"What's your name?"

"Nurse Strachan."

"Yes, I know that, but if we're going to get to know each other well enough for you to bathe me, I'd like to know your name."

"Emily."

"Emily... I like that. It suits you."

"Thank you... And what should I call you, fighter pilot?"

"Harry."

"Harry?"

"Yes... It's what I prefer."

"Well if you prefer it, Harry it is," Strachan said with a shrug, and Harriet smiled at her.

"How long do you think I'll be here?"

"I don't know, long enough for you to recover properly, I should think."

"I don't even know what that means. What exactly is wrong with me? Is it my arm and mouth?"

"Well they're the obvious things, but not the only things."

"Then what?"

"Exhaustion."

"I still don't understand. You mean that I'm tired?"

"Your body's tired. You were already injured from your crash, and your mouth, throat, and lungs were burned by the hot air in your aeroplane, that makes it difficult to breathe properly, which makes it difficult to get oxygen around your body. Then you spent hours in cold, oily water. Reducing your body temperature, shutting you down, and preparing you to die. It was close..."

"I do feel tired..."

"It's not surprising. Maybe you can get some sleep when I'm finished?"

"Maybe... Do you think if I'm feeling better soon, they'll let me go back to my squadron?"

"I doubt that. The doctor has already said that he's sending you home to convalesce. You need to get your strength back before you can go back to flying. No, you'll likely have to go home for a while, wherever home may be?"

"A long way from here."

"Mine too."

"I noticed your accent. Scottish, isn't it?"

"Very good, can you guess where in Scotland?"

"Sorry..."

"Up on the west coast."

"Why did you move down here?"

"It's warmer..." Harriet let out a giggle as Emily gave her a mischievous smile. "There," she said after finishing the bed bath. "Wasn't that bad, was it?"

"I suppose not."

"I'll try not to take that as a criticism of my bathing skills."

"Maybe you need more practice."

"I'll remind you of that when you're next complaining about having to be bathed..."

"I could get used to having a servant bathe me."

"Careful," Emily smirked. "Now get some rest, and I'll be back to check on you later."

"You're leaving?"

"Why, are you going to miss me?"

"I don't think so."

"Good. Now rest." Emily lifted the pillow and Harriet snuggled down into the bed again, then wriggled and got comfortable as Emily left the room. She stared at the ceiling a while, then quickly and unexpectedly drifted into a deep sleep.

The routine repeated in the afternoon, mostly anyway, the bed bath excepted. She had a lunch comprised of chewy brown bread and mild cheese with a cup of tea; followed by a check over by the doctor on his afternoon rounds. Then back to bickering with Emily about the ridiculousness of having to use a bedpan instead of being allowed to go to the toilet properly, then falling asleep again. The evening had no inspection, just a meat and potato stew, a wash, and being tucked in to sleep solidly through the night, disturbed only by the repetitive cycle of miserable dreams about burning in a Hurricane, or seeing Nicole burn in a Hurricane, or the new addition of Cas sitting at the bottom of the Channel strapped into his Hurricane. If anything, she'd prefer to have been woken for a bath than to live in the dreams, but she wasn't, so she stayed in her dreams until the morning routine started again, with Emily preparing her for the morning inspection by Doctor Goode and the grumpy Sister. She was on her best behaviour this time, not wanting to make Emily's life difficult. Doctor Goode was as pleasant as ever, he talked briefly about flying and about pilots, he checked her mouth and throat, and her burn; then had her wound cleaned and dressed again, with the addition of more fresh honey.

"Nurse Strachan tells me you struggled with the bacon yesterday?" he asked.

"Yes, sorry. I'm very grateful for it; it's just that the salt burned my mouth and throat."

"I see... Yes, yes, well it would, I suppose. I hadn't thought that through, and I can only apologise for your discomfort."

"It's really not a problem. I appreciate you thinking of me."

"I have an idea of how we can help your throat, though I'm not sure you're going to like it."

"I'm not even sure I like the sound of it," Harriet said nervously.

"We shall see later. For now, I'm sure Nurse Strachan can arrange something a little less uncomfortable for breakfast, then maybe she could take you for a walk in the grounds? It's a lovely day, a little cool so you'll have to make sure you're wrapped up, but I'm thinking that the fresh air will help your lungs a little. What do you think, Nurse Strachan, do you think we can make that happen?"

"Yes, of course, Doctor Goode."

"That's it agreed then, I'll check on you later. Good day." He left the room with the frowning Sister in tow, who hung back just long enough to complain at Emily about the dust on the flowers at the end of Harriet's bed before she left and closed the door firmly behind her.

"Did she really just tell you off because there's dust on the flowers?" Harriet asked.

"I'm sorry, I must have overlooked them," Emily replied with a frown.

"Did you really just apologise to me because there's dust on the flowers?"

"I thought they were clean..."

"You have to clean the flowers?"

"I'll be back in a moment with your breakfast," Emily replied. She was clearly distracted by the dust.

"Emily, stop it!" Harriet demanded.

"Excuse me?"

"Stop it. I don't care about dust on the bloody flowers!"

"The rooms must be clean, any dirt, or dust, can be a risk to your health, and I can't allow that. Now, remain in bed while I fetch your breakfast, then we'll scrub the room, and you, before we go for our walk." She quickly left the room and left Harriet with an uneasy frown on her face. She sat and thought for a while. The Sister reminded her of Section Officer Finn, the bully of a WAAF officer who'd tried to discipline her and Nicole when they arrived at the squadron in France; and of some of the older girls at school when she'd first arrived from England. She hated bullies. After simmering for a few minutes, she pulled off the blankets and swung her legs out of the bed while sitting upright. She felt a little dizzy, and even more light headed when she stood. A minute or two of steadying herself and she made her way across the room, uneasily and unsteadily, until she reached the flowers. The doctor had been right about her being exhausted, just crossing the room had made her breathless as though she'd climbed a mountain. She grabbed the vase and carried it over to the window, which she fought to open, then with a big smile she swung the vase and watched the flowers and water launch out of the window. She stepped forward and bent under the window frame to look outside, just in time to hear a shriek from below. The Sister was staring up with a face of fury, as water dripped over her uniform and a rose nestled in her hat.

"What on earth do you think you're doing!?!" she scolded angrily.

"Dusting!" Harriet replied with a smirk, before retiring inside and heading back to her bed where she collapsed, feeling a sense of accomplishment. She rolled back under the blankets and stared at the ceiling with a smug grin on her face. She knew the Sister would be galloping up the stairs at full speed, and she didn't have to wait long for the inevitable confrontation. The door opened, and the Sister marched in, drenched and angry, and carrying a mess of flowers in her shaking hand.

"What is the meaning of this?!" She demanded as she held the flowers in front of her.

"Spring cleaning," Harriet replied defiantly.

"Excuse me?"

"You heard. Emily is an excellent nurse, and she's doing a wonderful job of looking after me. She doesn't need you making her feel bad because there's dust on the flowers!"

"How very dare you!"

"You don't even want to know what I dare!"

"You are an ignorant young lady."

"And you are a bully."

"I am a Sister, and it's my job to maintain standards, of discipline and cleanliness, both of which are very important in a hospital. Not that I'd expect somebody like you to know anything about that!"

"Somebody like me?" Harriet asked.

31

"Yes, somebody like you."

"And what am I?"

"A delinquent!"

"A what?"

"A delinquent! Maybe if you'd spent more time educating yourself, like a young lady should, instead of messing about flying around the sky pretending to be a man, you'd know what that means!"

"Oh, I know what it means, thank you very much, and I studied at a very, very good school. I speak French and Latin fluently, and I had the best maths and science scores in the entire school. Oh, and if that's not enough for you, I can strip, repair, and rebuild the most complex engines Rolls Royce make, and fly the most advanced aeroplanes in the world, in combat, against trained and experienced German pilots. So, if you want to talk about education, pick your subject, and your language, and we'll get started."

"You may have those things, but they do not make you a lady!"

"I may not be a lady, but I know that dusting flowers has absolutely nothing to do with being a nurse; and everything to do with being an angry, bitter, miserable old snapdragon, who likes to bully her younger, more skilled, more efficient, and significantly more attractive nurses!"

"You!" The Sister flushed every colour before storming out of the room and colliding with Emily, who she sighed at irritably before marching off, and leaving Emily to enter the room and see Harriet sitting in her bed with her arms crossed and a smug smile on her face.

"What just happened?"

"The Sister and I had a difference of opinions."

"A difference of opinions? Why was she wet and carrying flowers?" Emily put the breakfast tray on the table, then turned and looked for the flowers on Harriet's dresser. "The vase is empty?"

"Well done."

"Why?"

"Because I'd grown tired of the flowers."

"What did you do?"

"Threw them out of the window."

"Oh, dear God."

"Well, I didn't know she was out there. It's her own stupid fault for being stood below the window."

"I suppose I shouldn't ask why you decided to throw the flowers at the sister?"

"Well, if we don't have flowers, they don't need dusting."

"Oh, Harry, I wish you hadn't."

"Too late, what's for breakfast?"

"Porridge... With strawberry jam."

"Thank you." Harriet took the bowl and took a small mouthful of the porridge then smiled, it was warm but not hot, and the sweetness helped soothe her mouth and throat as the milky oats slipped down. "It's perfect."

"I'm happy you like it."

"Sorry I don't have any bacon to share with you today."

" I'm sure I'll live, thank you. Anyway, less talking and more eating. I need to bathe you before we go for a walk." Harriet rolled her eyes and sighed at the prospect of having to be bathed again, quite against her will. She ate and drank her tea, then laid back with a look of frustration while Emily went about her business, before leaving her for a couple of hours to rest and snooze; before returning and subjecting her to the further indignity of being dressed in socks and a thick dressing gown. She was moved to a wheelchair, where she was piled with blankets, before Emily put on her cape and drove Harriet out of her room and along the corridor to the waiting lift which took them down to the ground floor, and out into the fresh morning air.

"Where are you taking me?" Harriet asked as the wheelchair rocked along the path, which was lined with trees and tall rose bushes which were blooming with yellows and pinks.

"You'll see."

"I'm not sure I like surprises."

"You'll like this one."

"What makes it so special?"

"Other than the company?"

"Obviously..."

"That," Emily said as she pushed Harriet through a rose lined archway and out onto a clifftop path. The view was incredible. Blue skies littered with fluffy white clouds and clear blue green seas, calm and almost motionless as the waves gently slid towards the shore below the steep cliffs. Birds swooped high overhead, bluebirds and swallows, darting around and catching flies, while a bumblebee buzzed its way through the wildflowers which lined the cliff top.

"OK..." Harriet said as a smile spread across her face.

"OK? Is that the best you've got?"

"Well, I've seen better views..."

"Oh, is that so?"

"Yes..."

"Name one."

"A few weeks ago, I took off from an airfield on the French coast just after sunset. As I climbed, I looked west and could see England. The sky was a mix of reds and purples, and the Channel between France and England glowed a deep, dark, shimmering red, sandwiched like a river of lava between the black of the land. It was incredible."

"OK, I'll give you that one..." Emily conceded. "Though having never been in an aeroplane at sunset, or at any time for that matter, I suppose I should take your word for it." She turned the wheelchair and strolled along the clifftop path.

"I'll show you one day."

"Will you now?"

"Yes, you'd love it."

"And how are you going to do that?"

"I don't know yet, but I'll think of a way."

"I won't hold my breath just yet."

"Don't you believe me?"

"Oh, I believe you'd like to, but I'm not sure the RAF are quite so keen on letting their pilots take nurses for joy rides. Besides, you're a fighter pilot, aren't you?"

"Yes, I fly Hurricanes. Why?"

"Don't they only have one seat?"

"I never said I'd take you in a Hurricane, who do you think you are?"

"I know who I am, young lady, I'm your nurse! So be careful, or I may just leave you out here on the cliff top."

"Promise?"

"What?"

"If you leave me out here on the clifftop, I'll be able to go back to my squadron."

"There's no stopping you, is there?"

"Nope."

"Why?"

"Why what?"

"Why do you want to rush back so desperately? Wasn't everything you've been through terrifying?"

"I don't know... Not really... You don't really get time to think, so you just get on with it. I suppose it's like any job, really," she replied like a seasoned veteran of many years of combat flying, and not the girl who first sat in a Hurricane just weeks before.

"Is that so?"

"It is."

"So, being trapped in a burning Hurricane wasn't at all scary for you?"

"Shut up."

"Excuse me?"

"You heard. I don't want to talk about that."

"So, if not that, how about being torpedoed and having to spend hours in the Channel waiting for help to come? That must have been a little scary, at least?"

"I wouldn't know, I can't remember it. I remember getting on the boat, then waking up here."

"You didn't really answer my question?"

"Because I told you I don't want to talk about it."

"Not that one. The one about why you're in such a hurry to get back to your squadron."

"It's my job."

"Is that all?"

"What do you mean?"

"I mean is there no other reason?"

"They're my family..."

"I've heard a lot of military people say that about their units, but there's always somebody at home waiting for them, too. Maybe that family would like to see you before you head back into the war?"

"They are that family... I don't really have anyone else."

"What? Nobody at all?"

"I don't think so," Harriet shrugged. "My parents were living in France when the war started, near Reims, right where the Germans broke through."

"Oh... I'm sorry, I didn't know."

"How could you know?"

"I'm sorry, anyway... So, there's nobody else?"

"Not that I can think of. I lived in France since I was young."

"I see. That's a shame. No grandparents, or aunts or uncles?"

"An aunt, maybe. I think she lives in Yorkshire somewhere. We lived nearby when I was young, but I don't really remember her that well." At that, Harriet looked up and around her.

"What is it?"

"An aeroplane... A Hurricane."

"Where?"

"I don't know, but I can hear it. Turn me around!" Emily quickly turned Harriet to face the sea, and she scoured the sky, then dropped her eyes down to see a Hurricane racing along at wave top height. "There, a Hurricane. I told you!" she said as she pointed. "It must be coming back from France." She smiled a huge grin as her tummy filled with butterflies while the Hurricane came closer. She strained to try and see anything recognisable, in a slight hope it was from her squadron. She waved excitedly as it neared the cliffs, as did Emily, and in response, the pilot pulled up into a slow victory roll low over their heads. The engine spluttered briefly, then the Hurricane resumed its level flight; and with a waggle of its wings it was gone, charging inland at hundreds of miles per hour. Harriet sat grinning as the engine hummed into the distance, then Emily continued their walk along the cliff path.

"The engine didn't sound too healthy when it flipped over, do you think it'll get back OK?"

"Oh, yes, that's normal," Harriet explained. "It's the fuel flow through the carburettor. It gets interrupted when the engine is upside down. It's OK as soon as you get it level again."

"That doesn't exactly fill me with confidence. What if the engine were to cut altogether?"

"You can always step out of the office."

"The office? What office?"

"I mean jump, use the parachute, though that would be a last resort. As long as there was somewhere clear and you had enough speed, it would always be better to try and land first."

"Jump? That sounds awful. I don't think I could do it."

"It's easy, really. You just unfasten your straps, open the cockpit, and flip upside down. Gravity does the rest."

"Stop it. You're making me sick just thinking about it."

"What?" Harriet laughed.

"That, falling out of the aeroplane. You haven't done that, have you?"

"Only once."

"Once is enough!"

"I suppose... I'm not in a hurry to do it again."

"Something we can agree on."

"You're such a scaredy cat."

"There's nothing wrong with being scared. Scared keeps you alive, it's what makes you fight for your life. People who don't get scared get dead pretty quickly, that's one of life's great truths." Emily said firmly.

"Do you really think so?"

"I know so."

"You could be right, I suppose... If I wasn't scared, I wouldn't have been able to smash my way out of my Hurricane."

"I can't begin to imagine how frightening that was for you."

"Everything around me was burning. The flames were everywhere. I think the canopy had buckled when I crash landed, and it wouldn't come open the way it should, so I was stuck. I thought I was going to burn. I couldn't breathe, so I had to pull off my oxygen mask, the smoke burned, but it was better than suffocating in the mask. My arm caught fire, and my boots caught fire, I've never been so scared. Then it shifted. Then I screamed and shouted and pushed, and the canopy finally shot open. The air rushed in, and the flames engulfed me totally, but I got out. A few minutes later and there wasn't an inch of the whole Hurricane that wasn't burning... But do you know what was even scarier than all of that?"

"I don't..." Emily said softly, captivated by Harriet's horrifying story.

"Only a few minutes before that, I'd watched my best friend shot down. Her Hurricane dived away through the clouds, trailing thick black smoke and engulfed in flames."

"I'm sorry."

"There was nowhere for her to run. She was trapped, and she burned all the way down to the ground. That's what truly scares me, knowing my best friend was likely screaming and crying as her skin burned from her body, and her lungs filled with smoke as she tried to get out, and knowing that I was powerless to do anything about it."

"Oh Harriet," Emily knelt beside the wheelchair. She held Harriet's hand and used a handkerchief to dry the tears from Harriet's cheeks. "I'm so sorry."

"You asked why I'm in a hurry to get back to my squadron..."

"I didn't mean to push."

"My parents are missing, my best friend is dead, and the last time I saw my squadron, the ground crews were heading for Dunkirk, and the pilots were flying headfirst into a fight with what must have been a hundred or more German aeroplanes, maybe more, we were badly outnumbered." Harriet stared at Emily. "The people who made me at home and welcomed me into their family could all be dead at the bottom of the Channel, for all I know. I've lost everything, and they're all I have left. I'm scared they're all dead, too, and I'm left alone." Emily moved closer and held Harriet while she sobbed, doing all she could to comfort her while she faced her demons.

"Hello? Nurse Strachan?" a voice called in the distance. Emily sat back and gave Harriet a smile, which was returned, then stood and looked down the path. A boy of fifteen or sixteen was riding his bike along the path and waving cheerily. Emily waved, then knelt again and dried Harriet's eyes.

"It looks like we have a visitor," Emily said quietly. Harriet nodded and smiled.

"Thank you," Harriet sniffed.

"Hush…"

"Though you're not supposed to see me like this, nobody is supposed to see me like this."

"Like what?"

"Crying!"

"Oh, don't be ridiculous. If I can't help you, who's going to? Now put a smile on your face while I see what this young man wants." She stood and turned Harriet to face the sea once again as the young man got close, then stood between her and him to make sure he couldn't see her.

"Are you Nurse Strachan?" he asked.

"I am, what do you want?"

"I'm Billy, Ma'am. From the village."

"I'm well aware of who you are, Mister Lester, but that's not what I asked."

"Yes, Ma'am. Your Doctor Goode told my dad that you've got a young fighter pilot down here just back from Dunkirk."

"Now is not the time for visitors, young man," Emily replied sternly.

"Dad sent these," the young man said as he got off his bike and pulled a small metal churn from the basket, before standing in front of Emily. "Doctor Goode said the pilot needed them on account of the burns he'd suffered to his mouth." He opened the lid of the churn and showed Emily inside, where two ice cream bars were packed in ice. "I want to be a fighter pilot when I'm older, a Spitfire pilot, so I thought I'd say hello to one of our boys while I was here, if that's OK?"

"Well there's a bit of a problem with that," Emily replied with a frown.

"What's that, then?"

"The boy you want to meet is a girl..."

"A what?"

"A girl... Meet Harry." She stepped aside and introduced Harriet, who simply sat and smiled uncomfortably. "Cat got your tongue?" Emily asked, and Billy frowned for a moment as he processed the scene in front of him.

"Good morning," Harriet said casually.

"You're a..."

"Don't!" Harriet said firmly.

"Lady fighter pilot," he continued, as a big smile spread across his face. "My sister is going to be so jealous."

"Why's that?"

"Are you a fighter pilot, for real?" he asked, stepping past Emily as though she didn't exist, and standing beside Harriet.

"Yes, for real. I fly Hurricanes. Now, what's this about your sister?"

"My twin sister, she's always wanted to be a fighter pilot. Everyone just tells her that girls don't fly aeroplanes, but here you are, a lady fighter pilot and I get to meet you. She's gonna be so angry."

43

"Do we have a visiting time?" Harriet asked Emily.

"This evening at seven, for one hour," Emily replied with a hint of a smile.

"I'd be happy to meet your sister if she wants to come and visit?" Harriet replied.

"You mean it?" Billy gasped.

"If Nurse Strachan is OK with it?"

"Only a brief visit, Harry is very tired after her trip from Dunkirk, and not too many questions."

"Yes, Ma'am!" he said with a smile. Then stood smartly to attention and handed Emily the churn. "I'd better get going. I've got deliveries to make. You can give the churn to my sister later..."

"Thank you, Billy," Emily said, maintaining her rigid and authoritarian demeanour. He picked up his bike and turned it around on the path.

"You shot any Jerries down, then?" he asked as he climbed onto his bike, ready to push off.

"Billy!" Emily growled sternly.

"Yes," Harriet replied.

"Blimey! How many?"

"Enough."

"Yes, it is enough!" Emily interrupted. "Billy, leave. Now!" he smirked and took off on his bike as Emily turned to Harriet. "And you stop telling war stories to young boys! You should know better."

44

"I didn't tell any war stories."

"Close enough. Now, I suppose you like ice cream?"

"I can't remember when I last had it."

"Well, here you go." She handed Harriet the churn. She looked inside and smiled. Before she could be stopped, Harriet stood from her chair, unsteadily at first. "What on earth do you think you're doing!?" Emily demanded.

"Sitting on the grass and having an ice cream. She walked to the cliff edge, laid the blanket on the grass, then stood and faced Emily.

"Oh, dear God," Emily muttered under her breath. "Can't you just do as you're told, just once?"

"Come and sit with me."

"I can't."

"Of course you can, it's easy."

"OK, then I won't."

"Why not?"

"Because I'm your nurse! I'm supposed to be caring for you, not socialising."

"If you were caring for me, you'd need to be over here with me. To stop me doing anything silly in my state of confusion, like this." She lifted one leg and hung it over the side of the cliff.

"Stop being ridiculous!" Emily jumped forward as Harriet wobbled a little. Emily grabbed her around the hips and pulled her back from the

45

edge. "Harry!" she exclaimed, as Harriet stared into her eyes and smirked.

"Nearly," Harriet said quietly, her eyes were sparkling with mischief.

"You're irresponsible!"

"Want an ice cream?"

"You're incorrigible!"

"Have an ice cream!" She reached into the churn, and held one of the paper wrapped ice creams in front of Emily's face, which was only inches from her own. "I can't eat both, and it would be wasteful to let one melt, especially when there's a war on." Emily's eyes narrowed as she bit her tongue to stop herself from exploding into a tirade of annoyance at Harriet. "You know it makes sense." Harriet continued. Emily rolled her eyes and let out the tension with a huge sigh, then released Harriet from her grasp and snatched the ice cream.

"This is wrong," Emily protested.

"Sit with me," Harriet sat down on the blanket she'd laid on the clifftop.

"You should be in your wheelchair."

"What's the worst that could happen?"

"We could be seen!"

"So what? I don't mind."

"I do! We'd both get in a lot of trouble."

"Just blame it on me, it's fine."

"I don't think it works that way," Emily said in resignation, as she sat beside Harriet and hung her legs over the cliff edge. "Oh well... I have a feeling I'm in for a very one sided conversation with Sister anyway, after your vase emptying exploits. I may as well enjoy an ice cream before I'm sent off to some horrible hospital in punishment. Though eating it makes me feel like a total fraud."

"Why a fraud?"

"I haven't earned it..."

"Don't be ridiculous."

"I'm not. You flew fighters over France, you've earned every mouthful, what have I done?"

"Looked after me..."

"Like you need any looking after!" Emily replied with a heavy dose of sarcasm. "I'm more like your handler, trying to keep you in line."

"You have looked after me... I know you've slept in my room every night since I arrived, managing my fever and looking after me when I wake with nightmares."

"What? How do you know that?"

"And I know you've kept my wounds clean, and kept me clean so that I can recover properly." Emily blushed and looked out to sea. "I know I've been delirious and knocked out most of the time, but in the moments that I was awake I remember you being there, and I know that the dark things in my head that were scaring me needed to come out, and you did that."

"It's my job," Emily said as she blushed some more.

"And I know I've been awful and got you into trouble with the Sister, and

47

I'm sorry. I'll fix it, I promise."

"Don't be silly."

"I'm not; I'll fix it."

"Honestly, Harry, you're right." Emily opened the ice cream and took a bite. "She is an old snapdragon. None of the nurses like her, you know?" She gave Harriet a smirk. "I wish I'd seen her face when you threw the vase of water at her."

"It was a sight..." Harriet smirked, and the pair laughed and enjoyed their ice creams, while listening to the waves crash against the beach below. "How come you're here on the south coast?" Harriet asked after a while.

"What do you mean?"

"You're Scottish, and about as far away from home that you can get without leaving the country,"

"I came down here with my husband..."

"You're married?"

"I was"

"Oh..."

"It's OK. He was a soldier."

"You're speaking in the past tense."

"I know."

"Is he...?"

"Missing, presumed dead," Emily replied firmly, then switched her gaze to Harriet. "That's what the message from the War Office said. He went on a reconnaissance mission last autumn and never came back. One of his friends visited me at Christmas to tell me about it, which was very kind of him, but there wasn't much to tell. He was liked, he was missed, but that's all they could say. A patrol went out to look for him, but they didn't find anything."

"I'm sorry."

"What for? You didn't kill him."

"I mean I'm sorry for your loss."

"I know, thank you. You'd be surprised how many times I've heard that. People think I'm fragile and they don't know what to say, so they just say, 'I'm sorry.' It's not like that, though, I'm not as fragile as some may think, how could I be when we're at war? We can't be fragile, and we can't live in the past. We've got to live for now and for the future, and live the type of lives that those who died have paid for. Lives worth living."

"I'd never thought of it that way."

"It's the only way we can think of it, don't you think?"

"I suppose..."

"Imagine those we've lost looking down on us and seeing us unhappy and miserable, and not living the lives in front of us? I know my husband would be furious, standing by the fireplace with his pipe and blustering as he did, 'What the hell was the point in me standing up to the bloody Germans, if you're only going to sit around and be miserable anyway?'" She did an impression which made her smile at herself, and her memories. Harriet smiled and suppressed a giggle. "He was a good man, and I miss him," Emily continued. "But he died doing what he loved, which is all any of us can ask, isn't it?"

49

"It is... Do you love being a nurse?"

"I think so. In a way."

"In a way?"

"Yes. I love seeing nice people recover and live their lives. Really live, I mean, I want them to laugh, love, cry, and do things that make them feel alive. If I can help make that happen, then maybe when it's time to face my own end, I can do so knowing that I've done my best."

"But why 'in a way'? What's missing?"

"Adventure..."

"Adventure?"

"Yes... Adventure. Like flying Hurricanes in combat..."

"I'm not sure that's what I'd call adventure?"

"What is it, then?"

"Terrifying, sometimes."

"And the other times?"

"Incredible..." Harriet said with a smile.

"Exactly. People like you get to fly and get all that goes with it, and you get the excitement and adventure. That's what I'm missing."

"It's not easy."

"I never said it was."

"It's dirty."

"So is nursing, believe me."

"It's exhausting…"

"So is nursing."

"Yes, but nobody's trying to kill you..."

"I'll give you that, I suppose. Though Sister will certainly give it her best effort if she catches me sitting on the cliffs eating ice cream." She smiled and stood. "Come on, let's get you back to the hospital."

"Just another five minutes?"

"We don't have another five minutes."

"Another three, then?"

"Right now."

"How about two minutes?"

"How about no?"

"You nurses are no fun!" Harriet sulked as Emily took her hand and pulled her to her feet. "Can I at least walk back?"

"What do you think?"

Emily pushed Harriet back to the hospital and saw her back to her bed, where she quickly fell asleep, despite her best efforts to stay awake. She was roused by the arrival of her evening meal, which she ate before having her wounds checked, then fell back to sleep. There was a visit from the grocer's daughter, which turned into an hour long conversation about all things flying, and saw Harriet becoming quite excited in explaining exactly how to fly, and writing the young girl a homework study schedule with a list of books, subjects, and activities she needed to practice if she wanted to be a pilot. Much to the displeasure of both Harriet and her new friend, Sister broke up the meeting and cleared all visitors, leaving Harriet to stare at the ceiling in boredom again before falling asleep. A sleep which, as with every sleep she'd had in the hospital, was filled with dreams of dead friends and burning alive. The next day was the same, a walk on the cliffs, with a little more walking on her own, and a long talk with Emily; who despite being a prime target for Harriet's teasing was perfect company, and somebody Harriet quickly came to enjoy being around.

The following day started the same, though it didn't include Harriet emptying a vase of flowers over the Sister, however tempted she'd have been if the Sister hadn't given her a very wide berth. After the morning routine, Harriet and Emily sat on the cliff tops eating ice cream that had kindly been delivered by the awestruck young man once again. Their conversation was light and fun, and in depth, and detailed, they talked about their losses, Nicole and Emily's husband, and how they were going to make the most of their own lives; they were both engrossed in each other until Emily noted the time and how late they were getting back. Emily hurried Harriet back into her chair, something she bluntly refused, leading Emily to agree to let her push her own chair back, slowly. They walked through the bushes into the hospital grounds, only to face the unwelcome sight of the enraged Sister, accompanied by a grey moustached Army captain.

"She looks happy..." Harriet said.

"Please behave," Emily replied.

"What?" Harriet protested as they walked closer

"You know what."

"It's not my fault that she's grumpy."

"I know... But all the same, if you wouldn't mind? I have to live here." Emily smiled politely as Doctor Goode walked from the hospital entrance to join them, and waved at them both excitedly as he did. The Sister's face filled with frustration.

"Looks like you've been saved," Harriet smirked. Emily rolled her eyes and sighed.

"Ah, there you are," Doctor Goode said.

"You're late! This is not acceptable!" the Sister blustered firmly.

"How are you doing?" Goode asked, totally ignoring the Sister, much to her irritation. "You seem to be walking much better, how are the lungs?"

"Improving, thank you," Harriet said politely. "Nurse Strachan has been helping me with controlled exercise. Encouraging me to walk a little more each time, but only while she's with me so she can monitor my progress and welfare. She's firm but fair, and she's taught me so much about physiology, and how my body is recovering from the injuries I've sustained."

"Is that so?" Goode asked Emily.

"Preposterous!" Sister bellowed. "You're a nurse, young lady, not a doctor!"

"Damned good show!" Goode said, taking Emily by surprise, and making the Sister turn several shades, and almost explode with rage. "That's exactly what a nurse should be doing, helping our patients recover."

"I was scared to even get out of the wheelchair, and likely wouldn't have if it wasn't for Nurse Strachan," Harriet added. "It was her who told me I needed to build the strength in my muscles, and insisted that I walk. She's magnificent"

"Yes, she is, isn't she!" Goode said with a huge smile, giving the now blushing Emily a nod of approval as he did. "I suspect we're not using your skills anywhere near as much as we should, Nurse Strachan. I'm meeting with Matron later; Sister is about to take some well deserved leave, and I think maybe I should be putting your name forward as her acting replacement. What do you say?" Emily stood staring in shock until Harriet reached behind her and gave her a nip.

"I'm honoured to serve our patients in whichever capacity you see fit," she replied politely.

"Good, good," Goode replied excitedly. "I'll pick it up with Matron, but first we have a more pressing matter to attend."

"Oh?"

"Yes. It would appear that things have turned from bad to worse over in France, and we have a large number of wounded men on the way. Which means we're going to need every bed we've got, even in our little country hospital."

"Yes, of course. I'll get to work on the preparations immediately."

"Thank you. The ambulance convoy should be with us in the next hour or so. However, before you get to that, we're discharging all patients who can convalesce elsewhere, and that includes you." He looked to Harriet, who instantly raised an eyebrow and smiled.

"I can go back to my squadron?" she asked excitedly.

"Certainly not!" the army officer replied formally, with the slightest twinkle in his old blue eyes.

"This is Captain Barrister, our local liaison officer," Goode continued.

"Liaison Officer?" Harriet asked.

"Yes..." Barrister replied. "Unfortunately, the War Office thought I was a little too old to send to the front, so when I was called up, I was put in charge of liaison with civilian hospitals. I tend to make sure the military know where all of our people are, in which hospital, and for how long, so their units can be kept up to date."

"I see..." Harriet replied.

"Sign here," he said as he handed her a book and pen. "Push hard; it needs to go through the carbon." Harriet took the book and pen and did as he asked before handing it back to him, then in return he gave her an envelope from his case.

"What's this?" she asked.

"Your pay award," he replied, as he packed the book and pen in his bag.

"My what?"

"Pay award... You're a commissioned officer wounded in France, and evacuated through Dunkirk. It's OK, I got your story from the doctor. As such, His Majesty's government expects that you'd have arrived back on these shores with only the clothes on your back?"

"Hardly even that," Emily added. "Her uniform was so badly damaged by the fire that burned her lungs and arm, that we had to cut most of it away." Barrister nodded solemnly.

"Yes... Well, the War Office in its wisdom has provided you with an allowance to buy clothes and replace personal effects, in addition to sending your pay arrears from your time in France, and a month's advance to get you through your convalescence." He pulled another envelope from his chest pocket and handed it to her. "And that's your rail warrant."

"My rail warrant?"

"Yes... I know you RAF types enjoy being flown everywhere, but I'm afraid the train is the best we can do at the moment. Times being as they are and all that. Not to worry, though, the warrant will give you unrestricted travel."

"I get that, but where am I going?"

"Home."

"Home?"

"Home. Your doctor has confirmed you're fit enough to travel, by train at least, and you're to go home and convalesce for one month, and not a day less! That's what you said, isn't it?" he asked Goode.

"That's right," Goode added excitedly. "Nurse Strachan; or Sister Strachan should I say, will help you get your things together. As soon as possible, if you please. Captain Barrister has offered to drop you at the train station. Probably best you ship out before the ambulances arrive." The Sister turned and left, marching across the gravel with the force of somebody significantly larger.

"Where is Home, by the way?" Barrister asked as he opened yet another book.

"France..." Harriet replied solemnly.

"Yes, well, I don't expect the warrant will get you back there. Somewhere safer, and less under occupation by the German army, perhaps?" Harriet scoured her mind.

"I have an aunt in East Yorkshire... I think...?"

"East Yorkshire. Good. OK, at least we'll know roughly where you are. A month from now just go along to the local recruiting office, and they'll arrange your warrant back to your unit."

"OK... But my unit..."

"Knows you're safe, and knows exactly where you are," he cut her off with a warm and confident reassurance. "They were informed the moment you arrived. The doctor let me know, and I let them know. I spoke to the duty officer myself, and they're happy you're safe and send their best wishes for a speedy recovery, not to mention a little ribbing for your time off." He gave her a wink and Harriet smiled. "Anyway, I need to leave shortly, so when you're ready..."

"Maybe you'd join me for a drop of medicinal brandy before you leave?" Goode asked.

"It'd be rude not to, I suppose."

"Twenty minutes, Sister," Goode said to Emily, who quickly nodded.

"I'll meet you by my car," Barrister said as he walked away with Goode, and pointed to the black staff car sitting by the hospital entrance.

"Come on," Emily said as she grabbed the chair.

"I think I've graduated from that now, don't you?" Harriet asked with a raised eyebrow. "Thanks to your bullying me to walk and strengthen my muscles."

"Whatever. Let's go, we need to get you ready!" Emily started walking, pushing the empty chair.

"You're welcome," Harriet replied as she walked after her.

"For what?"

"Telling them what a wonderful nurse you are."

"You lied."

"Did you, or did you not spend the last few days telling me how my body works, how it recovers, and the importance of rehabilitation?"

"Shut up."

"You're welcome."

"You're boring."

"Lucky I'm leaving in that case."

"Isn't it?"

Emily left Harriet in her bedroom to wash and prepare herself, and ten minutes later arrived with a grey kit bag slung over her shoulder, a pair of smart black shoes with a two inch heel, and a hanger of clothes, which she laid on the bed.

"What's this?" Harriet asked as she looked at the clothes.

"Your trousers and blouse were badly damaged; they're laundered, but they're little more than rags and you can't wear them home. I've put them in the bag with your flying boots and jacket, which are in no better condition. I stitched the sleeve of the jacket and got most of the smoke out of it, but you'll probably need to air it some more when you're home."

"The clothes... They're..."

"Mine. You're a little taller than me so they won't be a perfect fit, but they'll be better than looking like a scarecrow. Come on, let's get you dressed," Emily started pulling at Harriet's clothing, much to her reluctant disapproval. "Really?" she asked in despair. "There isn't an inch of you I haven't seen, so let's do away with the pretend shyness, and let me help you get ready before the car leaves, and I get stuck with you," she said while standing with her hands on her hips. Harriet stopped resisting, and soon after pulling on the borrowed underwear, which was tight and fit worse than anything else, she was looking at herself in the mirror. The narrow blue skirt sat just above her knee and the white blouse, too short to tuck properly, sat neatly over the waistband. The shoes accented her defined calves, and gave her hips a curve when she turned slightly and looked herself up and down. "You actually look like a lady," Emily said as she stood behind her.

"Don't be so surprised..."

"I'm not. You look good, Harry. Really good."

"Thanks to you... Thank you for putting my hair up, too, and for the lipstick."

"It's my pleasure," Emily said as she smiled into the mirror, and put a hand on Harriet's shoulder. Harriet put her hand on hers, then turned and looked Emily in the eyes.

"Thank you, Emily. Thank you for everything."

"It's time you were going," Emily said with a deep breath, as she moved to walk away. Harriet grabbed her and hugged her tight, taking her by surprise and paralysing her for a moment, until slowly she hugged back. They stood in silence, not needing to say a word, then Harriet let go, straightened herself and turned for the door, which Emily rushed to open for her, grabbing the kit bag as she passed and handing it to Harriet as she winked and walked out of the room confidently. People stopped as they walked through the hospital, patients, orderlies, even some of the nurses. As she stepped outside, she was greeted by the Matron standing in front of her. The Sister was nowhere to be seen, of course.

"Well, well," Doctor Goode said as he stepped out with Captain Barrister. "You'd better be careful, young lady, you'll be giving us a reputation for being a transformation factory." He laughed playfully and shook her hand. "No offence meant, of course."

"None taken, doctor," Harriet replied with a smile. She was feeling ten feet tall with confidence.

"Good. I only mean to say that the young lady standing before me now is a long way from the smoke and blood stained scarecrow that was delivered to us."

"Thanks to you and Emily, and the rest of your staff," Harriet said with a smile.

"Oh, and don't forget to take this with you." He handed Harriet a small polished cedarwood box which he pulled from his pocket.

"What is it?" Harriet asked with a raised eyebrow.

"Why don't you open it and see?" She did as he suggested and felt a wide smile stretch across her face as Cas' watch shimmered it's pearlescent colours as the sunlight caught it. "It was a little worse for wear when you arrived, so I had a friend of mine in the city have a look at it. He did a good job, but couldn't get that scratch from the glass without replacing the whole thing, which due to the rarity of the piece he suggested would do it more harm than good. Anyway, it's working and almost as good as new."

"I thought I'd lost it…"

"Sorry about that, we wanted it to be a surprise. He put it to the top of his work list when he found out you were a pilot; and handed it over last night when we met for dinner."

"It's a wonderful surprise… I really don't know how to thank you." She fought back the tears of joy that were welling and about to roll down her cheek.

"Well, you could do me a favour?"

"If I can?"

"When you get back to your squadron and get back into the air, give Jerry a punch on the nose from me." He gave her a wink and handed her another small parcel. "Medication, dressings, and honey. Keep those wounds clean and keep resting."

"I promise," she smiled and shook Goode's hand.

"We can't hang around all day," Barrister said as he walked to his car. "Make it quick."

The Matron stood in front of Harriet. She was an older woman, and very austere looking. Serious, hard, and terrifying. Harriet had seen her around the hospital, watching from a distance and keeping an eye on her, but never intervening in her care.

"It's been an experience having you here, young lady," the Matron said without breaking a smile. "It's not every day one of my patients empties a full vase over my Senior Sister."

"Yes... About that, I'm awfully sorry..." Harriet replied. "I think I was a little dazed from the action. I really wasn't myself."

"I'm sure..."

"Sorry..."

"You were a challenge for Nurse Strachan, though I knew you would be. After all, it's why I gave you to her."

"Oh?"

"We needed a new Senior Sister, and I supposed that if she could manage you, she could manage my nurses without any bother. It's nice to see that I was right." Harriet felt herself blush. "Good luck, young lady. You're a credit to your service." The Matron held out her hand, they shook, then with the smallest smile she turned and left.

"Well that was unexpected," Emily said as the Matron disappeared out of sight.

"That she used me to test you?"

"That you made her smile..."

"Funny."

"I know... Besides, how could the other be a surprise? Anyone who knows you must know that you're a challenge."

"I won't miss your poor sense of humour."

"I won't miss your rampant insubordination."

"Yes, you will."

"Maybe a little..."

"Anytime today, young lady!" Barrister bellowed.

"I have to go."

"I know..."

"Thank you."

"You're welcome."

"I mean it. You saved my life."

"You're being dramatic."

"I'll miss you."

"Write to me? Let me know you're OK?"

"I promise."

They hugged; then, as Bannister revved the engine and sounded the horn, Harriet threw her bag on the back seat. She climbed into the front and moments later they were rolling down the road.

Chapter 2

The North

The drive to the train station had been pleasant, made memorable by the moment Captain Barrister's old fashioned character got the better of him and he pointed out, as expected, that Harriet was a girl. She smiled politely and raised her eyebrows in acknowledgement of the ground breaking fact, which appeared to be all that was needed to get Barrister in a fluster. He apologised profusely for bringing attention to her gender and went on to explain how he'd never met a female pilot before, let alone a combat pilot. He wasn't ignorant about it, just a little surprised, and as their conversation progressed he became quite open about his admiration for the RAF in allowing women to be part of the fight where the metal meets the meat, as he put it. This phrase, he explained, was something his old Commanding Officer had used frequently when rallying the troops, before fixing bayonets and going over the top in the last war. Harriet was quite welcoming of Barrister's comment really, it broke the ice and allowed them to relax and talk about the war, among other things. Barrister had been working at the bank since leaving the army as a Major in 1932, having served as a junior infantry officer in France during the war; before moving around the world to places such as Mesopotamia and Egypt, with time in India, and even Argentina as a military attaché to the ambassador. When war was declared again, he volunteered his services, which were politely declined on the grounds of his advancing years. However he was retained for administrative duties, which included liaising with hospitals on the south coast, should they be needed once the fighting started proper. He asked Harriet what the battle was like in France, and she told him what she could, having seen most from a bird's perspective, and he wasn't impressed. He'd seen the injured lists, and the increasing number of casualties arriving at the local hospitals he was looking after. He'd wondered whether his seniors were telling the truth when he was told that his sector was bearing the brunt of the casualties as they were the closest to Dover; and that things really weren't all that bad in France. When Harriet told him of her experiences at Dunkirk, he almost cried. He'd seen the war in France the last time, he'd fought at the Somme, not too far from Dunkirk, and he felt for the soldiers he knew were in trouble over there. His rant about the idiocy of the generals was only broken by the solemn sight of a small convoy of ambulances heading in the opposite direction; carrying the wounded and dying to the hospital they'd recently left, in trucks smeared with bloody handprints, giving a brief insight into what lay inside. Harriet thought back to her own journey to the hospital, and she still didn't remember a thing. She only just remembered being in the sea. She shrugged and looked away from the ambulances, instead deciding to enjoy the sun on the endless fields of green and gold, and thought back to happier times, of being an excited eleven year old flying over the fields of northern France. She smiled. It seemed like a century ago.

Barrister said his goodbyes at the station and gave her the large paper bag of cherries that he'd bought from an elderly man who'd been selling them on the roadside not far from the hospital. Then, with a warning to keep what was happening in Dunkirk to herself, for reasons of morale, he shook Harriet's hand and wished her the best of luck for the future. He drove off with a wave from the window of his black car. He left Harriet to shoulder her kit bag and walk a little unsteadily into the train station on the heels she was unaccustomed to wearing. She was greeted by the station master, who kindly put her on the right train to London, and gave her exact instructions on how to get to King's Cross station for her journey north.

The hectic bustle of the city shocked her when she arrived in London, she'd never experienced anything like it. People everywhere, bumping and shoving in the early summer sun, and if that was bad, King's Cross station itself was worse. There were so many people coming and going, businessmen, soldiers, sailors, and a few dots of Air Force blue here and there, that it looked like a giant ant nest. Everyone bustled and shoved to get where they were going, it was quite intimidating, and not at all to Harriet's liking. She much preferred the countryside, and never had liked being around crowds. Going with her family to the market in Reims had been bad enough, but London was too much.

"Can I help you, miss?" a Policeman asked, as she walked straight into him and bounced away again. He was a tall lean man, made all the taller by his dark blue helmet with blackened metal badge. He looked down at her from under the peak, while she surveyed the medal ribbons above his left breast pocket. He was an older man, and a veteran of the last war, no doubt.

"I... I'm looking for the train north, to Yorkshire."

"Yorkshire? What are you going there for?"

"I'm going home. I'm on leave from my squadron."

"Your squadron?" He raised an eyebrow in disbelief.

"Yes, I'm an officer with the RAF!" She held out the travel warrant, in the hope that it would prove her identity enough to prevent an in depth conversation about female pilots.

"Oh, I see. You mean you're a WAAF Officer?" he said with a smile as he glanced over the warrant.

"No, I mean RAF. I'm in the Volunteer Reserve."

"Is that right?" he asked with the slightest frown.

"It is, and I'd be grateful if you could tell me where I can find the right train home!"

"My apologies, Ma'am. I didn't recognise you, with you not being in uniform and all."

"What's left of it is in my bag, the rest of my possessions are still in France..."

"I do beg your pardon, Ma'am." The Policeman straightened up and appeared even taller. "I didn't realise. Come this way, would you? I've

66

got an idea." He led her through the crowded station, to a platform gate manned by an army officer and a Sergeant. "' Ere, your troop train's heading north, isn't it?" the Policeman asked.

"Yes... To York, why?" the young officer replied as the train sounded its whistle.

"This young lady is one of yours, Air Force Officer just back from France.
Any room for her?"

"I don't know; we're quite full. Do you have a warrant?" he asked with a frown. Harriet handed it to him, and after a brief examination, he nodded and handed it back to her. "Very well, but I hope you can run?" The train whistled again. A long, loud blast that echoed through the station. The train shuddered and jerked as the brakes eased off, and the wheels spun and gained traction on the tracks.

"Come on, Ma'am, we'll need to be quick," the Sergeant said as he took her kit bag from her and started walking quickly.

"Thank you!" Harriet said to the Policeman and officer as she joined the Sergeant. The train shuddered and rolled slowly along the tracks.

"Can you run?" the Sergeant asked.

"I can try," Harriet replied. She hitched her skirt up her thighs and started running, and windows along the trains either side of the platform opened, and soldiers appeared, shouting and cheering as Harriet and the Sergeant sprinted towards the train, with the occasional whistle at Harriet's long shapely legs, which were on display as she hitched her skirt higher to allow her to run full speed. The guard waved excitedly, and leant out of his van to catch Harriet's bag as the Sergeant threw it, before he reached back and grabbed Harriet by the hand, then with all his might threw her forward to the guard so he could pull her aboard. She grabbed the railing and smiled up at the guard while catching her breath. A huge cheer roared through the spectators, and the whistles sounded in applause. She turned and waved to the Sergeant, as the train gathered speed and pulled out of sight.

"Welcome aboard, Miss," the guard said in a strong Yorkshire accent. He was an older man with grey hair, and a big grey moustache.

"Thank you," Harriet said as she straightened her clothes and smoothed out her skirt. She let out a cough as her throat and lungs burned like they were on fire, and steadied herself for a moment as a wave of dizziness hit her.

"In a hurry to get somewhere, are we?"

"Yorkshire."

"Aye, it's a big place. Anywhere in particular?"

"Cottingham? It's in the east. I think"

"You think?"

"I haven't been there for a very long time. Since I was a little girl."

"Well, we're heading to Yorkshire. Nowhere near Cottingham, though."

"You know it?"

"I've been on trains all my life, lass. There isn't a station in Yorkshire I've not been through more than a couple of times. Of course I know it. Up near Hull, it is."

"I've no idea how to get there..."

"Don't worry, lass. I'll see you right when we get to York, and get this noisy lot disembarked." He gestured his head back towards the train. "Best get yourself settled for now," he said as they entered the darkness of a tunnel, and the warm yellow light from the brake van beckoned them

68

inside. Harriet took a seat on the small leather cushioned bench. "Make yourself comfortable, lass." She sat and relaxed as the train rocked and clattered down the track, and before long, her regular routine had caught up with her, and she was asleep.

By the time they arrived in York, it was late in the afternoon, and Harriet had slept most of the journey, waking only for a cup of tea and a biscuit with the guard. The train system was working, but it was slow, with troops and equipment being transported all over the country as the government prepared for the total loss in France, and the potential invasion of Britain. Most civilians didn't know how bad things were, as the newspapers weren't allowed to report the truth for fear of causing panic, so as the guard led Harriet through the busy York station, she was able to overhear much grumbling among the portly businessmen whose trains were now delayed or even cancelled 'just to taxi the army around.' Harriet frowned in dismay and exhaustion, she couldn't really be bothered with people, especially not miserable people who were clearly comfortable and well fed, while soldiers, sailors, and airmen and women were dying just across the Channel. She just wanted to get back to her friends in the squadron, but instead of that she was in York and heading to the middle of nowhere to meet, hopefully, an aunt she hadn't seen in years.

"Alright there, Jonesy?" the guard said as he called up to the engine sitting at the head of a train of coal carriages.

"Now then, Colin. What can I do for you?" the Welshman replied.

"Heading for Hull tonight?"

"Aye."

"Wouldn't mind dropping a parcel off in Cottingham for me, would you?" He looked at Harriet and winked. She smiled politely as the engineer pursed his lips.

"I'm pretty sure your parcel would be a little dirty by the time it gets there," came the reply. "We're pulling coal, so no carriages, and even the brake van is full of some army types heading east. The only space I can offer is up here on the footplate, and, well, you know how that is."

"What do you reckon, lass? You want to get home dirty tonight or clean tomorrow?"

"I've been dirtier," Harriet replied with a smile.

"What do you reckon, Jonesy? Room for a small one."

"I take no responsibility for damaging those pretty clothes you're wearing, but alright. Come on, then." He reached down and took her kit bag from the guard, who she thanked profusely before getting a hand up onto the footplate. She stood in awe of the multitude of red valves and blackened pipes, and the glowing hatch where the fire burned. "Now, don't you be touching anything," he said. "Have a sit down on that bench out of the way." He pointed to the dusty bench at the back of the engine cab, which she wiped the coal dust from before sitting on her bag. The fireman arrived shortly after, raised an eyebrow at her presence, then went about stoking the fire. She watched both men as they prepared for their journey, then with a few final checks and a whistle for the guard, they were on their way, and she was on her third train journey of the day.

Harriet stood and excitedly watched the scenery pass as they whistled through the countryside and villages in the early evening sun, and she was even allowed to drive the train for a short time, which put a huge smile on her face. They finally slowed into Cottingham, and she climbed down to the platform and was handed her bag before the train quickly continued its journey into the warm orange and blue sky. The station master greeted Harriet, unexpectedly, as the coal train didn't often stop there. He was as pleasant and welcoming as the others, and he soon had her heading in the right direction to where she thought her aunt's house was. Others in the streets, children mainly, though some adults were wandering around, too; all looking at her suspiciously in her coal dusted smart clothes as she looked around and guessed her way through the station master's directions and her own foggy memories, until she turned up what she thought was the right driveway. She marched up the gravel, then with a deep breath, she knocked on the heavy door and waited. She felt sick with nerves and turned briefly, deciding instead to go somewhere else, anywhere else. She had no idea where she was, where anything was, or what she would do if she left, so she decided to stay and turned to face the door just as it opened.

"Hello... I'm sorry to disturb you, but..." she mumbled through an increasingly dry mouth, drier than any time when she was in combat.

"Harriet?" the lady facing her, who looked remarkably familiar, said with a slight frown of disbelief. "Is that you?"

"Hi, Aunt Mary," she said with an awkward smile.

"My God, Harriet." Aunt Mary put her arms around Harriet's shoulders and hugged her tight. "I can't believe it." She pulled away with tears in her eyes and a smile on her face, then with a look to the heavens mouthed a silent 'thank you'. "Whatever are you doing here? How did you get here?"

"I..."

"Oh, do come in, you must be exhausted. Come and sit down." She took Harriet by the arm and pulled her into the house, closing the heavy door and walking through to the large kitchen. "Put your bag down. Let me get you a drink, is tea alright?"

"Thank you..." Harriet said as she looked around, a little overwhelmed by the greeting. She half remembered the large kitchen from when she was young. A huge table sat in the centre surrounded by chairs, with a cooking range in the middle of the wall. She glanced up to the clock above the windows that looked out over the drive. It was past seven in the evening.

"Your parents are going to be so happy." Aunt Mary continued, while she poured hot water from the large simmering kettle into a teapot. Cups and tea were put on the table, along with the milk, and she sat looking excitedly at Harriet where she'd sat at the head of the table.

"My parents?"

"Yes, I had a telegram from them just today... Oh, Harriet. I'm so happy to see you. We all thought the worst."

"The worst? My parents? Where are they?"

"Oh, my dear girl, you won't know, will you?"

"Know what, Aunt Mary?"

"Your parents are in Switzerland."

"Switzerland? What? How?" Harriet felt a flutter of excitement in her tummy.

"They only just escaped when the Germans came. They got to the embassy in Paris, who tried to send them home, but instead, they took the train to Switzerland to wait for news of you."

"They're alive?"

"Yes. Yes, they're alive." Aunt Mary poured tea, and Harriet felt tears run down her cheeks. "You poor thing. They're alive, and now you're safe in England, they'll be able to come home too." Harriet nodded while she fought to compose herself. "I'll send them a telegram first thing in the morning. They'll be delighted, and ever so relieved." Harriet nodded again. "Harriet, how did you escape?" Mary asked after they both spent a minute sipping tea. "How did you get here? How did you even remember your way? You must have been eight when you were last here?"

"Train..." Harriet replied.

"But from where? How did you get out of France?"

"On a boat from Dunkirk..." Harriet was struggling to process her thoughts properly. She'd all but given up her family as dead or captive.

"You always were so matter of fact," Aunt Mary smiled. "Anyway, it seems you've brought half of the train with you, too." She pointed at the coal dust on Harriet's blouse.

"The train from York was a coal train; the only place they could give me was upfront on the footplate. Otherwise, I'd have had to sleep at the station until tomorrow."

"What's that?" Mary asked as she saw the bandage under Harriet's sleeve.

"A burn. It's OK, I've had an excellent nurse looking after me," Harriet said with a smile, but Aunt Mary's frown returned.

"A burn? What sort of burn? Let me have a look. If you've been on trains all day the coal dust or smoke could have got into the wound, I should check it for you." Mary stood and retrieved her first aid kit from the cupboard, along with a bowl of hot water from the giant kettle.

"It's OK, really," Harriet protested, not wanting to be any bother.

"I'm sure it is. Now, let me see," Mary unbuttoned Harriet's sleeve and raised it, then took off the bandage which had indeed started to blacken with coal dust. Harriet winced as the last layer peeled off the honey coated wound and pulled at the flesh. "Harriet, what's this?" she asked as she looked at the scale of the injury.

"A burn, like I said..." Harriet shrugged nervously.

"A big burn. What on earth happened?"

73

"It's OK; it's been well looked after. The new skin has started to form, and the honey has helped keep it clean. I have some in my bag, and some spare dressings."

"Have you indeed? That doesn't explain how you got burned?"

"I had a bit of an accident with an aeroplane. It's a long story."

"I'm sure it is. Let's get this wound cleaned and dressed; then I'll show you to your room."

They talked while Aunt Mary dressed the wound, and when they'd finished their tea, Harriet was shown up the wide staircase and into a bedroom, which looked out over the very neat and well tended garden. In the distance, she could see the smoke from the factories of the city of Hull in the dimming evening light. It was quite a view and incredibly peaceful. Harriet took a bath, being careful to keep her dressing dry, and washed the coal dust and smoke from her hair before putting on the pale blue summer dress Aunt Mary had laid out for her. It fit well and flowed lightly over her body, keeping her cool, and it was a lot less restrictive than the very nice but very close fitting skirt and blouse Emily had given her. She went downstairs and joined Mary out on the patio in the cool evening air.

"Feel better for that?" Mary asked.

"Much, thank you," Harriet replied, as she settled herself into the chair, listening to the twittering of the birds around the garden. The fragrance of the late spring flowers was soothing, helping her to finally relax. "I'm sorry to impose on you this way, but thank you for letting me stay."

"Don't be silly, you're family," Aunt Mary replied. "For all intents and purposes, this is your home, and you'll stay as long as you like. Besides, where else would you go?"

"To my squadron..."

"Your what?"

"My squadron... I joined the RAF while I was in France."

"You've done what?"

"Joined the RAF. They sent me on leave until I'm feeling better, and in a month I'm to report to the local recruiting office to collect a warrant so I can go back." Harriet said excitedly.

"I don't understand, do your parents know?"

"I..."

"Of course they don't. I can't imagine a world where your father would let any daughter of his join the RAF, that would be far too demeaning. The last I heard about you was in a letter from your mother explaining you'd agreed to train as a nurse, and something tells me you're not a nurse in the RAF?" Harriet shook her head, and half smiled nervously. "He'll have kittens when he finds out." Aunt Mary smirked.

"Maybe he doesn't need to find out just yet."

"Oh, don't worry, I won't be telling him."

"Thanks, Aunt Mary, you know how he can be."

"He's my brother, and I know exactly how he can be. I love him dearly, but he's such a snob!" Harriet let out a snigger. "Besides, I'd much rather see his face when you tell him in person," Aunt Mary gave her a mischievous wink.

"Don't, please. I haven't even thought about it."

"I'm thinking about it right now. He'll turn every colour of the rainbow."

"Maybe we can keep it between us, for now?"

"You'll have to tell them sometime."

"I know, but maybe not just yet."

"Should I dare ask what you do in the RAF?"

"Fly..."

"Oh, Harriet, this is wonderful. You're a pilot?"

"Yes, though he knows about that. Kind of..."

"Kind of?"

"Mum knows I fly. My friend's grandfather was a pilot in the last war, and he taught us both. That's why the RAF accepted us, because we could already fly."

"I didn't know girls were allowed?"

"Neither did anyone, but we did, I did. I flew Hurricanes in France. That's how I was injured; in fact, I was shot down and crashed on the beach at Dunkirk." Aunt Mary's expression changed from one of disbelief and humour to deep focus and intrigue, as Harriet talked about some of her experiences. She found herself talking at length, and Aunt Mary hung on every word, until a distant rumble disturbed them, followed by a slow escalating whine. "What's that?" Harriet asked.

"They're early tonight," Aunt Mary replied. "Come on. We should go inside."

"Who's early?" Harriet asked as she followed Aunt Mary into the house and up the stairs, then through a door and up more stairs to the attic space. "Who's early?" Harriet asked again as Aunt Mary beckoned her to follow. "The Germans," Aunt Mary replied quietly, as she pushed the window open and climbed out onto the roof. She helped Harriet out, and they walked along the narrow lead walkway to the south of the house, above Harriet's bedroom. They stood and watched as the city started to glow red from the rumbling explosions that lit up the sky, which was crisscrossed with beams of light from the searchlights and pocked with small fiery explosions as the gun crews sought to deter the invisible German bombers. "I like to come up here and watch."

"Is it safe?"

"Yes... They don't come this far, they're after the docks," Aunt Mary replied as she pointed south. Harriet watched as the red flashes illuminated the inky blue sky, followed seconds later by the thunder of explosions travelling on the wind. It reminded her of being back in France, sitting with AP as the French town to the west of their airfield was bombed mercilessly through the night. She got lost in the thoughts, especially those of AP, who had stayed behind to keep the squadron fuelled and flying right to the last minute. The Germans were already closing the circle around Dunkirk when Harriet arrived. The squadron had got through and been evacuated, but there was no way AP's group could have made it in time, not before the circle closed entirely. Had they been overrun? Had they been captured? Had they been shot? So many questions, and absolutely no way of answering them. One thought led to the next, and as quickly as she pushed thoughts of AP into the back of her mind before they became overwhelming, they were replaced with thoughts of Max. He'd rescued her from the beach, but she'd left without him. Did he get off? If he did, did he get home without being sunk and drowned? So many more questions and so many unknowns. At least with Nicole she knew. She'd seen her burning Hurricane spinning out of control towards the ground. No parachute, no sign of control, experience suggested she was dead at the controls long before the fire took hold. Probably. "Hello?" Aunt Mary asked.

"Oh, hello," Harriet replied with a smile, having been dragged out of her daydreams.

"Are you OK, Harriet?"

77

"Yes... Yes, sorry. I was just thinking."

"You don't have to come if you don't feel up to it?"

"Come where?" Harriet asked in genuine confusion.

"Oh dear, you were away with the fairies, weren't you?"

"I..."

"It's OK. It's probably been a long day for you. I'd asked if you wanted to help me take cocoa to the trekkers?"

"The who?"

"Oh, Harriet. Come on, let's go." Harriet shrugged and followed Aunt Mary through the house to the kitchen, where the oversized kettle was still simmering away on the range. Aunt Mary poured it into a large dented metal billy can and threw in a generous scoop of cocoa powder and a jug of fresh milk, then she handed Harriet a large ladle, and they headed out of the house and through the yard gates to the main road from the city. Across the other side, in the pasture, Harriet could see the black outlines of people and hear the hushed voices of men and women, with the occasional childlike giggle and cry of a baby. Under a large old oak tree were three canvas tents, and sitting outside them were a couple of large families. "They've started early tonight," Aunt Mary said as she approached the group.

"Aye. It's gonna be a long night," an older man replied. "Thought we'd come up and stay out of harm's way."

"Probably a good idea, especially with the little ones around. Anyway, we've brought you some cocoa."

"That's very kind of you Ma'am, I have a few pennies..."

"I won't hear of it. I can't do it every night, but when I can, it's my pleasure. Come on, get your mugs," Aunt Mary said warmly. The family gathered their tin cups, and Harriet ladled the rich hot cocoa into each. "This is my niece. She's just home on leave from the RAF. She was with them in France, you know?"

"My boy's in France with the Yeomanry," one of the women said. "Rumour is that there's a lot of fighting going on over there?"

"Yes..." Harriet replied nervously.

"We'll put the Germans right, though. We did in the last war."

"What the bloody hell do you know about it?" an older man grumbled.

"Well we won, didn't we?"

"I was there, in the trenches, and I don't reckon anyone won."

"You made it back, didn't you? You grumpy old bugger."

"Aye... I did. Many of the other lads didn't, though."

"This is different. The Germans haven't got the army they had. Anyway, my Johnny and his mates will sort them out. Isn't that right, love? You were there, you tell him."

"Oh... I'm sorry, I didn't see much of the fighting on the ground," Harriet replied, as innocently as she could. "I burned my arm, so got sent home to hospital." Barrister's words of wisdom warning her not to talk about what was happening in France were at the front of her mind, and now she could see why. This woman's son was in France, and she believed he was safe and fighting the good fight, and how many more mothers were in the same position? None of them needed to know that their sons and husbands were either dead, captured, or running scared. Barrister had a point.

"Sorry to hear that, love. I hope you're better soon."

"Thank you. I'm sure I'll be fine. Aunt Mary, I'll be back in a minute," Harriet said. Aunt Mary nodded, and Harriet ran back to the house to retrieve the bag of cherries Barrister had bought her from the roadside in Kent. She quickly ran back to the group and offered the bag to the families.

"Cherries?" a woman said excitedly. "Where did you get cherries from at this time of the year?"

"Kent," Harriet replied. "Picked fresh this morning."

"Are you sure you don't mind sharing?"

"Please, there's more than enough for everyone," Harriet protested, and the woman smiled gratefully then handed the bag around. The families ate the cherries and drank the cocoa while talking with Harriet and Aunt Mary. After a while, they finally said their goodbyes and headed back to the house. "Where are they from?" Harriet asked.

"Hull," Aunt Mary replied. "When the bombing started, lots of people decided to spend their nights in the countryside to stay safe. They used to do it in the last war when the Zeppelin raids came over, though I think these raids are a bit different to those, and a lot worse." Harriet forced a smile, then yawned unexpectedly. "I bet you're exhausted after all of your travelling, why don't you get yourself to bed? We can walk to the village post office in the morning and telegram your parents, and let them know you're safe?" Harriet nodded.

"Thank you, Aunt Mary. For everything."

"Don't be silly. Here, take yourself some cocoa and wrap up warm. The house can be cold on a night."

They said their goodnights and Harriet made her way to her room, where she stood looking out of the window while sipping her warm cocoa. The raid was over, and the sky had darkened from blue to black, with a flickering red glow hovering over the city. Whatever the Germans had hit with their bombs was burning bright. Maybe the docks? Maybe an oil tank or something? Harriet soon felt tiredness overtaking her as she drained her cocoa, so quickly slipped out of her clothes and between the cool, clean, and welcoming sheets. No sooner had she laid her head on the soft feather pillow than she slipped into a deep sleep.

Chapter 3

Fools & Friends

A month after her arrival on Aunt Mary's doorstep and the day had finally come for Harriet to visit the local RAF recruiter, and collect her desperately desired rail warrant so she could head back to the squadron. She'd enjoyed her time staying with Aunt Mary, but she was so far beyond bored that she could hardly contain her excitement in the week leading to the big day. She'd helped around the house, and she'd helped the gardeners, she'd even painted the seemingly endless wooden fence which ran around her aunt's house. She'd done everything she could to be useful, and to keep herself occupied, but there was no escaping the yearning desire to be back in the air. The day after she'd arrived she'd gone to the post office with Aunt Mary, as planned, and telegrammed her parents in Switzerland. The same afternoon she received a reply telling her she was to go to Switzerland to be with them, as they were staying in Geneva so her father could monitor business and be ready to redevelop the French office as soon as the fighting was over. She'd declined, of course, and over a series of telegrams, it was agreed that she could stay with Aunt Mary until the autumn when her parents would return to England for a visit, as her father was due a meeting with the head office at home. Aunt Mary was a little irritated, not at having Harriet stay with her, she enjoyed the company, and she got on very well with Harriet; she was angry with her brother, Harriet's father. She had a significant rant over a glass of wine that evening, about how he could possibly stay in Switzerland after all Harriet had been through. He'd wired money to Mary for Harriet's keep, which Mary immediately gave to Harriet. Harriet tried unsuccessfully to give it back, and eventually put in her underwear drawer and forgot about until the morning she and Aunt Mary headed into Hull on the train to visit the recruiting office. She'd come across it while looking for Cas' watch, which she'd kept in the bottom of her drawer to keep it safe, frightened of damaging it more than the scratch she'd put across the glass when trying to escape her burning Hurricane. She was determined to keep her promise and return it to Cas if he was still alive, and as she'd convinced herself that it had kept her alive in France, she put it on for luck before leaving for Hull.

With a deep breath to compose herself, and contain her excitement, Harriet marched confidently up the steps of the City Hall. The main door was held open for her by the Military Police Corporal standing guard outside with a pair of soldiers. He gave her a welcoming 'Ma'am' and a lingering gaze as he watched her pass. Aunt Mary raised her eyebrow at him, making sure he blushed with embarrassment at being caught eyeing a young woman.

"Excuse me?" Aunt Mary asked the army Sergeant standing with a clipboard in front of a small group of soldiers.

"Yes, Ma'am?"

"Where's the RAF recruiting officer?"

"Door behind you Ma'am, all officers are in there." He pointed to the door at the opposite end of the entrance hall, she nodded her thanks and led Harriet. They knocked and waited, and knocked again. "I'd just go in, Ma'am, if I were you." The Sergeant shouted over. Aunt Mary nodded and opened the door into a large office. Directly ahead was a desk with a Navy Commander seated at it; to the right, an Army Major sat behind a heap of paperwork. They closed the door and walked over to the desk on the left, the RAF desk.

"Yes?" the ageing Squadron Leader asked as he looked up from his paperwork, peering over the top of his half moon glasses.

"Are you the recruiting officer for the RAF?" Aunt Mary asked.

"I am..."

"Good, my niece would like to speak with you,." She stepped back, and Harriet stepped forward. The Squadron Leader didn't change his expression.

"I'm Cornwall, Harriet Cornwall."

"Squadron Leader Herten. What can I do for you, Miss Cornwall? I'm a busy man."

"Yes, I don't doubt that," she replied politely. The Squadron Leader simply stared, unmoved. Harriet straightened up and blushed a little. "Anyway, I was told to come here to get a rail warrant."

"Oh?"

"Yes."

"And where is this rail warrant supposed to take you?"

"Well, to my squadron, of course."

"Your squadron?"

"Yes. I was evacuated from France through Dunkirk and sent here to recover from my wounds. The liaison officer at the hospital said you'd give me a rail warrant when it was time to go back."

"Did he now...?"

"Yes, so if you could give it to me, I'd be most grateful. I'm keen to get back."

"Back where, exactly?"

"My squadron..."

"Yes, I got that. Where?"

"Oh... I'm afraid I don't know where they are."

"I see... Which squadron?" He sat back in his chair, clearly irritated at being disturbed.

"I..."

"You don't know...?" he asked in a low and unwelcoming tone.

"Of course I know! 508 Squadron Auxiliary Air Force, The Wild Geese!"

"The Wild Geese? Of course... And what do you do with the Wild Geese?"

"I'm a pilot."

"A pilot?"

"Yes"

"I don't think so..."

"Excuse me?"

"There are no female pilots in the RAF."

"I beg to differ."

"I'm sure you do. However, I am a busy man, so if you wouldn't mind..."

"Mind what?"

"Good day." He picked up his pencil and returned to his paperwork.

"What about my rail warrant?" Harriet demanded. The Squadron Leader put down his pencil and looked up at her with exasperation.

"There is no rail warrant, as you don't know where you want to go to. There is no rail warrant, as you don't even know where the squadron is that you supposedly belong to, and lastly, but in no way least, there is no rail warrant as there are no female pilots in the RAF! Auxiliaries or otherwise! Now, good day!"

"How dare you!" Aunt Mary blustered. "My niece has fought bravely for her country, she was almost killed when she crashed her Hurricane at Dunkirk, and you have absolutely no right to talk to her in this way. Who is the senior officer here? I demand to speak to him!"

"I am the senior officer here, Madam, and I do not have time for the pranks and dreams of silly little girls! There's a war going on, and I'd expect a lady of your maturity to understand that, instead of indulging the fantasies of a child!"

"You, Sir, are rude!"

"And you, Madam, are wasting my time. So if you please, I have work to do. Essential work. War work!"

"I demand to speak to your superiors!"

"London."

"Pardon?"

"The Air Ministry in London. You'll find them there. Now, good day," he said, and went back to his work.

"You are the most..."

"Good day!" he repeated, cutting her off.

"Come on, Harriet," Aunt Mary took Harriet by the arm, and led her away from the desk.

"Excuse me, Miss," the Royal Navy Commander said, just as they reached the door. They turned to see him standing and walking around his desk.

"Yes?" Harriet asked, biting her tongue and refusing to let the tears of anger and frustration find their way out.

"Did you say you were a pilot over Dunkirk?"

"Yes, why?"

"I was at Dunkirk." He walked over and stood in front of them. "My boat was sunk not far off the coast." He raised his left arm, which was stiff and rigid, the hand covered in a black leather glove. "Crushed all of the nerves in my arm in a hatch when abandoning ship, and had to have it off. Apparently not having an arm means you're not allowed to command a ship these days. It didn't stop Nelson, of course, but their lordships at the admiralty know best, I suppose..."

"I'm sorry. I injured my arm there, too," Harriet said, touching the right sleeve of her dress. "When I crashed."

"Terrible over there on the beaches, wasn't it?"

"Oh, I wasn't there long. Just a night."

"Long enough though, right?"

"Right..."

"You know... There was a rumour going around the beaches when I was there."

"Oh?"

"Yes... About a squadron of women pilots who took on a massive German air raid. Outnumbered ten to one, they forced the Germans back and saved several naval vessels at the harbour and in the Channel." Harriet blushed a little as he talked.

"How did anyone know they were women?"

"Well, that's the other rumour... The story goes that one of them was shot down over the beaches, and when she was brought to the Naval Beach Master organising the evacuation, she was on the receiving end of a hard time from a pompous old army type, so she pulled a pistol and stuffed it in his mouth until he apologised."

"Is that so?" Harriet asked as her cheeks started to burn.

"Well, that's the rumour... Nobody seems to have met anyone who was actually there."

"I'm sure there were plenty of witnesses if it actually happened."

"I'm sure there were... Anyway, as I said, that's just a rumour. However, rumours and old war stories are almost always born in truth, to a degree, so I'm of the mind that it would be a terrible disservice to the country in its hour of need if we didn't at least entertain the idea that you could be one of those Amazons, and give you a chance to get back in the air," he smirked and nodded towards his desk. Harriet followed him as he sat and filled in a travel warrant. "There you go!" He handed her the piece of paper. She blushed even more, and looked a little shocked as she took it. "London. That's where you'll find the Air Ministry, which is where I believe my colleague over there said you should go."

"Thank you... Thank you so much!" Harriet said excitedly.

"You're welcome, Ma'am. It's open for a return back here, should you need it, and if you do, please call in and talk to me. If the RAF doesn't know a good thing when it sees it, I don't doubt that we can find something for you."

"As a pilot?"

"Sadly, that's highly unlikely. The Navy hardly have enough aeroplanes for the pilots we already have, but something's better than nothing, and we need highly motivated officers."

"I'll keep it in mind, thank you so very much."

"My pleasure. I wouldn't recommend travelling today, though, you'll have missed the early train, and the later ones may not get you to London until early evening when the Air Ministry is closed for business. Maybe catch the morning train tomorrow, it leaves at five. It'll have you in London mid morning at the latest, and get you to the Air Ministry before lunch." He gave a polite smile as Harriet and Mary thanked him again, then turned and headed for the door.

"The army is open to an approach, too. Should the senior service not fit..." the Major added without looking up from his desk as she passed. Aunt
Mary gave her a wink, and Harriet held in a giggle. They left the office and ran down the steps excitedly, and walked quickly towards the train station; but before they got there Aunt Mary pulled Harriet into the large department store across the road, where quite to Harriet's surprise Aunt Mary insisted on buying her the most beautiful sapphire blue suit with emerald threading, which depending on the light could make the fabric look either green or blue. Harriet was in love with it at first sight, as she was the pair of elegant heeled shoes that matched the clothes perfectly. She protested at having it bought for her, of course, and naturally, Aunt Mary would hear none of it. Suit, blouse, shoes, bag, and hat, all new, all the perfect fit, and all neatly hung and packed for Harriet to carry, which she did as far as the tea shop where she and Aunt Mary had tea and a scone before heading home.

That night Harriet packed her things and had a long bath before helping Aunt Mary take cocoa to the trekkers in the paddock, as yet another early raid bothered the city. They talked a while, the news about Dunkirk had finally broken, and the country was finally under no illusion as to how bad things were. The city's people were courageous, but they were understandably nervous. Germany had rolled across Europe almost unchecked, and it was difficult to see how Britain could stand alone. Harriet and Aunt Mary returned home and shared some cocoa, before Harriet climbed the stairs for the final time, and stood at the window watching the Hull burn again. Part of her would miss Aunt Mary and her life in Yorkshire, but another part couldn't wait to get back, and maybe to be away from the bombing, and the panic and worry it caused in the city she was so close to. Finally, she climbed into bed, leaving the curtains and blackouts open so she could watch as the flickering red glow filled her room and danced on the ceiling above her.

The morning came after a long night of tossing and turning, and after a good breakfast, Aunt Mary travelled with Harriet to Hull, where they made their way to the morning train to London. There were lots of military personnel. Army, Navy, RAF, they were all there, along with lots of businessmen.

"Are you nervous?" Aunt Mary asked.

"No," Harriet replied with a smile. "More excited than nervous. It feels like I'm going home."

"You know you have a home here anytime you want it, don't you?"

"I do, and I can't thank you enough for all you've done for me."

"Don't be ridiculous! You're family, my family; and more than that, in a way you've become a very good friend, it's been a pleasure getting to know you as a woman. I'll miss having you around."

"I'll miss you."

"Write to me?"

"I promise," Harriet said.

"I'll always reply. Oh, and I have something for you."

"What is it?" Harriet asked. Aunt Mary smiled and pulled a small box from her pocket and handed it over. Harriet raised an eyebrow then opened it, and immediately blushed. "It's beautiful."

"It was my grandmother's," Aunt Mary said. Harriet pulled the sparkling flying goose brooch from its box and stared at it as the lights of the station glinted off the green and white stones. "It's diamond and emerald, and it'll match your new suit."

"I really can't..."

"You can and you will, or I'll be insulted. Besides, it's destined to be. You told the recruiter your squadron is called the wild geese, it's like it was meant to come to you all along." She took it from Harriet and pinned it to the lapel of her suit jacket. "There, perfect." Harriet felt a tear on her cheek and quickly wiped it away while rolling her eyes in disappointment at herself for crying. They hugged as the guard blew his whistle, signalling the imminent departure of the train, followed by a loud 'all aboard!' "Go quickly. Don't you dare miss your train now!" They hugged once more, and Harriet climbed on the train and walked along the passageway until she found a compartment with an empty seat by the window. She put her kit bag in the rack above then took her seat, before standing again as soon as the train lurched into life. She waved to Aunt Mary out of the window. She waved and waved until out of sight, then she settled and watched the rugged bomb damaged streets roll by, and the heavy grey silhouettes of the barrage balloons hanging ominously in the distance. She sank into her seat, disturbed only by the conductor checking tickets. The journey was slow and unremarkable until finally the mass of London's barrage balloons came into sight and the train wound its way through the endless streets of people, before passing through the tunnels she'd remembered from her journey north, and arriving at King's Cross station. She'd made it. There was just the small matter of navigating the underground to the Air Ministry. She walked confidently down the Kingsway, dodging the many businessmen, military personnel, and tradesmen, all buzzing around looking as though they had somewhere to be. Finally, she arrived and walked towards the door where she found a large Military Police Sergeant standing in her way.

"Can I help you, miss?" he asked.

"I'm looking for the Air Ministry," she replied.

"You've found it."

"I know, thank you. Could you please move out of my way?"

"That depends."

"On?"

"On why you're here?"

"The recruiting officer in Hull sent me here."

"Ah, I see. My mistake, Miss. There's a door about halfway down the side of the building. You'll see my Corporal there, tell him you're here for recruiting, and he'll see you right."

"I'm not here to join the RAF, I'm already in the RAF, I'm a pilot, and I'm reporting for duty."

"You're a girl."

"Well done, go to the top of the class. Now, if you'd just get out of my way..."

"Girls don't fly."

"This one does."

"Wait here... Blythe, make sure she doesn't follow me inside." He rolled his eyes as a Corporal replaced him while he went into the building, returning a few minutes later with an RAF officer in tow.

"What's going on here?" the officer asked.

"I'm reporting for duty."

"So the Sergeant tells me."

"Then why can't I come in?"

"Because you're not the first young woman we've had here telling us she's going to be a fighter pilot, and you won't be the last I'm sure, but the fact is the RAF doesn't recruit female pilots. I'm sorry, but there it is."

"I don't need to be recruited. I'm already a serving pilot."

"I don't think so."

"This is ridiculous!"

"We thank you for your interest, but maybe the WAAF would be able to help you?"

"I'm a pilot."

"I'm afraid not. Good day."

"Really!"

"Good day, and please move along. Otherwise, I'll have the Sergeant call for a Policeman to remove you," he said as politely as he could. Harriet let out a roar of frustration then stormed down the steps. "Parade ground suffragettes," the officer muttered in amusement to the Sergeant. Harriet turned and fired him a fierce stare, before marching off around the corner, and down the side of the building.

"I'm here to see the recruitment officer!" she hissed at the Corporal guarding the door. Without argument, he showed her into a large room full of young men in suits, mostly waiting quietly on seats along the wall. In the centre of the room was a large desk, and sitting behind it was a grey haired Japanese man dressed smartly in an RAF uniform. He stood and bowed courteously as she approached. Harriet was taken by surprise and found herself bowing her head slightly in reply, though she was still shaking in anger. As she looked up, she noticed the wings on his chest, Royal Flying Corps wings, similar to those Cas had worn, sitting neatly on top of a row of medal ribbons.

"Flight Lieutenant O'Kara at your service, Ma'am," he said very formally.
"How may I help you?"

"Hello, I'm Harriet Cornwall. I was with the RAF in France and injured at Dunkirk," she blurted, then took a breath before continuing. "The hospital sent me home to convalesce, and I was told I could return to my squadron when I'd recovered, which I have, but nobody seems to want to help me, or believe me."

"I see... This is something of a quandary," he replied thoughtfully. "Unfortunately, this is the pilot selection board, and I'm not sure how I can help?"

"I am a pilot."

"Oh?"

"Yes... I know I'm a girl, but I'm also a pilot, and I just want to fly!"

"I know you're a girl, Miss Cornwall," he said with a polite smile. "It's a pleasure to meet a fellow pilot." He held out his hand, to Harriet's surprise. She shook it politely. "Where in France where you?"

"South of Reims, at first, before moving south."

"Ah yes, Reims, I remember it well from my time there in the last war."

"It's a beautiful place, or it was." Harriet sighed as she remembered her time there.

"Indeed. Which squadron were you with?"

"508 Squadron Auxiliary Air Force... Though the recruiter in Hull wouldn't believe me."

"That must be a difficulty."

"It is. It's like I no longer exist. I volunteered in France, and I was told that as I'm a pilot, and I'm of Norwegian descent, I could fly. I flew Hurricanes against the Germans." A few sniggers came from behind her, and she turned to see a couple of young men laughing at her story.

"Is there something I can help you gentlemen with?" O'Kara asked. "Excuse me, Miss Cornwall." He walked over to the young men and looked down at them.

"No, Sir," one of them started. "It's just that, well, we all know they don't let girls fly, why are you humouring her? She's clearly pulling your chain."

"Pulling my chain?"

"Yes," the other young man joined in. "It's an English expression, you know?"

"I know all too well what it is, Sir. Tell me, do you know what these wings signify on my tunic?"

"You're a pilot, of course."

"Of course... A pilot who served in France for two years in the last war, in the British Royal Flying Corps, and the Royal Air Force, and while I may still maintain some of my native Japanese accent, I can assure you that my English is of an exceptional standard."

"Yes, Sir. Sorry, Sir."

"Don't be sorry, young man, be wise. Wise enough to know that you know nothing other than what you think you know in this moment." Both young men looked at him, confused and sheepish. "The Royal Flying Corps, in the early days, didn't appoint pilots other than those of white European heritage. Yet here I am, wearing the wings of a Royal Flying Corps pilot, and the ribbon of the Distinguished Flying Cross, which the King himself presented me with after I shot down five German aeroplanes in one single combat. The Royal Air Force didn't commission non white European officers at first either, yet here I am standing before you and wearing the rank of a Flight Lieutenant. We only know what we think we know in the moment, gentlemen, and accepting that will, I guarantee, help you when you face a German aeroplane in combat for the first time! I can promise you that the experience will be nothing like you expect, and your enemy will not behave as you expect. If your mind is closed, he, or she, will kill you. Assuming you make it through this selection board, that is." The young men fell silent and nodded respectfully as O'Kara turned back to Harriet. "If a young Japanese boy can fly in combat for the British, and meet the King, it's entirely possible that a young lady of Norwegian stock can do the same." He gave a short bow and a smile. "I have an idea, Miss Cornwall. Why don't I put you in front of the head of pilot selection? He's a reasonable man. Convince the panel, and who knows what could happen?" He pulled a piece of paper from his desk, and Harriet helped him fill it in with her details, then he left the room, and she was asked to take a seat among the young men. O'Kara returned after a while, smiled, and returned to his paperwork.

"Harry Cornwall?" a Sergeant called from the passageway behind O'Kara a short while later. Harriet paused a moment, then stood.

"Here," she replied confidently. The Sergeant frowned at her for a moment.

"This way please, Ma'am." He showed her to an office where he announced her. "Harry Cornwall, Sir."

"Send him in, Sergeant." The Sergeant stepped back with a half smirk and waved Harriet into the room, where three officers, all of them pilots, were sitting behind a long desk with a lone chair in front of it. All three stood immediately as Harriet entered, and the Sergeant closed the door.

"Can I help you, Miss?" the senior officer asked.

"I'm Harry Cornwall," Harriet replied.

"Excuse me?"

"Harriet Cornwall. I'm a pilot, and I want to fly."

"I don't doubt that you do."

"Good." She sat down in the chair, and they followed her lead, after looking exchanging startled glances.

"We... The RAF, that is, doesn't recruit female pilots, I'm afraid," the senior officer said, almost apologetically.

"It has done before."

"I assure you, Miss..."

"In France. I was there when the Germans came. My family have Norwegian ancestry, and I'm a good pilot, and the squadron let me fly Hurricanes with them."

"You flew Hurricanes?" he asked in intrigued disbelief.

"Yes. A senior officer said it would be allowed, and that I would fly in the Royal Air Force Volunteer Reserve as a foreign pilot."

"I see... I'm afraid it's the first I've heard of it."

"It's true, I swear. Mister Singh was the Commanding Officer, and Mister
Salisbury was the Adjutant."

"That's quite some story, young lady."

"It's not a story."

"And what would you like me to do about it?"

"Nobody will see me, and nobody will believe me, they just keep telling me that girls don't fly. The officer at the main door here said I should be a WAAF, and the recruiting officer in Hull told me I was making it all up, and said if I wanted to join the RAF I should come here, so here I am."

"Sergeant, ask Mister O'Kara to join us, will you?" The Sergeant quickly did as he was asked, and soon O'Kara stood by her side and politely bowed. "Mister O'Kara, what do you mean by putting this young lady in front of us?"

"She's a pilot, Sir. I believe she has the right to state her case."

"Do you now?"

"We need pilots, Sir, and if Miss Cornwall is as she says, the country could make use of her services."

"You are as astute as ever, Mister O'Kara. But what to do... You know as I do that we may not recruit a female pilot."

"Yes, Sir, but if Miss Cornwall has indeed already been recruited under emergency war powers, that's not something that should stand in our way."

"Yes... Yes, good. OK, why don't you ask your assistant to cover your desk, while you head upstairs and see if you can find some supporting evidence for Miss Cornwall's claims? Miss Cornwall, no promises of course, but if we can get the evidence we need, we'll talk further. Could you wait outside, please?" Harriet stood and smiled politely, and O'Kara showed her back to the waiting room, where she waited as the young men were summoned one by one. Some came back and left looking downhearted, and some didn't, she waited long enough to see more than a few go through. Finally, O'Kara returned and disappeared again, then after another wait, she was called back in front of the selection panel. "Thank you for waiting, Miss Cornwall," the senior officer said warmly.

"You're welcome."

"Look, I won't beat around the bush, it's bad news I'm afraid." Harriet's heart sank. "Mister O'Kara has discussed your situation with the records officer, and I'm afraid there's no record of your commission, or of you at all."

"But...!" Harriet protested. The officer waved his hand downwards to calm her.

"Let me finish, Miss Cornwall."

"Yes, Sir."

"Now, the Air Ministry has rules, and one of those rules is that we cannot recruit female pilots. Whether or not that rule is righteous or even sensible is above my pay grade to say, but the fact remains that it's a rule I'm not able to bend. However..."

"Yes?"

"You say you're a pilot."

"I am."

"Well, we'll soon see. I'm prepared, with your agreement, to recommend you for flying duties with the Air Transport Auxiliary, subject to you passing their flying assessments. It's not the RAF, I know, and it's not combat duties, but it is flying. If you're any sort of a pilot, you'll snap my hand off to take the opportunity to join the organisation which is transporting our much needed combat aeroplanes around the country to our squadrons. What do you say? Want to give it a try? It's the best offer you're going to get today." Harriet looked at O'Kara, and he gave the slightest encouraging nod.

"That would be very kind of you, Sir. Thank you."

"I know it's not what you want, young lady, but it's what you have. Besides, who knows what the rules will be a year from now, or even six months from now. If Hitler turns his invasion eyes in this direction, which we're expecting he will, we'll soon need every pilot we can get our hands on. God knows, they may even put me back in a cockpit, then we know we're in trouble!" The other officers laughed politely. "Mister O'Kara, give Miss Cornwall a warrant to get her down to the ATA specials on the coast, and get a telegram off letting them know to expect her."

"Yes, Sir."

All of the officers stood, and the senior officer leant forward on the desk. "It's up to you now, Cornwall. They're pretty hot on their flying assessments, and if you're not the pilot you say you are, they'll soon have you heading home."

"Thank you. Thank you all, I won't let you down," Harriet said as O'Kara showed her out.

"Good luck," they called after her. She smiled as she walked by O'Kara's side.

"I'm sorry I couldn't find more information," he said as they walked.

"It's OK. I appreciate your efforts. You've done more than anyone else so far, and at least I'll be flying."

"That you will, which is more than some of us can say."

"Do they not let you fly?"

"Sadly not. I'm too old, apparently. At least I can do something, though, by helping get the new generation of pilots in the air."

"It's a noble job."

"As is delivering aeroplanes to the front line squadrons. Remember that."

"I will. Thank you." Harriet let herself smile, despite being a little downhearted. O'Kara produced the travel warrant and sent a Corporal to send a telegram, then he showed Harriet to the door and stepped outside with her. "I have a question, though I'm not sure I should ask," she said.

"If you don't ask, how will you ever know the answer?"

"What if it's insensitive?"

"Are you intending to be insensitive?"

"I'm not."

"Then, you should ask."

"You're Japanese."

"I am."

"But you have an Irish name."

"Ah, that," he laughed. "As a young man, I wanted adventure and excitement, so I travelled to see the world, and when war broke out, I volunteered for the British Army. I studied metallurgy under my father, a master swordsmith, and the army sent me to the cavalry as a blacksmith and farrier. However, when the recruiting Sergeant asked my name, and I replied Akara, he registered me as O'Kara. I later asked for it to be corrected, and was told that I would likely not be taken seriously with such a foreign name, so the name change stuck, especially after my flying assessment when they passed me without even seeing what I looked like. Had they known they were assessing a Japanese person, I likely wouldn't have been allowed through the door.

"I don't know if that's terrible or wonderful."

"It's whatever we want it to be. Even though they're good men, the panel wouldn't have seen you if Harriet had been on your application, instead of Harry." She felt a blush on her cheeks and a smile on her face.

"I can't thank you enough."

"You already have, Miss Cornwall. Good luck."

Chapter 4

'ATA Girl

Following the instructions O'Kara had given her, Harriet had made her way across London and found the train which took her to a small aerodrome on the south coast of England. The last stage of her journey was on a small bus, which rocked and rolled along the country lanes while Harriet gazed out of the window at the beautiful scenery, occasionally glimpsing the turquoise sea as it sparkled in the summer sun. She stepped off as the driver called her stop, then straightened her clothes, and marched confidently to the gate.

"Good Morning, Ma'am," the RAF Policeman greeted.

"Good Morning, Sergeant," Harriet replied as she handed him the letter O'Kara had given her. He read it and handed it back, then stepped aside and waved her through the gate.

"Follow the road, and you'll find the dispersal hut; you can't miss it."

Harriet found herself smiling as she walked along the road. It was the first time she hadn't been questioned or obstructed in what felt like a long time, and she felt like she was heading in the right direction. As the airfield came into view, a Tiger Moth biplane circled above, and she watched it wobble a little as the pilot tried to keep the wings level. More Tiger Moths were lined up on the grass in front of the dispersal hut, where a young woman, dressed smartly in a pristine blouse and dark trousers, stood on the veranda and watched the flying. The gold braid on her epaulettes glinted in the sun and caught Harriet's eye, and matched the woman's golden hair and lightly tanned skin.

"Hey there," the young woman greeted Harriet in a confident American accent.

"Hello," Harriet replied. "I'm looking for the ATA."

103

"Well, you've found us, honey. What can we do for you?"

"The Air Ministry sent me..." Harriet handed the young woman her letter.

"You're a pilot?"

"I am."

"That's good. We need pilots. Hey, Penny?" she called into the office. A commanding woman somewhere in her thirties, and with much more gold braid on her shoulder, stepped out into the light. The young woman handed her the letter. "The Air Ministry has sent us a gift."

"Harriet, is it?"

"It is, friends call me Harry."

"Well, Harriet, this letter says that you're a pilot."

"I am," Harriet replied with a sense of foreboding, for no other reason than the woman chose to call her Harriet, and not Harry.

"It takes more than just being a pilot to fit in around here, I can assure you. Flying whatever low powered toy you learned on back home is entirely different from the powerful warbirds my girls fly every day."

"I think I'll be OK."

"Oh, you do? Fortunately, we don't rely on the word of amateurs around here. We've worked far too hard to have our name tarnished by poor judgement and poor flying. If you get past Lexi, we'll talk"

"What's Lexi?"

"Me," the glamorous American said with a smirk. "Lexi Lexington, at your service." She stood with her hands on her hips and looked Harriet up and down. "You got any pants with you?"

"I'm wearing them," Harriet replied with confusion.

"Trousers, honey. Trousers. I don't mean your panties."

"Oh... No, sorry. I only have what I'm wearing." She felt herself blushing.

"Well, I hope you ain't shy, let's go." She marched off in the direction of a bright yellow Tiger Moth parked on the grass.

"You've got to be in the aeroplane if you're going to prove yourself," Penny said sternly and nodded her head in the direction of the Tiger Moth. Harriet dropped her bag and pulled off her suit jacket, which she dropped on top of it before running after Lexi.

"Flown a Tiger Moth before?" Lexi asked.

"No..."

"OK, well, let me give you the grand tour, then we'll get in the air." She did exactly that, showing Harriet round while throwing out bullet points of handling characteristics. Harriet's brain was spinning, trying to keep up and take it all in as the golden American talked. They stopped by the wing after completing a lap. "That's just about everything, you ready to fly?" Harriet nodded excitedly. "That's the right answer. Climb in the back seat, and I'll finish the tour." Harriet hitched her skirt to her hips without a thought and climbed up the wing and into the cockpit. Lexi smirked, then leaned in the cockpit and gave her the once over. "Nervous?"

"No."

"I would be, I'm not easy to impress," she said with a smirk. "Put your helmet on, then give me a minute to spin the prop so you can get her

105

started. Then I'll get strapped in, and you can show me what you've got." Harriet looked around the cockpit and familiarised herself with the controls. They weren't as simple as the old Nieuport, but there was a lot less to think about than with the Hurricane. "Ready?" Lexi shouted.

"Ready, clear prop!" Harriet shouted. Lexi spun the blade, and Harriet caught it the first time. The propeller spun as the engine spluttered blue smoke and buzzed into life. The vibrations travelled through the airframe, and Harriet instantly felt at home, though slightly unnerved at not hearing the comforting roar of a Merlin engine. "I'm guessing I don't have to get her off the ground for you?" Lexi asked over the intercom.

"No," Harriet replied, quite bluntly.

"OK, well, take us around to the end of the runway, then you can take off and get us up to five thousand feet."

"Five thousand feet, got it." Harriet looked around for obstacles, checked for traffic, and noted the wind direction. Then she revved and taxied smoothly to the end of the runway, where she turned into the wind and conducted her last power tests before lining up. No traffic, wind on the nose; she had one last look around, then hit the throttle, and the Tiger Moth bounced along the grass strip. It was a lot different to the Hurricane, she felt as if she could walk quicker, but soon enough the bounces were lifting a little more. In a move that Nicole's grandfather had shown her, she eased the stick forward to lift the tail into the airstream. All of a sudden, the air rushed underneath the wings and lifted them off the ground and into the sky.

"Nice move," Lexi commented, giving a thumbs up from the front seat. "Now get us up to five thousand and get a feel for the controls." Harriet put the nose into a steady climb, then set about working the stick and pedals as she went through a few climbing turns and slips, and she was soon feeling comfortable. The controls were light but not as responsive as the Hurricane, and the smaller aeroplane didn't seem as stable or robust. She'd thrown the Hurricane all over the sky, and apart from the carburettor problem, it had always felt safe. The Tiger Moth felt a lot

106

more precious and vulnerable. "OK, level off," Lexi instructed. "How are you feeling?"

"Fine."

"OK, that's good. The floor's yours, honey. The Tiger Moth is designed for principle flight training, and it'll stand up to pretty much anything you throw at it, so thrill me but don't kill me."

"Yes Ma'am," Harriet replied politely, feeling a smirk spreading across her lips. "Are you strapped in tight?"

"I'm brave but I ain't stupid, honey. I'm flying with a new pilot; would I be anything else?"

"Good!" Harriet smiled, then pushed the stick over to the left and flipped the moth half on its back, then pulled back on the stick and dived at the ground, rolling as she went. Gauging the altitude just right, she stopped the roll and pulled up out of the dive, gently at first, so as not to rip the wings off the fragile looking Moth. The speed faded as the moth struggled to maintain the ascent then, timing it perfectly, Harriet let the wing drop in a stall. She kicked the rudder bar hard and pushed the stick to flick the tail over their heads, before falling into a screaming straight down dive. They rolled tighter and tighter as the ground got closer and closer, then fighting every instinct she pushed on the stick and flattened out of the dive fifty feet from the ground, upside down. She let out a scream of laughter and joy as she shot over the airfield, before flipping over and starting another powerful climb; which she quickly made into a loop that she rolled out of at the top. Once again she flipped the moth on its back, fully this time, before diving steeply back to the deck, where she proceeded at full speed before pulling up into a victory roll.

"OK that'll do, put her back down," came Lexi's instruction, which sounded a little forced and flustered. Harriet did as she was asked, and after a quick check for traffic, she made a steep turn into the approach and quickly scrubbed off speed and height, before touching the ground as

107

light as a feather. She rolled the moth to where she'd found it and shut down.

"Come on," Lexi said as she removed herself uneasily from the front cockpit, and steadied herself against the wing for a moment. She threw her flying helmet onto the stick, then ran the back of her hand against her sweat soaked forehead. She didn't seem as bright and confident as when they'd first started, and Harriet looked at her nervously with an unwelcome mix of knots and butterflies in her tummy. She started to consider exactly how much she'd overdone it on her test flight, and whether she'd messed it all up. She took off her helmet and climbed from the cockpit, then straightened her clothes and followed sheepishly behind Lexi, who was marching towards Penny.

"Well?" Penny asked.

"Give her a set of wings and a uniform. There's nothing I can teach that girl about flying," came the American's reply. She turned to Harriet and winked. "Though for a moment I thought I'd pissed her right off, and she was trying to kill me." Harriet felt a smile on her face as the tension left her stomach.

"How's your map reading?" Penny asked, trying to hide her smirk.

"Pretty good," Harriet replied. "I can find my way most places in an aeroplane."

"Good... Come and see me in station headquarters after lunch, and we'll talk about what happens next."

"Thank you!" Harriet replied, trying hard to contain herself and stop herself from jumping up and down with excitement.

"Come on, honey. Let me buy you lunch," Lexi said. Penny nodded, and Harriet followed at Lexi's side as she walked around the dispersal hut. "Where'd you learn to stall turn like that?"

"Back in France..."

"Maybe I should've done more flying in France." She gave Harriet a wink, then climbed on the large red and chrome motorcycle standing behind the dispersal hut. "Jump on." Harriet hitched her skirt once again as the engine roared into life, then straddled the motorbike and got as comfortable as she could while pushed tight against Lexi. "Put your arms around my waist, don't be shy," Lexi ordered. Harriet held tight, and they left in a roar of smoke, skidding on the grass a little as they joined the perimeter road, then steadying and going so fast Harriet was sure they'd take off. She was equal parts terrified and exhilarated and loving it. It was almost as good as flying. They pulled up and parked, and the pair of them climbed as gracefully as possible from the motorbike.

"Something I can help you with, Mister?" Lexi shouted at a passing airman, who was staring wide eyed at Harriet's legs as she straightened her skirt. "No Ma'am," he replied with an instant blush and stammering a little, not expecting to be challenged by a fiery young woman.

"No Ma'am indeed. You wouldn't look at your mom or your sister like that, so don't do it to young women here. Especially not officers!" He scurried away, and Lexi gave Harriet a wink. "Keep them in their place," she said. "Call them out on the spot, and they'll run a mile. Better they learn they'll catch hell if they mess with you than behaving like a damned animal."

"Thanks..." Harriet replied. She'd never met anyone quite as confident as Lexi; not even Nicole was as fierce. Lexi was a woman who had been around a bit, enough to know how to manage people with confidence. She wasn't old, not by any means, in her mid twenties at the most, but Harriet was instantly in awe. They walked into the building, past the comfy leather chairs in the reception. Harriet signed the visitor's book before being led to a dining room not dissimilar to the senior's canteen at her school in France. A waiter appeared with a jug of water, then brought them each a cup of tea. "What is this place?" Harriet asked as the waiter returned a third time, carrying two plates of cheese and lettuce sandwiches.

"The officer's Mess. It's where we live. Well, in an annexe anyway," Lexi replied. "All ATA pilots are commissioned officers, and as we don't have an ATA Mess, we stay as invited guests of the RAF. Besides, they like us, we deliver their aeroplanes so they can focus on fighting and not shunting. Not that there are many pilots on this station, it's mainly a handful of ground officers and us. There's a Communication Fight who are nice enough. Then there's a flight of Lysanders who disappear off at all hours of the night. Their crews are usually here at odd times as they're sleeping in the day and flying at night. Anyways what about you? Where did you learn to fly like that?"

"In France, my friend's grandfather was a fighter pilot in the last war. He had his own aeroplane, and he taught us how to fly in return for our help keeping it running."

"You can fix them too? Not bad, honey."

"What about you, where did you learn to fly?"

"I learned back home in California. I never was one for playing with dolls and settling for a girl's life. Daddy is in the mining business and had a pilot to fly him here and there to check on things. He used to take me on his trips, much to Mom's annoyance, but I nagged him so much he eventually let me learn. He thought it might keep me out of trouble, and steer me away from the motorcycle racing I'd taken to. One thing led to another, I flew in aerobatics displays for a while, and flew the mail in the prairies, then one time for fun I flew from California to New York, right across the country."

"Wow... That's incredible."

"Yeah, it's been pretty good," she replied with a twinkle in her eyes. "Anyway, I was over here for a motorcycle race. I couldn't leave it alone, I just love the speed so much, and when war broke out, Penny found me and asked if I wanted to be part of it. I was hoping to be a fighter pilot, but I guess you know the story there. Girls don't fly and all that."

110

"I've heard that once or twice."

"Oh me too, honey. Me too. Anyway, this isn't so bad. I get to fly Spitfires.
Not many can say that. Men or women."

"You've flown Spitfires?"

"You bet. It's what we do here. We're a small outfit, an all female detached flight from the main pool north of London. The Supermarine factory where they make the Spitfires is just up the coast. We move their specials around the country, though sometimes it's just regular Spits going up to the engineers at the support fields, to be armed and equipped before they go to their squadrons."

"Specials?"

"Yeah, the smart guys at Supermarine and the Air Ministry are always thinking up something new, and we're often tasked with taking the modified Spitfires out to be field tested somewhere, or collecting them after testing, and taking them back to Supermarine to be tweaked or scrapped. Sometimes we even collect Spitfires that have been ditched by their pilots when they've had an engine failure. The mechanics go out and get it going, then we go and collect it, and drop it wherever it needs to be for a full overhaul."

"That's really amazing."

"You bet. I've been here for two months, and there's almost a Spitfire a day in my logbook. We have days off, obviously, but there's a war on, and Spitfires need moving. Besides, there's nothing quite like flying a Spitfire.
It's kind of addictive. You're gonna love it."

"I really can't wait."

"It's a fun job, you never know where it'll take you, it could be anywhere. Hell, one of our girls even flew a Hurricane out to France while the fighting was raging a short while ago, and was asked to bring a PR Spitfire back, a big blue camera ship used to take photos and spy on the Germans. You probably won't get to France, but you'll certainly get to know a lot of the airfields in England. You'll be popular, too, so you'd better get used to that."

"Popular?"

"Yeah, popular. You're a girl in a uniform, and the fighter boys are gonna swarm around you. I'm telling you now, so be ready for it, and be prepared to put them right in their place if they cross the line. Or maybe let them put you in their place if you like them." She gave Harriet a wink and laughed. Harriet instantly blushed and raised her eyebrows, while trying desperately to hide her embarrassment. It was the first time in a long time she'd blushed that way, not since Nicole's teasing. "Oh, don't worry. They're perfect gentlemen and know when to take no for an answer if you're not interested."

"I'm not... I just want to fly."

"Well, you'll get plenty of opportunities for that. Come on, let's go and see Penny in her office. If you've finished?" Harriet nodded and gulped down the last of her tea, before following Lexi out to the motorbike for another whirlwind ride to the station headquarters.

"Finished lunch?" Penny asked as they entered the office.

"Yes, all done," Lexi replied. "Hello, Mister Thomas," she said politely to the smartly dressed older gentleman sitting in a chair facing the desk. He stood quickly and bowed respectfully.

"Ladies," he greeted them formally.

"Mister Thomas has come to measure you for your uniform," Penny said to Harriet as she walked him to the door. "If you wait next door she'll be in directly, and thank you again for coming at such short notice."

"Not at all, Penny. I was in the area anyway, and it's on my way back to London. Besides, it's always a pleasure to see you."

"And you, Mister Thomas."

"Shall I put the uniform on the account?"

"Please do."

"I'll have it ready in no time," he looked Harriet up and down. "I think you're about right with your estimates." He smiled and left the office, closing the door behind him. Harriet joined Lexi standing in front of the desk.

"I've talked with headquarters," Penny started, as she sat in her green leather chair and looked up at Harriet. "And going by the Air Ministry's recommendation, and Lexi's assessment of your flying, they're happy to take you on the roll as a Ferry Pilot in the rank of Third Officer."

"Thank you," Harriet said while trying to contain her excitement.

"You'll be based here with us for the time being. Do you have anywhere to stay locally?"

"No... The closest thing I have to a home is in Yorkshire."

"I see. In that case, you'll have a room in the Officer's Mess Annex. You'll have to share, but the girls are all quite pleasant."

"I don't mind sharing at all."

"You'll be paid weekly in arrears, and I'll arrange for the cost of your uniform to be deducted weekly over your first year. It'll hardly be noticeable. Otherwise, your money is yours, except for your Mess bill, which you'll find in your pigeonhole. Make sure you pay it on time. The RAF are very gracious landlords, and we have an excellent reputation as tenants, which I'd like to keep."

"Got it."

"On that note, we, as female aviators, are in a precarious position. Our commandant fought long and hard to convince the powers that be that we should be allowed to fly in contribution to the war effort. It took a lot of strings being pulled with a lot of contacts in very high places to get them to agree, and even now many would like to see us fall on our faces so they can close us down. Which all means that we have to do it better than our male counterparts in the ATA, as we're being watched very carefully, and held to higher standards."

"I'll do my best, I promise."

"I expect so, too. Do what you want when you're off duty, but in the air, you need to be the best pilot you can be." Harriet nodded in agreement. "Good. Now, I brought your bag down from the dispersal and sent it up to your room. Call in next door for Mister Thomas to measure you up, and then you can both hop over to Supermarine. They have a special that needs to go up to a maintenance unit for fitting. That'll be the last job for today, so you can stand down when you're back."

The girls left the office, and after stopping in the next room to be measured by Mister Thomas, they headed out to the motorcycle. "Welcome aboard," Lexi said, giving Harriet a firm handshake. "I'm happy you're staying with us, though I didn't doubt it."

"You didn't?"

"Not for a second. The Air Ministry don't send pilots straight to us. Usually, they recommend assessment up north first, at the main headquarters, and if you meet the standards, they'll decide what to do with you. A letter recommending you straight to us isn't just unusual, it doesn't happen, so I kind of guessed there must be something about you, and I was right. Not many fly like you, honey. It's a gift!" Harriet felt herself blushing again and settled onto the back of the motorbike with her arms around Lexi's waist. Soon they were roaring along the road of the airfield back to the dispersal hut, where Lexi handed Harriet a pair of white overalls more suited to flying than her skirt, and a pair of old boots which just about fit. Lexi showed her through the sign out procedure with the duty clerk, a pleasant young girl from London. Then they headed over to the Avro Anson taxi aeroplane. Lexi showed Harriet around, talking her through the controls and flight parameters. They sat side by side as Lexi took them up away from the aerodrome, and into a wide circuit, pointing out local features and navigational marks for Harriet, before heading out to the coast while Harriet navigated with her map. "Just remember, most of the aeroplanes we fly aren't fitted with radios, so we're kind of on our own once we're off the ground. Your navigation needs to be hot, as there's nobody to tell you where you're going wrong. Stay low, too. If you go too high, you risk finding a stray German. They tend to stay up above fifteen thousand feet, so if we're down at treetops, they're unlikely to see us, or even be bothered with us if they do. Now have a read of the pilot's notes for the Spitfire while we're flying. It's how we learn in the ATA, and there's no specific type training beyond single engine, multi, fours, and seaplanes, so you're expected to fly anything within your rating. For you, that's anything with a single engine, for now. It could be a Tiger Moth; it could be a Spitfire. Everything operates differently, but they're all pretty much the same, you'll pick up the differences from the pilot's notes and from asking around." They flew along the coast and finally put down at the Supermarine factory airfield where Lexi parked in the visitor area near the tower, then showed Harriet in to report their arrival and collect their orders from the duty dispatcher.

"Miss Lexington, it's a pleasure to see you as always," the balding civilian dispatcher greeted as he walked over to the counter. "And who's this you've brought with you; I don't think we've met?"

"Harry Cornwall," Harriet replied, offering her hand.

"Harry? I like that. A pleasure to meet you, Miss Cornwall. Will you be a regular visitor?"

"It's likely, she was posted to us today," Lexi replied.

"Good. Good... Well, if there's anything I can ever do, just say, won't you?" He stared at Harriet with a broad smile from under his moustache.

"You've got something for us, I'm told?" Lexi continued.

"What? Yes, yes, of course," he replied. "A Spitfire needs to go to the satellite maintenance unit at Biggin. She's waiting out on the dispersal for you."

"Anything fun, Mister Byron?"

"Now, now, Miss Lexington, you know we don't talk about those sorts of things." He leant forward and lowered his voice to a whisper. "She's got a modification to the underside, though, a rack for a bomb and a release in the cockpit by the throttle. Just so you don't go touching anything you shouldn't..." He smiled and gave them a wink.

"We'll make sure we don't," Lexi smiled. "Thank you. See you next time." They left the control and headed out to the beautiful beast of a Spitfire that was parked out in front. In the distance, an engineer appeared from a hangar in his overalls and started walking over slowly.

"Don't mind Byron, he's cute," Lexi said quietly. "He was a fighter pilot in the last war. It's why he has a twinkle in his eye when he sees a pretty girl. They just can't help themselves; all fighter pilots are the same." Harriet giggled as Lexi laughed.

"It's so beautiful," Harriet said as they stood in front of the Spitfire.

"It sure is. It's the most beautiful airplane I've ever seen, and I've seen plenty."

"What are they like to fly?"

"You're about to find out."

"What?" Harriet asked in shock.

"Have you ever flown a twin engine airplane before?"

"No..."

"Well, they're a little different to a single engine, in lots of ways. Besides, you work for us now, and you remember Penny's rules, you only fly what you're rated to fly, and you're rated for single engines so saddle up, girl, you've got a Spitfire to fly." Harriet's stomach tensed with excitement and nerves, and her heart started to pound. Lexi showed her around the external checks then helped her up to the cockpit where she climbed after fastening on her parachute.

"Do you need any help up there, Miss?" the mechanic asked as he stood ready with his fire extinguisher.

"No thanks, we're good," Lexi replied, before returning her attention to talking Harriet through her cockpit checks. After making sure she'd done all she could she marked the maintenance field on Harriet's map. "Once you start the engine, don't hang around," she advised. "It'll overheat really quick if you do. Get to the end of the runway, do your power checks, then get up. Oh, and make sure you swing her ass as you taxi! You ain't gonna see nothing over the nose until you're in the air, and you don't want to crash before you take off. Keep some rudder on when you're running the field, too! That big old Merlin engine is so full of torque that its gonna want to drag you right over, so you've got to keep it straight."

"Got it," Harriet replied nervously, going over everything she was told and trying to make it stick in her memory.

"Good. Finally, we have one strict rule in the ATA that stands over all others."

"What's that?"

"The pilot is more valuable than any airplane." Harriet raised an eyebrow. "The factories can have another airplane built in less than a week, but there ain't no building another good pilot. They take years to make, and the best pilots are unique and one off, and can't ever be reproduced, pilots like you. So if anything goes wrong, don't try and be a hero, use your parachute."

"OK..." Harriet said, feeling a little nervous. "Is anything likely to go wrong?"

"Who knows?" Lexi smiled, then walked down the wing. "I'll see you when you get there, and try not to break your first!" she laughed and left Harriet to look around the cockpit and refresh her memory on what the many switches and dials did. It wasn't too different from a Hurricane. She looked out of the cockpit and checked the mirror to make sure the area was safe. Lexi was standing by the engineer, who wasn't filling her with confidence in the way he was holding his fire extinguisher.

"Clear prop!" Harriet shouted, then with the magnetos and fuel on she hit the ignition. The three blades of the propeller flicked over before a shot of fire flickered from the exhaust stubs and for a moment illuminated the blue smoke they coughed out before it was blown away by the spinning prop. The aeroplane vibrated, and Harriet felt herself smiling as she went through her checks. She took a deep breath then waved the chocks away. Lexi waved her off as she rolled past, gently easing the rudder to pull the nose so she could see what was in front of her. Finally, the moment came.

Harriet turned into the wind and did her final checks, then after a quick spin of her head to check the circuit she straightened up and slowly pushed the throttle open. The mighty Merlin engine roared, and the Spitfire lurched forward. The power was incredible, and she had to push harder than she expected against the rudder bar to stop the nose yawing and pulling her off the runway. She was pushed back in her seat by the force of the thrust, and before she knew it, the Spitfire leapt into the air. Harriet couldn't help but smile. Finally, she was flying a proper aeroplane again, more than that she was flying a Spitfire. She switched hands on the stick and raised the undercarriage, then went through her checks as she climbed up to one thousand feet, high enough to jump if she needed to, and low enough to stay out of the way of any stray Germans. The speed was incredible, as was the handling. It took the lightest touch, and the Spitfire responded gracefully; it was almost as if it knew what to do before even being told. A moment of madness took over, and Harriet pulled up into a long climbing loop, which she barrel rolled out of with ease before descending back to one thousand feet and getting her bearings. The Spitfire was a dream. So similar to the Hurricane in so many ways, yet so very different. She could see what all the fuss was about in just a couple of minutes, and she couldn't help thinking that the Germans wouldn't stand a chance against such an aeroplane. She snapped out of her daydream and checked her map, then set her heading and dropped down, skimming the treetops and enjoying the sight of people waving at her from the fields.

Every second was a moment of absolute, unrestrained pleasure, and it was over too soon when she reached the maintenance airfield. She joined the circuit before lowering the wheels and slipping into the final approach for a quick landing, having already made a note of the dispersal area so she could taxi to an empty spot, spin into line with the other Spitfires and Hurricanes there, and cut the engine. She'd done it; she'd flown her first Spitfire. She shut down and climbed up out of the cockpit as a smile stretched from ear to ear. Standing at the base of the wings were a couple of RAF Corporals. Both smirked as she climbed onto the wing and raced forward to offer their hands to help her down. She took hold of both and was almost lifted down gently.

"Good flight, Ma'am?" one of them asked.

"Every flight in a Spitfire's a good flight," she replied with a smile, instantly loving the feeling of being the centre of attention. Other airmen soon turned up, and a small group formed around her asking all manner of questions about flying. She felt like a film star as the mob guided her to the dispersal office, where she finally broke loose of them to report her arrival to a young female WAAF Corporal. "Spitfire for you from the Supermarine factory." She handed over the delivery chit, which was signed, and a copy handed back to her while the other was hole punched and put into a file.

"Thank you, Ma'am. Do you need a ride home?"

"No thank you, my friend is on her way to collect me in an Anson. She should be here any minute." She smiled and stepped back outside into the afternoon sun. The airmen had returned to their many duties on the line of aeroplanes, including the Spitfire she'd just delivered. She watched the buzz of activity and thought back to France, when AP, Lanky, and all of the other ground crews would swarm over the aeroplanes as soon as they landed, refuelling, rearming, patching, and repairing. It was a little different here. The mechanics were working, but in a relaxed manner, without the urgency of France. It was a different world, though, or so she supposed. The ground crews and aircrews probably had comfortable beds to go to at the end of the day instead of camp cots or fields, and they weren't flying four or five sorties a day just to keep pace with a German onslaught. Life was a bit easier. There was lots of talk about an invasion, but the Germans hadn't done so yet. It was late June, and while they were testing the defences and bothering convoys along the coast, they weren't showing any signs of invading. The sound of the Anson stopped her daydreams before they went places that she wasn't ready for, and she was soon aboard. She bounced with excitement for the entire journey back to their small aerodrome on the coast, and after hanging her parachute in the equipment store and changing back into her skirt and heels, Lexi took her back to the Mess and showed her to her room. They agreed to meet in the bar for drinks in an hour, then Lexi left her to it. She went in to find two beds, one either side of the room, two lockers, and two chests of drawers. On one of the beds was a set of flying kit, all neatly laid out, flying jacket, boots, helmet, and on the other a petite

120

figure reclined, half hidden by a newspaper, which was slowly lowered to reveal a familiar face.

"Hello again," the petite blonde said, as a smile spread across her face, and her dark blue eyes sparkled. Harriet looked for a moment, then smiled back as she recognised the young woman. She was the Spitfire pilot she'd met in France.

"Hello... I think I'm your new roommate," Harriet said.

"I think you are," the blonde replied as she put down the newspaper. "Penny told me to expect you."

"Harry," Harriet stepped into the room and closed the door, offering her hand.

"I remember..." the small blonde replied. "Abby," she introduced herself, and they shook hands politely. "Penny said we had a new pilot, an English girl who learned to fly in France. I wondered if it might be you."

"It's nice to see you again."

"And you. I hear you almost made Lexi sick with your aerobatics."

"I don't know about that..."

"It's all over the flight. Lexi's the best of us by a long way, so if you pushed her to the edge you can't be a bad pilot; but then we already knew that, didn't we? After all, you flew with the RAF in France, a combat zone, that can't have been easy?" Harriet felt herself blushing. "Here, Verity put your things in your locker for you." Abby showed her to the wardrobe against the window wall, inside was the most beautiful uniform, as dark as night with gold braid and beautiful golden wings on the chest. Harriet took it out and looked at it. "He's quite efficient, is Mister Thomas," Abby said as Harriet pulled on the tunic, it was a perfect fit. "It arrived a short while ago, sent by courier from Saville Row in London."

121

"It's beautiful."

"Yes, it is. You're going to need it tonight."

"I am?"

"Yes. We're celebrating."

"What are we celebrating?"

"Your arrival, it's a tradition we've adopted."

"Oh..."

"You'd better get ready. The bathroom is through there," Abby gestured at the door next to her locker. Harriet smiled and nodded, then opened the door to see a large roll top bath, a toilet, and a sink and mirror, and it was all spotless and inviting.

"Who's Verity?" Harriet asked as she returned to her locker to find her wash bag, which had kindly been unpacked for her.

"Our batman."

"Our what?"

"She looks after us. Kind of like a surrogate mother away from home. It's an RAF thing. The officers generally have batmen, and mostly they're older men who have served and retired. They know the service and know how things should be. Verity is very much the same. She sewed your wings on your tunic for you, and your rank braid."

"I should find her and thank her."

"Not now, you have a bath to have. We have an appointment in the Mess," she smiled, and Harriet disappeared into the bathroom for a luxurious hot bath.

Chapter 5

A New Home

Harriet took her time in the bath, which involved a great deal of daydreaming about how she'd officially made it as a pilot, at long last. It wasn't what she'd wanted when she'd arrived in London, but she'd only been with the ATA for an afternoon, and already she'd flown a Spitfire, and had a most beautiful uniform made for her in London. It wasn't the RAF, and it wasn't a fighter squadron, but it was something that couldn't be taken from her by people who didn't believe she could fly. Now she could confidently say she was a pilot, and it was undeniable. She had the uniform and the wings to prove it. She had to be knocked out of the bathroom by the softly spoken and ever polite Abby, who gently reminded her of their date. Harriet smiled and finished cleaning up, then did her hair and makeup, and dressed in her new uniform, which fit like a silk glove, and they went down to the Mess. It was busy, there were lots of RAF and Army Officers around, and a large table to one side with nine seats, two of which were empty. Harriet and Abby took their places, and at the nod from Penny, who was at the head, the King was toasted before any other business; which was no surprise to Harriet, having done the same at the improvised Mess dinner in France.

"Thank you, everybody, for gathering to celebrate our new arrival," Penny said, "I give you Miss Harriet Cornwall." The gathered pilots applauded. She looked around at them while trying to fight a blush, they were all young, except for Penny, and some had gold wired shoulder flashes showing their country of origin. Lexi had the USA, Abby had Argentina, another girl had Poland and another Ireland. "Welcome to the ATA, and welcome to our detached flight, the specials! Named both for the special duties aeroplanes we fly, and the special nature of each and every one of our members. May your wings carry you high. Cheers!" The group cheered and drank and started the meal.

"I hear you made our Lexi a little green around the gills earlier?" an Irish girl called Erin asked Harriet with a knowing smirk.

"For your information, Erin," Lexi replied, as she pointed her full wine glass at the flame haired young woman who'd commented. "Harry here made me turn several different shades of green." She winked, and they all burst into laughter. "She's a good pilot, not bad for flying an old biplane in France."

"Oh she flew more than that," Abby said.

"More how?" Erin asked.

"She flew Hurricanes in France," Abby continued.

"You flew Hurricanes?" Lexi asked, her eyes wide in surprise.

"One or two," Harriet replied nervously.

"Remember I told you about a girl I met at the airfield when I took that Hurricane over the Channel?" Abby continued.

"I remember, but I didn't believe you," Lexi said. "I even asked my friend in the RAF, and he knew nothing about any girls flying for the RAF in France." She looked at Harriet with a frown, "Is this little mischief pulling my chain?" She pointed her glass at Abby.

"No..." Harriet replied. "We met when I collected the Hurricane she brought to France and took it to the squadron I was working with."

"Why didn't you say you'd flown Hurricanes?" Penny asked.

"Nobody believes me," Harriet replied with a shrug. "I tried telling people, and they just said I was lying. I didn't tell you because I thought you wouldn't believe me either, and if you thought I was a liar, it would jeopardise my chance of flying for you."

"My dear girl, you're a pilot and a damned good one. The fact that you flew Hurricanes in France just makes you even more of an asset," Penny said warmly.

"Thank you," Harriet replied with a blush she was no longer able to contain.

"I'll talk to my contact at the Air Ministry and see if I can get your records.
It could help with your promotion."

"You flew Hurricanes in France?" Gabriela, the Polish girl, asked bluntly. She had ice white hair and crystal clear blue eyes. "I flew a P11 against the Luftwaffe when they invaded Poland; and a P37 for the French. In combat. Not delivering aeroplanes like you, like here. I flew in Polish Air Force, and after that the French let me fly. Five Germans I killed over Poland and France. Five. Then the French gave up and stopped fighting."

"Gabriela stole a French P37 and flew it to England when the squadron she was with surrendered," Lexi explained. "And she ain't happy."

"They won't let me fight!" Gabriela said irritably. "I'm a good pilot. I should be shooting Nazis, not ferrying aeroplanes for men to take to battle."

"Unfortunately that's the rules for all of us," Penny interjected. "I'm sure we'd all rather be fighting if we could."

"Well, I guess this explains how you made that Spitfire dance right after you took off this afternoon," Lexi added.

"You saw?" Harriet asked with a blush.

"Damn right," she replied with a smirk. "I knew there was something about you."

126

The drinks flowed, and the party continued into the early hours. Harriet's new family couldn't have been more welcoming, every one of them was kind and friendly, and they all told their stories as the night progressed. They wanted to fight, desperately, and were frustrated at being refused, something they had all experienced more than once. It was partially why they'd all been grouped together; they were passionate about flying, but they were passionate about more than that, they craved more, they weren't scared by danger, and that meant they were ideal to be right in the middle of it. The rest of the ATA were dotted around the country at different places, but these women were stationed on the south coast, on the front line of the likely invasion grounds, where German reconnaissance flights and nuisance raids were becoming more frequent. They were right in the middle of the danger zone. They were a close group, and they made Harriet one of their own immediately. They were also hard drinkers, and as the night went on, they found themselves around the Mess piano with the rest of the station's officers and singing the hours away.

That night, after finally going to bed, Harriet woke in tears and terrors. It was something that had happened less frequently since she'd been home, but it was still every bit as intense when it did happen. It could have been the alcohol or the new environment, or flying a fighter again, but whatever it was had triggered the thoughts of being trapped in a burning cockpit. When she finally woke from the horror of the nightmare, Abby was holding her and soothing her. She didn't have the thought or strength to feel embarrassed. She felt safe, and that's all that was important, so she just went with it and fell asleep again until she woke the next morning snuggled in Abby's arms. She slipped out of her bed and into the bathroom, where she washed and cleaned up, and gulped cold water to try and fight off the rapidly approaching hangover.

"Good morning," she said as she went back into the room to see Abby sitting up in bed.

"Good morning, how are you feeling?" Abby asked.

"I think I have the world's worst hangover coming on..." Harriet replied sheepishly, receiving a giggle in return. "I'm sorry about last night."

"About what?"

"The nightmare. I thought they'd stopped."

"Don't worry about it. I mean that. It's what friends do; and what happens in our room stays in here, deal?"

"Deal, and thank you." Harriet smiled. They got dressed, had breakfast, then took the morning transport down to the dispersal hut, where they checked in and picked up their assignments for the day. They all looked a little delicate after the previous night but were able to function. Harriet and Abby were detailed to collect a Spitfire from a field near Dover, just above the cliffs. The pilot had belly landed after the propeller had been shot off in a run in with a 109, and the mechanics had been up all night getting it airworthy. They were to collect it and take it to a maintenance unit. Before they left, Abby took Harriet to the main hangar, where they received a knowing look from one of the RAF Corporals, Paul, who showed them into a room of oxygen bottles and test masks. "What's this?" Harriet asked.

"It's where they test the oxygen systems for the aeroplanes," Abby explained. "Put a mask on." She handed Harriet a small green oxygen bottle with a mask attached. She pulled the strap around her head and pulled the mask tight, then Abby turned on the oxygen. "Deep breaths." Abby did the same, and the two of them stood in the quiet room and breathed deeply. Ten minutes later they were leaving, and the hangover was all but a memory.

"That's like magic," Harriet said under her voice.

"I know," Abby smirked. They took the Anson, and Abby soon had them circling the field of the crashed Spitfire. She lined up and put the Anson down in the limited space she had available, managing to stop just short of the hedges and spin the aeroplane around to taxi back towards the

128

gathered airmen. She stopped and shut down before the pair of them climbed out. The Sergeant in charge talked them through what had happened and the repairs they'd done, then Harriet climbed aboard and prepared for flight. Checks done, she managed to start the engine with no difficulty. The drive shaft had been shot through and had jammed, vibrated and then seized, ultimately wrecking the propeller and forcing the engine to blow a piston. The propeller spun, and the engine hummed. There wasn't anything obvious to worry about, so she waved the mechanics away before taxiing to the edge of the field, where she checked the power, then let go of the brakes and sped with bump after bump towards the opposite hedgerow, which she was rapidly approaching. With a final bump and a pull on the stick, she was up. She quickly retracted the gear and banked around over the field, giving everyone a wave. She climbed in a wide and slow circuit until Abby got the Anson off the ground, and side by side they headed for the maintenance field.

About fifteen minutes into the flight, the engine started to run rough. Harriet adjusted the mixture, but nothing helped, she throttled back and then forward, but nothing appeared to make a difference. The roughness got worse, and the aeroplane started to shake violently. The temperature gauge climbed quickly, and speed started to scrub off. The cockpit suddenly started to heat up, and Harriet started to get nervous, she knew what could happen, and she didn't fancy it. She started to look around for somewhere to land. Then it happened. The aeroplane lurched, the engine seized, and the prop shuddered. What came next froze Harriet. It was her worst nightmare. A jet of flame shot out from the engine and engulfed the cockpit and fuselage.

"Oh God, no" Harriet muttered again and again, as her entire body trembled. The intensity of the flames increased, and an orange and gold glow enveloped the cockpit entirely as fire surrounded her. A voice deep inside her screamed 'Do something, or you're dead!', and in a moment her mind was back. She cut the fuel and switched everything off, and seconds later the flames died away back to the engine cowling, where they stubbornly flickered and licked. Harriet took a deep breath and steadied herself, the fire had decreased, but she was still in a dangerous position, made worse by the flames having blackened the canopy so she couldn't see a thing in front of her. It wasn't her first choice, but after a moment of flying blind, Harriet pushed the canopy back, instantly cooling the oven like cockpit and letting her breathe. It was a calculated risk, if the flames started up again, she'd be roasted alive, but if she didn't open the canopy, she'd have no idea of where she was going, which would undoubtedly hasten a high speed meeting with the ground, and her inevitable death. Finally, with a little gentle rocking, she spotted a field on the outskirts of a village which was long enough for her to get down, or so she thought. A little adjustment and lining up, and she guided the silent Spitfire through the rushing air until she met the ground with a gentle bump and rolled to the far hedge, where she was able to circle the Spitfire without looping the nose into the ground and come to a halt. Quickly she checked everything was off, before unclipping her harness and jumping out onto the wing. The flames around the engine had flickered to nothing more than sparks, but she wasn't confident the full lot wouldn't go bang any minute, so she grabbed her parachute and ran off the wing, and in the direction of the group of uniformed children running towards her from the gate connecting the field to the village school. She held up her hands to stop them.

"It could blow," she said, "Better not get any closer." She took off her flying helmet and shook out her hair, to the gasps of the gathered children.

"It's a woman pilot," one of the older girls said in amazement.

"Girls don't fly Spitfires!" a boy of about thirteen exclaimed.

"Well it didn't land itself," Harriet replied firmly, to the sniggers and giggles of the other children. She then spent her time answering questions about flying, about Spitfires, and about how young ladies can fly them. The boys were just as enthusiastic, and once she'd set the first straight, they were accepting of her as a pilot, and very keen in wanting to know how to be pilots or mechanics. Their teacher joined them, and gave an impromptu lesson on the principles of flight, the ATA, and the RAF, until finally the Anson appeared and rolled to a halt in the field. Abby joined Harriet and joined in the questions and answers before they were both invited back to the school for tea, which they enjoyed after telephoning the dispersal to tell them what had happened. The school caretaker had already called the local RAF station to let them know of the crash, and by the time the tea was finished, a recovery crew had turned up. Harriet and Abby were able to get on their way back to the station, after saying goodbye to the children. In an unusual and unexpected moment, they found themselves signing autographs and posing with the entire school for a photograph in front of the Spitfire.

"Are you OK?" Abby asked as Harriet sat quietly beside her in the Anson.

"I think so..."

"What happened?"

"The engine seized and caught fire. I was worried for a moment."

"I bet you were, I'd have been terrified."

"I was... But something happened. I was surrounded by fire, but the Spitfire didn't burn, not like Hurricanes do, it kept me safe and practically flew itself until I was on the ground."

"They're incredible aeroplanes, and they really do fly themselves; it's like they know exactly what to do," Abby replied warmly. They flew back to the airfield where they made their way to Penny's office to report what had happened. Penny listened intently to the details, then without a word to either of them, she picked up the phone and asked to be put through to the Officer commanding the recovery team that had handed the Spitfire over to Harriet.

"What exactly do you mean by handing one of my pilots a Spitfire that was quite patently unserviceable?" she demanded. "I'm sure I don't care whether she signed for it, she's not the chief engineer, and she doesn't get to sign it off as airworthy, that's your job!" She listened impatiently for a

131

minute. "Let me stop you right there. My pilots are invaluable, and worth their weight in gold, and you put one of them at risk today. If it weren't for her supreme skill, we'd have lost a much needed Spitfire and an irreplaceable pilot. This will go to the Air Ministry, and you'll have to explain yourself. Good day!" She put the phone down sharply. "As for you," she said to Harriet, wiping the half smirk from her face and giving her a knot in the stomach, the likes of which she hadn't experienced since back in France. "What you did today was incredible, impossible even, and you've saved the RAF a very expensive Spitfire. However, what you should have done is jump!"

"I couldn't..." Harriet protested.

"Couldn't? Or thought you were something special and didn't have to follow orders?"

"Couldn't, Ma'am. The cockpit was engulfed in flames, if I'd tried to open it, I'd have been burned alive; and when they finally abated the stick was virtually dead, and the aeroplane was pulling right. If I'd have jumped it would likely have crashed into the village. Not that I'd have been any better, I didn't have the height for my parachute to open. I stayed in the aeroplane not because I wanted to save it. I just hoped I'd be able to get it down without hitting the village, regardless of what happened to me."

"I see..."

"The aeroplane was a mess," Abby added. "It was virtually black from the burning, and I expect it would have made a mess if it had hit the village." "I don't doubt it," Penny replied, her face softening a little. "Miss Cornwall, you're a very good pilot, and I'd quite like to keep you around if you don't mind?"

"What? No, no, I don't mind at all. I love it here."

"In that case, please try and keep yourself alive, and try not to worry me quite as much. I haven't lost one of my girls yet, and I intend to keep it that way." She smiled, and Harriet felt a wave of relief pass over her body. "Now, get yourself some tea, then if you're feeling up to it, there's a special at Supermarine that needs moving." She gave them both a wink, and they left excitedly.

The days turned into weeks, and Harriet became part of a small and successful family with the best reputation in the ATA for their professionalism and skill for moving Spitfires. She travelled the country, delivering Spitfires to Scotland, and collecting them from Wales. She visited many RAF stations, mainly in the north, sometimes staying over as an invited guest, and being part of the rowdiest of Mess parties. She lived, and she enjoyed every minute, she even learned to ride one of Lexi's motorcycles, a chrome and metallic turquoise 1939 Harley Davidson Knucklehead that had been imported for her tour of Europe. Harriet was a natural, and the two of them spent long summer nights racing up the coast.

Sadly things were changing for the worse. Churchill announced preparations for invasion in July when the Luftwaffe increased their harassing nuisance raids around the coast, and by early August the intensity of their attacks against Channel convoys and coastal defences was at a peak. The airfield had been left alone, but that didn't mean they hadn't suffered. Penny's wish to not lose one of her girls was dashed when Erin, the fiery Irish redhead and a very talented pilot, was shot down near the Isle of Wight by a marauding patrol of 109s. She'd out flown them by a considerable margin, according to the eyewitnesses who'd seen the fight from the ground, and the naval convoy below; but being unarmed she was at a significant disadvantage, and eventually, they closed her down. Her body was pulled from the Channel the same day. Her loss was felt by everyone in the flight and the ATA as a whole. There was talk of the flight being withdrawn north, out of what was fast turning into a fierce combat zone, dubbed Hell's Corner by the fighter pilots tasked with defending it. The flight's operations were being increasingly curtailed by the German raids; and with the country fearing invasion along the south coast somewhere, the powers that be weren't comfortable having a flight of female pilots in such a risky position. It wouldn't look

133

good in the papers if they lost more unarmed women in the air, or so they were told.

The summer was warm, the warmest England had experienced for years, and an early August afternoon of sunbathing on the hangar roof, out of sight of the 'erks on the ground, was followed by a night out with the girls in the local pub. Harriet was dragged from her bed first thing the following morning for an urgent job flying Abby out to collect a Spitfire, which had put down on the Kent coast in an emergency landing. She splashed herself with cold water, before dressing and calling into the oxygen bay for a gasp of the hangover gas, as they'd come to call it. Their task proved to be uneventful, and they spent much of the day sitting on the nearby beach while the recovery crew worked to get the Spitfire airworthy. It was a welcome break after the late night they'd had in the Mess, and an opportunity for the pair to top up their tans while watching Spitfires and Hurricanes chase German raids out above the sea. It was time for themselves, and to just relax and enjoy each other's company away from the world. By mid afternoon the Spitfire was ready to fly, and the girls were back home at the dispersal hut before the evening, where Harriet received a message from Lexi summoning her to Penny's office.

"Ah, Harry, do come in," Penny greeted her, showing Harriet to the seat in front of the desk before taking her own. "How are you doing?"

"Good, thank you..." Harriet was a little nervous. It was rare to be summoned to Penny's office in the station headquarters. Usually, it was the preserve of the girls who'd been caught out doing something they shouldn't, which generally resulted in a threat of instant dismissal and a week of the worst jobs.

"Enjoy the night out with the girls last night?"

"Yes... They're a great group."

"They are, they are..."

"Is there something you wanted me for?" Harriet asked cautiously.

134

"Yes. Yes, there is," Penny replied with a smile returning to her face after she'd drifted off for a moment. She hadn't been the same since Erin had been shot down the week before, she'd become even more protective of her girls, and even more furious with anyone who put them at risk, including the girls themselves when they did something careless. "They've got their way, you know. The headquarters staff that is, we're being moved north next week."

"Oh..."

"Don't tell the rest of the girls, though. Not yet. There's no need to ruin the rest of the week for them."

"I won't, of course." Harriet raised an eyebrow. She wasn't entirely sure where the conversation was going, or why she'd been summoned.

"Of course... Anyway, that's not why I called you here," Penny said. "I've always thought there was something special about you, Harry, right from the moment you turned up at our door with that unusual letter from the Air Ministry. It was like they'd sent us a blessing. A talented pilot and leader, exactly what our little section needed." Harriet felt herself blushing as Penny talked. "You've brought young Abby out of her shell, that's undeniable, and given Lexi somebody on her own skill level to play with."

"I'm just happy to be here," Harriet replied. "They're great girls and great friends."

"They are... Anyway, before I digress any further, I expect you're wondering where I'm going with all this?"

"A little," Harriet shrugged nervously.

"Well, things move slowly at headquarters, often slower than I'd like, but it would appear that the personnel department has found you at last."

135

"Found me?"

"Yes. Your commission to Third Officer was registered while you were in France earlier this year, but some fool had filed you in the deceased section. You were only found when poor Erin's death in service was being processed."

"Oh..." Harriet's heart raced.

"It means that we have your records, Harry. I know you like to keep quiet about what you went through in France, but I also know you did a lot more than you've let on. If we have these records, we can maybe trace the rest of your service records and get you the recognition you so rightly deserve for what you did over there!" Harriet's eyes opened wide. She'd put France to the back of her mind, but now it was all there, as though it was yesterday. "It also means you're due a few weeks of back pay, and a promotion based on your previous service. So it'll be First Officer Cornwall as of today, as agreed by headquarters."

"But I thought Lexi was your First Officer?"

"She is, but when we move north, we're going to be picking up a few more girls, and I'm going to need another senior officer to help keep them in line. If you're up for the job?"

"You're sure?"

"Do I ever joke about serious matters?"

"I accept!"

"Good. I've already processed the paperwork, and you'll need to get some new gold braid sewn on your tunic." Harriet smiled excitedly. "But before that, I've got a job for you. There's a job lot of Spitfires at Supermarine that need ferrying to the maintenance unit at first light tomorrow. It'll likely take a few hours. Pick four to go with you, and I'll see you later for a celebratory drink in the Mess." Harriet thanked Penny profusely before leaving the office and making her way to the Mess for something to eat, unable to wipe the huge smile off her face. She told the others while they ate, then set about her task for the following day as the officer commanding a Spitfire ferry. The downside of the job was that she wouldn't be flying a Spitfire. Instead, she'd fly the Anson, which she'd quickly been trained and authorised on, and move her pilots back and forth until the job was done. Such was the responsibility of command.

Chapter 6

Pink

The operation had gone well, and for her first time in command, Harriet was particularly happy with herself. With her four pilots, they'd moved sixteen Spitfires to four different maintenance units. In addition to their scheduled task, they'd also managed to return eight Spitfires to Supermarine for modification, all in all, a good day's work had been done before mid morning. The skies had been a more dangerous place than usual, and the Germans had been about quite a bit, which meant the pilots had to fly very low and very fast to get the job done. Finally, Supermarine had one last request. A Spitfire needed to go out to a station in the South West of England and another was to be returned. A small job which Harriet was happy to take on! It was something that her rank gave her the authority to do; and something which in the past had got the flight a bottle of whisky as thanks from the Supermarine staff for doing an extra. Harriet dropped Abby at Supermarine to collect the Spitfire, then dropped her other three pilots back at the airfield before taking a leisurely flight back to Supermarine ready to collect Abby on her return trip. She parked the Anson, then following in the footsteps of Lexi she made her way to the dispersal office in the tower, so she could graciously accept a bottle of whisky, should one be lying around. As she walked across the dispersal, she could hear a furious argument rumbling inside.

"It's pink!" a man bellowed from inside, clearly ready to, if not actually blowing his top. She stepped in to see a male ATA pilot, a Third Officer, arguing with Mister Byron.

"It's a Spitfire!" Byron argued calmly.

"Well, I'm not bloody taking it." The ATA Officer turned and marched for the door, barging into Harriet as he went.

138

"Hey!" she exclaimed. He looked down at her and rolled his eyes before turning back to Mister Byron.

"There you go, a girl pilot. Maybe she'll drive your clown kite!" He stormed out of the room.

"What on earth was that all about?" Harriet asked, a little shocked at what she'd just witnessed.

"Oh dear, Miss Cornwall. Are you OK?" Byron asked.

"Yes, are you?"

"Yes, yes. Just something of a disagreement over the special your ATA gentleman was supposed to be taking down to the Kent coast for us. Apparently, it falls short of what he considers to be acceptable."

"That's ridiculous. He doesn't get to choose what he will and won't fly. It's his job to move aeroplanes."

"I know that Miss Cornwall, and you know that. Unfortunately, Mister Henderson tends to do exactly as he likes, when he likes. He has something of a reputation for being rather troublesome."

"I see... And they still let him fly?"

"His father is very senior in the War Office. It tends to make your headquarters types a little nervous about funding and support."

"That seems to happen a lot in this country."

"Quite... Anyway, that's my problem, Miss Cornwall. What can I do for you?"

"You could show me the Spitfire he's refusing to fly. I'm a little intrigued."

"Why not?" Byron said. "Oh, and here's a little something for your girls, to thank them for the extra work they put in today." He pulled a bottle of whisky from behind his desk and handed it to her with a wink. Then he led her to the adjoining hangar where a dusty pink Spitfire was waiting for them.

"Oh my God," Harriet said as she saw it, instantly smiling and even giggling as Byron led her to the front of the aeroplane. "It's pink!"

"Yes... Apparently, the colour doesn't agree with our friend. He seems to worry that his manhood would be questioned if he were to arrive at a front line air station in it. I don't entirely blame him if I'm honest, I know those fighter boys can tease terribly when the mood takes them, I was one of them once." His eyes twinkled for a moment. "Still, that doesn't solve my problem of getting it there this morning ready for its trials."

"Why is it pink?" Harriet asked.

"It's a twilight interceptor," Byron explained. "An upgraded Merlin for speed and power, and two half inch cannons, one on each wing. The idea was taken from the photographic reconnaissance kites, or dicers as they're known."

"Why dicers?"

"Because the missions they fly are so dangerous they dice with death every time they go up. Anyway, the pink blends in perfectly with the oranges, pinks, and reds that come with sunrise and sunset, making it almost impossible to spot until it's on top of you, not to mention that it's damned difficult to spot in grey cloud. At least that's what the PR boys report. The theory is for it to fly into dawn and dusk raids with its cannons and break up the Germans before they even know what's hit them."

"Will it work?"

"There's no reason it shouldn't, but we won't know until it's been put into practice properly, and the boys down on the Kent coast, being as close to the Channel as we can get, have agreed to do just that. If we can get it to them."

"I'll take it."

"I know you would," he smiled.

"I mean it, I'll take it."

"We both know that ATA girls aren't allowed to deliver to front line stations. Their Airships would hit the roof if they knew."

"Who's going to know? I'll leave my flying helmet on and hide my hair, and probably take off my lipstick. They won't care as long as they get the Spitfire. I'll leave the Anson and Abby can come and collect me. Easy."

"I don't know..."

"I've flown plenty of Spitfires for you, Mister Byron, you know I can do it."

"OK..." he said with a sparkle in his eyes. "You're on, but if anyone asks, you came in here pretending to be a male pilot, and I didn't know any better."

"Deal!" Harriet said excitedly. "Now show me around and tell me what's different."

"Well, it's simple, really. The engine is a little more powerful, but you won't be using the boost, so that's not something to worry about. Otherwise, the only difference is the guns. You don't have any, just two dirty great cannons, one on each wing. Now, you must be careful not to touch the gun button, the cannons are live and loaded with experimental explosive ammunition, high grade incendiary stuff that'll burn a Jerry bomber down from the inside, after ripping the airframe apart that is."

141

"OK. Give me five minutes to check my maps and do a walk around, and
I'll take it."

"Thank you, Miss Cornwall. I'm grateful. Why don't you jump in, and I'll have the boys push you out of the hangar when you're ready so you can shoot straight off."

"So nobody sees a girl climbing into it, you mean?"

"Well... If you could wear your oxygen mask, that would be helpful?" She smirked and nodded, then went around the aeroplane to do her checks, before climbing into the cockpit and making herself comfortable. She had a quick check of her map, not that she needed to, she'd passed over her destined aerodrome more than a few times, though she'd never actually landed. Byron returned with his ground crew, and the Spitfire was moved out to dispersal. After getting the all clear, Harriet fired up the engine and enjoyed the roar as it shot a cloud of blue smoke past her before the propeller blasted it away. Pre flight checks were done, and she gave the chocks away signal before rolling to the end of the runway, swinging the tail left to right so could see over the long nose of the Spitfire as she went. Once in position, she ran through her final checks and tested the power one last time, then with a check of the circuit for traffic, she was off. The Spitfire felt faster somehow, even though Byron had said she likely wouldn't feel the extra power; and without asking it lifted from the ground and carried Harriet up into the air faster and more seamlessly than she'd ever experienced before. Undercarriage up, and she pointed east as she climbed.

The Spitfire was a dream to fly, hardly a vibration to disturb her as she climbed and hid in the fluffy clouds a few thousand feet above the ground. She didn't need to make a target of herself for any Germans that were hanging around, and clouds were always a good place to hide. As she weaved in and out, threading holes, and generally enjoying herself, she could see the coast below her. For a moment, she drifted back to her time at the hospital and the ice cream she'd enjoyed with Nurse Emily while sitting on the cliffs. It all seemed so long ago, but in reality, it had only been a couple of months. She'd kept in touch with Emily and regularly wrote to tell her of the adventures she was having. Emily always wrote back, and always asked when, or if, Harriet would come and visit. She intended to do so as soon as she had a few days, something which hadn't really been possible due to the increasing intensity of the war over England, and the associated increase in the need for Spitfires to be moved around by skilled ATA pilots. She did want to visit Emily, though, and had often written in her letters how she'd turn up in an aeroplane one day and take Emily for a ride. Harriet was dragged out of her daydreams by the sight of condensation trails ahead of her. They were out to sea and fifteen thousand feet above her at least, but there were lots of them, looping and diving, and generally chasing each other around the sky. There wasn't any immediate danger, but it wouldn't take much for a German to spot the big pink Spitfire from above; so Harriet adjusted her course and headed inland, just to be safe. There was a bank of scattered clouds a few thousand feet above, so she pulled back on the stick and pushed forward on the throttle and headed for them. The detour would only add a few more minutes to her trip, but it was worth it to avoid trouble and make sure she actually got where she was going. As Harriet approached the closest cloud, she had a quick look around her for signs of other aeroplanes, then checked her rearview mirror. A shadow caught her eye, not in the mirror but right in front of her. Suddenly a Hurricane dived out of the cloud, coming straight for her with a trio of 109s swarming on its tail. The Hurricane pitched up as the pilot saw her, then rolled and dived as soon as it was clear, and the 109s went to follow. Instinctively Harriet switched the gun button to fire and gave it a push as the last 109 filled her windscreen ready to flip and dive after the others. The cannons were nothing like the eight machine guns of the Hurricane. No sound of ripping canvas with these, just a thundering thump, thump, thump, that shook the entire aeroplane. It took her by surprise, and she released the gun button after only a second of firing, but it was too late for the 109, the experimental incendiary cannon shells lit up the sky like glowing lances extending from the Spitfire and ripping into the 109 with bright flashes. Five shells had been fired and all five hit home, at least one of which must have torn open and then ignited the main fuel tank, as the 109 exploded into a ball of orange and black. There wasn't time to respond, and Harriet passed through the turbulent air where the 109 had just blown apart, and debris rattled off her canopy as her Spitfire shook and bounced. A quick check proved all to be OK, so she pushed the stick over and pulled back, determined to help the Hurricane. She searched the sky, but it was gone, as were the 109s. Surely they couldn't have knocked it down and scarpered already, could they? When she dipped her wing to check below, she saw the Hurricane. It was spinning and rolling its way towards the ground, still trying to lose the two 109s which were following its every move. There was nothing for it, Harriet pushed the throttle through the gate, snapping the mechanic's locking wire and forcing the engine up to maximum boost. The Spitfire lurched with the powerful increase of speed, and soon Harriet was cruising well over three hundred and fifty miles per hour, and the needle was still climbing. With a gentle nudge of the stick, the nose dipped, and Harriet went over the cliff into a steep dive which pushed the speed well beyond what she'd imagined possible. She was dropping even faster than the dive in France which almost killed her. This time the carburettor wouldn't be a problem, all of them having been modified in the factories following the formal adoption of an enhanced version of AP's modification, and the dive was on full power. The airframe started to shake as the ground got closer. The Hurricane was now down at treetop height, and Harriet started to pull out of the dive, making the airframe shake and vibrate even more, as her head squeezed with the pressure. At last, she was level with the ground and closing on the 109s so quickly that she hardly had time to think of what she was going to do next. She lined her sight on the rear 109 and fired, this time ready for the thunder of the cannons and holding her thumb tight on the button. The shells glowed and streaked brilliant white trails as they reached out for their target, streak after streak as the cannons shook the Spitfire and vibrated Harriet's chest. Then they hit. The 109's wing exploded and sent the rest of the aeroplane spiralling downwards and bouncing into the ground, so hard it almost buried in the field. Already the remaining 109 had filled Harriet's windscreen and was disintegrating from the repeated hits of her cannon. Harriet pulled up to avoid the remains, and carried on right over the top of the Hurricane before dropping down in front of it, then waggled her wings while watching it in her mirror. The Hurricane waggled in reply as Harriet rocketed away from it, still on full boost and keeping her eyes on the rolling farmlands below, making sure she didn't become part of them. As she checked for any more Germans, she watched the Hurricane pull away to the north. She smiled to herself and pulled back on her stick to head back for the clouds, which she reached in next to no time thanks to the engine still being at maximum power. A quick course correction and it was time to back the throttle off again and spare the engine while checking the gauges which, despite the few minutes of unexpected combat, were showing as absolutely fine. She pulled off her oxygen mask and gasped. Her heart was pounding, more so since the action was over. She hadn't had time to think when the Hurricane appeared, and when she'd tried to think she drew nothing but blanks anyway, but now it was over she could feel how it had impacted her. She could feel the sweat running down her spine in torrents, and her hands were shaking. She was also smiling, grinning in fact, quite unintentionally with a smile that stretched ear to ear. It was like France was only yesterday. The patrols, the dog fights, the cockpit stinking of smoke and sweat. It was terrifying and exhilarating, and the few short minutes she'd just experienced had reignited a passion deep inside her, a nagging desire to fly and fight. After losing Nicole, Harriet didn't know how she'd feel about combat again; and throughout her short time with the ATA she'd even convinced herself that she was happy away from the war, but the smile on her face was telling her otherwise. The smile quickly turned to a frown when she thought of her frustrated efforts to do anything other than be a ferry pilot. She'd written to the Air Ministry several times in her first few weeks with the ATA, and only ever received one reply, which simply informed her that the squadron was aware of her work and wished her all the best for her future in the ATA, the home where she belonged. It was enough to break her heart at the time, and she felt sick in the pit of her stomach. After all that she'd shared with them, that's all she got! Not even a thanks, or an invite for tea. She didn't feel angry at the pilots themselves, but she did feel sad, she thought she'd meant something to them. The thing that helped her move on was the conversation she'd had with Cas that night in the Mess in France; when he'd given her and AP the quietest and politest telling off that she'd ever had. Had she arrived anywhere else in the RAF in Sully's aeroplane she'd have been thanked, put in a car, and driven off to who knows where? She'd been part of things when they were going wrong in a foreign country, great things, but now that she was in England, she was dealing with the proper RAF, the RAF where girls don't fly. It had been enough to put the idea, and the squadron out of her mind. Until she'd got into a Spitfire and shot down a German again, that is. She couldn't leave the thought alone, though, and she decided to track down the squadron when she'd delivered the Spitfire. She was going to a fighter command airfield, not a maintenance unit or factory, and she was going to ask where to find them. She wanted to face them, and she wanted to face Cas. Especially after all of that nonsense that he'd given her about getting back to England so she could be trained properly for the fight against the Germans. He, more than anyone, needed to explain himself. He'd put her in harm's way and used her as a pilot when it suited him, but now they were back in England he didn't need her anymore, so all she'd got was an 'enjoy your home at the ATA'. She felt herself getting agitated, annoyed even. She'd given that squadron everything, she'd offered her life, and they'd taken Nicole's. A friendly letter would be the least they could do.

Harriet was so riled with annoyance that for a short while she forgot her mission altogether. It was only when she saw the sun glinting off the sea to the south through a gap in the clouds that she was able to pull herself together with the sound reasoning that she loved the ATA, and loved the girls she flew with who'd become sisters to her. Regardless of how shoddily the RAF had treated her she couldn't take it out on them. She had a responsibility to do a good job, for them as much as for herself, which meant getting the Spitfire down on the ground and finding a reasonable excuse for the cannons being fired. At that moment she saw the airfield, or so she thought. She checked her instruments and dropped to the base of the cloud, where she circled a couple of times to make sure she'd got the right place, having been a little distracted in her navigation during the trip. Once she was sure she was safe, she throttled back and started to lose height as she dropped from the last ghostly wisps of cloud into the clear daylight below. A few minutes and she'd be on the ground and explaining the cannons, or not, if she could just leave it with them and run away before they noticed. An idea she toyed with. Perhaps for once, she could use being a girl in her favour, and hide her flying kit then deny all knowledge of the mysterious pink Spitfire. It was worth a try, at least. As she circled the airfield, she dipped her wing and saw a line of

146

Spitfires near a dispersal hut and a few vehicles. Further along the airfield were the hangars, then much further away was the domestic site with accommodation and offices. She assumed that the dispersal would probably be the best place to park. Before she could do anything else, a slow moving glowing ball caught her attention as it floated in the air right in front of her. She was mesmerised by it. In a way, it felt familiar, but she couldn't imagine where from, until it exploded into a cloud of fire and smoke around the nose of her Spitfire. The engine pitch increased as it tried to spin a propeller that was no longer there, before it shuddered and coughed out a cloud of oil and black smoke just ahead of it seizing. Another explosion shredded her right wing and flipped the Spitfire upside down. The gauges had given up as Harriet fought with the heavy controls to try and make them do something. Eventually, her screaming and shouting and riving at the controls started to pay off, and the Spitfire began to roll as it descended. More explosions erupted around her, close enough to shake the airframe but not close enough to make things any worse, which would be difficult to do even if they hit her straight on, as she was too low to jump. As the wings levelled, she dropped the undercarriage, pulled open the canopy and lined up with the centre of the runway. The undercarriage indicators weren't showing, so there was no telling what was under her, but it wasn't something she had the time to worry about. She was approaching stall speed, and the ground was rushing up to meet her at a startling rate. She pulled her harness as tight as it would go and closed her eyes as she saw the individual blades of grass and waited. The wheels bounced as the Spitfire met the ground, and she quickly opened her eyes again and guided the near useless controls to pull the nose back into line and wait for the second bump, which came soon enough, and this time held her to the ground. The Spitfire rolled and rolled, then a loud snapping sound rang out as the right undercarriage leg gave way, and the wing dipped and buried itself into the ground, spinning the entire aeroplane to the right and onto its nose, and flinging Harriet tight against her harness. The left undercarriage leg gave way and the Spitfire dropped flat on its belly, where it lay motionless, hissing and creaking, as clouds of black and grey smoke entwined and climbed into the sky above. She breathed deep for a moment and tried to compose herself, her head was hurting as though she'd hit it, but she couldn't remember when or how. As her eyes started to focus again, she looked up at a smiling face that slowly became sharper, and more recognisable.

"You are in so much trouble when she sees you!"

"What? Lanky? Is that you?"

"Welcome home, Harry," Lanky smiled as she reached in and released Harriet's harness, before taking her hands and helping her stand, which was a slow affair due to her dizziness. As Harriet steadied herself, she pulled off her flying helmet and wiped the sweat from her eyes. "Better late than never."

"Well, I'll be damned..." a familiar American accent exclaimed. Lanky stepped to one side to reveal the pilots and ground crew gathering around her Spitfire. At the front of them was Max.

"Another of your wonderful understatements, old boy?" Archie said as he moved through the gathering to stand by Max's side. "Get lost, did we?" he called up to Harriet.

"Shut up!" Harriet replied with a half smile as she fought to make sense of what was happening. She rubbed her eyes, and her head, maybe she'd hit it harder than she thought? Or maybe she was dead?

"Come on, Harry," Max said as he appeared by the cockpit, and helped her step out onto the collapsed wing with a huge bear hug. "God damn, it's good to see you."

"They shot me down," she said with a frown.

"Oh I wouldn't take it personally; they took a pop at Kiwi this morning, and his aeroplane isn't even pink," Archie said as she and Max joined him. "Good to see you, old girl. We thought we'd lost you." He shook her hand warmly and gave her a welcoming smile. "We were shouting at them when we saw it was a Spitfire they were shooting at, again. The skipper had to call the battery commander to tell them to cease fire, a little late, unfortunately." He looked over her shoulder at the creaking and smoking very dirty pink Spitfire. The group of pilots who'd been hanging around outside the dispersal hut were now gathered around her. Murph and Dolph both patted her on the shoulder and welcomed her back, as did Hugo and Pops, the French and Polish pilots who'd escaped with the Blenheim and joined the squadron in France on a more permanent basis.

"You're supposed to be dead," Grumpy said as he stood in front of her.

"Sorry..." Harriet replied. "I'll try harder next time." She looked back at the broken Spitfire regretfully. "Though I'm not sure how much harder I can try..."

"I'm not sure that's what he means," Archie said. "We were told you were dead, drowned when the ship carrying you from Dunkirk was torpedoed."

"Oh..." Harriet's heart skipped a beat as she momentarily remembered being in the water, and instantly felt a chill up her spine.

"It's been quite a rollercoaster," Archie continued. "We thought we'd lost you over Dunkirk, then when Max got home and said he'd seen you we were relieved."

"Until we were told you'd drowned," Max added. "But here you are." He pushed the smile back onto his face. "We're gonna have a big party to celebrate this!" A cheer went up, and the pilots talked excitedly, all firing questions at Harriet.

"Hi!" a giant of a pilot said as he stood right in front of Max and offered his hand to Harriet. He was young, or his face was at least, with dimples and mischievous brown eyes. He raised his eyebrows a couple of times and gave her a big smile. "Pilot Officer Jonny Isaac, at your service. Can I be the first to buy you a drink later? I've heard all about you."

"Steady, lady killer," Max said as he shoved the young man out of the way. "Ignore the boy, he's got an eye for the ladies but hasn't had the time to learn a thing about them."

"The boy wouldn't know what to do if he caught one," Archie added. "Besides, if he were anything of a gentleman, he'd be finding the lady a drink right now. Considering the manner of her arrival, I think she's earned one." The pilots laughed as Jonny looked around with an embarrassed smirk on his face. Harriet looked at him, and then past him to the quiet old man staring at her from the doorway of the dispersal hut. Cas. He didn't say a word, just looked her in the eyes like he'd seen a ghost.

"I think you'd better see this, Sir," he said as he leant back into the shadow of the hut. A moment later Singh appeared. He was wearing his blue RAF tunic and a sapphire blue silk scarf, along with his Mae West and ever present turban. He stood in the doorway and smiled, then walked over through the gathering of pilots, which parted to let him through. He stood in front of Harriet and looked her up and down.

"Miss Cornwall..." he said quietly.

"Sir..." she replied nervously.

"It pleases me to see you again." In a rare moment of emotional display, he let a wide smile spread across his face, the first she'd ever seen. If that wasn't enough to surprise her, the uncharacteristic hug he gave her left everyone speechless. A phone rang from inside the dispersal hut, and the entire gathering turned and looked.

"It's a squadron scramble!" Cas shouted as he reappeared.

"Don't be ridiculous!" Singh said as he strolled towards Cas. "We haven't been down ten minutes; we're still refuelling and rearming. Get me the duty controller." A distant rumble drew the eyes of the pilots across the airfield to the fiery black plume of smoke and earth jumping into the air, followed by another, and another. The aerodrome was being bombed.

"Don't just stand there, get one up!" Singh yelled as he ran through the pilots towards his Spitfire, while Cas rang the squadron scramble bell. The air raid sirens started to wind up and the pilots scattered, heading for their aeroplanes. The ground crews, which had been busy rearming and refuelling the Spitfires after their recent sortie, already had the engines started. Harriet watched impatiently, almost dancing on the spot with nervous energy as the adrenaline which had rioted through her body following being shot down was topped up with the excitement of a squadron scramble, and the imminent danger of an aerodrome being bombed. Her mind quickly fell back to the attack on the airfield on France, when she and Nicole had fought off the attacking Stukas. One by one the Spitfires rolled from their neat row, quickly increasing speed to the centre of the airfield for a quick getaway before the bombs reached the dispersal.

"Harry! Let's get to the bomb shelter!" Cas shouted. Harriet turned and looked at him briefly as he walked out of the hut towards her, then began to run before stopping in her tracks and instinctively looking back at the Spitfires. As she did, she watched Jonny Isaac trip over his own feet as he ran, and hit his head on the wing edge. "Harry!" Cas repeated as he got closer. The ground crew jumped from the Spitfire and shook Jonny. He was motionless. "Harry, no!" Cas shouted as he started headed towards her, and she started running towards the now lone Spitfire sitting by itself with the prop spinning and the prone, unconscious pilot by the wing. The crewman looked up at Harriet in surprise as she approached, he'd been with her in France, and they'd talked a few times. She jumped over Jonny and grabbed his parachute before running up the wing and climbing into the cockpit, throwing the parachute in ahead of her. The crewman followed her onto the wing. He gave her a nod and fastened her harness while she quickly went through her checks. All the time the bombs were getting closer, as the last of the Spitfires climbed up through the fire and smoke. She gave the crewman a nod, and he jumped from the wing. A look around showed the way ahead to be clear, apart from the closing bombs, then a quick look over her shoulder showed Cas shaking his head and waving frantically. She couldn't hear him over the engine noise, though he was shouting something. She looked forward and pushed on the throttle, making the Spitfire lurch as it quickly gathered

151

speed and bounced her along the grass. There was no time for any more checks, or to get into a reasonable spot for take off, so she opened the throttle and pushed it through the gate, going straight to full boost as soon as she had speed enough to avoid being tipped on her nose by the surge of power. She was pushed into her seat as the Spitfire eased into a hard sprint through the thickening smoke. She couldn't see in front of her, thanks to the high nose of the Spitfire and the blackness surrounding her, until one of the falling bombs lit up the darkness ahead, turning her windscreen a glowing orange and gold. She swallowed hard and pulled back on the stick, the nose lifted, and she felt her stomach dip as the Spitfire jumped from the ground, not a moment too soon as another bomb exploded, throwing dirt up in the air and rocking the Spitfire, almost flipping it upside down. Had she not got off the ground, the bomb would have killed her instantly. The bomb smoke spiralled around the wings as she climbed hard to clear the airfield. The undercarriage came up, and she was searching the sky for the rest of the squadron, they'd gone, and there was no sign of them. She could see the direction the bombs were falling though, which gave her an idea which way the bombers were heading, and she reasoned that's where the squadron would be heading too, so she turned and did the same while maintaining the steepest and fastest climb she could. As she climbed, checking constantly for signs of the Luftwaffe or the squadron, she fought with the parachute, pulling the harness around her and securing it into place. Her ponytail blew in the wind rushing past the open cockpit, and she realised that she'd left her flying helmet in her recently crashed Spitfire and had absolutely no way of communicating with the squadron. It didn't bother her that much, and she was used to flying without a helmet anyway. The Spitfires that she'd moved around with the ATA hardly ever had radios fitted, as that was usually done at the squadron; but on this occasion, she would have liked to have been able to talk to somebody. She continued to search the sky as she raced upwards on full boost, until finally she passed through a scattering of clouds and saw a web of white condensation trails following the mess of black dots heading south, and out over the Channel. She corrected her course and maintained the climb, heading towards the dots as fast as the light and responsive Spitfire would carry her. As she closed on the battle, she was left frowning as she tried to work out what was going on. A squadron of 110s were circling a few thousand feet below; literally, nose to tail in the tightest circle they could manage, protecting themselves by preventing any of the four rapidly closing Spitfires from getting on their tails. Further below, and further away were a huddle of bombers being chased down by more Spitfires. A quick scan showed there were no other aeroplanes around, at least none she could see, so she pulled back on the stick and climbed harder to put herself even further above the circling 110s. The Spitfires were already trying their luck with them, but being thwarted by the defensive circle, unable to break in without risking being shot down, and forced to come back again from a different angle with the same result. The Spitfires were keeping the 110s circling, which was stopping them from diving down on the other Spitfires attacking the bombers. Another minute of watching the Spitfires tease and test the 110 circle, and she was above them. One final look around and over her shoulder, and she pushed the stick over to the left and flipped the Spitfire on its back, pulling back on the stick to send the aeroplane into a steep dive aimed straight at the circle. The four Spitfires below had split into pairs, and each pair was turning in a wide curve to line up for their next run at the circle. Harriet lined up her sights and rolled as she kept them on one of the 110s, then at two hundred feet she was aiming just far enough ahead of its tight and predictable circle and pushed the gun button. The Spitfire shook as the guns buzzed, and burning tracer rounds reached out like long deathly white fingers towards the 110, at first appearing to curve away, then all of a sudden rattling into the cockpit and along the fuselage. It immediately began streaming smoke and flames, rolling upside down before falling out of the circle at the same time as she rocketed through in her Spitfire, only just missing the next 110 in line as it broke to the inside of the circle and dived to avoid the wreckage of the one ahead. Harriet's speed gauge wound up while the altimeter rapidly unwound, as glowing tracer bullets from the diving 110 she'd overtaken weaved around her fuselage. A pull of the stick and kick of the rudder, and she pulled out of the dive while slipping to the left and avoiding the cannon shells, which had somehow hit every inch of air around her without even scraping the paintwork. As she turned, she watched the diving 110 continue downwards, heading for the ground and a quick escape. The 110 she'd shot down was arching off into the distance with a stream of flames and black smoke as it nosedived towards the ground. A

153

quick scan of the sky and her mirror showed nobody was chasing her, so she opened the throttle again and gave chase. The engine roared as she dived after the heavy twin engine fighter, whose rear gunner was already taking shots and sending streams of tracer up towards her Spitfire, and thankfully missing. She returned fire, though she was further away than she was used to in combat. A few of her bullets clipped the 110s airframe, which was enough to rattle the pilot into pulling up to avoid her fire, and in doing so, presenting himself large in her windscreen. She fired, and his left engine coughed and spluttered out black smoke. He rolled over and headed down again, twisting and turning to avoid her guns. She fired and fired, sometimes rattling him and sometimes missing, as he threw the heavy fighter around the sky to avoid her; while all the time the gunner returned her fire, finally finding home as a stream of bullets rattled her wing while arcing towards the cockpit. Harriet pulled back on the stick and pushed it right while kicking the rudder bar to avoid the stream of bullets and quickly entered a tight roll. Eventually, the tracer bullets stopped passing the cockpit, and she finally let out the breath she'd been holding since she started the manoeuvre. She looked around and checked her mirror, and the 110 was far in the distance, its smoking engine leaving a black smudge behind it as it dropped to the deck and headed for home. She breathed deep and wiped her eyes, only now realising sweat was pouring down her face and soaking her. After composing herself, she pointed the nose of her Spitfire upwards to head back to the circle, to join with the rest of the squadron, but they weren't there. Nobody was. The whole battle had gone, and the sky was empty, except for a few fading smoke trails. She looked around frantically, nothing, until finally in the distance she picked out dots heading towards France. She shrugged and checked her instruments, and everything was as it should be. So, with one final scan of the sky she slowly turned back towards the distant lines of black smoke which gave away the airfield's position, and set a course for home, throttling back to save the engine, and dropping down to the deck to skim the fields as she headed back to safety. As she arrived at the airfield, she saw Spitfires on the ground already, and others in the process of landing. Her mouth was dry. The adrenaline had started to ease, and her thoughts started to centre around how much trouble she was probably in, again. The day wasn't yet over, and she'd already flown two different Spitfires in combat, shot down four

Germans, written off a Spitfire, and taken one without permission. Now she was heading back to the ground to explain herself, which she wasn't entirely sure she could. Leading her to the same revolving thought of how she'd be lucky to keep even her ATA wings this time, despite how out of character Singh had been in showing how happy he was to see her. Flaps down, scrub off speed, slip into the approach, canopy open, and she was lining up to land along the airfield boundary hedge. She touched down lightly, and the Spitfire rolled along the grass to the dispersal line, where she parked at the end of the row of Spitfires already there. Her pink Spitfire was still where she'd left it, though it was now being inspected by an officer she didn't recognise, Cas, and a mechanic in white overalls. She knew in her stomach she was in trouble. The mechanic was no doubt expecting a new secret weapon to check over before sending it up for testing, and now he had a crumpled wreck. She looked along the line of Spitfires. Some were shutting down, and some pilots had already alighted and were at the dispersal hut giving their reports to the officer waiting to greet them. Harriet cut the engine of her Spitfire, then slumped into the seat and closed her eyes, thankful to be back on the ground and still trying to think of a single phrase that was going to get her out of trouble.

"Where the hell have you been?" a familiar voice demanded as the sunlight was blocked and the cockpit darkened. Harriet looked up to see AP frowning down at her while reaching in and unfastening her harness.

"I didn't break anything..." Harriet replied with an awkward smile. "At least not this one, anyway." AP pulled her up and hugged her, quite unexpectedly.

"Are you OK?" AP asked, as she finally released Harriet and looked in her eyes.

"Yeah..." she replied. She was trembling as the adrenaline finally let her emotions start to kick in.

"Well you'd better smarten yourself up, your company has been summoned."

155

"Summoned? What?" Harriet asked nervously. AP nodded over to the mechanic as she helped Harriet out onto the wing of the Spitfire. "Oh..."

"Yes. Oh... What on earth did you do?" She helped Harriet out of her parachute and slung it over the wing, before helping her smarten herself up, the best she could. Her hair was matted with sweat, and her tunic was a little crumpled.

"Broke a Spitfire?"

"Come on," AP rolled her eyes. "You'd better not keep him waiting any longer than you already have." She led Harriet around the Spitfire, and in the direction of the broken one she'd left piled into the ground not much earlier.

"He? The mechanic in the white overalls, you mean?"

"Yeah, the mechanic..." AP said with a look of disappointment. "God alone knows how they ever let you in the RAF."

"What?"

"Just be polite, and don't argue." AP straightened her own clothes as they approached. "Sir," she said loudly, catching Cas' attention.

"Section Officer Kaye," he replied formally, before looking Harriet in the eyes. She squared her shoulders and stared at him fiercely. She was still angry at him for the way he'd used her in France, and then abandoned her. "Miss Cornwall."

"Mister Salisbury," she replied curtly.

"Who's this?" the mechanic asked as he stepped away from the Spitfire wreckage and stood by Cas' side.

156

"This is your Spitfire pilot, Sir," Cas replied, keeping his eyes locked on Harriet for a moment, before slowly turning to look at the mechanic. The mechanic raised an eyebrow at Cas, who in reply nodded without a word.

"But she's a..." the mechanic said firmly.

"Yes, Sir, she is."

"Was he going to say I'm a girl?" Harriet asked, breaking the silence. AP raised her elbow sharply and nudged Harriet. "What?" she demanded.

"Shut up!" AP whispered.

"Yes, I was, as a matter of fact, and what of it?" the mechanic asked confidently as he stepped forward. Cas cringed a little and put his hand to his forehead. "You are a girl, aren't you?" he demanded as he looked her up and down.

"I certainly hope so," Harriet replied.

"Good. Now we've got that cleared up; you can tell me what you did to that Spitfire?" he asked as he pointed to the pink wreck.

"My best," Harriet replied after a deep breath. The adrenaline was starting to pump through her system again.

"Oh? How's that?"

"I got it here in one piece as I was asked to," Harriet continued. "It was the idiots operating the guns here who shot me down and almost killed me in the process when I came in to land. If it wasn't for them, your precious Spitfire would still be in one piece. Mostly."

"Mostly?"

"Well, this Hurricane was having a bit of a thing with some 109s on the way, and I stopped to help. So the cannons were fired, and the engine ran at full boost for a while longer than it probably should, but that's all."

"That Hurricane?" He pointed over to the Hurricane parked by the dispersal hut.

"Maybe," she shrugged, recognising the code on the side and knowing full well it was.

"Maybe indeed..."

"Look, I'm very sorry for any damage I've done, but it was quite unavoidable; and as for the other Spitfire I just took up, I did it because the airfield was being bombed and I know how valuable Spitfires are. I didn't want it to be destroyed on the ground, and I'm a pilot trained on the type, so I took it up."

"So you did..." the mechanic replied.

"It's in good condition, Sir," AP added. "A couple of holes in the wing, but she brought it back in one piece."

"I don't doubt that she did," the mechanic replied. "My office this afternoon, Mister Salisbury, and you'd better bring this little spitfire with you."

"Yes, Sir," Cas replied.

"We'll continue our conversation later," he said to Harriet. "I have to get back to Uxbridge and try to find out what the hell the Luftwaffe are up to." He gazed up to the sky briefly and muttered under his breath. "Hannibal ad Portas."

"Dulce Periculum," Harriet replied without thinking, having remembered her Latin.

"Indeed..." the mechanic said with a half smile, before turning and marching in the direction of his Hurricane, following a smart salute from Cas, and leaving him looking at Harriet and AP He shook his head then turned to watch another couple of Spitfires coming in to land. The Hurricane spluttered into life as Cas turned back to Harriet.

"Are you OK?" he asked. Harriet nodded. "You're sure?"

"I'm sure," she said firmly. "Can I go now?"

"Excuse me?"

"I'd like to freshen up before the taxi flight arrives to collect me, so if there's nothing else?" She paused for a moment, then turned and started to walk away.

"Have I done something to wrong you, Harry?" he asked. She stopped and turned to face him, then reached under her sleeve and pulled off his watch, which she placed firmly in his hand.

"Yours, I believe. Thank you for the loan, I shan't be needing it anymore." She turned again and straightened her shoulders confidently before marching away without answering, fearing that if she did, she'd say something horrible. AP shrugged as Cas looked at her with a pained expression, then gave her a nod and she turned and walked after Harriet. "What's wrong with you?" AP asked as they walked. Harriet bit her tongue as she could feel her emotions getting the better of her, and her eyes were watering, much to her annoyance.

"Nothing," Harriet replied.

"Harry!"

"Just leave me alone!" She marched faster, straight past the dispersal hut and towards the trucks parked up beyond it. Not knowing where she was going, just desperate to get away from people before she cried in public, which was strictly against her own rules. Before she could take another step, AP grabbed her by the arm and dragged her between the trucks. "Get off!"

"I'll get off when you stand still and tell me what the hell's wrong with you?"

"Just shut up!"

"No I won't shut up, and if you won't talk, you can listen. That man out there tore himself to pieces when he lost you. We all did, but none more than him. He took you to battle against his better judgement, and he lost you, shot down over Dunkirk. Then a few days later Max turns up and says you survived, that he found you on the beach and you were injured, but you made it. Then you didn't. Then the boat you were on was reported sunk with no survivors. Then we lost you all over again, until you fall out of the sky in a pink bloody Spitfire, alive and kicking as though nothing had happened! It almost broke him, Harry. Then when he sees you're alive, you ignore him and treat him like dirt!" The tears were now streaming down Harriet's cheeks.

"I'm sorry," she sobbed. "I didn't mean to..."

"Where have you been, Harry? Why didn't you come home?" AP pleaded.

"They told me you didn't want me..."

"What? Who did? What are you talking about?"

"I woke up in a hospital on the south coast, and they told me they'd reported to the Air Ministry that I was safe and that my squadron would be informed. Then I was sent to stay with a relative while I recovered, and after that nobody wanted me. The recruiting office wouldn't even talk to me, and I ended up going to London, to the Air Ministry, who didn't want me either. Finally, I got a letter from them, the Air Ministry, saying the squadron wishes me the best with my future. I felt... I

160

thought... I thought you didn't care, any of you. I thought I'd been used and forgotten. I thought Cas had forgotten about me."

"Oh, Harry..." AP hugged Harriet. "We were told you were dead." She stood back again and looked Harriet in the eyes. "The Air Ministry said you were dead, missing in action. Cas even went there himself with Singh's blessing and was given a copy of the official document posting you as missing. We even had a wake for you in the Mess."

"I don't understand..."

"Neither do I, and I honestly don't care right now. All I care about is you being here, being alive." She smiled uncharacteristically. "If you can get that into that thick, stubborn, head of yours, maybe we can go and talk to Cas and sort all of this out." Harriet smiled, and half laughed through her tears.

"He must think I'm such a bitch."

"You are."

"Harsh." They both laughed. "I mean it, though," Harriet continued "I don't even know how to fix this."

"Well, you'd better find a way before this afternoon."

"Why? What happens this afternoon?"

"You really are hard work, Harry." AP sighed.

"What?"

"Well unless I was listening to a very different conversation, the AOC just ordered Cas to have you at his office this afternoon, so you'd better be on talking terms otherwise it's going to be an awkward trip to Uxbridge and back."

161

"I have no idea what you're talking about."

"The man in the white overalls who pointed out that you're a girl, remember?"

"The mechanic?"

"The what?"

"The mechanic in the overalls, the one who'd come to check over the Spitfire?"

"Oh dear God. Harry. That was the Air Officer Commanding of the entire fighter group. He's in charge of every Spitfire and Hurricane in the whole of the south east of England and reports directly to the Commander in Chief of fighter command."

"Why on earth does he want to see me?" Harriet's eyes opened wide.

"Because when he turned up in his own personal Hurricane shortly after you'd taken off, he was looking for the pilot of a pink Spitfire who'd saved him from three Messerschmitt 109s that had jumped him while he was up checking on the battle."

"Oh... Oh. " Harriet said as she realised, and her mouth dropped open.

"Yes, Oh. Cas filled him in on the pilot, in detail. Almost."

"Oh," Harriet repeated.

"Yes. He was keen to meet you when you landed, and you tore a strip off him."

"I'm not having the best day, am I?"

"You're alive, aren't you? Anyway, where did those bullet holes in the wing of that Spitfire you took up come from?"

162

"I really couldn't say... Anyway, I should probably go and talk to Cas, shouldn't I?" she said as she adjusted her tunic. AP pulled a crisp white handkerchief from her pocket and handed it to Harriet, who took it with a smile and wiped her eyes. With a deep breath, AP walked her back to the dispersal hut. Some of the pilots were still landing on the bomb strewn airfield, and those that were already down were huddled around the intelligence officer giving their reports. Cas was still standing by the crumpled pink Spitfire and watching a group of airmen as they went about trying to attach slings so the wreck could be lifted onto the flatbed of their truck.

"I thought you had somewhere to go?" Cas asked quietly as Harriet approached, while keeping his eyes fixed firmly on the airmen.

"How did you know it was me?" she asked as she stepped from behind him and stood by his side.

"Well we've had quite a few new faces join us since we left France, but I don't recall any of them wearing Chanel." He looked at her briefly to see a frustrated half smile on her pursed lips, as she remembered borrowing some of Lexi's perfume earlier that morning. She and Nicole had taken a few drops each of Nicole's grandmother's Chanel on the fateful day they'd met Sully, and their adventures had begun. She'd told Lexi how much she liked the smell when they'd had a drink in the Mess the previous evening, and Lexi had insisted she wore some the next morning.

"It could have been one of the other girls on the squadron."

"You're the only one I know who wears Chanel."

"Oh..." She blushed a little while gathering her thoughts, having been distracted from her prepared speech. "I'm sorry," she blurted unceremoniously. "For being rude, I mean. You see, I didn't know. About what the squadron had been told, that is." Her words were just falling out of her mouth in no particular order, and with what felt like next to no control. "They told me you knew and wished me all the best. So I was angry. I felt like I'd been forgotten."

"My dear girl, what on earth are you talking about?" Cas asked as he turned to face her.

"I didn't know the Air Ministry told you I was dead..." she said with a heavy heart.

"Yes... They were quite unhelpful."

"I know. I wrote to them asking for information on the squadron, and I received a reply telling me the squadron was happy I was safe and wishing me the best in the future. I felt..."

"Forgotten?"

"Yes. It's stupid, I know, but I loved being part of the squadron in France and thought I belonged. It hurt to think I didn't."

"What are we going to do with you?" He smiled and shook his head.

"Forgive me?" she asked awkwardly. He reached into his top pocket and pulled out his thin silver flask, which he handed to Harriet. She took a swig and coughed as the brandy burned her throat. "Thanks," she gasped as she gave it back to him. He took a swig and put the flask away in his pocket.

"Better?" he asked. She nodded and coughed again. "Good. Now let's go and call your boss and let them know where you are. There's a bit of a flap on today, so they're bound to be a bit worried." They turned and strolled towards the dispersal hut.

"What flap?"

"The Germans are hitting airfields all across the south coast, by all accounts. They've been keeping themselves to the Channel for the last

164

few weeks, bothering convoys and the likes. Today's something different; the plan's changed. The squadron has been up three times already, and, well, you've seen the state of the airfield."

"Yes..." She looked around at the destruction.

"So, you're an ATA pilot?"

"Yes. They're the only ones that would have me. The Air Ministry turned me away."

"Maybe they just need to get to know you," he replied with a smirk. "I see the Latin isn't too rusty."

"They made a big thing about it at school. Apparently, it's useful."

"You don't think?"

"Not really. What good is it unless you're a doctor or a lawyer?"

"Well, it just put a smile on the AOC's face. That has to count for something," he said with a smirk. They entered the dispersal hut, and he asked the airman orderly to get him through to the ATA headquarters. He took the phone and waited. "Hello, Flight Lieutenant Salisbury here. Look, one of your pilots, a Miss Harriet Cornwall, dropped into our airfield a short while ago when she ran into a load of Germans. She's absolutely fine, but things are a bit dicey around here at the moment, so we're going to keep hold of her for the time being, then get her back to you as soon as it's safe if that's OK? No, don't bother, we'll fly her over when things settle down." He put the phone down and turned back to Harriet. "There, that'll stop them worrying. They've all been grounded anyway, so you'd have had to go back on the train. Besides, we have a meeting to go to later."

"That's everyone back," Singh said as he entered the hut. "Where's Isaac? He was nowhere to be seen when we took off, and didn't answer the radio when he finally showed up!"

"Do you want to tell him, or should I?" Cas asked Harriet, who shrunk into herself and felt the familiar blush on her cheeks.

"Tell me what?"

"Mister Isaac is in the sickbay with Simon, having knocked himself out cold when he tripped running to his Spitfire. Again."

"That boy is a liability!" Singh sighed as he hung his Mae West on the back of his chair. "So who was flying his aeroplane?" he asked with a frown as he realised that Isaac's Spitfire was in the sky without its owner. Cas simply looked at Harriet and raised an eyebrow. "Is this true?" Singh demanded.

"I didn't want it to be destroyed on the ground," Harriet said shyly.

"I appreciate your efforts, Miss Cornwall, and we do need every aeroplane we can get. Especially Spitfires. However, next time could you please just hide in a cloud somewhere, and not dive through a defensive circle of Messerschmitts. You'll live longer."

"Yes, Sir."

"You dived through a defensive circle?" Cas asked.

"It seemed like the only way to break them up."

"You certainly did that," Singh replied. "Better add her kill to The Spy's tally."

"I'll make sure it's counted," Cas said. "The AOC called by while you were up."

"The AOC? Here? What did he want?" Singh asked with surprise.

"To talk to the driver of that pink Spitfire outside, or what remains of it."

"What did you do?" Singh asked Harriet.

"Caused the AOC a headache, I think" Cas replied with a smirk. "Apparently our young friend here intercepted a German patrol hell bent on shooting the AOC out of the sky, and he wanted to say thank you."

"I don't remember him doing that," Harriet added.

"Quite," Cas continued. "Anyway, he's asked me to deliver her to his headquarters this afternoon, if that's OK with you?"

"I don't think a lowly Squadron Leader can exactly say no to the AOC, do you?"

"Probably not."

"Well, she can't stand in front of the AOC dressed in smoky flying kit. Why don't you take the Tiger and fly her back to her aerodrome to freshen up a little, then head up to Uxbridge?"

"Good idea, we'll push off. Are you sure you don't need me here?"

"We've been up three times since first light; I expect we'll be stood down in a few hours to get ourselves together. Get yourselves off. Oh, and Miss Cornwall. Welcome back." Harriet beamed a huge smile as she followed Cas out of the dispersal hut and past the group of pilots, some of whom were still talking through their recent combat and filling out their reports, while others were sprawled on the grass recovering, some even sleeping.

"Leaving already?" Max asked as he looked over.

"I hardly blame her," Archie added. "Look at the reception we put on."

"I'll be back," Harriet replied with a confident smile. She followed Cas to the Tiger Moth, which the squadron held as a communications aeroplane that was mostly used as a run around. Harriet climbed in and made herself comfortable while Cas went to the front to swing the propeller, which he did a few times, enough to get up a sweat before stopping and looking up at Harriet.

"Are you going to start the bloody thing, or am I just fanning you to keep you cool?" he demanded. Harriet bit her tongue as she remembered he'd asked her to start the engine when she'd climbed aboard, and she'd totally forgotten just seconds later. She waved, and he went back to swinging the propeller and this time she ignited the engine and gave it a good rev. "Sticky ignition button, was it?" he asked as he climbed up the wing and into the rear seat. She smiled in reply as he raised his eyebrows before getting comfortable. A quick look around for obstacles and they were pulling away from the squadron lines, being waved off by a group of the pilots, before taxiing to a clear spot on the runway. A quick power check and they were bouncing along the bomb cratered grass and climbing into the rough air. Harriet looked out over the airfield and through the haze of black smoke. Repair crews were already out filling in craters, and vehicles were running in every direction as the station went into action to return it to operational as soon as possible. She also laid eyes on the gun positions and made a silent vow to have words with the officer commanding them if she ever got the chance. Harriet had given Cas details of her home field, which he knew well, so all she had to do was sit back and relax and keep her eyes open for German aeroplanes while Cas flew them practically at ground level along the Kent coast. A swarm of bombers and fighters passed many thousands of feet above them, heading back towards France. Harriet watched them closely, but at their height they likely never even noticed the camouflaged old Tiger Moth hedge hopping its way west, and even if they did it was unlikely that they'd bother to come down for such a slow and easy target. Especially when there was the chance of Spitfires and Hurricanes waiting around for them. It wasn't long before they were approaching Harriet's field, which was made all the more visible by the spirals of black smoke winding their way up from the fires along the perimeter. Harriet looked all around, but there was no sign of Germans. Cas did the same before doing a circuit and lining up for a soft landing. Harriet directed him to the ATA dispersal, where he parked next to the yellow Tiger Moth and cut the engine. As Harriet climbed from the cockpit, she looked over to the dispersal hut where two familiar faces were waiting for her, Lexi and Abby. She waited for Cas to extract himself and throw his flying jacket in the cockpit, before straightening his blue uniform and putting on his service hat, then together they headed to the hut.

"We were worried about you until we got the call from HQ," Abby said as she stepped forward and hugged Harriet.

"Then the Luftwaffe paid us a visit," Lexi added as she joined them. "So we decided to worry about us for a while instead."

"Are you all OK?" Harriet asked.

"We're fine," Abby replied. "They bombed the other side of the airfield and hit an old truck and the scrap dump."

"Yeah, some real skill right there," Lexi said. "Missing an entire airfield and hitting a scrap pile."

"I suspect their aim will improve next time," Cas said.

"Well hello, flyboy," Lexi said as she stood in front of him and eyed him from top to bottom, and back again. She stepped closer and ran her fingertip over his medal ribbons. "Thank you for bringing our friend back... Can we buy you a drink in the Mess to show our gratitude?" Cas smirked and looked her firmly in the eye.

"It was my pleasure to fly Miss Cornwall home, but it would be rude to decline your very kind offer. A quick brandy, perhaps?"

"Quick is always good for me, honey," Lexi smirked back at him.

"Really?" Harriet said in disbelief at Lexi's uninhibited flirting.

"Why don't you get cleaned up and changed into your best uniform?" Cas said. "I'll meet you in the Mess for a drink before we head up to Uxbridge?"

"Whatever," Harriet said with a roll of her eyes.

"Can I get a ride with you?" Abby said. "We've been grounded because of the raids, so I may as well go back and get changed, too."

"Sure," Harriet said as she marched past Cas and Lexi, who both turned and followed her. She dropped her kit in the doorway of the dispersal hut, then headed behind it and climbed onto her borrowed shining motorbike, which was parked up by Lexi's. Abby climbed on behind her and held tight, while Cas unceremoniously climbed on behind Lexi who looked over to Harriet and winked.

"Last one to the Mess puts a drink behind the bar," Lexi shouted. Both bikes roared into life, and the race was on. They left dust trails behind them across the camp all the way to the domestic site where the Mess was located, safely away from the airfield. Lexi tore off, using her experience of motorcycle racing to her advantage, but Harriet chased hard all the way, to the irritation of the station warrant officer who was left spinning in the road as the bikes passed either side of him in a roaring blur. It wasn't the first time they'd done that to him, and likely wouldn't be the last. He shouted and blustered every time and threatened God's retribution until Lexi fluttered her eyelashes and turned him bright red. She had a reputation for being a man eater, though it's rare that anyone saw her go any further than teasing men mercilessly and having them eating out of the palm of her hand, regardless of age or rank. They parked up, and Lexi waved with a mischievous giggle as she led Cas to the Mess. Harriet and Abby dismounted and watched them disappear inside.

"Is he a friend of yours?" Abby asked as they walked towards the Mess and their room

"Something like that," Harriet replied.

"Well, I hope he can look after himself, she's on top form today."

"He shot thirteen Germans down in one battle in the last war, and led a head on attack into a swarm of bombers raiding Dunkirk earlier this year." Harriet continued as they walked up the stairs. "He's brave, intelligent, and a peerless strategist."

"You're worried about him, aren't you?"

"In Lexi's company? Absolutely!" Harriet opened the bedroom door and stepped in, still blustering about Lexi. "She's hopeless. I love her, but she drives me to distraction at times." She stopped and fell silent as she saw the uniform hanging on her locker. "Whose is that?" she asked Abby as she looked at the smart tunic with the gold braid of a First Officer.

"Yours, of course," Abby said with a giggle. "Lexi got on the phone with Mister Thomas in London as soon as she heard of your promotion, it arrived earlier this morning."

"She is so annoying... All my ranting about her and she's gone and done this for me."

"She can be like that. Anyway, you need to get cleaned up and get into it. Otherwise, your friend may not last in the bar alone with Lexi."

"Somebody should rescue him."

"Hurry up, then." Harriet nodded and headed into the bathroom, where she kicked off her flying clothes while the sink filled with hot water. She looked at herself in the mirror for a moment. Her face was black with smoke and sweat. Her mind drifted back to the last time she'd looked this way in the mirror, back to France when Nicole was still with her. She frowned as one memory linked to another, and then another until she was watching Nicole's Hurricane diving towards the ground, out of control and burning. She caught herself heading to a dark place, and quickly splashed a handful of water over her face to distract herself, then got on with scrubbing herself clean. The water was black when she'd finished, and that was the third filling of the sink. Her skin was filthy and her hair was matted, it had been a while since she'd been in combat, and

171

she'd forgotten how much it made her sweat. She dried herself down as she went back into the room, where Abby was finishing changing into her best uniform.

"Going somewhere?" Harriet asked.

"On a rescue mission," Abby said with a wink and a smile before leaving the room, still fastening her tunic.

"Give me strength..." Harriet said as she rolled her eyes to the ceiling. "Not you as well?"

"See you in the bar," Abby giggled cheerfully as she closed the door behind her. Harriet quickly changed underwear and dressed in the newly decorated uniform, after towel drying her hair and combing it back into a smart bun. She fastened her goose brooch to her lapel, checked herself in the mirror, then grabbed her hat and ran out of the room. Once moving through the Mess, Harriet walked as quickly as she could while remaining dignified, driven to get to the Mess bar with an urgency she couldn't explain. As she hurried down the corridor, she heard laughter and voices, lots of voices, coming from the bar. She took a deep breath and stepped through the doorway. Facing her was a sight she didn't expect. Cas was standing against the bar, laughing and smiling, and enjoying being surrounded by every woman on the flight; all of whom were dressed in their smartest uniforms, and all hanging on his every word. They laughed and talked until he looked up and caught Harriet in his sight. He smiled and gave her a small nod, a gesture which signalled her arrival to the rest of the group, and they all turned to look at her in the doorway. The group fell silent. Penny stepped forward from the group, surprising Harriet a little as she didn't expect to see her fawning over Cas in the same way as the others. She started a slow clap which had Harriet confused. The others joined in until they were applauding loudly. Harriet looked around behind her, then as she turned to look in the bar again, Cas was walking over to her.

172

"Shall we?" he asked as he held out his arm. She nodded and put her hand on his forearm and allowed him to lead her graciously to the applauding girls of the flight.

"What's going on?" she asked him quietly as she approached the others. "What have you done?"

"I'm sure I don't know what you mean," he replied as he delivered her to her friends.

"You flew Hurricanes in combat?" Lexi asked.

"I told you I did," Harriet replied.

"No, Ma'am. You told us you flew Hurricanes in France, not that you shot down highly decorated Luftwaffe pilots!" Harriet felt herself blushing.

"I knew there was something about you," Penny said.

"Brandy?" Cas asked as he offered her a glass. Harriet quickly nodded, took it, and downed it in one to the rousing cheer of her fellow pilots.

"Mister Salisbury has been telling us about your exploits," Penny continued.

"Has he...?" Harriet asked, trying her best to hide the mixture of embarrassment and irritation building inside.

"He has," Cas said. "However, he must now pull you away before things get going, as you're due at Uxbridge. It's not good to keep the AOC waiting. He's a busy man."

"You're flying there in a Tiger Moth, are you?" Lexi asked.

"How else would you suggest we get there?"

173

"It'll mess up your uniforms in those open cockpits, and your hair. Why don't you use our Anson? Hell, I'll even fly you there myself, if that's OK with you, Penny?"

"I suppose," Penny shrugged. "Then, when you get back, we can have a few drinks to celebrate Harry's war service. It's not every day you find out that one of your girls is an ace."

"Not every day?" Abby asked. "It's never happened before. It's not any day!"

"Well yes, that's certainly true," Penny replied with a giggle, which made Abby raise an eyebrow to Harriet at the way their usually austere and professional leader had become every bit the schoolgirl in Cas' presence. Harriet simply rolled her eyes in disappointment. "Why don't you go for a ride out with them, Abby? You can keep Lexi out of mischief while she waits with the Anson. HQ has stood us down until tomorrow at the earliest. You may as well make the most of it."

"Is that OK?" Abby asked Harriet.

"We're going to a busy RAF station, she'll need somebody to keep an eye on her," Harriet replied.

"That's it agreed, then. We'd better get going," Cas said as he finished his brandy. "Thank you all so much for your hospitality. It's been a pleasure meeting you."

Chapter 7

Nineteen

Having successfully navigated around London's balloon barrage, and followed Cas' instructions on finding the expertly camouflaged air station, which even boasted a stream painted across the runway, Lexi landed and parked with the other visiting aircraft by the tower. Northolt was a busy operational station, and being just a few miles down the road from Uxbridge, the Headquarters for 11 Group Fighter Command, visitors of all types would regularly fly in for a multitude of reasons; and the Anson joined a line of Tiger Moths, Hurricanes, and Spitfires, the expensive, fast and efficient taxis of the RAF.

The duty officer, a young Flight Lieutenant with a pilot's brevet and a look of disdain, had greeted Cas in a formal yet dismissive manner, before reluctantly arranging for a vehicle to take the party to Uxbridge. Even Lexi's charms didn't sway his cold and miserable derision, and he hardly registered Cas' row of medals, something that generally garnered a little civility from other pilots, if nothing else. Cas simply frowned and ignored the officer, choosing to leave the matter and join the others in boarding the transport. On arrival at Uxbridge, Lexi and Abby were dropped at the Officer's Mess, where they all agreed to meet afterwards, and Harriet and Cas headed to Group Headquarters.

"I think I got a distorted view of the RAF when I was in France," Harriet said as they walked towards the large mansion house which housed the Group HQ.

"Oh, why's that?" Cas replied.

"Almost every officer I've met since I've been in England has been miserable. It's not at all like the squadron," she said with a frown. Cas let out a stifled laugh before holding the door open and following her inside. "Why are you laughing? I'm not joking!"

175

"I know you're not joking, Harry. The RAF can certainly appear a strange creature to those that don't know it, and I dare say that it is quite peculiar even to those of us that have known it for its entire life. Though for now, all you need to know about the RAF is that very senior officers don't like sarcasm or witty comments from their subordinates, and they certainly don't stand for any talking back." They stood in front of the Orderly Sergeant at his reception desk. "Flight Lieutenant Salisbury and First Officer Cornwall to see the AOC." The Sergeant checked his paperwork and made a short telephone call.

"Yes, Sir. If you'd like to follow me, I'll show you the way." Cas gave Harriet a wink, and they followed the Sergeant to a small waiting room where they were left to sit in silence.

"Why does it have to be so formal?" Harriet whispered. "It reminds me of school." Cas gave her a reassuring smile, but before he could reply, the door in front of them opened and an officer marched out, giving Cas and Harriet a brief nod and smile before leaving the waiting room. Another officer followed him a minute later, another pilot, not as young as Harriet, but not as old as Cas. He had a couple of medal ribbons under his wings, and a distinguishing scar on his cheek.

"The AOC will see you now," he said politely. He gestured them into the office. They both stood, and Harriet followed Cas' example in straightening her uniform, before walking smartly at his side through the door; which was closed behind them by the officer who remained almost ominously at the back of the room. Cas nodded to the spot next to where he'd stopped in front of the large wooden desk, and Harriet took her place, copying him in standing smartly to attention while the officer sitting behind it looked through a file while simultaneously listening to the telephone. Harriet recognised him, or at least she thought she did; it was the mechanic. Though he no longer looked like one. Gone were the white overalls, replaced by a smart RAF uniform complete with pilot's brevet with several rows of medals underneath, and more than enough braid on his cuffs.

"OK, thank you," he said in his faintly antipodean accent, then put the phone down. Harriet glanced questioningly at Cas in the continuing silence, and Cas remained facing forward, rigid and silent like a guardsman. "Nineteen!" the AOC finally said as he looked up from the file he was reading, and looked Harriet in the eyes with a stare that made her instantly nervous.

"Eighteen," she replied before anything else could pop into her head. "Though I am nineteen this year." Cas frowned and winced, still keeping his eyes forward.

"That's as may be, young lady, but if your rather intense service record is to be believed, you'll be lucky to reach that age with the way you attract trouble."

"My service record?" Harriet asked, ignoring absolutely everything else he'd said. "You have my service record?"

"You are Probationary Pilot Officer Harriet Cornwall of the Royal Air Force Volunteer Reserve, formally of the Norwegian Army Air Service?"

"Yes, Sir! It's just... I was told there was no record of me."

"Yes, well, I had to do some digging and speak to many different people at the Air Ministry, but it was finally found in the deceased section, the 1918 deceased section, to be precise, and under the entirely wrong letter. Though how it got there is another matter." He continued his emotionless stare as he talked. "Now, if you'd be good enough to allow me to continue without further interruption?" Harriet nodded and blushed while fighting the huge grin that was making her cheeks ache as it tried to spread across her face. Somebody had finally found her record. "Nineteen enemy aircraft destroyed in the air in combat is what I was trying to say," the AOC continued. "That's quite some record, and I can see why Air Vice Marshal Bristol both authorised your commission; and recommended you for the Distinguished Flying Cross for your actions in putting your life in extreme danger to defend the bomber on which he, his staff, and a number of other personnel, including several injured

177

airmen, were travelling; against an entire squadron of the enemy. A recommendation which was approved, I should add." He flicked a page in the report and read from it. "In addition to being mentioned in dispatches, twice, for your actions in the air defending your squadron's airfield, and being awarded to the Légion d'honneur by the French government, France's highest award for bravery, on the recommendation of General Calvert of the French Army; who credits you for engaging the superior enemy forces attacking his position, both bombers and fighters, and breaking up the attack despite being outnumbered at least ten to one. In doing so, allowing many civilians to escape, and enabling the General to fortify his position and slow the German advance to the coast," he paused before resuming. "Last, but not least, we have a bar to your Distinguished Flying Cross. An award recommended by Captain Anderson of the Royal Navy, who cites you as following a lone German bomber at low level through the Navy's anti aircraft flak barrage at great risk to yourself, and shooting it down before it had a chance to release its bombs on the Captain's cruiser. A boat which at the time was carrying over two thousand service personnel being evacuated from the beaches of Dunkirk. An action which left your own aeroplane severely damaged and forced you to crash land on an enemy held beach. A recommendation seconded by both the Beach Master at Dunkirk, and Vice Admiral Dover." Harriet had started paying attention and felt her cheeks burning with embarrassment from hearing her exploits read out publicly, in addition to feeling sick deep in her stomach as she remembered the person who was with her through almost all of it. Nicole. Her mind wandered as she replayed every action, every twist and turn, every word shouted between her and Nicole as they fought above France, and how Nicole had saved her life one last time over Dunkirk and lost her own in the process. "Well?" the AOC's voice cut through her daydreams and pulled her back into the room.

"Sir?" she asked.

"Do you care to explain yourself, Miss Cornwall?"

"I'm not sure I understand, Sir?"

"Where have you been since leaving France?"

"I was sent to stay with a relative when they discharged me from the hospital in Kent. They said they'd told the RAF where I was, and that I'd be able to return to my squadron after a month's convalescence. Only, when I tried to report to the RAF, nobody had heard of me. No records, nothing. A nice Japanese Officer at the Air Ministry, Mister O'Kara, finally found a way of sending me to the ATA so I could at least still fly. I tried to contact the squadron, but all I got was a letter from the Air Ministry thanking me for my service, and wishing me the best for my future on behalf of the squadron..."

"I see... What do you have to say about that, Mister Salisbury?"

"Much to the regret of the entire squadron, Sir, among whom Miss Cornwall had become very popular in her short time with us. The Air Ministry informed us that Miss Cornwall had been lost at sea; when the minesweeper she was evacuated from Dunkirk on was torpedoed and sunk. I even went to the Air Ministry myself to try and find news of her. Had I known she was alive; I'd have moved heaven and earth to get her back to us."

"And you'd want that?"

"Sir?"

"To have this spitfire back with your squadron?"

"Absolutely, Sir. Miss Cornwall is, without doubt, the finest fighter pilot I've ever seen. She's a natural, better even, whatever that may be. We'd be lucky to have her."

"That's quite the accolade, especially from such an incredible pilot as yourself, Mister Salisbury."

"It's quite true, Sir," Cas replied humbly. "It's an opinion shared by the entire squadron."

179

"I don't doubt it, Mister Salisbury. I don't doubt it..." He switched his gaze back to Harriet and nodded his head slowly while setting the file down on his desk and sitting back. "As you'll both no doubt know from the fun and games at your airfield this morning, after a while of keeping themselves amused by annoying convoys in the Channel and bothering some of our coastal airfields, it's finally our turn. The Germans have launched raids right across the south, hitting airfields, depots, and production facilities with massed bomber forces escorted by large numbers of fighters. The consensus is that invasion is imminent, but to cross the Channel the Germans must neutralise the RAF first, so it's on us, particularly Eleven Group. Unfortunately, what happened in France has drained us of hundreds of much needed Hurricanes, and more importantly, we lost almost as many irreplaceable experienced pilots. So, that said, I suppose now's your chance, Miss Cornwall." Her eyes opened wide in anticipation. "You can either return to your Flight with the ATA, with a letter of recommendation from me, and the genuine heartfelt thanks of the RAF. Or, and I've agreed this with the CinC Fighter Command and the Minister for Air as you arrived, your commission can be reinstated, and you can return to your squadron, subject to conditions, of course." Harriet stood gobsmacked. Her mind was spinning, and she was struggling to keep up and process what was going on. Was he really letting her go back to the squadron? "Well?" he continued.

"Sir?"

"The ATA or the RAF Miss Cornwall. I don't have all day. There's a war to fight."

"RAF, Sir!" she replied excitedly.

"Good... Now, the conditions attached to the reinstatement of your commission. You'll need to pay attention too, Mister Salisbury, she's your problem now. "

"Yes, Sir," Cas replied.

"First. I don't have the time to send you to Cranwell to learn how to be an officer, or even learn how to be in the RAF, as much as I would like to; so every minute of spare time you have, you'll be learning the ropes from Mister Salisbury. I expect the highest standards of my officers." Harriet and Cas nodded in unison, though her nod was much more excitable than his. "Second. There'll be no flying until you're passed fit by the doctor, and given a rating by the Chief Flying Instructor, the same as any other pilot. As luck would have it both are available today, so you can head straight over to the WAAF hospital when I've finished with you, and subject to you getting through that part you can head to the dispersal at Northolt. The instructor will be expecting you. Fail either, and your flying career stops. Understood?" Harriet nodded excitedly again. "Third. I can make you a fighter pilot, but I can't keep you a fighter pilot. As soon as the media hear about a female fighter pilot, you're going to be famous; and as such you're going to make a lot of enemies."

"Enemies?" Harriet frowned. "I don't understand?"

"I'm sure I don't need to tell you that we've never had a female fighter pilot before, Miss Cornwall, and it'll be no surprise to you that there are many who would keep it that way. I know because I was one of them." Harriet raised an eyebrow. "Oh, it's true. I didn't even want WAAFs on my stations, for a number of reasons, and the thought of a female fighter pilot was so fantastic it hadn't even crossed my mind. Until that is, I heard rumours of female fighter pilots riding around France in Hurricanes and getting into trouble during the retreat. Rumours which were later confirmed by Air Vice Marshal Bristol, who I believe you've met." Harriet nodded. "Sadly, there was no trace of you. No records, no documents, no names. Nothing. Until now, that is. Anyway, I'm not the only fool in high places to think that way. There will be those out to see you fail, and if they don't see it, they'll encourage it, I guarantee you. As the first female fighter pilot, you'll carry the unfortunate, unjust, and lonely burden of having to be better than your male peers in every aspect of your life. If you drop your standards, they'll crucify you, and likely me with you, so you can be sure that if you step out of line, you'll hear it from me first!"

"I won't let you down, Sir. I promise."

"I won't give you the chance, Miss Cornwall. Fail me, and you'll find yourself sweeping rain from a runway in the Highlands of Scotland for the rest of your inglorious career."

"Yes, Sir."

"Now, one final thing. That uniform you're wearing."

"Yes, Sir. It was made in London by Mister Thomas, at least I think that's his name. He's the tailor who supplies our uniforms."

"I see..." the AOC said with a slight smirk. "Well, you're incorrectly dressed, and that won't do at all. Once you've finished with your medical and flying assessments, you may want to ask Mister Salisbury if he can help find you one more appropriate. Unless he's changed so much in the years since I last worked with him, he'll know exactly where to find something in your size." He looked over to Cas enquiringly.

"Oh, I think I can rustle something up," Cas replied casually.

"Good. Make sure it's not too shabby. The Norwegian Ambassador is very keen to meet the young lady of Norwegian descent who he kindly adopted to make all of this happen; and it would be an insult after all of his graciousness to turn up in something the dog slept on. Besides, she'll need something for her trip to the palace when the gongs come through, better make sure the ribbons are on before then. She's been Gazetted, so it's all above board. While you're there you could also pick up some regulation RAF wings to replace those RFC antiques you appear to be wearing." He gave Cas a firm stare and pointed at the pilot's wings on his chest, then handed Harriet an envelope. "Here are your papers, Flying Officer Cornwall. Mister Salisbury will make sure all is in order with your squadron. Good day."

"Flying Officer?" Harriet repeated as a broad smile spread across her face and lit up the room.

"My thanks for this morning," he replied. "Now, if you don't mind, I have to get back to the bunker. Good luck, Miss Cornwall." He smiled and nodded. Cas saluted and showed Harriet to the door which was being opened by the AOC's assistant.

"Sir..." Harriet asked as she stopped and turned to look at the AOC from the door.

"Yes?"

"There was another girl with me in France, another pilot, my friend. I don't suppose...?"

"I'm sorry, Miss Cornwall. Miss Delacourt's Hurricane was seen to crash in flames some miles beyond the Dunkirk perimeter. Medals have been conferred, and if you have an address for her family I'll make sure they know of her loss and receive her medals as soon as the war is over." Harriet nodded and forced a smile. She knew the answer before she'd even asked, but she needed to know, for it for to be final. "It's a shame, Miss Cornwall.
We could have done with her. I could do with a whole squadron of female pilots if they're half as good as you both."

"I can't get you a squadron, but I can probably find you a Flight," Harriet replied confidently.

"Excuse me?"

"My ATA Flight, Sir. All female from all over the world. All with many hours in Spitfires and some of them are better pilots than I could ever hope to be. We lost one girl a couple of weeks ago, Erin, she was shot down after out flying three 109s for over five minutes while on a ferry mission. If she'd had guns on her Spitfire she'd still be alive, and the Luftwaffe would have three fewer fighters."

183

"I'll keep that in mind, Miss Cornwall. Thank you." He smiled and nodded, and Harriet and Cas left and walked through the headquarters.

"Happy?" Cas asked as they walked

"What?" she replied.

"What?" he echoed.

"Stop it. What do you mean?"

"I mean, are you happy now that you're a fighter pilot?"

"I've been a fighter pilot for a long time."

"Not officially... Besides, you haven't passed your medical yet, or your flight test. Fail those, and you may be posted somewhere as a squadron Adjutant."

"I'm not old enough..." She looked out of the corner of her eye at him and smiled. He rolled his eyes and shook his head in mock disappointment.

"You realise I'm your superior officer, don't you?"

"Senior," she replied while stifling a giggle.

"I didn't miss you," he said as he opened the door and they stepped outside into the daylight.

"That's mutual," she replied.

Chapter 8

Tried and Tested

The medical was carried out in a consultation room at the WAAF hospital, a place where they were used to dealing with female service personnel, which meant that for once Harriet didn't have to endure any raised eyebrows about her gender. Harriet had gone through a medical when she was accepted to the ATA, and despite her lungs still burning a little when she was breathing hard, such as when she went for a run, there were no concerns about her physical health. Her confidence was well placed as she passed with flying colours, even if she did have to stifle a coarse cough induced by having to blow the ball up the pressure tube that reported her lung capacity and function. Fortunately, that was the last of the tests, and while she watched nervously as the doctor signed her medical paperwork, she smiled politely and held in the cough. When she made it to the ladies room, as far away from the consultation room as she could get, she proceeded to cough so hard she thought her lungs were trying to escape. She soon calmed and composed herself, and then after checking herself in the mirror she made her way to join Cas at the main reception. They collected the others from the Mess before being taken back to Northolt and dropped off at the dispersal for Harriet's flying grading. This went better, although she had a rocky start when she was met by the young duty pilot who wouldn't accept why she was there. Luckily the instructor, a Wing Commander who'd just finished his time at the Central Flying School and come fresh from a meeting with the AOC, stepped in to help Cas settle the apparent confusion. The Wing Commander was similar in age to Cas, and the two of them obviously knew each other and spent some time reminiscing before Cas introduced him to Harriet. He was pleasant and professional, and his only concerns were whether or not she could fly, not what she had between her legs. Which is exactly what he told her before they headed out to the waiting Tiger Moth, which Harriet threw around the sky with a confidence she hadn't previously felt. She did everything asked of her and more, and on landing, with a huge smile on her face, the instructor simply climbed out without a word and walked over to Cas, who'd been joined by Lexi and Abby in watching the display, and told him without hesitation that Harriet was exemplary. Her logbook was signed, and after Cas and the Wing Commander made plans to meet up in London, he threw a sly smile in Lexi's direction, and was gone.

An excited party of four were taken to the train station by the duty driver, and they were in the centre of London in time for a late lunch at the Ritz; an extravagant celebration at Cas' insistence, and expense, to mark Harriet's acceptance into the RAF as a fighter pilot. Cas seemed to know everyone, and the Maitre d' at the Ritz welcomed him like an old friend, as did the doorman, both asking how he was doing and both engaging happily when Cas asked after their families. This continued in the restaurant, and other officers of all services waved and smiled, and some even came over to say hello during the meal. All were polite and very proper, and more than a few seemed just a little jealous of Cas being surrounded by three very glamorous young ladies in their very smart ATA uniforms. He casually made sure they all knew he was enjoying it, too. It was a celebration that made Harriet's heart glow. She was with friends, she was a fighter pilot, and she was eating in the most exclusive restaurant she'd ever set foot in, which despite there being a war on still made the most exquisite food. When they finally left, Cas took them to Saville Row, London's most exclusive tailoring district. Then led them into a tailor's on the corner, where once again he was welcomed like an old friend into the luxurious surroundings by Mister Thomas, the very kind gentleman who'd measured Harriet for her uniform the day she'd arrived at the ATA. The group were shown upstairs, and Harriet was guided into a large and almost regal changing room with mirrors on every wall, and facing her, hanging under a spotlight, was the most beautiful uniform she could have imagined. A ladies cut tunic in RAF blue with rank braid around the cuffs, medal ribbons, and pilot's wings. A small brass VR was pinned to each lapel, and on the top of each sleeve was a simple, elegantly embroidered name tape showing the word 'Norway'. Harriet slowly stepped out of her ATA uniform, which she hung on the spare cedar wood hanger, then dressed equally as slowly. The skirt, as with the tunic, was lined with turquoise silk and felt smooth against her legs, which were now wrapped in the soft silk stockings that had been presented in a box beneath the uniform. Their softness was only equalled by the pale blue blouse which kissed her skin as she fastened it. On went the black soft leather shoes, again with turquoise silk interior, then the black tie, and finally the tunic. Harriet looked at herself in the mirror and felt her eyes fill with tears. The fit was perfect. She couldn't believe what she was seeing or feeling. She was so proud. She wanted her Aunt Mary to see her, she wanted her parents to see her, and Nurse Emily. She wanted Nicole to see her. For a moment she looked upwards and thanked Nicole for saving her life, for making her life, and promised she'd do her best to make her sacrifice worthwhile. A gentle knock at the door brought Harriet back into the room from her prayers. She checked herself and dried her eyes.

"Yes?" she asked, and the door opened a crack.

"Are you OK? You've been gone for ages," Abby asked.

"Yes. Yes, I'm fine. Come in. It's OK."

"Oh, Harriet..." Abby gasped as they faced each other. "You look incredible."

"Thank you," Harriet replied with a blush. "It's the perfect fit."

"Cas said he called ahead while you had your medical. Mister Thomas already had your measurements from your ATA uniform, and put everyone to work preparing for you at Cas' insistence."

"They've done a good job," Harriet said, trying her hardest to be casual. "An amazing job, in fact."

"So have you..."

"Don't be silly. I only had to put it on."

"You know what I mean," Abby smiled. "You did it. You made it as a fighter pilot. The first female fighter pilot and I can say I know her."

"I hope you more than just know me. I didn't do this. I'm here because of my friends, people like you. We both know I was a mess when I first arrived, and that it was you that got me through the nightmares." It was now Abby's turn to blush.

"Turn around, let me see you," Abby said, breaking the silence and changing the subject. Harriet did as she was asked, and Abby whistled playfully.

"Stop it!" Harriet blushed.

"Go show the others," Abby insisted. "I'll bring your things." Harriet nodded, picked up the service cap from the stool, and headed out to meet the others. Their conversation immediately hushed as Cas, Lexi, Thomas, and his staff all turned and looked at the now furiously blushing Harriet. Cas smiled and nodded his approval, and Harriet walked over to join them. She thanked the tailors profusely, before turning to Cas.

"Thank you so much for organising this. I don't know what to say."

"You heard the AOC's orders," he replied casually. "You need to do it better than everyone else. That starts with looking the part."

"I'll pay you back," she insisted. "And you, for the ATA uniform," she said to Lexi.

"No way, honey. I'd be insulted if you did!" Lexi replied playfully.

"Don't be ridiculous," Cas added. "You'll do no such thing. Now, there's just one more thing."

"What?"

"This…" He pulled his watch from his pocket and put it on her wrist.

"But we agreed…" she half stammered.

"You're a fighter pilot now, Harry, a proper one in a proper fighter squadron. You need it, and you'll accept it graciously as my gift to welcome you home." She blushed more, not thinking it was possible, and simply nodded in agreement. "Good!" Cas said confidently. "Now, if you're ready, we need to get these ladies back to their station and you to your squadron. You've got a lot of learning to do." Mister Thomas wrapped Harriet's old uniform and bagged it with the spare shoes, trousers, blouses, and everything else Cas had ordered. Harriet and Cas thanked Mister Thomas again before joining the others in heading to the train station and back to Northolt, and their waiting Anson. Lexi had them home in no time, resuming her high intensity flirting with Cas as he had her fly low to the ground to avoid the interest of the Luftwaffe; whose continued presence was advertised by the hundreds of vapour and smoke trails crisscrossing the late afternoon sky south of London. Penny was waiting to meet them and congratulated Harriet excitedly as she entered the dispersal hut dressed in her new RAF uniform. Harriet thanked her for everything, then said her goodbyes before changing into her trousers for the Tiger Moth flight back to the squadron. Lexi gave Cas a lingering goodbye kiss on the cheek which had Harriet rolling her eyes again, then did the same to Harriet which made her tense and frown at the unexpected physical contact, amusing Lexi even more. Harriet hugged Abby goodbye and promised to return for her kit and to stay in touch, then she packed herself into the Tiger Moth's cockpit with the four bags from the tailors, strapped herself in, held tight, and let Cas fly them along the cliff tops.

As they flew back to her new home, Harriet found herself daydreaming as she watched the last of the day's sunlight dancing on the sea. She couldn't imagine what was ahead of her, no matter how hard she tried. So she filled the unknown with her memories of the squadron in France; and was only briefly disturbed from her distant thoughts as she recognised the hospital she'd stayed in and waved excitedly at the nurses standing outside. She couldn't see them clearly but hoped one was Emily. She'd already written a letter in her head telling of her recent adventures, and she couldn't wait to share her news; but having seen the hospital and how relatively close it was to the aerodrome, the idea popped into her

189

head that she would try and fly there and see Emily in person sooner or later. Finally, they joined the circuit, mercifully left alone by the gunners this time, and put down safely and softly before coming to a halt at the squadron dispersal hut. Their Spitfires were crawling with ground crew, but the pilots were nowhere to be seen. The duty airman informed Cas that the squadron had been stood down, after one more scramble to intercept a German raid in the early afternoon. They weren't due back until the following morning, so Cas loaded the bags in the back of his fire engine red Aston Martin sports car, then raced them both to the Mess and introduced Harriet to the Mess Manager. He then left her to be shown to her room in the WAAF extension, with instructions to meet him in the Mess bar that evening.

Harriet sat for a while in the quiet of her first floor room. It had been a day of days, to say the least. Six months ago she was just a girl with dreams of being a pilot, living with a reality of those dreams being crushed by years of service in a job she didn't want to do, and the inevitable servitude in a marriage she didn't want to be in; but how that had changed, how the world had changed. She'd been to war, she'd flown, she'd had adventure and excitement enough for a hundred lifetimes, and she wanted more. Fate had made her a pilot, and whatever the future held now, there was no going back. The RAF could disown her, her parents could disown her, and none of it mattered. What she'd done was now a matter of public record, and what she did was a matter of personal choice. People like Lexi and Abby had shown her what could be done, and if the old world didn't want her, the new world would. Thoughts of the future excited and scared her equally. She knew she wanted it. She just couldn't see it, and she had no frame of reference or passion for anything out of the present. When she did think on it further, it was quite worrying being part of an organisation she didn't understand, with nobody by her side. She'd always had Nicole until she came to England, and even then, she had Emily, and then Abby and Lexi, but now she was alone in what she'd been told in no uncertain terms was a man's world. She shook off the worry and ran a bath, which she enjoyed thoroughly before preparing herself for the evening. Penny had packed an overnight bag for her and had it waiting at the dispersal hut with a promise of having one of the girls deliver everything else in the Anson the following day, or by road, if flying was still off the menu, so she had everything she needed. After drying her hair, brushing it, and making it look as glamorous as she could, she dressed in her stockings, skirt, and blouse, and finally her tunic. Desperate not to let Cas down, she constantly checked the mirror, determined she would look the part. The AOC had placed responsibility for her squarely on his shoulders, and while she'd be furious if she let herself down, she'd be outraged if she let him down, especially after all he'd done for her. A knock at the door put an end to her mirror gazing, and a few seconds later a young WAAF Corporal stepped into the room, dressed smartly in her best uniform.

"Good evening, Ma'am," Daisy said formally and politely.

"Daisy? Is that you?" Harriet said excitedly, as she recognised the young Corporal from her time in France.

"Yes, Ma'am," Daisy replied with a smile.

"Stop calling me that and come in!" Harriet said as she pulled Daisy into the room. "What are you doing here? How are you? How's your injury?" She looked at the scar on Daisy's cheek that she'd received when the headquarters house collapsed around her in France.

"Steady on," Daisy laughed. "I'm good, Ma'am, and looking at that uniform you're wearing, I'm thinking you're not doing too badly yourself!"

"Stop calling me Ma'am. It's Harry, remember?"

"Sorry, Harry. It's just that we're not in France anymore, and things are a bit different on a proper RAF station. People are expected to know their place, so to speak, you don't last long around here otherwise. Officers included."

"Well, this is my room, so it's my rules; and if I understand this whole officer thing, you have to do as I say. So it's Harry, right?"

191

"Right..." Daisy laughed. "Look at you, in uniform all of five minutes, and already you're throwing orders around, I can see you're gonna be hard work," Harriet smirked in reply and instinctively hugged Daisy, something neither of them was expecting.

"It's good to see you," Harriet said quietly.

"And you," Daisy replied, as they broke the hug and faced each other. "We were worried, we thought we'd lost you at Dunkirk."

"I thought the same!" Harriet smiled as she looked around her room. "I'm sorry, I'd offer you a drink, but I don't appear to have anything."

"That's something I think I can help with."

"Oh?" Harriet asked as she looked at the small bag in Daisy's hand, which was being held out in front of her. "For me?"

"For you. Cas asked me to bring it up to you as I was coming here anyway."

"Why were you coming here? Do you live in the same accommodation block?" Harriet asked as she took the bag labelled 'Harrods.'

"Of course not, I'm not an officer! Us workers don't get to live in places like this, you know. I'm your batman."

"My what?"

"Your batman. Well, batwoman I suppose, technically anyway."

"I don't really think I need one..."

"You're gonna be hard work, Harry."

"It's hard work trying to figure out what you're talking about."

"Officers are traditionally entitled to an assistant, somebody to help keep them, a bit like a servant, I suppose."

"Yes, I know, but don't be ridiculous. I can look after myself perfectly well, and I certainly don't need a servant! What century is the RAF living in?"

"Well, that's good because I wouldn't be your servant if you paid me. I do, however, want to be your batman. Woman. Whatever."

"I really don't understand..." Harriet pleaded.

"That's why I volunteered," Daisy smiled. "You could've been assigned somebody; usually junior officers share a batman, but Cas was worried that your route into the RAF was a little unorthodox. Which would make it difficult for you to fit in with what happens and why, so to speak, so he cleared it with the Station Commander for you to have your own batman, and I volunteered for the job."

"Why on earth would you volunteer to be somebody's servant?"

"I'm not your servant..."

"Batman?"

"Better. Anyway, it made sense. I know you, and I've been around the RAF long enough to know it and how it works, and how it doesn't."

"Well, it's very kind of you, and if there's anything I can do for you in return, you just need to tell me."

"You already are doing something for me."

"How?"

"My posting from the squadron had come through, I'd been requested at Group Headquarters to work down the hole, and I can't think of anything worse."

"Down the hole?"

"In the command bunker. It would probably have led to promotion, and it's an important job, but I can't imagine spending my life in an underground bunker. Besides, I love being around aeroplanes, and by volunteering to look after you, I get to stay around a bit longer. I may not be next to the aeroplanes, but I'll be with the first female fighter pilot, so it's close enough," she laughed. Harriet smiled, then opened the bag Daisy had given her. It contained two small boxes. "Come on. I'm dying to see," Daisy said excitedly. Harriet put the bag on her bed and took out the first box. She lifted the lid to reveal a small, narrow silver flask. She took it out and threw the box on the bed so she could look at it closely. The front was engraved with the RAF crest, and on the rear a simple inscription, 'Your friends will never forget you, no matter what.' She smiled and felt herself glowing. She'd been so worried about being forgotten, but that seemed so long ago. "He had me fill it with brandy before bringing it up," Daisy whispered. Harriet opened it and took a swig before handing it to Daisy with a smile, as the brandy made her eyes water, at least that would be her explanation if asked. "It's supposed to be for you!" Daisy protested.

"Isn't there something in the RAF about following orders?" Harriet smirked. Daisy rolled her eyes and took the flask, while Harriet pulled the second box from the bag.

"I've no idea what that one is," Daisy said after taking a swig of brandy and screwing the cap tight. Harriet smiled and continued to open the box. Inside was a bottle of perfume, Chanel. She felt a smile stretch across her face. "Very nice! What does the card say?"

"Welcome home..." Harriet replied. She gave herself a spray, then without warning, she sprayed Daisy, who let out a small shriek of surprise and stepped back.

194

"Bloody hell, that smells gorgeous!"

"I know, it's my favourite."

"You'll look and smell the part tonight. Speaking of which, we'd better get you to the Mess. You're expected." Daisy tapped her watch. Harriet nodded, gave herself another spray, then put the perfume on her bedside table and slipped the thin flask into the inside pocket of her tunic.

"How do I look?" she asked.

"Perfect," Daisy said with a smile. "Absolutely perfect. Come on." She opened the door and led Harriet out of the accommodation, and to the Mess bar where she straightened Harriet's tunic as they stood by the closed door.

"Aren't you coming in?" Harriet asked nervously.

"I'm not an officer. It's not my place."

"I'm not sure I like that rule."

"What makes you think I want to drink with a load of officers anyway?" Daisy gave Harriet a wink. "First lesson." She took Harriet's hand and lifted it so she could point at the blue rank braid stitched onto her cuff. "This light blue line sandwiched between two thick blue lines means you're a Flying Officer, it's a rank similar to a First Lieutenant in the army. A light blue stripe sandwiched between thin dark blue lines is a Pilot Officer, the most junior rank. You're higher than them, just, and they get to do as you tell them. Or at least that's the theory. Anyone with more light blue stripes than you is senior, and you need to call them Sir until they tell you to do otherwise. It's much more complex than I made it sound, but for now, that'll do you. Any questions?"

"Are the WAAF Officer ranks the same? Is there a Ma'am I need to know about?"

"They're not the same, but there's nothing to worry about, the highest we've got here is a Section Officer which is the same rank as you, one stripe. Got it?"

"I think so."

"Oh, and remember that anyone with badges on their arm, like me, whether it's stripes, propellers, crowns, or otherwise, is a lower rank. They call you Ma'am; you call them by their surnames. It's not impolite. It's discipline."

"If you say so. OK, here goes. Wish me luck!"

"You're the first female fighter pilot in the RAF, and that makes you a film star among pilots. I don't think you're going to need any luck."

"Thanks..."

"Oh, there is one thing..."

"Yes?"

"I'll put it bluntly."

"Please do. Anything more than that will be too much for my poor confused brain."

"Fighter pilots are known to be, well, hot blooded."

"Hot blooded?"

"Boisterous."

"I'm not sure what you're getting at?" Harriet asked in genuine confusion.

"I'm not doing very well at being blunt, am I?"

"It doesn't feel like you are."

"OK..." Daisy took a breath and rolled her eyes. "I'd bet my next pay packet that more than one of them will try to sleep with you."

"Sleep with me?" Harriet frowned, then she blushed as the penny dropped, and her eyes opened wide. "You mean...?"

"Yes."

"Oh..."

"Yes... Anyway, it's the summer of love. The general consensus seems to be that we'll be invaded before the autumn, and most of us will be dead and long gone before then, so what does it matter? We may as well enjoy ourselves and make the most of the time we've got, right?"

"Daisy!"

"I said it's consensus, not common practice. What I'm trying to say, and failing miserably at, is do what you like and enjoy yourself, but look after yourself!"

"I..." Harriet protested. Daisy gave her a wink and a smile, then opened the door to the bar and gave it a shove. It swung open with a crash, just as she stepped to one side to leave Harriet standing in the doorway, facing the raucous bar.

"Good luck, I'll see you later," Daisy whispered with a smile before nudging Harriet forward and pulling the door closed, leaving Harriet in the lion's den.

"Gentlemen!" a voice called out, followed by a loud cough from the back of the wall of smart blue suits. "And ladies... Three cheers for Flying Officer Cornwall, DFC and Bar!" The Mess erupted with cheers, and finally, as Harriet's cheeks burned with embarrassment, Cas stepped forward from the crowd to rescue her.

"You got my gift," he said with a smile as he twitched his nostrils.

"Yes, thank you. You shouldn't have…"

"I'm sure I don't care," he replied mischievously.

"Congratulations, Miss Cornwall," Singh said with a firm handshake as he joined them, along with Max and Archie who offered their hands and congratulations. "Cas called ahead and told us to expect you, so tonight's in your honour. Though try not to drink too much, we're on standby at first light, and you'll be flying as my number two. We'll have a proper party when we're stood down." Max pushed a pint of beer into her hands, and there was an instant call for her to 'down in one'. She looked to Cas for help and received a shrug and a nod in reply, and a muttering about 'tradition'. A chair was placed in the centre of the Mess, and Singh took her hand and guided her up on to it, then with the crudest song about 'why was she born so beautiful' to support her efforts, she tipped her head back, put the glass to her lips, then poured the bitter ale into her mouth. One thing Harriet knew she could do was drink. When growing up she'd drink milk by the pint and, after a few accidents resulted in her being drenched, she'd learned how to satisfy her thirst by pouring it straight down her throat and into her stomach. She confidently drained the beer and held the empty glass aloft, much to the enthusiastic cheering and singing of her colleagues. Having passed that particular test, she was helped down from her chair, and the party continued in full swing. A succession of officers were introduced, Matthews, the squadron intelligence officer, or 'The Spy' as Cas called him, Yeoman the engineering officer, known as Spanners, Timmons, the supply officer, and even the Reverend Alan, the Padre, made himself known. Some she knew, like Simon, the doctor, who waved from across the room, as did some of the pilots she recognised, though there were more new faces than old. Finally, she was dragged away by Max and Archie to be introduced to the pilots. Murph, Dolph, and Grumpy MacDonald were all there, drinking hard, and very happy to see her, as was Kiwi. The drinks flowed, and war stories were told, mostly humorous with much laughter. After a while, Harriet excused herself and went to the toilet, using the time to check herself in the mirror and make sure she was still at her best.

"That's a nice uniform," a familiar voice said from behind. She looked over her shoulder in the mirror, straight at AP, who was dressed in her best uniform.

"Yours too," Harriet replied, then turned and looked her friend in the eyes.

"I wondered where you were. I've been looking for you."

"I had some work to finish off on one of the aeroplanes before knocking off.
You didn't think I'd miss your welcome drinks, did you?"

"Is that what's going on in there?"

"Any excuse for a drink, I suppose."

"Not you, though?"

"I've only just arrived."

"They made me stand on a chair and down a pint."

"And you did it?"

"Easily."

"Good. We'd better get in there before they come looking for you." They headed back to the increasingly rowdy bar, where drinks were pushed into their hands before the door had closed behind them.

"Hello again," Jonny Isaac, the giant pilot who'd knocked himself out said as he stepped in front of them, and stared straight at Harriet with a big smile on his face and a twinkle in his eye. "I thought maybe I'd buy you that drink at last."

"Go away," AP said firmly.

"Oh come on, AP, don't be like that. I'm only being polite," he protested.

"When you've learned how to fly properly, you can buy her a drink, but for now you're not fit to polish her shoes."

"Harsh," he mumbled with a frown.

"Really? How was that sortie you flew this morning when the airfield was bombed?"

"I..." Isaac blushed.

"Unless you're going to say, 'I was asleep because I'm a great clumsy oaf who can't even climb into a Spitfire without knocking myself unconscious', I'm not interested. Now be a good boy and bugger off!" Isaac smiled sheepishly and backed away out of AP's sights.

"Daisy warned me about pilots..." Harriet whispered as they walked across the Mess to a space near the window.

"Oh? What did she warn you?"

"That they'd try to sleep with me."

"I doubt it."

"Why not?" Harriet asked with a frown, straightening her back and feeling a little insulted.

"Nothing against you, you're beautiful. It's them."

200

"I'm not following."

"Daisy is right. Usually, they're all over anything in a skirt, and to be fair everything in a skirt is usually more than happy to try and catch themselves a fighter pilot; they're the glory boys, the film stars of the war."

"Usually?"

"Yes, usually. They're confident, talented, even arrogant sometimes; but they can also be a little fragile as a breed."

"I'm still none the wiser, AP."

"I honestly don't think their egos would let them dare try it on with a pilot of your calibre. Those pretty ribbons on your chest are quite intimidating."

"Oh..." Harriet smiled and almost laughed to herself. "But what about him?" She pointed over to Jonny Isaac, as he stood among his peers cheering and drinking.

"He's all mouth and no trousers. He's genuinely lovely, and I'll kill you if you ever tell him I said that, but in all honesty, I don't think he'd know what to do with a girl if he got one. I like to think of him as a big puppy. Excitable, silly, and easily frightened into line with a firm bark. He came to us when we were refitting up north after Dunkirk. He's not a bad pilot, considering he has to squeeze his giant frame into a Spitfire, he's just clumsy. As you've seen."

"Yes…" Harriet laughed. "What about you? Is that pretty little ribbon on your chest intimidating?"

"No..." AP smiled. "I intimidate them all by myself." They both laughed as more beers were delivered.

201

"What's it for?" Harriet asked. "The ribbon, I mean?"

"It's the Air Force Cross. It was recommended for my stupidity."

"Stupidity?"

"Yes, for volunteering to stay behind when the squadron retreated to Dunkirk. The little bronze oak leaves are a Mention in Dispatches for more stupidity, specifically 'rescuing a downed pilot in distress.' Or coming to save your arse, in other words."

"A medal is better than being kicked out of the Air Force, I suppose."

"Maybe..."

"How did you get away from France? When I was at Dunkirk, the Germans had all but closed the bag. I couldn't imagine how you could get out."

"We went south. Sergeant Oliver and his men got us out, with a lot of help from the French anti aircraft artillery boys. It was close, though. We had to fight through the advancing German flank to get to safety, and we lost a few on the way. Fortunately, they were so busy focusing on their push west to the coast that they weren't expecting anyone to try and get through their sides, it could have been worse."

"I'm happy you made it out."

"I'm happy you did, too. We got back a while after the squadron and joined them up north. It was a shock to hear about you and Nicole." Harriet forced a smile. "I'm sorry about her. I know you were close."

"We were like sisters."

"I know. It was a bad day for the squadron when we lost you both."

"Cas introduced me to the engineering officer. I thought that was your job?" Harriet said, as she quickly tried to change the subject.

"It was. I was listed as missing, so somebody else was assigned, somebody senior, and to be fair to Yeoman it is a senior position, and he's an outstanding engineer."

"So are you."

"I know. He's got more experience of the job, though. He came from another squadron where he'd been engineering officer for a while. He's pleasant enough, and when the strings were pulled to keep me on staff, he agreed to take me as his apprentice, so to speak, and teach me the ropes so I can be promoted in the future. I'm not bitter about it. He's a good boss. Anyway, it was either that or be posted to the WAAF depot to train new girls, and you know what my people skills are like."

"I like your people skills."

"You'd be the only one. Ice Queen is the current favourite behind my back."

"Maybe they just need to get to know you."

"That makes it sound like I want to get to know them."

"You let me get to know you."

"You're different."

"I am? Why?"

"You're more irritating than most. I thought it better to get to know you so
I could try and find a redeeming quality..."

"You really know how to make a girl wish she were back in the hospital covered in bandages." Harriet rolled her eyes, and AP smirked in response.

"Bandages, are you OK?"

"I was until I started talking to you!" Harriet frowned. AP let out a rare giggle, which set them both laughing as the piano burst into life with the musicality of a tone deaf gazelle, and the pilots started a rowdy rendition of their squadron song. "My God, that's terrible," Harriet laughed.

"Hang around much longer, and the words will get much worse."

"I meant the piano playing!"

"That's Archie. He swears he was classically trained, though we're not sure in what."

"Even I can play better than that, and I haven't played in years!"

"Is that so?" Max asked as he appeared from behind them.

"What?" Harriet asked nervously, her eyes opening wide as her stomach knotted with a very uncomfortable feeling. "Max, no!" she protested as she saw the mischief in his eyes.

"Hey, Archie, knock that noise off for a moment, would you?" he yelled across the Mess, and the room fell silent as Max dragged Harriet through the crowd towards the piano.

"If you're referring to my highly skilled and classically trained playing of the piano, I shall be mortally wounded," Archie rebuked.

"Not as wounded as we are by your hammering those poor ivories. Now get out of the way and let a professional show you how it's done."

"Max! Max, no!" Harriet protested quietly, whispering as firmly as she could as he pushed her forward into the circle of staring eyes.

"A pianist as well as a decorated fighter ace, is there no end to your skills?" Archie smirked, then rose from the piano stool and waved her forward.

"I'm really not a pianist at all," Harriet continued to protest. "Max is just being silly, so please carry on, and I'll go back to my drink." She tried to turn as her cheeks burned with embarrassment.

"Not a chance, I'm rather intrigued..." He ushered her onto the stool and stepped back to join the silent circle of officers who'd gathered around the piano. Harriet shook nervously. She fought to breathe while wishing she was flying in combat against fifty 109s instead of sitting in front of a piano with a boisterous crowd of drunken officers watching her and expecting something good. Slowly they started chanting, quietly and slowly at first, 'Harry, Harry, Harry.' Cas stepped forward and stood by her side. She looked up at him pleading for help with her eyes, and he handed her a small glass of brandy, which she took and downed in one before handing him the empty glass. He gave her a wink of support, and she nodded, then looked down at the keys as he waved his hand to quieten the chant. Harriet laid her fingers on the keys. Then with the brandy burning her throat and spinning her head, she played the piece she'd learned when she was young and had played over and over, practising until she'd perfected it and become the best in her year at school. The delicate melody of Beethoven's Für Elise echoed around the Mess, and the officers stood and watched, captivated by the notes as they danced flawlessly on the air. When she'd finally finished, she looked up to Cas, who'd remained by her side throughout, and he nodded with warm smile.

"Oh God, was it that bad?" she gasped.

"It was probably the most beautiful thing I've ever heard..." he replied as his smile warmed his face.

"Now that, ladies and gentlemen, is classically trained," Archie said, before starting an applause and cheer which raised the roof of the Mess and made Harriet blush fiercely, while smiling in a way she didn't think was possible. "Got anything else in the bag, Harry?" She nodded and ran her finger across the keys, getting another cheer, before playing the very familiar tune which the squadron song had been worded around; and playing it much lighter, and much faster than she'd heard Archie play it only a few minutes before, and the Mess erupted into song. Finally, after another hour of increasingly boisterous singing and drinking, Singh put his foot down and sent everyone to bed, a disappointing decision which was reluctantly accepted by everyone. They dispersed to their rooms, Harriet and AP holding each other up as they attempted to remain ladylike and professional while stifling giggles and trying not to attract attention. They said their goodbyes and Harriet fell into her room. Her bed was made and pulled back, and a pair of blue and white striped pyjamas were laid out waiting for her. She undressed and fell into bed, falling instantly asleep as soon as her head hit the pillow.

Chapter 9

Welcome Home

Daisy had woken Harriet long before first light, much to her disgust. The cup of tea she'd brought with her hadn't made the rude awakening, or the hangover any better. At Daisy's insistence, Harriet immersed herself in a cold bath. First standing in it, then sitting down quickly and sliding under the freezing surface. It wasn't perfect, or pleasant, but the shock was enough to scare the hangover from her and send her dashing into her room while shivering violently. Daisy had laid out her uniform for the day, including the flying jacket, boots, and helmet that had been collected from the stores. Harriet quickly dried herself, and Daisy helped her dress as her frozen fingers shook and fumbled. She was soon pulling on her long, rich cream woollen socks and flying boots, and slowly starting to thaw. A cold glass of milk from Daisy helped settle her stomach, and then she was handed her blue and white diamond pattern silk scarf, freshly laundered and pressed. She tucked it into her pocket then gave herself one last check over before following Daisy down to the truck. A hand reached out of the darkness, and Jonny pulled her aboard to take her seat. The tailgate was closed, and they bounced their way to the dispersal hut in silence, where they dragged their hungover bodies inside for their pre dawn briefing from Singh, who'd been there long before them for his own briefing from Spanners and the Chief. Cas was busy checking the map wall, studying it meticulously and looking as fresh as a daisy in comparison to most of the pilots.

"Everyone here?" Singh asked. A group mumble assured him they were. "Good. We're not long from first light, and we're on standby. Mister Maxwell, you'll lead A Flight, Mister Russel, B, six in each as usual. Miss Cornwall, you'll fly as my number two today. It's going to be a busy one if it's anything like yesterday, so rest when you can, and make sure you get enough to drink. The meteorologists are suggesting it's going to be hot up there by late morning, and I don't want anyone dehydrating, You'll lose seconds off your reaction times, and that's the difference between life and death! As for operations, I expect we'll be vectored to intercept any incoming raids over the coast, the same as yesterday, and try and put them off going any further inland. We get less notice here than anywhere else, so we'll likely have to climb fast and attack from below. I'll lead the squadron in, and direct the flights as appropriate until we engage. Remember, don't fly straight and level for more than five seconds once the guns start firing, and as soon as your ammunition is spent, you're to drop to the deck and get home. Should the raid get through, we're likely to be sent back up to hit them again on the way home, so we need to be ready. Dress jackets and ties are optional, Mae Wests are mandatory, we'll be over the Channel at some point, and you may end up needing them. Any questions?" The room was silent as the pilots looked at each other. "OK, get outside and check your aeroplanes over, breakfast will be up at six. Carry on." The pilots broke away, leaving Harriet standing alone with Singh, Cas, and the duty airman in the dispersal hut. "Miss Cornwall, you haven't flown number two before, not in a squadron formation anyway." Singh continued. "It's not that much different to what you did with Miss Delacourt in France, so there's nothing to worry about. I'll lead, and you stay on my left wing. Once the fighting starts, you're to stick to me like glue, and keep any Germans off me so I can control the battle, understood?"

"Understood"

"Any questions?"

"Yes, what am I supposed to fly in?"

"I was hoping you'd ask that," he smiled. The door opened, and AP entered right on cue, looking as fresh as Cas. "Good timing, AP. Take Miss Cornwall and get her acquainted with her new steed if you would?"

"Come on," AP said without a smile. Harriet grabbed her kit and followed her out into the fresh morning air.

"How do you look so fresh?" Harriet mumbled as they headed to the line of Spitfires.

"How do you not?" AP replied. "That was a mild night. You should see it when we're not on first light standby."

"Oh God, it gets worse?"

"Much... I didn't tell you this, but while you're doing your checks, sit in your Spitfire and take some oxygen for a few minutes, it'll help."

"Thank you..."

"Don't use much, though. You'll need it when you're flying."

"I won't."

"We thought this would suit you," AP smiled as she showed Harriet her Spitfire. "We have a squadron code now, but it still kind of fits. On the side of the Spitfire were the large dirty cream letters HU, and an H the other side of the roundel. "HU is the squadron code, H is the aeroplane, H for Harry."

"I like it."

"You should, it's a brand new mark two, straight from the factory. It runs like a dream, so you'd better not break it!"

"I won't, I promise."

"I mean it! They're not as easy to patch up as a Hurricane." They walked around and checked the Spitfire over outside, then Harriet climbed in. Already Merlin engines were coughing into life and fire was flickering from their exhausts, illuminating the morning darkness like fireflies dancing in a neat line. Harriet looked around the cockpit and got comfortable, moving her parachute harness into place so she could leave the parachute in the seat and fasten it around her once she was airborne. The dials glowed in the darkness, and for a moment, despite the roaring engines running up to speed all around her, she felt quite alone. AP plugged in the radio and oxygen and, after a quick shout of 'clear prop',

Harriet pulled the mask over her face and breathed deep, while flicking the magnetos and master switch, and hitting the ignition. The mighty Merlin coughed, and then roared, blasting smoke past the cockpit and setting the exhaust stubs fluttering with fire in the darkness. She ran through her checks, then ran through them again, all the while breathing deep and sucking the oxygen into her lungs. One by one the engines cut until only Harriet's was running. AP gave her a tap on the shoulder, and she shut down. After extracting herself from her cockpit and leaving her helmet and mask hanging off the rearview mirror, she made her way across the grass to the dispersal hut. Pilots were already sitting in deck chairs, with the sheepskin collars of their Irvin jackets pulled up around their faces to keep them warm in the chilly morning air. Not much was being said, just the occasional murmured conversation.

"Looking for a seat?" Max asked in the darkness. Harriet looked around and saw the empty wicker chair next to the big American. She nodded and joined him.

"What do we do now?" she asked as she made herself comfortable.

"Welcome to our new favourite game," Archie said from the next seat. "We like to call it, hurry up and wait."

"Wait for what?"

"For that phone to ring," Max replied. "We're one of the closest stations to France, so we're the first in line if a raid is coming anywhere between the south coast and the Thames Estuary. When we're scrambled you run like hell to your ride, take off, and climb fast. The ground crew will have it started for you; all you've got to do is get her up."

"If the Hun are going to be civilised," Archie continued. "They'll let us have breakfast first." At that, the phone rang in the dispersal hut, and every head turned to look. The air was full of anticipation.

"Miss Cornwall," Singh said as he stepped out of the dispersal with his flying kit.

210

"Sir," Harriet replied as she stood.

"Let's go. We've been asked to have a look for an intruder heard buzzing around in the Channel."

"Go get 'em, Harry," Max shouted as she joined Singh in marching through the darkness.

"Leave some for the rest of us, Harry," Archie called after her.

"Remember you're my number two," Singh said quietly as they headed to their Spitfires. He waved and put one finger in the air, and his Spitfire was started for him. Seconds later, Harriet's was started too, as AP saw her approaching. "Stick to me like glue and do exactly as I say. If we get split up, drop low and head home fast. The Kent coast is no place to be hanging around by yourself at the moment."

She nodded, then climbed up the wing and into the cockpit. AP was waiting to strap her in while she went through her checks.

"Remember what I said," AP warned quietly as Harriet put on her helmet.
"Don't break my aeroplane!"

"Aren't you a little senior to be here?" Harriet asked. "Don't you have paperwork to do at a desk somewhere?"

"Get going, or he'll leave without you," AP said with a smirk. "You may as well get some more oxygen while you have the chance, you look awful."

"I don't think I like you anymore," Harriet said with a smile. AP closed the cockpit hatch and jumped from the wing. A quick look around and Harriet was taxiing forward and chasing Singh, swinging the Spitfire left to right so she could see over the nose which stretched up in front of her like a pointed black mountain climbing into the darkness. Seconds later

211

and she was smirking to herself as the engine roared and the Spitfire bounced along the grass at speed. A hard push on the rudder bar stopped the nose swinging with the torque of the propeller, and kept it pointing straight forward. A bounce and a gentle pull back on the stick and there it was, she was airborne. Throttle forward a little, switch hands on the stick and undercarriage up, then hands back in place and she eased forward to come into line with Singh, who gave her a nod as she took her position. He gave coordinates, and they climbed hard at full throttle. The sky to the east was glinting as the first light drove away the darkness and lit up the English Channel, making it look like a river of liquid silver snaking between England and France. Dover passed beneath them, with its dark and threatening barrage balloons, and soon they were over the water and still climbing hard.

"Goose Leader to Silver Control. Any ideas where our friends are?" Singh asked.

"Control to Goose Leader. Bandit should be nearby," Control replied.

"There!" Harriet said after a few more minutes. "Heading west, behind us and following the coast." She spun her head and dipped her wing to get a better look. "Five o'clock high, angels two zero, a twin engine bomber by the looks of it, dipping in and out of the clouds."

"Good eyes, Harry, I've got him. Looks like a reconnaissance flight. OK, on my mark, let's turn and follow him." Harriet followed Singh in the steep turn to the right, keeping a watchful eye out for any other aeroplanes she'd missed. She was thankful she'd decided to take off her tie and replace it with her Bavarian silk scarf, her neck would have been raw without it. Singh led them up to the cloud base, and they sat underneath it as they chased closer and closer to the lone German aircraft. The German didn't see them, despite their Spitfires being silhouetted against the lightening eastern sky, and there was no attempt to change direction or evade the attackers in any way, even when they were close enough to see the rear gunner at his post. "OK, drop behind me," Singh instructed. Harriet instantly complied. "I'm going to have a go at him, keep your eyes open for his friends." Singh lined up and opened his throttle, dragging the bomber closer. Suddenly a long line of tracer shot out from the rear gunner and circled Singh's fuselage, but it was too late. He fired and his eight machine guns sent streams of light into the gunner's position, silencing him instantly, before drifting across the right wing and sending sparks and debris into the air from the engine, which coughed out a stream of white smoke. The bomber rolled to the right and went into a dive as Singh and Harriet overtook it, keeping their height and watching it pass underneath. Singh led them into a wide diving turn, all the time keeping his eyes locked on the bomber. Its turn steepened and tightened as it crossed over the coast. A black blob slipped out of the fuselage, followed closely by another, both quickly blooming into white parachutes which glowed like lightbulbs against the darkness below. Singh led the Spitfires in a wide circle as they watched the parachutes float down after the bomber, which finally crashed into the ground in a ball of flames. "Goose leader to Silver Control. Raider down at my position, two parachutes spotted. Unless you have any more trade for us, we're going to hang around a few minutes before heading home for breakfast."

"Well done, Goose leader. Thank you for your business. No more trade for you at the moment, enjoy breakfast."

"We may as well make the most of the opportunity to have a look at your flying skills," Singh said as the pair followed the coast, which was starting to glow in the first silver light of dawn as the sun approached the horizon in the east, and cast a soft, warm light over the French fields just behind them across the Channel. "See how lazy being a ferry pilot has made you."

"Yes, Sir," Harriet replied, feeling a little nervous at the unexpected change in plans.

"OK. I'm going to get on your tail, and you're going to try and get away from me. Understood?"

"Understood..."

"Fly straight and level and count to thirty, then start your lookout."

"Understood, Goose Leader." She frowned as she watched Singh pull up and turn out of sight. She did as she was told, but kept an eye in her mirror, and glanced around a few times to keep an eye out for his silhouette; which she caught briefly passing underneath her and turning to come at her tail from underneath. She counted, and at thirty seconds Singh was approaching rapidly. As soon as he closed to firing distance, Harriet flipped her Spitfire on its back and pulled back on the stick, pulling her Spitfire into a tight 'split s' manoeuvre, which made her stomach flip and squeezed her head with pressure. Halfway through the dive, she pulled up and rolled left into a turn so tight that her sight dimmed to a narrow cone, which made it difficult to see anything in the morning twilight. She kept the turn tight and opened the throttle, and seconds later she was on Singh's tail at close range. "How's that, Goose leader?" she asked.

"What? How did you do that?"

"I'm not sure..."

"OK, well let's see you try that a second time. Watch your tail." He pulled up and once again, Harriet watched him curve away. This time her nerves had eased, and she felt herself smiling as she counted. Singh tried a different tactic this time, and turned his curve away into a beam attack, changing direction and coming straight back at her. She waited until she was sure he was committed to his attack, then at the last moment pushed her stick hard left and pulled into a tight turn to face Singh head on. Instinctively he pulled up, she rolled and followed in a sweeping climbing curve, and latched on to his tail as he curved to come back at her. She closed to firing distance again before talking.

"On your tail, Goose Leader," she said casually.

"What? What the...?" Singh's Spitfire rocked as he looked around to see her. "OK, this time I want you to attack me," he instructed.

214

"Understood, Goose Leader," she said with a smile, before pulling away and keeping her eyes on his silhouette. She held him in sight, dropped her speed and dropped below him, using the dark ground to hide her silhouette as she opened her throttle again to catch him, stalking him as she chased to keep ahead of the expanding dawn and stay in the last shadow of night. She positioned herself in his blind spot, almost perfectly mirroring him from below and slightly behind. When she was ready, she slowed and pulled up and sat on his tail, right behind him and close enough to fill his mirror. He instantly rolled, and she followed, sticking to him like glue and matching every roll, turn, dive, and climb like she could see exactly what he was going to do before he'd even thought of it. There was no shaking her. Had she been a German, she'd have been in the perfect firing position a dozen times, and Singh would likely be in his parachute, if he were lucky.

"OK, Goose one, I think you've earned your breakfast. Follow me home."

"Roger, Goose Leader," she said with a smile so big it made her cheeks hurt. They flew together side by side, all the time keeping watch for unfriendly followers, until eventually they put down at the airfield, and taxied to the dispersal where they parked up and shut down.

"Any luck?" AP asked as she jumped up on the wing and started unfastening Harriet's harness.

"Singh got a reconnaissance bomber, I think, a big two engine thing."

"Good. How about you? Everything OK?"

"Yes, fine. I just sat on his tail and watched."

"You sat on his tail and did nothing?"

"Yes, that's what he told me to do," she said with a frown as she stood, then froze and her eyes opened wide. "That's what he meant, isn't it? I wasn't supposed to do something else?" She was instantly worried she'd missed some sort of RAF procedure, and taken instructions too literally, instead of following some unknown routine.

"I'm pretty sure you're fine. I was just a bit surprised you'd done as you're told. It's not one of your strong points."

"Hilarious." Harriet rolled her eyes, and AP laughed to herself while helping Harriet out of the cockpit.

"But true. Go and get breakfast, it's just arrived." AP smiled, and Harriet jumped to the ground then ran to catch Singh as he headed for the dispersal hut, where a wagon had brought bacon sandwiches and tea for breakfast.

"Good flying, Harry. It seems you haven't lost your touch," Singh said with a smile.

"I'm a bit rusty," she replied casually, feeling both confident and mischievous.

"Is that so?" He raised his eyebrow questioningly as he looked at her.

"I think so. I should be back to it soon enough."

"Good..."

"Get anything?" The Spy asked as he greeted them.

"An eighty eight reconnaissance kite. He was looking around the coastline not far from Dover and came down inland. I let Silver know where the crew bailed out, so the army can pick them up."

"Great news! Good show, skipper! I'll get the news up to Group and see if we can get it confirmed for you."

"Go get yourself some breakfast," Singh said to Harry. "I think you've earned it." He gave her a slap on the shoulder and a smile. Harriet made

216

her way over to the folding table that had been set up by the visiting cooks and took a bacon sandwich and a tin mug of tea before joining Max and Archie who were talking with Grumpy.

"The old man not let you play?" Max asked.

"No..." Harriet replied regretfully. "It's OK, there was only one of them, and he was in the perfect position to take a shot. Besides, it was my job to cover him in case any fighters turned up."

"No fun watching, though, is it?"

"Not really," she frowned.

"You've got to learn to play with others," Archie added. "You can't take on the entire Luftwaffe on your own. It's not polite. Some of us spent several years training for this..." Harriet smirked and took a bite of the salty half cold bacon sandwich, which after the excitement of her flight tasted wonderful. The dispersal phone rang, and the many breakfast conversations dulled as the pilots turned and looked.

"A Flight scramble!" the orderly screamed out of the window, before running out of the hut and ringing the large brass bell.

"Bloody Germans have no sense of decency!" Archie scowled as he placed his bacon sandwich carefully on his seat, before running towards his Spitfire, which the ground crew were already starting. "Don't touch my bacon! I'll be back!"

"What do I do?" Harriet asked Max. Her stomach was fluttering with nervous energy.

"Eat your breakfast," Grumpy said casually.

"Yeah, you can't go up every time," Max added. "You'll burn out if you do." They watched and ate as the Spitfires roared, and one by one rolled across the grass before heading off into the dawn. Harriet felt a twinge of

217

jealousy and a longing to be with them. Standing around and eating breakfast while they were flying off into battle didn't seem right. She finished her sandwich and tea and almost immediately felt unexpectedly tired. As Max and the others took to their deck chairs, and the wireless Cas had bought for the dispersal hut played soft and relaxing music, she sunk into her seat, pulled up her collar, then closed her eyes for a moment.

For a while, Harriet fought with the brightness shining through her eyelids, determined to ignore whichever idiot was shining torches while she was trying to rest her eyes. Finally, she broke and opened one eye a little, and was surprised to see blue skies dotted with heavy white clouds. She blinked and sat up. Max was still snoozing in the chair next to her, and the remainder of the pilots were scattered around the place as the music played. She arched and stretched as she stood, looking towards the familiar buzz of Rolls Royce Merlin engines. Six Spitfires circled the airfield, then touched down as she went to the urn for more tea. A Flight had returned, all of them. Singh, Cas, and The Spy appeared from the hut to greet the returning warriors, who one by one shut down after taking their places, before dismounting and heading back to the dispersal.

"Get anything?" The Spy asked.

"Hungry!" Archie replied. "All that fuss and noise before breakfast, and the inconsiderate buggers had the cheek not to be where they were supposed to be when we finally arrived."

"Nothing?" The Spy sighed.

"Nothing at all," Archie replied with disappointment. "They had us parade up and down around Dover for over an hour, and all I saw flying was a bored looking seagull."

"Better luck next time," Cas said. Archie raised his eyebrows and shrugged then headed for his chair and the bacon sandwich he'd left.

"You know, I think this sandwich tastes better than when I left it," he said as he looked up to the skies. "Maybe the Boche are onto something." The three went back to the hut, and Harriet went back to her deckchair.

"No luck, huh?" Max asked without opening his eyes.

"I'd take it personally if I wasn't so bloody hungry."

"Enjoy your sandwich, and maybe try to keep the noise down. Some of us are trying to sleep."

"Some of you haven't had to fly yet this morning. Not like the real workers around here, isn't that right, Harry?"

"I think I'm ready for lunch," she replied.

"See, the girl's been here five minutes, and she's already done enough to work up an appetite. Don't worry, Harry. You'll soon get used to our colonial cousins; they don't like to get their hands dirty before lunch."

"Why bother when we have people like the two of you to do the work for us?" Max replied. The three settled as the morning news was reported, waiting, and eventually sleeping off the extravagances of the previous night in the Mess. They snoozed until late morning, when once again Harriet fought with the light shining through her eyelids, then instantly jumped awake and sat up as she heard an engine nearby. The others did the same, and soon the entire squadron were searching the sky for aircraft, and totally missed the turquoise and chrome Harley Davidson sweep around the side of the dispersal hut until it came to a halt in front of them. Harriet's face lit up as she recognised Lexi, sitting on the big motorbike in her Irvin sheepskin flying jacket. She had a kitbag swung over her shoulder and hanging down her back. She smiled as she cut the engine and casually kicked the bike onto its stand. Cas and Singh had stepped out of the dispersal hut to see what the noise was about, and some of the pilots were already making their way over to the golden haired and very glamorous looking motorcycle rider.

"Hey flyboy," she greeted Cas with a playful wink. Harriet slumped back into her chair and rolled her eyes at the overt flirting.

"Miss Lexington," Cas replied. "It's a pleasure to see you again so soon."

"I'm sure the pleasure's mutual, flyboy."

"Good morning, Ma'am," Jonny Isaac said with an accompanying wiggle of his eyebrows, as he practically elbowed Cas out of the way to stand in front of Lexi.

"Oh, for God's sake!" Harriet mumbled as she pulled herself up.

"Well, good morning to you, sweetie," Lexi replied to Jonny in her most alluring manner. "And what's your name?"

"I'm Jonny... I'm a fighter pilot, Spitfires," he said proudly. All six feet, four inches of him were almost trembling with excitement.

"Is that so?"

"Yes, Ma'am."

"Tell me something, Jonny," she said in a low and seductive voice that silenced the other pilots and made him move in close. "Does your momma know you're playing pilot?" The assembled pilots burst into fits of laughter as Jonny frowned and blushed. "Now where's my pretty girl?" she asked as she looked around and locked her eyes on Harriet, who was already walking towards her. "There you are!"

"Hello... What are you doing here?" Harriet asked.

"Is that any way to treat the girl who taught you how to fly Spitfires?"

"You know what I mean!" Harriet felt the slightest tingle of a blush in her cheeks. "How come you're here?"

"I brought your things," Lexi said as she handed over the kitbag.

"Oh..." Harriet blushed more. "That's very kind of you."

"It's only your essentials. Abby is flying over this morning to bring you the rest, and to pick me up."

"Pick you up? Will your motorbike fit in the Anson?"

"It won't need to. It's staying here."

"I don't understand."

"Well, I got to thinking last night that I have five motorcycles with me here in England, and only one ass to ride them with, so I was hoping you'd maybe look after this one for me?" she smiled.

"What? For real?"

"Why not? You love riding it, and it makes sense that you'd get some use out of it, rather than it sits in a storage shed somewhere. Besides, I ain't gonna have much time to look after them all since some big mouth told the RAF about our cosy little number down on the coast."

"What on earth are you talking about?"

"Penny got a phone call yesterday. The rest of us are being sent to the RAF Central Flying School to have our skills assessed. It seems the powers that be want to know if we can do what you can do..." She smiled as she talked. "Apparently the RAF needs experienced pilots."

"Oh my God!" Harriet exclaimed. "Really?"

"Really... So I suppose giving you one of my rides is my way of thanking you for opening the door. All we've got to do now is walk through it, I guess."

"Really, I didn't do anything, and even if I did, it wouldn't deserve your Harley."

"Well, you don't get to decide that, pretty girl," Lexi said confidently, her quiet and genuine tone fading as her boisterous and confident armour returned.

"I'll pay you for it. I've got some savings."

"You pay me for a gift, and we won't be friends much longer!" Lexi said firmly, then gave Harriet a playful wink. "Seriously, it's a gift from all of us specials." Harriet felt her cheeks burning fiercely. "Anyway, I'm doing you a favour. You ride like a child, so you're going to need all the practice you can get." The dispersal phone rang, and Harriet immediately turned to look at the hut.

"Squadron scramble!" the orderly yelled as he appeared at the door and started ringing the brass bell, which sat beneath a sign on the hut wall inscribed 'Don't just Yell! Ring the Bell and Run like Hell!' Which is precisely what Harriet did. Lexi stood and watched as the pilots sprinted at full speed to the row of Spitfires already barking into life. Harriet leapt onto the wing of H for Harry after collecting her parachute from the wingtip, then threw it inside and jumped in after it as AP climbed out of the cockpit, then reached in and helped strap Harriet in while she checked her instruments over.

"She's good to go!" AP shouted. "Good luck and bring her back in one piece!" Harriet nodded and smiled, then received a wink before AP ran off the wing. Singh rolled forward, and Harriet rolled after him. One by one the Spitfires rolled in their pairs and made ready to take off, then, as one, the full squadron opened their throttles and roared across the grass together in a thunder of Merlin power which pulled them off the ground and up into the blue grey cloudy sky. Harriet's stomach was in knots as she looked around anxiously, desperate to keep her place and not crash into any of the other Spitfires which were climbing all around her. It was the first time she'd been part of a squadron scramble, and it was a new, exhilarating, and quite scary experience.

222

"Hello Goose Leader, Silver here," the controller said over the radio. "Make angels two zero, and vector Dover. We have some trade building up for you." The voice focused Harriet's mind and stopped the nervous checking of everything inside and outside of her Spitfire.

"Understood, Silver Control," Singh replied firmly. "Goose Squadron form abreast and make angels two zero." Harriet took her place on Singh's wing and watched as Max took A Flight to the left in loose pairs, and Archie took B to the right. The fourteen Spitfires were an incredible sight as they charged up through the clouds, and Harriet couldn't help but feel both proud and excited to be part of it as she forgot the nerves of taking off. They climbed hard, as steep as Singh could push them while still keeping enough speed to get them to height before they reached whatever was waiting for them at Dover. Harriet found her mind wandering. What was there? What would happen? She thought of the earlier sorties. What if there was nobody there like for Archie and his flight earlier? What if there was only one reconnaissance bomber, who would take it on? Would she get the chance to fight? Could she fight? What if it was like Dunkirk again? The questions cycled through her brain as she climbed up through a large swathe of grey cloud; which wrapped around her wings and for the briefest of moments made her feel all alone when it obstructed her view of the squadron. Finally, Singh gave the instruction to level out, and as they did, Harriet was able to see what looked like a swarm of gnats in front of her windscreen. She blinked and shook her head; how could it be gnats that far up and moving that fast anyway? She focused and her brain made sense of what she was seeing.

"Right on the nose, boss," Pops called. "88s, maybe fifty or so." The Luftwaffe twin engine bombers, Junkers 88s, were advancing west in waves towards Dover at about fifteen thousand feet.

"Fighters above them. 110s," Archie called. "There must be a hundred or more." As the Spitfires made their way towards the enemy, the sky was almost black with aeroplanes, and Harriet's heart pounded as a voice in the back of her mind started to ask over and over 'where do we even begin?' She was lost as to what to do over Dunkirk when they faced fifty or so aeroplanes, and now there were close to two hundred coming at them. "Hurricanes, ten o'clock low," Archie added. Harriet looked over and saw a squadron of twelve Hurricanes hurtling with unflinching confidence at the bombers in vees of three aeroplanes lined out abreast. It was both awe inspiring and terrifying. A wall of fighters, maybe thirty or more, dived in unison to intercept the Hurricanes, still leaving more fighters staggered above them.

"Max, keep A Flight up here and watch our backs," Singh instructed.

"You got it, skipper!" came the American's confident reply.

"OK Goose Squadron, let's look after our Hurricane friends and hit those fighters!" Singh called. "Tally ho!" He pushed into a dive which Harriet followed perfectly, and the eight Spitfires launched into the unsuspecting fighters. Harriet's heart was now pounding so hard she could hear it in her ears over the roar of her engine. "Stick to me like glue, Harry, and keep my tail clear!" Singh called before firing as they closed. Chunks flew off the closest 110 before white smoke streamed from the engine, he'd hit the coolant. The 110 steepened its dive, and almost instantly the crew bailed out and took to their parachutes. Harriet pulled up to miss the closest German, who stared into her eyes with fear as her wingtip narrowly missed slicing him in two. Singh pulled them up, then down into a wide diving curve to come around and have another go at the remaining 110s. Meanwhile, the German crews maintained steely discipline and continued their dive into the Hurricanes, while their comrades were intercepted and shot up by the Spitfires. By the time Singh had lined up on his next target, the sky was a scene of chaos. The 110s were among the Hurricanes, who were among the 88s. Aeroplanes twisted and turned as the sky filled with tracer and smoke. Harriet stuck on Singh's tail as he worked through the melee, putting a short burst into a passing 110 and knocking it off its course to intercept a Hurricane, which let the Hurricane finish off the 88 it was chasing down. Down below, an 88 had broken from the fight and was turning to run at Dover harbour. "Come on, Harry, let's go bloody his nose before he hits the harbour!" Singh shouted, and the pair of them started in a shallow dive to intercept the bomber. The sky started to fill with the familiar black

224

cotton wool balls of ack ack fire, which hung in the sky before glowing orange and expanding into a raging explosion. "Steady... Steady..." Singh said. All the time, Harriet was keeping a sharp look out for the enemy. It wasn't long before she saw a 110 break from the fight and follow them down, closing quickly on the pair, who'd had to throttle back a little so they could catch the 88 and not overtake him.

"110 coming in from behind!" Harriet shouted. Her mouth was dry, and sweat started to run down her back.

"Keep him off me, Harry!" Singh replied.

"How long?" she asked.

"Another ten seconds... Just a bit closer!"

"OK. Stay straight, and on my mark dive right!" Harriet instructed as she throttled back and dropped back behind Singh, before swinging right and putting herself between him and the chasing 110. A line of tracer followed her as she passed high over his tail, then quickly slipped left again, keeping the 110 focused on trying to chase her around the sky instead of Singh. She watched in the mirror and watched the tracer, then watched as Singh put his bullets into the 88 and sent it straight down into a steep dive.

"Done!" Singh yelled.

"OK..." Harriet replied. "Three, two, one, now!" Singh pulled right and into a dive as Harriet had instructed, while at the same time she throttled all the way back to idle, dropped her flaps, and pulled hard on the control stick, burying it in her stomach as she pulled the Spitfire up hard, and almost stood it on its tail. The full aeroplane shuddered as the speed scrubbed off so quick the wings were almost flapping. The 110 passed straight underneath her in a dive to the right, exactly as she'd planned, ducking underneath the obstacle she'd made of herself and chasing Singh. As soon as she saw his course, she throttled forward and pushed the stick hard forward, retracting the flaps and flipping the tail upwards,

225

and pointing the spinner straight down at the 110. Her stomach churned and flipped, and her eyes bulged with the g forces, and as soon as she was lined up, she hit the fire button and raked the 110 with bullets. Her target shuddered, and a jet of flame shot from the right engine before expanding and engulfing the entire aeroplane in a massive explosion, which there was no way Harriet could avoid. She was enveloped in blackened orange, gold, and red flames, and for a moment, she felt like she was in the very definition of hell. As her aeroplane shook and rocked, her mind went back to Dunkirk, and the burning Hurricane as smoke started to fill her cockpit. It felt like she was in it for hours, though in reality, it was no more than a second or two until she was facing the fast approaching green waves below. A pull of the stick and she let out a gasp of relief as the controls responded and the Spitfire levelled out. She was soaked in sweat and gasping for breath. A quick look around showed her to be alone, so she pulled back the canopy hood and gulped in the cold air, appreciating the feel of it on her sweat streaked face. She counted to ten and checked her mirror, nothing. She was more composed. She pulled the canopy closed, then turned and pointed the nose upwards while starting a slow turn to head back in the direction of the battle. She searched the sky, but there was nothing to be seen, except for lines of white and black smoke and a landscape below dotted with burning and smoking wrecks. How could two hundred aeroplanes just disappear? She climbed up over Dover and looked around, she continued through and above the clouds, still watching her tail, but there was nothing. Nobody. She flew around searching the sky until she finally saw another Spitfire, which she chased until finally, she could see it was Singh. With a gasp of relief, she sat on his wing and gave him a wave. He nodded and smiled.

"Let's go home," he said. Harriet nodded and followed as he led them back to the aerodrome. A quick circuit showed a few Spitfires had already arrived before them. She pushed her canopy open then followed Singh down to the grass, where they bumped gently to a halt outside the dispersal. She checked her instruments then shut down and pulled off her flying helmet, which was soaked with sweat, then slumped in her seat and closed her eyes for a moment. She was exhausted.

"Are you OK?" AP asked urgently.

226

"Yeah..." Harriet replied as she half opened her eyes and looked up. She reached under her jacket and Mae West and pulled out the flask Cas had given her and took a sip of brandy. She offered it to AP, who shook her head.

"Are you sure you're OK?" AP asked again as Harriet put the flask back in her pocket.

"The sky was full of them," Harriet said after a moment. "Then, they were gone." She looked AP in the eyes. "How do two hundred aeroplanes disappear in a matter of minutes?"

"Hundreds?"

"It looked like hundreds."

"That's the biggest raid so far... Oh well, come on. You can't stay in there." She unclipped Harriet's harness and pulled her to her feet. Harriet stepped out onto the wing and unfastened her parachute. "Give it to me, and I'll put it inside and keep it ready for you. If raids are getting that big, I'm thinking you'll be needing it again before you're stood down." Harriet nodded then handed the parachute over, before walking down the wing and jumping down to the ground. The sky was still a mix of blue and grey, but the heat and humidity of the morning were climbing quickly, and Harriet started to feel like she was overheating. She pulled off her Mae West and jacket, then unfastened her tunic as she headed over to dispersal. Lexi ran over and hugged her tight as Harriet dropped her jacket and Mae West and accepted the hug happily.

"You OK, honey?" Lexi asked as she finally pulled away a little. Harriet nodded and smiled. "You're soaked!"

"Yeah... That can happen," Harriet said with a smile. Lexi picked up her kit and walked at her side towards the dispersal.

"The boys that got back before you said it was crazy up there."

"That's one word for it," Harriet laughed, as she felt her head start to decompress and her humour return. "I thought I was going to have to swim home for a moment."

"Stop it! You're not funny!" Lexi said sternly. She was clearly worried about her young friend. Harriet just smirked at her and gave her a wink.

"Bloody good show!" Singh said as he greeted her. "She stood her kite on its tail, then dropped down and shot the 110 on my tail into smithereens," he said to The Spy.

"You saw it?" The Spy asked.

"Yes, it's confirmed, alright. I got one, too."

"He did," Harriet said. "I saw the crew jump out this side of Dover."

"OK, well get writing!" The Spy handed them report forms and pencils.

"Good show?" Cas asked.

"There had to be two hundred of them, bombers and fighters," Singh said. "It's the biggest raid we've seen so far. It was so busy it was hard not to crash into one."

One by one the pilots made their way back, though after some time it was evident that three were missing, including Archie. The others were a Pilot Officer and a Sergeant, both relatively new to the squadron having only arrived a couple of weeks before Harriet. Jonny had seen a Spitfire go down, but he couldn't be sure who it was, and at the peak of the battle the sky was full of parachutes, so many it looked like an invasion. Everybody had an opinion or an idea, but ultimately nobody had a clue what had happened to the missing pilots. Cas went to ring around local units to see if they had news, while everyone else got themselves a drink. Harriet separated herself from the others. She walked with Lexi and

Abby, who'd arrived while they were gone, and talked excitedly about their upcoming flying assessments at the central flying school. She tried to give them any advice she could think of, racking her brain from her own test the day before, and trying to pull anything from all of her combat experience. She was rambling and stuck firmly on trying to think of more ways to help them.

"Hey..." Lexi said, putting her arm on Harriet's and stopping her talking. "I think we're gonna be OK."

"I've been babbling on, haven't I?" Harriet asked with embarrassment.

"Not at all," Abby said with a warming smile. "On the contrary, you've been a great help."

"Will you be staying? I know the boys would love to buy you a barrel load of drinks in the Mess later, and I'm sure I can arrange a room..."

"We can't, I'm afraid. We're due for our assessments first thing tomorrow, and we have to go back and finish packing our kit."

"I understand... I suppose I'd better let you get on your way in that case."

"I suppose."

"Though you could both do me a favour before you go?"

"It'll have to be quick," Lexi replied.

Harriet nodded and led them over to the line of Spitfires where AP was busy organising the fitters, riggers, armourers, and all manner of ground crew to make sure the Spitfires were ready for the next scramble.

"What do you want?" she asked as Harriet, and her friends approached.

"I've got something for you."

"Not now, can't you see I'm busy?"

"Yes now," Harriet replied. "Go on, tell her," she said to Lexi.

"What?" AP demanded, hands on hips.

"Our friend here tells me you're a pretty handy flyer?" Lexi asked.

"I'm OK, so what?" AP shrugged.

"So the RAF have just summoned the two of us and five of our friends to the central flying school for a flight assessment."

"Don't mock me," AP replied as her eyes narrowed. "It's going to be a busy day, and I don't have the patience."

"I ain't mocking anyone, honey. When they made Harry a fighter pilot, they decided to see if any other girls can fly like her," Lexi and Abby both smiled.

"Did you put them up to this?" AP blustered at Harriet.

"Nope," came the simple reply. "They're due there tomorrow morning for an assessment. If they pass, the RAF is going to look at making them pilots." AP's eyes opened wide. She looked at all three of them in turn, and all three smiled warmly.

"We gotta fly, honey," Lexi said as she put her hand on Harriet's shoulder.

"Thank you both for everything," Harriet replied. "And good luck tomorrow, you'll both pass with flying colours, I'm sure."

"Well, we're both better flyers than you, so I'd hope so," Lexi winked. "Take care of yourself."

230

"Do as she says," Abby said as she hugged Harriet. "I'll let you know what happens." The pair left Harriet and AP standing side by side and headed for the Anson.

"Don't ride my motorcycle the way you fly your aeroplane. You'll stay alive longer!" Lexi laughed, and Harriet smiled then turned to look at AP, who was just about holding herself together.

"Go on, then," she said, surprised AP had lasted that long. AP immediately turned and started sprinting towards the dispersal hut, with Harriet running in her wake. She bounced inside and ran through the closed door to Singh's office, clattering it against the wall, and stood in front of Singh, Cas, and Max, who were jarred out of their conversation.

"Is everything OK, AP?" Singh asked, frowning and looking around while the others looked out of the window to check for signs of a bombing raid.

"You need to send me to the central flying school!" AP blurted. She was as far out of character as it was possible to be, she was never flustered, and nobody had ever known her not be precisely clear in whatever she was talking about. So when the three senior officers of the squadron were faced with her breathless and demanding to go to the central flying school, they were more than a little confused.

"Whatever for?" Cas asked curiously.

"Assessment," AP replied. "Harry, tell them!" she demanded as Harriet stood by her side. The three men shifted their gaze to her.

"Apparently the AOC has sent my old ATA flight to the central flying school for an assessment tomorrow, with a view to training them as RAF pilots like me, if they make the grade." Harriet shrugged. "They're all female."

"I see..." Cas turned to Singh and raised an eyebrow.

"And why should I send away my best engineer?" Singh asked.

"Because you have an engineering officer, and he's a good one, which means I'm here running the dispersal and getting in the way of the Chief. I'm in the way here, and surplus to numbers, or needs."

"If that's the case, there are plenty of other squadrons who would bite my hand off for an engineer of your calibre."

"Sir!" AP protested.

"Right now, AP, I think you have Spitfires to get ready for when that phone rings again."

"But...!"

"That'll be all AP," he said firmly. She opened her mouth as Harriet put her hand on her shoulder and gave her a gentle pull, turning her quickly and leading her from the office as her face reddened with a mix of upset and frustration. Harriet smiled politely then closed the door as she guided AP outside to the dispersal. She had tears in her eyes for the first time. She looked around at the pilots. Some looked back, and some were already snoozing, then she started walking away slowly in the direction of the Spitfires. Harriet stopped her and pulled her over to the tea urn, where AP fought hard to keep her tears inside.

"They didn't say no," Harriet said as supportively as she could.

"You heard them... I'm an engineer. Forever."

"You're a good engineer."

'Is that enough?" AP shrugged and looked dejected. "I mean, for me? All I've ever wanted to do is fly, and I can fly, but because I'm an engineer I don't get the chance to do what I love. It's not fair, Harry."

"I know... But maybe this will be the start. If they get through the assessments, maybe the RAF will go with it and recruit more? If that happens, they can't say no, can they? If recruiting females is official?"

"Maybe," AP replied sadly. "Just... How can I be content fixing them when other girls are flying them? I accepted you doing it. You're exceptional. You're the best pilot I've ever seen, male or female, but the others? I know they're your friends, but there can't be another seven exceptional pilots. Good, maybe? But if they're good, so am I, and it's only fair I should have the chance to prove myself, isn't it?"

"Yes..." Harriet replied. "Yes, it is, and I hope you get that chance. You deserve it more than anyone else I can think of."

"It's not even a case of deserving, Harry," AP said as she started a slow walk towards the Spitfires. "I just want a fair shot. I wouldn't even mind if they didn't let me fly fighters, as long as they let me fly."

"If they don't, why don't you transfer to the ATA?"

"I told you, they'd be reluctant to let me go."

"But you have a right to request it. I know that much, the girls in my flight told me so, in fact, one had been a WAAF Officer before they started taking girls in the ATA."

"I'm going to. I'm going to ask today." AP said firmly.

"Don't do anything impulsive."

"I don't care anymore, Harry. In fact, I'm going to ask as soon as I get these Spitfires finished. Singh can't just keep me here because I'm a good engineer."

"AP!" Cas shouted from the door of the dispersal hut. The girls stopped and turned to face him.

"Sir...?" she replied as politely as she could manage.

"Get your kit packed," he said with a slight smirk. AP's eyes opened wide with excitement. "I'm taking you to the CFS later today." AP was frozen to the spot; the only sign of life was a slight tremble in her hands and face. "Well? What're you waiting for, a written invite?" He turned and went back into the dispersal hut.

"Did that just happen?" AP asked.

"I suppose you need to be careful what you wish for," Harriet replied with a shrug and a smile.

"Oh my God. Harry! Is this real?"

"It sounds like it is."

"Can I do it?" AP asked as her eyes narrowed, and the excitement was replaced by focus.

"Yes," Harriet replied without pausing for thought. "Absolutely."

"What's it like? The assessment, I mean?"

"Nothing you can't do. Just do as you're asked with confidence and if you get it wrong, explain what you did wrong right away and ask for the opportunity to correct it. That's all you can do. Oh, and don't try and show off."

"I'm not you..."

"Hilarious. Haven't you got kit to pack?"

"Yes... What kit?"

"Ask Cas. He'll know." AP smiled the biggest smile Harriet had ever seen, then ran off excitedly and left Harriet to wander over to her deckchair and settle down with her cup of tea.

"You're a good pilot," Jonny said from his chair a few places away.

"Thanks," Harriet smiled as she got comfortable.

"I mean it. I thought you were just another girl when you turned up, you know?"

"I don't think I do, Jonny, what's just another girl to you?"

"I don't know... Mum always told me to respect women, and I do, I promise, it's just that as soon as I sewed these wings on my chest, I had girls throwing themselves at me. I didn't know what to do? I just went with it and, I suppose the girls I met weren't anything like the girls that mum talked about. Honestly, they scared me a bit, so I just acted up to them instead." Harriet smiled at him. The gentle giant was genuine as he sat forward in his chair. He'd ditched his flying jacket and sat in his unbuttoned tunic and Mae West and looked at her with his soft brown eyes. He looked like a tired young boy with his hair sticking in every direction and a smudge of dirt on his face, but his eyes seemed more aged and not as innocent as she imagined they were not too long ago. "You're not like those girls, though. You're a scrapper."

"I'm going to take that as a compliment."

"You should. I saw that manoeuvre you did with Singh when you slammed the brakes on and came down behind that Jerry. That was inspired."

"It was lucky."

"You are lucky. That's what the others who were with you in France said. When I got here, they all talked about this incredible pilot called Harry. I thought you were a man. Who wouldn't? Anyway, I suppose

235

what I'm saying is sorry if I've been a bit of an arse. Can we be friends? I mean proper friends, that drink in the Mess and stuff, nothing else."

"I'd like that."

"Me too," he smiled and sat back in his chair.

"And if you misbehave, I'll get your mum's address from Cas and tell her what you get up to."

"Oh, God, please don't do that. She'll kill me quicker than any German." Harriet smiled then closed her eyes and instantly dropped into a deep sleep.

The bell was rung twice more during Harriet's first day on standby. The first was for a single flight to scramble and look for a phantom raid coming in over Dover, and on the second the squadron was sent up to intercept three bombers. One of which was shot down by Jonny, who in doing so logged his first aerial victory; and another was damaged by Kiwi. When the squadron was finally stood down, they'd been called up five times in one form or another, and Harriet had flown on three of the sorties. They'd claimed five fighters, one bomber, and one reconnaissance bomber destroyed, two probables, and five damaged. In return they'd lost three pilots and their Spitfires, including Archie, one of their most experienced and most popular pilots in the squadron; and they'd had two Spitfires damaged badly enough to need a major repair at the factory. Harriet was exhausted. She'd returned to the Mess on her new motorcycle and dropped her kit bags on the floor of her room, before collapsing into the chair by the window and falling asleep. When she came to, Daisy had taken off her boots and unfastened her tunic and pulled a blanket over her to keep her warm. Harriet smiled to herself before heading to the bathroom to get cleaned up, which made her feel much more alive and much more human. After dressing in her best uniform, she made her way to the Mess where she had something to eat, then headed to the bar, determined to have a quiet drink before going to bed for an early night. She was relieved to see it was nearly deserted, and after being served with a beer, she found her way to a comfortable leather armchair in a corner. She picked up a newspaper and started browsing; though she wasn't really reading, just glancing over the pages enough to give her brain something other than the day's flying to think about.

"Harry, old man! There you are!" Harriet looked up from her newspaper at the handsome man with salt and pepper hair standing in front over her. She raised an eyebrow as she tried to imagine who he might be, but she was drawing a blank. She looked at the lines of braid on his cuffs and quickly remembered Daisy's advice about braid and seniority.

"Sir?" she asked questioningly as she stood.

"Sit, sit," he waved his hand excitably. "Do you mind if I join?" He pointed to the chair opposite and started to move it closer to the small table, which he'd already put his beer on before she could reply.

"Please," Harriet said politely, as she sat down a little uncomfortable about what was happening.

"Oh, Dickie, be a good sport and bring us a sherry each, would you?" he called over to the old barman, who nodded and mumbled something to himself. "And make sure they're the good stuff, I'll have none of your games, or you won't be paid!" He gave Harriet a playful wink, as though they were best friends and she was in on the joke. The barman was German, of all things, but had lived in England for most of his adult life, and even served in the RAF in its early years; before retiring and agreeing to run the Mess bar. Harriet had been told all about him during the previous evening's celebrations. He had a habit of pouring the cheap stuff when the pilots became excessively inebriated, to save his stock and turn a small profit for the Mess bar. "So, how are you settling in with the squadron? Raj treating you well?"

"Erm, yes, Sir. Very well." She was a little surprised and not expecting the conversation.

237

"Good, Good. He's a good man, is Raj. Fearless in the air, and a damned good leader. We're lucky to have him."

"Yes, Sir. I couldn't ask for better."

"Oh, I don't think we need to be formal when nobody else is about. Alastair is fine. Keep saying Sir, and I'll be forever looking over my shoulder for the AOC," he said casually, as Harriet's eyebrow raised further. "At least while nobody's around."

"Two of the finest sherries, Group Captain Saltire, Sir," Dickie said in his most formal, and heavily accented voice, accompanied by a smart Germanic click of his heels.

"Don't be naughty, Dickie, and thank you very much. Give us a few minutes and bring us another, there's a good chap." He let out a chuckle as Dickie rolled his eyes and walked away. "I must admit, Harry, when the AOC called yesterday and told me you'd be coming to stay with us, I was more than a little excited. Our very own celebrity here on my station, and flying in one of my squadrons." He handed Harriet a glass of sherry, and before she could move it, he clinked his against hers and drank half. She followed suit. Her eyes watered a little as it caught the back of her throat.

"Celebrity?" she asked innocently.

"The first ever female fighter pilot in the RAF, and a bloody good one too, if the legend is to be believed!"

"I don't know about that..." Harriet protested as a blush spread across her face in a combined response to the conversation and the sherry.

"Don't argue with your Commanding Officer, Harry, it's not nice," he said with a mischievous twinkle in his eye. He took another swig and finished off the sherry, then waved his glass in the air at Dickie, while encouraging Harriet to do the same. "I've been looking forward to meeting you," he continued. "I wanted to come over and say hello before now, but there's a bit of a war on, as you know. Anyway, I got to listen to your scrap this morning, at least."

"Listen?" Harriet asked as another round of sherries arrived, and another was ordered.

"Yes, I was in Ops listening to the squadron chat as it happened. Raj filled me in on the details this afternoon, which helped me fill in the blanks and paint a picture. It seems you did a sterling job of keeping the Huns off his tail."

"I did my best."

"Yes, you did, my girl. Yes, you did! I can see how you earned the ribbons on your tunic!" Harriet glanced down and smiled. "Speaking of which, I've got the dates through for your trip to the palace. Early September, I think. I'll confirm them with Cas, and he'll let you know."

"The palace?"

"Yes, the King is looking forward to decorating you for your services. He's quite keen to meet you, too."

"The King?"

"Oh do keep up, Harry old man. You've got to get your gongs pinned on sooner or later, and when it's a double hitter like yours, the King likes to do the job himself. Besides, as we've already discussed, you're something of a celebrity, and I think he'd like to say he's met you." Harriet felt herself blushing again as she drank the second sherry. "Anyway, Harry. I think it's important that you know that my door is always open to you. Anything you need, just come and say hello." At that, the Mess door opened, and the squadron pilots poured into the bar led by Max, cheering excitedly. "I say, what's the din in aid of?" Alastair asked as he stood from his chair and looked over to the group, all of whom instantly fell quiet.

"We've had some good news, Sir, so we're having a bit of a celebration," Max replied.

"Do tell?"

"It's Mister Russel, Sir. He's turned up in a hospital down the coast."

"He's OK?"

"Shot in the behind by the Home Guard when he bailed out near Dover, Sir. All the parachutes had them thinking it was an airborne raid, so they started shooting before asking questions, and Archie caught one right in the derrière."

"Well that's just marvellous," Alastair said excitedly. "Dickie, whiskies all round, and make them doubles!" Another cheer went up, and Alastair turned back to Harriet. "Come on, Harry. Celebrations are afoot!" Harriet stood and drained her sherry glass as she followed Alastair to the bar. She was instantly ecstatic and filled with life at the news that Archie was alive, as was everybody else; and the celebrations soon descended into something to eclipse the previous night's, mostly thanks to Alastair's insistence on flooding the pilots with the best whisky. Everyone was happy.

Chapter 10

Flowers

The next morning Harriet found herself face down in the bathroom with her arm around the toilet. She was wearing her pyjamas, which was something of a relief considering Daisy was standing in the doorway with a pot of hot black coffee. Which, after she'd helped Harriet stand, she mixed with some cold water before forcing Harriet to drink, while she busied herself filling the bathtub. Harriet stared in fuzzy minded fear as she watched Daisy at work, but complied without argument when she was told to strip and climb into the bath. The icy water was up to her knees, and already she was shaking from the cold. On Daisy's instruction, she let out a sigh then sat and ducked herself. The cold was horrific, but it did the job, and after a few more duckings Harriet let out a stream of profanities as she climbed out of the bathtub, shivering like a leaf. After towelling dry, she drank more coffee while getting dressed in her flying kit. Daisy smirked for most of the episode, while Harriet muttered her displeasure, which was received with polite, courteous, and respectful mocking and teasing, for the self inflicted discomfort she'd visited on herself with a late night of heavy drinking in the Mess. She thanked Daisy, in a roundabout way; then instead of taking the transport truck to the dispersal, she mounted her motorcycle and roared through the darkness by herself, letting the cool pre dawn air chase away most of the remaining hangover which was still clinging to her. By the time she'd parked outside the dispersal hut she was feeling alive enough to tolerate conversation with people. She entered the hut for the morning briefing, before heading to her Spitfire to give it the once over ahead of the day's inevitable fighting. AP had moved Lanky to Harriet's crew, and she was joined by a Corporal named Holland, an older man who'd been in the service from long before the war, and knew his way around every inch of every aeroplane he'd ever worked on. He was a good mechanic, if a little grumpy. She sank into the cockpit and after finishing her checks started the engine, then pulled on her oxygen mask and breathed deeply while she went through the last of her checks.

"You'll miss it when you need it if you use it all down here," Holland complained, as she shut down and extracted herself from the cockpit. She nodded and smiled politely yet dismissively, before putting her parachute in place and tidying the straps ready for a quick getaway. A couple of minutes later and she was slumped in her deckchair next to Max, with her warm collar pulled up around her face. Another couple of minutes and she was asleep. There she stayed until being rudely awakened by the ring of the dispersal phone, which cut through her fuzziness and instantly brought her to full alertness. She joined the others staring in wait. 'Squadron scramble!' came the yell, followed by the ringing of the bell.

"Get out of the bloody way!" she yelled as she jumped up onto her wing. Holland was still slowly extracting himself from the cockpit after starting the engine. She pulled on his shoulder and jumped in while helping him out with a shove. Lanky appeared and fastened her harness while she ran through her checks, then with a wink and nod which sent Lanky running down the wing, Harriet released the brakes and started rolling. Singh eventually caught her, and the pair led the squadron across the grass at full speed and climbed into the silver gold dawn sky. Harriet felt her stomach squeeze with excitement as she listened to the vectoring from Control, then followed Singh into the sunrise to look for a formation of German bombers. Nothing materialised, but nerves were clearly jangling at Control, so the squadron remained in the sky, flying up and down the coast and finding nothing. When they had less than fifteen minutes of fuel left, they were finally ordered to land, having seen nothing more than a glorious sunrise.

After breakfast, they settled again, before being called up mid morning to patrol the coast between Dover and the Thames Estuary, where they bumped into a raid of Stukas seemingly flying unescorted. The squadron got among them immediately, knocking four down, and damaging four more, before what remained of the dive bombers scurried home across the Channel. Throughout the engagement, Harriet had sat on Singh's wing without leaving him for even a moment. All her focus was on searching the sky for fighters which never came, and she engaged in nothing aside from a brief moment when she got her guns on a Stuka that Singh had already had a blast at, silencing the increasingly accurate and troublesome rear gunner. The squadron mostly returned together, with the stragglers finding their way back shortly after, all except another of the new faces from B Flight, a Pilot Officer called Philipson. A young man who'd been quite full of himself in the Mess and who Harriet had only ever said a handful of words to. He'd last been seen chasing the Stukas to France, despite Singh's instructions to the contrary before the engagement; and by early afternoon he was still unaccounted for. They didn't have much time to dwell on it before they were called up again, this time to join two squadrons of Hurricanes in intercepting a massive raid north of Dover. It was a brief, intense fight which saw Harriet getting in the way of a 109 who'd come head on at Singh. She left it trailing smoke as it ran for home while she returned to her station on her Commanding Officer's wing. Singh had full confidence in her ability, allowing him to do his job in leading the squadron, safe in the knowledge that she was there to watch his tail, something he'd very quickly come accustomed to. The full Squadron returned home this time, only to find the airfield smoking from a small raid that had come in over the treetops and bombed the far side of the airfield, hitting a fuel bowser which had left a large crater near the perimeter hedge. Harriet was furious when she found out that the anti aircraft gunners hadn't got a single shot off at the three German bombers who'd flown away over the coast unmolested. It was only a few days earlier that they'd been so eager that they'd shot her out of the sky while she was flying a Spitfire, but for the three German bombers, there was nothing. She was still complaining bitterly, though only to herself, when they were called up for the fourth time to patrol the Dover coast again, where they caught a group of German fighters heading home after being in a fight further inland. Dolph scored another, making him an ace, and Kiwi shared one with Murph, but it was a short interaction, and they were soon called down again, where the call finally came to stand them down in the afternoon.

"Harry, you got a minute?" Max asked as the pilots prepared to disperse. She nodded and walked over to join him. "Fancy a ride out to the coast?"

"What, now?" she asked with a frown, not entirely sure where he was going with his question.

"Yeah, unless you've got anything better to do?"

"I was thinking of getting cleaned up. My hair is thick with sweat, and I stink."

"Well, why don't you go get freshened up and meet me back here in thirty minutes? The skipper's sending us on a diplomatic mission."

"Now I really don't know what you're talking about."

"We're gonna fly that little old Tiger Moth up the coast to the hospital where Archie is busy taking it easy and enjoying life and ruin his afternoon."

"I'll be back in thirty minutes," she said with a smile. He nodded, and she ran to her motorcycle and sped back to her accommodation, where Daisy was waiting with a bath ready for her, a hot one this time, and her spare trousers and blouse neatly ironed and hanging ready. Harriet stripped as she ran to the bathroom. "Daisy, you're a lifesaver. Please leave my things where I throw them, and I promise I'll tidy them later." Daisy smiled and casually ignored Harriet as she dived into the bathroom and followed along, picking up her clothes and throwing them into a laundry bag. "I said to leave them!" Harriet yelled.

"I know," Daisy replied, still ignoring Harriet, who was now under the water, nervously hiding herself from Daisy and feeling herself blush. "You're really shy about me being in here?" Daisy asked while rolling her eyes.

"I'm not used to being naked in front of people, especially not close enough where I can have a conversation about laundry with them."

"Harry, I swam naked with you in that river back in France, I don't think you've got anything I haven't seen before."

"Still..." Harriet protested. "That was different. It was a river in France, not a bath in my room."

244

"And how do you think you got into your pyjamas last night?" Daisy asked as she put her hands on her hips and stared Harriet in the eyes. "The pyjama fairy?"

"Oh... I thought..." Harriet's blush went into overdrive.

"You couldn't even stand up, and the closest you'd got to putting your pyjamas on was putting an arm in one leg, and trying to squeeze your head through the other. While still wearing your uniform."

"I really don't have time to discuss this..." Harriet said as she went about scrubbing herself, changing the subject entirely and doing her best to show she wasn't in the least embarrassed. "I was only trying to save you a job. If you want to clean up after me, go for it!" Daisy laughed, then continued collecting clothes.

"You've missed a spot," Daisy said with a mischievous smirk as she looked over the bath side into the water.

"Seriously!" Harriet blustered. "Do they take women in the infantry?"

"Why?"

"Because as soon as I've finished in here, I'm going to ask Singh if he can transfer you there!"

"I'll leave some fresh knickers on your bed. See you soon." Daisy giggled as she left the bathroom and closed the door behind her. Harriet let out a cry of frustration, then sunk under the water to rinse herself. Daisy had been the perfect choice to look after her. She was worldly and confident, and wouldn't be silenced by Harriet's blustering, no matter how hard she tried, and Harriet appreciated her all the more for it. She finished washing, dried, quickly put on lipstick and tied up her hair, then dressed in her fresh, clean clothes. A squirt of perfume and she was ready to go. She looked at herself in the mirror and made a note of a few sweat marks on her very nice tunic, she was going to need to fly in something else, or she'd ruin it. It was a spare, and not her best, but it was still of exceptional quality, and she hated dirtying it. Otherwise, she felt she was looking good, if not a little different in tunic, trousers, and shoes. In trousers, she'd usually wear flying boots, and in shoes, she'd typically wear a skirt. She was happy with how she looked, though. She opened the door to see Daisy just about to come in.

"Hat," Daisy said.

"Excuse me?"

"You look incredible, Ma'am, but you'll need your hat if you're going off station." She passed Harriet and collected the blue service cap from the top of the locker and handed it over. "Wear it outside, and don't forget to salute them if they have more than a couple of stripes on their cuff…"

"Got it," Harriet said. "Thank you. I'll see you later."

"I'll have your pyjamas ready."

"And I'll talk to Singh about your transfer to the infantry," Harriet replied as she ran down the corridor. She was soon on her Harley, and after whizzing through the station and blow drying her hair, she arrived at the dispersal where she parked and joined Max, who'd changed out of his flying kit and freshened up. As soon as they'd said their greetings, they were in the Tiger Moth and heading up the coast at treetop height. Harriet found herself smiling as she recognised the hospital that she'd stayed in, and she smiled more when Max lined up to land in the extended field behind it.

"You OK?" Max asked as she excitedly climbed to the ground. Already a small group of nurses and wounded servicemen were gathered outside watching their unexpected visitors.

"It's where they brought me after Dunkirk."

"No way? You were this close to us the whole time?"

246

"I suppose..." Harriet said with a frown.

"Tough break. Shall we go see his Lordship, and ruin his day?" he smirked, and she nodded and smiled, and put on her hat, then walked at Max's side towards the hospital.

"What's the meaning of all this noise?" a familiar stern voice asked, making Harriet smile as she looked through the gathering crowd, which parted to let the small Matron pass through. "This is a hospital, not an aerodrome!"

"I'm sorry, Matron," Harriet said politely, standing smartly to attention as she talked. "We came from along the coast to see our friend. We were told he was brought here after being shot down." The Matron looked closely, then let half a smile break the fierceness of her face.

"I recognise you," the Matron said as she walked forward. "You're that feisty young girl who threw a vase of flowers at one of my senior sisters..."

"Yes..." Harriet replied nervously, while Max looked at her in surprise with raised eyebrows. "Again, I'm truly sorry about that. I really wasn't myself."

"If you say so... I see you found your way back to your squadron."

"Yes. Yes, thank you. I fly Spitfires now."

"I knew you would," the Matron said warmly, then stepped forward and shook Harriet's hand. "It pleases me to see you again, and I know somebody else who will be equally happy to see you. Follow me, and we'll see if we can find them and your friend. You can even bring this handsome young American with you if you'd like." She gave Max a wink that made him blush, and Harriet choke down a laugh. They followed her as she marched through the gathered crowd. "You nurses have work to do, and if you young men are well enough to be standing looking at aeroplanes, you're well enough to go back to your units!"

247

"I say, I think that pilot's a girl!" a recovering soldier wrapped in bandages exclaimed to a group of his similarly afflicted friends.

"That bomb really rattled your brain," his friend replied.

"I'm telling you, look at her hair and her lipstick."

"Bloody hell, you're right!"

"That pilot's also an officer," a nurse reminded them sternly from behind.

"Ma'am," the soldiers said in unison, as they all stood as close to attention as they could muster as she passed. Harriet bowed her head in recognition and smiled politely. "A bloody pretty one she is, too," a soldier whispered not so quietly as she passed. Harriet felt herself blush.

"Would you look at that," Max said in dismay.

"What?" Harriet asked as she looked around.

"Here's me, a Flight Lieutenant, and they're standing to attention for you, a newly promoted Flying Officer."

"Not my fault they know who the boss is," she said confidently.

"Uhuh..." he replied as they stepped into the hospital.

"The name of the person you're here to visit?" the Matron asked as she led them.

"Flight Lieutenant Archie Russel, Ma'am," Max replied.

"I should have known," the Matron sighed as she led them up the stairs, and on to a ward full of young men in various states. She pointed to the bed in the corner, where Archie was lying face down with his bandaged behind pointing to the ceiling.

248

"Well ain't that a pretty sight," Max said as he stood beside Archie's bed. "I should have brought you a flower for that vase."

"Oh bloody hell," Archie groaned, as he recognised the voice and raised himself on his elbows to look at Max. "There goes the neighbourhood!" He then looked at Harriet, who was smirking and doing all she could to stop herself laughing out loud at his predicament. "And you had to bring her?" he continued.

"Hey, don't be bitter, she wanted to see you..." Harriet shrugged and nodded, still stifling a laugh. "Though I doubt she expected to see quite this much of you." That was too much for Harriet, who finally let out a laugh, as a tear ran down her cheek.

"Go on, make the most of my plight," Archie said as he rolled his eyes.

"How bad is it?" Max asked, "You coming back to fly with us anytime soon?"

"Honestly, I've no idea, old boy. Apparently, the bullet twanged a nerve somewhere. Trust me to find the only good shot in the whole bloody Home
Guard!"

"That's a tough break."

"Tough? The buggers were going to use me for bayonet practice until one of them recognised the uniform, then they became all apologetic. I wouldn't mind, but they didn't even have any good whisky in the local pub, so I had to do with tan coloured paint thinners while I waited to be picked up." He looked back at Harriet, who'd now stifled her giggles and composed herself. "Better for getting that out of your system?" he asked.

"Yes, Sorry. I just..."

"Oh, I know, don't worry, had it been anyone else I don't doubt I'd have been positively unbearable," he smiled. "And the way this war is going, I could well have that laugh sooner rather than later, if you end up in here too!"

"She's already barred from this hospital," an unexpected voice said from behind. Harriet turned quickly to see Sister Emily. Her eyes widened with excitement, and Emily smiled as she looked Harriet up and down. "That uniform suits you."

"Thank you. I've missed you! Max, Archie, Emily was my nurse when I was here. She saved my life."

"Don't be dramatic, Harry!" Emily scolded. "We write to each other every week; how can you possibly miss me?"

"It's not the same... Anyway, how's the patient?"

"Living up to his wound and being a pain in the posterior!" Emily said as she moved to Archie's bedside.

"Ah, Sister, there you are," Archie said warmly. "Have you given any thought to us going out for that drink?"

"Mister Russel, if you can't even lie on your back, you've no chance of standing, and I think that going for a drink with anybody may be a long time in your future." She popped a thermometer in his mouth. "Better," she said.

"Is it that bad?" Harriet asked.

"He's lying with his backside in the air in front of God and everyone, how good can it be?" Emily gave Harriet a wink, then took the thermometer from his mouth. "Still a bit of a temperature, we'll keep an eye on you for infection."

250

"I can't think of anyone else's eyes I'd rather have on me," Archie replied confidently, and Emily rolled her eyes.

"Max..." Harriet asked with a frown.

"What's up?"

"How long are we staying?"

"Why? You had enough of the view already?" he chuckled.

"Very droll," Archie replied.

"No, I was just wondering if you'd mind me taking the Tiger Moth for a spin..." She looked at Emily as she checked Archie's dressing.

"Wonderful idea," Archie said. "Do say yes, old boy, she does grate, and I could do with a break."

"Sure..." Max replied. Harriet's face lit up. "Hey, stay close, and stay low, and don't do anything stupid. It's me who has to fill in the paperwork if anything happens."

"Yes, Sir!" she said smartly while clicking the heels of her smart, highly polished parade shoes together.

"I thought you were French, not German?" Archie asked.

"Norwegian, actually," she said as she stepped forward and showed him the country flash on her shoulder. "Technically, at least."

"Millions wouldn't believe," he sighed. You're about as convincing as a Yank pretending to be Canadian... Anyway, aren't you supposed to be buggering off for a while so that I can chat with my friend in private?"

"Happily," she replied. "Emily, have you got a minute?" Emily finished checking Archie over, nodded, then followed Harriet across the ward to

251

the Matron, who was busy instructing a young nurse. "Excuse me, Matron?"

"Yes, Miss Cornwall?"

"I wondered if you might give Sister Emily a break for thirty minutes or so?"

"What?" Emily asked in surprise. "I'm sorry, Matron, I had no idea what she was going to ask." The Matron looked at them both for a moment.

"It's only I have something for her, a thank you present for looking after me."

"Very well," Matron replied with a playful sparkle in her eye. Harriet grabbed Emily's hand and ran excitedly from the ward.

"Harry, what are you doing?" Emily demanded as they ran.

"You're going to need to take off your hat," Harriet said, as she looked at the traditional white nurse's bonnet Emily was wearing on the back of her dark brown hair. Emily pulled out the hairpins and slid off the hat, then left it on the reception desk with the porter as she ran outside.

"Where on earth are we going, Harry?"

"There," Harriet pointed at the Tiger Moth, which was being carefully inspected by a small group of bandaged patients.

"You're joking!"

"I'm not! You're going to need to lift your dress to get in."

"Harry..."

"Watch out!" Harriet shouted at the patients, all young men with various injuries, standing in their pyjamas, slippers, and dressing gowns.

252

"Who are you?" one of them asked in a very upper class accent.

"The driver," Harriet said. "Now shift out of my way."

"Don't be preposterous," he argued. "You're a girl!"

"Thank you for pointing that out, I wondered why my tunic was tight around the chest," she replied casually. He blushed and stepped aside, much to the sniggers of his friends. "Who are you?"

"Captain Howard, Coldstream Guards."

"Well, Captain Howard, Coldstream Guards. If you're a gentleman, you and your friends will turn and look the other way while I help this girl into the cockpit of my aeroplane; and considering this particular girl is one of your senior nurses, with power over your recovery and daily comfort, I expect you'll make the right choice!" Harriet helped Emily up the aeroplane and told her exactly where to stand.

"What? Oh. Oh yes, yes, obviously. Turn around, chaps," he turned his group, and Emily hiked up her dress and climbed into the front cockpit. Harriet put her flying helmet on Emily's head and strapped her in, then flicked the switches in the cockpit before going forward and spinning the propeller until the starter caught. She quickly ran into the cockpit, strapped herself in, then checked around her as she revved the engines.

"OK, you can clear out, Captain Howard," she yelled. The group quickly waddled and limped to a safe distance, and Harriet taxied the Tiger Moth to the far side of the field, facing the coast, from where the wind was blowing off the sea. "Ready?" she shouted through the communication tube to Emily.

"Are you sure we should do this?" Emily replied.

"Hold tight and ask me again in a few minutes." Harriet pushed the throttle forward, and they quickly bounced across the grass, before climbing up into the sky and shooting out over the cliffs.

"Oh my God!" Emily screamed with excitement as they launched into the air. The next fifteen minutes were spent skimming the fields and buzzing around the local villages. At one point Harriet had Emily take control for just a few minutes, and fly in a long wide circle over the countryside, before Harriet finally landed them back in the field by the hospital, and taxied to a halt exactly where they'd left from. Captain Howard and his friends had watched intently and gave a polite applause as the engine cut. Harriet jumped out and waved her finger in the air to signal they turn their backs, which they dutifully did, while she helped Emily extract herself from the front cockpit and straighten her dress. "Harriet, that was incredible!" Emily said. "I tried to imagine what it would be like, but it was better." Harriet smiled, sharing the excitement. She felt the same every single time she flew. "Thank you so very much."

"Thank you for keeping me alive."

"Don't get all dramatic again!" Emily blushed.

"It's not dramatic. It's the truth. I know you stayed with me when I was asleep, instead of going to bed, and I know you looked after me when I couldn't look after myself. A quick flight doesn't go anywhere close to repaying that, but it's a start." Emily simply smiled and hugged Harriet.

"You're very kind."

"As are you. Now let's get back and check on your patient." They headed back to the hospital to the polite nods of Howard and his friends, and after straightening her clothes and pinning her bonnet back in place, Emily took them back to Archie in time for tea, before finally, they said their goodbyes. After a final hug, Emily watched Harriet and Max fly off into the evening sun. Harriet smiled all the way home and thanked Max when they landed and handed the Tiger Moth back to the station communication flight, from whom they'd borrowed it. There was still no sign of their own Tiger Moth, which Cas had taken to the central flying school the day before to get AP in place for her flying assessment, but they hadn't yet returned. She mounted her motorcycle, then headed back to the Mess, where she ate with Kiwi and Murph before heading to her accommodation to find that Daisy had run her another bath. She was maintaining her slightly unnerving knack of knowing exactly where Harriet was, and when she was due back at her room.

"Going to the Mess bar tonight?" she asked as Harriet took off her tunic.

"I don't think so; I could do with a night off and a proper sleep."

"Well, I suppose it'll make getting into your pyjamas easier..."

"Aren't you supposed to be my servant? I thought servants were supposed to be polite and respectful?"

"Yes Ma'am, sorry Ma'am, three bags full Ma'am."

"Don't you have somewhere to be?"

"Yes, looking after you, and I'm here."

"I mean somewhere else. Seriously. What do you do when you're not here?"

"Go to the NAAFI, I suppose, or out to the local pub."

"Why don't you do that tonight?"

"I don't know... I have things to do."

"Would it help if I made it an order?"

"Probably not."

"I don't need a babysitter."

"Well, that's lucky, because I'm not a childminder."

"I just want you to be able to enjoy yourself."

"Who says I'm not enjoying myself being here?"

"Really? Ironing my clothes and running me baths is enjoyable?"

"Why not?"

"Why?"

"Maybe I enjoy the company?" Harriet frowned in surprise at the response.
"Besides, I like to think I make your life a bit easier."

"You do..."

"Then I'm happy."

"Don't you miss your old job? The communications and radios?"

"A bit, maybe. Anyway, less questions, your bath will get cold."

"Do something for me?"

"What?"

"Go and see Dickie in the Mess bar and bring me a couple of large sherries."

"Are you joking?"

"No. Put it on my tab and bring them up. If I'm going to stay in tonight, I may as well have something to sip on. I'll see you when you're back, thanks for running the bath." Daisy rolled her eyes and left Harriet to undress and bathe, returning a while later when Harriet had dried off and dressed in her blue and white striped pyjamas.

"There you go, two sherries," Daisy said as she pointed to the glasses on the dresser. She'd tidied the room and hung Harriet's uniform. Harriet smiled and offered a glass to Daisy.

"What's this?" Daisy asked with a frown.

"If you're going to stay, you're going to have a drink with me. Unless you think it's acceptable for me to drink alone?"

"I don't know..."

"You don't like sherry?"

"I love sherry, I just don't like officers," she said with a wink.

"Oh, grow up!" Harriet blustered.

"Seriously, though, it's so against the rules. If I was seen drinking in the Officer's Mess, even in the accommodation, we'd both be for the high jump."

"We'd better make sure we don't tell anyone in that case," Harriet said with a smile as she gestured with the glass again. Daisy smiled and took the glass, they said 'cheers' then sipped. "You may as well sit down," Harriet pointed to the chair by the window before sitting on her bed. Daisy nodded and took a seat, and a few minutes later, she was relaxing. The two were talking like old friends, which of course they were. They'd known each other since France, and Daisy had taken a shine to Harriet the minute she stepped into the WAAF tent armed with Champagne and cigarettes. A heavy knock at the door silenced the conversation, and Daisy quickly jumped to her feet, hid the sherry glass, and straightened herself as she headed to the door before Harriet could say a thing. Harriet adjusted herself and nodded, and Daisy opened the door to reveal AP. She was shaking with nervous energy.

257

"Ma'am?" Daisy said cautiously.

"Harry?" AP asked. Harriet was already at her feet and joining Daisy at the door.

"AP, are you OK?" she asked. AP just nodded. "Come in..." AP did as she was told and walked across the room to look out of the window.

"I should probably go," Daisy said.

"No... No, it's OK," AP muttered. "Please stay." Harriet gave Daisy a nod, and she closed the door.

"AP," Harriet said softly. "Are you OK? What happened?" AP finally turned to face the pair, she had tears in her eyes, and Harriet felt her heart squeeze.

"I passed..." she said quietly. "I passed the flying grading and was sent immediately for an interview with the AOC."

"Well?" Harriet demanded impatiently, while at the same time trying to remain warm and supportive, worried that something terrible had got in the way of AP flying.

"They're transferring me to the RAF Volunteer Reserve and sending me on an advanced training course. I'm going to be a pilot." Harriet immediately hugged AP "I'm going to be a pilot!" she repeated, overjoyed. "Oh my God, Harry, I'm going to be a pilot!"

"Bloody hell!" Daisy said excitedly as she walked over and hugged her friend. "Sergeant mechanic to pilot, you're my bloody hero!"

"Daisy, do one more thing for me," Harriet asked.

"What's that?"

"Get down to the bar and bring a bottle of whisky. Put it on my tab. We're going to celebrate!"

"You should go down to the bar and celebrate with the others," Daisy replied.

"You're not allowed in the Mess bar, and you're part of the celebrations. Go and get the whisky!"

"Ma'am!" Daisy smartened up and left quickly.

"I'm still shaking," AP said. Harriet handed her the silver flask from her tunic so that she could sip on the brandy. "The flying was a piece of cake. I thought I'd messed up and missed something it felt so easy. Then I was taken to an office where the AOC was waiting. He'd been there to see the results himself. He asked me a load of questions, about what I'd done in the service and what I'd like to fly. After discussing it with another officer and the flying instructor I was told my transfer is going to be processed, and I'm going for advanced refresher training somewhere up north before being assessed for which command I'll fly in."

"AP, that's incredible."

"It's better than incredible, Harry. It's my life dream. I'm going to be a pilot!"

"Yes you are, and you'll be great at it!"

"I'm going to be a pilot, and it's all down to you!"

"Don't be silly! You're the one that did it."

"I'm not. It's true. Remember what I told you in France? It's all down to you. You showed them what girls can do, and when they didn't pay attention, you grabbed them by the scruff of the neck and made them sit up and take notice! Without you, this wouldn't happen. It couldn't happen. I wouldn't be going to flight school, and neither would your friends from the ATA! All of us owe it to you."

"Wait. What? They passed too?"

"Every one of them. We're all going to advanced training together. We've done it, Harry, you were the first, but now look. Female pilots are finally going to be allowed to do their part. The Germans won't know what's hit them!"

"I can't tell you how excited I am for you."

"You're excited? I've been shell shocked since I was told. I'm lucky I had Cas to get me home. Otherwise, I'd have been stuck there unable to move, or think, or anything."

"When do you leave for training?"

"I don't know. The AOC said my orders would be sent through as soon as my transfer had been processed. Until then, I'm back here doing my normal job."

"I'm going to miss you, but I wouldn't have it any other way."

"I haven't gone yet."

"It doesn't stop me missing you..."

The door opened, and Daisy entered carrying a bottle of whisky on a silver tray, complete with a jug of water and three glasses.

"I'm not sure I can afford that bottle of whisky..." Harriet said as she looked at the bottle. She'd seen it before, a business client had bought one for her father after a particularly lucrative deal had been signed, and while he didn't drink whisky, he did appreciate the rarity and expense of the one he'd been given.

"You don't need to," Daisy said. "Compliments of Mister Salisbury. He saw me in the bar and insisted I bring it up so you can celebrate AP's news."

"Even better..." Harriet said with a smile.

"I should leave you both to it," Daisy said as she put the tray on the dresser.

"You'll do no such thing," AP said sternly. "I'm your superior officer, and I'm ordering you to stay and drink with us."

"And you're my servant, so you have to do as I say," Harriet added. "And I say you stay and drink."

"But..." Daisy protested.

"But nothing," AP said as she poured the whisky. "You and I have been in the same squadron since before the war, and you're my longest standing friend. If I can't celebrate with you, I don't want to celebrate with anyone else."

"That's you told," Harriet said with a smile. Daisy obligingly smiled and took the whisky; it was going to be a long night.

Chapter 11

IT

The days ran into each other over the next week. Every morning the squadron was on standby, and every morning they were called up at first light, either to intercept or to patrol; but whatever the start of the day, even if it was a quiet patrol, there was always more to come. Most days they were called up four times during their duty, sometimes more but rarely less, and each day the airfield became more of a target for the Luftwaffe. The damage was so bad it was getting difficult to land when the exhausted pilots returned from their missions, much to the frustration of Singh. He would frequently be heard ranting into the telephone about the lack of effective airfield defence, and threatening to leave one section behind on every scramble to protect the airfield so they could get back down. His anger boiled over into a heated phone call to group headquarters when a young Pilot Officer, Clarke, hit a fresh shell hole after dragging his badly damaged Spitfire back from Dover. He was killed, burned alive upside down in his cockpit in front of everyone who'd run to help him after his Spitfire flipped. He wasn't the only casualty in a week of intensifying combat, as the Germans increased their efforts to destroy the RAF both in the air and on the ground, in a prelude to the expected invasion from across the Channel. In just seven days, the squadron had lost five Spitfires. One pilot made it back home after taking to his parachute not far from the airfield, one broke his leg after escaping his stricken Spitfire over Dover, and three were posted missing presumed dead. The pilots were permanently exhausted, and the arrival of the replacements to fill their ranks didn't make the job any easier. Every new pilot was fresh out of training, and few of them had more than single figures in hours flying Spitfires, none of which were in combat; and as keen as they were, it was generally considered that they were a liability to themselves. The training programme had been trimmed to the minimum, and it was considered the squadron's responsibility to train the newly qualified pilots in combat. However, the cruel fact was that the squadrons were in battle four or more times a day, and they simply didn't have the time for training new arrivals. Of course, this made the experienced pilots on the squadron feel even worse because they couldn't do anything to help, and that got people killed. One young Pilot Officer, in particular, was shot out of the sky on his first scramble, before anyone had the chance to learn his name. Some of the old hands helped as much as they could. Max did his part, as did Singh, as the senior officers on the squadron they found thirty minutes here and there to take the new boys up and give them at least a little extra time preparing for the hell of combat. Another new face was Flight Lieutenant Ian Timothy Oakland, or 'IT' as he quickly became known, who'd been posted from one of the squadrons based in Yorkshire to replace Archie as Flight Commander. He was a regular pre war RAF Officer with a chip on his shoulder and a reputation for being awkward, something made worse by his seething anger at being appointed as Flight Commander, a demotion in his eyes, after his time as acting Commanding Officer in his previous squadron. He was noticeably short and older than most on the squadron with prematurely greying hair, all of which he carried as though they were afflictions, something which made him all the more determined in his skin crawling attempts to engage anything female when in the Mess. In almost a week with the squadron IT had become immensely unpopular and was considered to be single handedly responsible for dragging the already battered morale of the squadron through the floor. Every pilot in A Flight had been reprimanded for something or another. All were small indiscretions which were violations of the rule book, technically, but nothing that wasn't overlooked across every front line squadron in the RAF. He'd even insisted that his pilots wear their ties when flying, an order which was overturned by Singh when he heard of it. He'd tried his tricks on B Flight at one point, a mistake soon rectified by Max who put him against the wall of the Mess and threatened to push his teeth down his throat, a threat which saw B Flight left alone, most of the time. Sadly, IT's bravado on the ground wasn't matched in the air, a deficiency which was noticed by all in the squadron, old hands and novices alike. He was lots of things, but a good pilot wasn't one of them. All in all, his arrival on the squadron had made an already difficult time almost unbearable. As they entered the last week in August, many on the squadron were long overdue a rest, even Harriet, who'd only been with them a couple of weeks, but had quickly become drained by the unsustainable combat. She'd done her job loyally, though, and kept the Germans off Singh time

263

and time again, while managing to damage a few 110s and shoot down a bomber.

"Come on, sleepyhead, time to get up and at them," Daisy said in her usual cheerful tones, as she entered Harriet's room and switched on the light. Harriet pulled her blanket over her head and turned to face the wall. "What do you want?" Harriet begged.

"It's morning."

"It's not."

"Don't be ridiculous. Get up; I've got some coffee for you."

"I don't like coffee."

"I know, but you need it."

"It gives me acid."

"You'll be fine once you get down to the dispersal. Besides, I brought some cream with it, that'll sort the acid." Harriet let out an angry groan and rolled onto her back.

"You know you're not making any friends around here, don't you?"

"Officers and Corporals aren't friends, Ma'am, I'm here to serve."

"Very well, servant, go fly my Spitfire for me while I go back to sleep."

"If only," Daisy replied as she put the coffee on the dresser, then whipped off Harriet's blanket in one sharp move. "Up and at 'em, the Germans won't shoot themselves down."

"If I'm lucky they'll shoot me down," Harriet said as she swung her legs out of bed.

"Don't talk like that!"

"Why? At least I'll get some rest and won't have you nagging me every morning." She stood and drank the coffee, screwing her eyes tight as she did, then went into the bathroom to splash herself with some cold water. She was soon as awake as she could be at that time and heading out, ready for her morning blast on her Harley, though the air coming through her window was heavy and humid, so she wasn't expecting it to rouse her that much.

"Hey," Daisy said as she left. Harriet turned to look at the petite blonde Corporal. "You be careful."

"I'm always careful."

"I mean it!" Daisy barked. Harriet smirked and closed the door behind her, then headed to dispersal for their morning brief.

The weather was forecast to be clear and hot, much to the disappointment of the pilots, most of whom were hoping for the type of rain and high winds that would put the Germans off for a day and let them rest. Once the briefing was complete, the usual routine commenced, and after checking over her Spitfire, Harriet slumped into her chair next to Max and pulled her flying jacket over her as a blanket. It was too warm to wear the jacket, even at that time in the morning. Instead she opted to fly in her tunic, blouse, and silk scarf, without her heavy and hot Irvin jacket, which she'd stopped wearing for sorties a few days earlier after almost melting during a patrol under the afternoon sun. She'd been nervous about ditching her jacket at first, due to Cas' warnings in France and her experience with the burning Hurricane, but the Spitfire was an entirely different animal to the Hurricane, it was aluminium, not canvas, and rarely burned anything like a Hurricane. Sleep was disrupted for a while as IT led A Flight in the morning exercises which he'd insisted were good for waking them ahead of combat. B Flight refused bluntly to play the game, smug under the protection of their confident American Flight Commander, and Harriet had been left alone since day one. Cas had one of his 'words to the wise' with IT about not bothering the CO's number two, and IT had uncharacteristically obliged without argument. Though whether Cas was the reason for his compliance, or his wandering eyes, which he frequently cast over Harriet, was hotly debated by some in the squadron, a conversation which made her cringe. She and Max watched as IT shouted in the darkness, instructing his flight, and scolding them when they weren't quite as spritely as he was demanding. Jonny Isaac was catching most of his criticism. The young man had stepped forward and politely intervened in the Mess the previous evening when IT had tried to pester Harriet inappropriately. IT hadn't taken the intervention well and bawled Jonny out before storming out of the bar.

"Any more guys like that turn up, and I'm switching sides to the Luftwaffe," Max said under his breath.

"Is there anything normal about what he's doing?" Harriet asked, confused as to why a Flight Commander would make his exhausted pilots run and jump around in the dark before they'd even started their day.

"There ain't nothing normal about him, period," Max replied.

"Mister Oakley, a word if you will," Cas called from the dispersal hut. IT shuffled over as his pilots made their way to their deckchairs. He disappeared inside, and the door was closed.

"Coffee without biscuits," Max said.

"I'll give him coffee," Grumpy muttered. "If I'd wanted to play silly buggers like that I'd have stayed in the army."

As silence finally engulfed the dispersal, the pilots dropped off to sleep until woken by the arrival of breakfast. Harriet extracted her stiff muscles from the chair with a pull up from Max and made her way over to the folding table, which was loaded with bacon sandwiches and hot drinks. She took Daisy's advice and took a coffee with milk, then made a start on her sandwich. It woke her, slowly, but her muscles still ached. Over a week of being crammed into a Spitfire four or more times per day with muscles as tense as rock while flying in combat were taking their toll. The phone rang in the dispersal hut, and the chattering pilots fell into silence.

"Squadron scramble!" came the shout, followed by the ringing of the bell. Harriet put down her breakfast and started sprinting. Already the mighty Merlin engines were coughing into life as ground crews fired them up for their pilots. AP was already out of the cockpit when Harriet jumped in, and instinctively reached in and fastened her harness around her.

"Bring my aeroplane back!" she shouted with a smirk.

"It needs a few ventilation holes to help with the heat, but I'll see what I can do," Harriet replied with a wink. She pushed the throttle forward and followed Singh into position, then with a nod from her leader they bounced along the grass and climbed hard into the pale blue sky. The sun was golden and gleaming, and there wasn't a cloud in the sky. It was going to be a hard day with nowhere to hide if things went wrong, and the pilots were going to have to be at their very best if they were going to get through.

"Goose Squadron from Silver Control. Make angels one five and vector Dover, we've got some trade building up over the Channel," Control called.

"Roger, Silver Control," Singh replied. At that moment a stream of black smoke trailed from his engine and his Spitfire shuddered. "Damn it. My engine is playing up. Red One, take over," he instructed. "Red One!" he called again.

"He's not with us," Kiwi replied.

"Very well. Blue one, you take the lead. Harry, take over as red one, you know what to do." Harriet's heart raced, what was he doing, leaving her in charge of a flight? She panicked for a moment, then took a couple of deep breaths and calmed herself. She'd watched Singh lead the entire squadron more times than she could remember from right on his wing where she'd seen every move and manoeuvre.

"Yes, Sir!" IT replied confidently. Singh pulled up and away and dived back to the airfield while Harriet manoeuvred into position to lead A Flight.

"Kiwi, watch my back and stick to me like glue," she instructed.

"Got you, Red One," he replied.

"Cut the chatter, A Flight!" IT barked. Harriet found herself rolling her eyes while turning her head and searching for the enemy. "They're not here!" IT cursed as the squadron arrived over Dover.

"Dorniers, twelve o'clock low," Pops called. He was almost always the first to see the enemy. A product of his combat in Poland, he'd fought the Germans without the aid of radar and the observer corps to guide him into the fight, and quickly learned how to spot the enemy at a distance. Harriet snapped her eyes on the target to see a vee of three bombers speeding across the Channel towards Dover harbour.

"OK, Goose Squadron. Let's go and get them!" IT said.

"What about the fighters?" Harriet asked.

"What bloody fighters?" IT replied.

"Their escort. It's daylight. They won't have come alone!"

"Pipe down, red leader. There aren't any bloody fighters, and if you don't shut up, we'll miss the bombers!"

"Bloody amateur," an unknown voice muttered.

"Everybody just shut up!" IT screamed. "Goose Squadron, B Flight follow me, A Flight get on our tails. You can have any scraps after we've finished!" Harriet's heart was pounding with fear, her mouth was dry, and her stomach was sick; what they were doing was against every instinct she had. She needed to say something, to find some way of stopping the madness.

"Sir, with respect, shouldn't A Flight stay up here and watch out for the fighter escort? B Flight can easily deal with the bombers without us, and we can keep you covered."

"Red One, you're already facing a charge of insubordination, you either follow me now or I'll court martial you for cowardice in the face of the enemy!" he barked, then started a diving turn which the squadron followed dutifully. Harriet was both furious and terrified. She felt positive that she was doing the wrong thing but couldn't think of how she could stop IT from leading them into a long winding turn which would put their backs to the sun with no top cover. "They'll never see us coming out of the sun!" he laughed. "Come on, boys, let's show the Hun how it's done!"

"Keep your eyes open for fighters, A Flight," Harriet instructed.

"Shut up about the bloody fighters, red leader, and pay attention to what's in front of you!" She felt sweat starting to run down her back, while she tried to look in every direction for the fighters she was sure were there.

"What's in front could be a decoy!" Harriet protested.

"Don't be so bloody stupid. This is why women shouldn't fly fighters. You're too bloody scared of a good scrap! Fighting is a man's game, not something for frightened little girls!"

"Fighters coming down!" Dolph shouted.

"Goose Squadron, break, break, break!" Harriet yelled. She pulled up hard with Kiwi on her wing, just in time to see a blast of tracer zip underneath her. The 109s were among them before anything could be done, diving out of the sun having watched the Spitfires turn away from them and chase the decoy bombers, just as Harriet had expected them

269

to. A Flight had responded instantly and broke formation in every direction, but by the time Harriet and Kiwi had turned hard out of harm's way and come back into position to attack the 109s, she counted four B Flight Spitfires streaming down towards the Channel in smoke and flames. They hadn't stood a chance. Harriet turned as hard as she could without blacking out and got on the tail of a 109 which was chasing a rolling and spinning Spitfire. She moved close enough to see the rivets and gave him a blast, shooting off his right wing which sent the 109 spiralling downwards. The fight was hard. Kiwi pulled around to shoot a German off Harriet's tail, clipping his wings and sending him home trailing black smoke. By the time Harriet was able to compose herself to look around, the battle had passed. The bombers had unloaded their deadly cargo over the harbour, smoke was climbing into the sky, and they were heading home with their fighter escort. It had been two minutes at the most since the German fighters had sprung their trap, and the fight was already over. "Goose Squadron, pancake," Harriet instructed. "Keep your eyes open, Kiwi, let's go through the gate and climb high, and make sure nobody follows us home."

"Got it," he replied and followed her as she pushed the throttle to maximum power and led her number two up high, where she had good visibility of the few Spitfires she could see below, hedge hopping their way home.

"Two o'clock, church steeple," she called.

"Yeah, I can see the bastard," Kiwi replied as he saw the 109 flying at low level and stalking a smoking Spitfire.

"Good. Go and get him, I'll watch your back."

"Roger, Goose Leader," he replied. Even in the pitched battle, she felt herself smile at hearing that response. She followed him down in a screaming interception dive.

"Don't overshoot," she advised. "You're coming in hot. Give yourself space to pull up after giving him a squirt!" Kiwi lined up perfectly and

270

held his thumb on the fire button, letting stream after stream of tracer cut through the 109, almost pushing it flat into the ground in a fiery explosion. It was done. "Good shooting, Kiwi, let's head home." The pair did a final sweep of the area, then sat high above the airfield while watching the remaining Spitfires come home and making sure no more 109s were stalking for an easy kill. The adrenaline was still coursing through her veins as she counted the squadron in. Of the fourteen scrambled only thirteen got off the ground, then Singh had to turn back with engine trouble leaving twelve Spitfires. Of those twelve she counted five home, making seven survivors including her and Kiwi. Five valuable aeroplanes and their even more valuable pilots lost in two minutes. "OK, you head in," she instructed. Kiwi complied immediately, and as soon as she was sure he was safe, she started her own descent. She gave the sky a thorough scanning before lining up for her final approach, lowering her flaps, dropping her undercarriage, then bumping along the ground towards the dispersal. The engine had only just cut when she was out of her seat and climbing onto the wing, having unfastened her harness as she taxied.

"Harry..." AP said as Harriet ran past her and off the wing, ignoring her with her eyes full of fury. "Harry!" AP called as she ran after her, knowing from her face and demeanour that there was something very wrong.

"Coward!" she shouted at IT, who was standing talking to Singh, Max, and Cas, all of whom were looking very perplexed. Cas recognised what was happening and tried to move to stop it, but he was too late. As soon as IT turned to see what the bluster was about, she landed a haymaker punch right on his nose, crushing it into his face and sending out a spray of blood. He staggered backwards with a yelp, while Max instinctively grabbed Harriet. He was using every inch of his broad six feet two frame to hold her back and stop her killing IT, who had steadied himself and was in the process of launching himself forward at Harriet. Cas stepped in his way and drove his fist into the pit of IT's stomach, winding him and making him drop to his knees and vomit.

"Enough!" Singh shouted. "I'll not have my officers brawl like common drunks!"

"He killed them! The incompetent, useless, ignorant, bastard!" Harriet shouted, while still trying to wrestle herself past Max to get her hands on IT again.

"Remember, you're a lady!" Singh warned. "And an officer in the Royal Air Force!" she gasped and tried to calm herself while Max held her tight to try and soothe her. "My office, all of you!" Singh marched into the dispersal hut and into his office. Cas pulled IT up roughly by his collar, while Max released Harriet from his grip and put his hands on her shoulders.

"Look at me," he said quietly. "Hey, look at me," he repeated as he drew her snarling attention from IT. "You OK?" She shook her head, then nodded, then felt tears from her eyes and furiously wiped them away.

"He led us into a trap," she said. "He killed five of our pilots because he wouldn't listen."

"OK, come on. Let's go inside and let the skipper sort this out," he said. She nodded and walked at his side toward the dispersal hut. "Whatever happens, bite your tongue and don't punch anyone!" She nodded and wiped her tears before taking her place beside the snivelling IT in front of Singh's desk. Cas was standing by Singh with an angry frown on his face, something Harriet hadn't seen before, and something that made her nervous. Max closed the door and stood silently by it.

"Do you care to explain what that was all about, Miss Cornwall?" Singh asked Harriet.

"She assaulted a superior officer!" IT blurted out from under the handkerchief he was using to try and stem the flow of blood from his now very swollen nose. "I want her charged with assault and insubordination, and put in front of a court martial for cowardice in the face of the enemy!"

272

"I'm not talking to you, Mister Oakland. Unless you've changed gender all of a sudden, or that punch has rattled your head enough to forget yourself."

"Sir..." he muttered.

"Well, Miss Cornwall?"

"I'm sorry, Sir. I've got no excuse for my behaviour," Harriet replied with genuine remorse.

"I never asked you to excuse your behaviour. I asked you to explain what that little display was all about. If one of my junior officers attacks one of my Flight Commanders so violently, I have a right to know why."

"Yes, Sir. It's simple, really," she started.

"Good, it shouldn't be so difficult for you to tell me, in that case."

"Mister Oakley ignored protocol and training, and led the entire squadron into a dive against three enemy bombers without giving any consideration to their fighter escort."

"There were no bloody fighters!" IT complained.

"Then what the hell shot down five of our bloody Spitfires?" Harriet raged, immediately escalating. Max's warning rang in her head and she clenched her fists tight to stop herself lashing out again.

"So, Mister Oakley, what did shoot down five of my Spitfires?"
"Messerschmitts, Sir. 109s. They came out of the sun, and we didn't even see them until it was too late. It was impossible even to know they were there."

"Impossible?"

273

"Yes, Sir. The sky was clear, and instead of being helpful, this young Officer was awkward and obstructive to the mission, then refused to engage the enemy when ordered." A knock at the door disturbed the conversation.

"What?" Singh demanded sharply. The door opened, and The Spy popped his head around the door.

"Ah, Sir, I wonder if I might have a moment of your time?"

"Not now, I'm a little busy. Can't it wait until later?"

"Not really, Sir. You see, I think it may relate to what you're busy with..."

Singh stood, clearly frustrated, and marched out of the room, slamming the door behind him hard enough to make Harriet jump. It felt like an age while he was out of the room. Nobody spoke, and nobody moved, except for IT, who whimpered from time to time as he pushed his handkerchief to his nose. Singh returned after a while and sat behind his desk, then stared at the pair in front of him.

"The pilots have reported their action to our intelligence officer, and they tell a slightly different story regarding the events," he started. "It would appear, from their unanimously agreed reports at least, that Miss Cornwall sought to advise and support you several times. Even offering to fly cover while you made your attack on the bombers when it was not possible to see if any enemy fighters were hiding in the sun. In fact, it's the general consensus that had Miss Cornwall not called the break when the fighters were reported; we'd have lost the entire squadron..."

"Nonsense!" IT blustered.

"Excuse me?"

"That's not how it happened! She ignored me and questioned me and refused to attack when I gave her a direct order. Those pilots are lying."

274

"And why would they do that?"

"Isn't it obvious? They're protecting her. They don't like it because a superior officer dared to challenge a girl, it makes them feel uncomfortable as men so they instinctively rush to protect her as they would a sister. It's exactly this reason women shouldn't fly! It destroys the cohesion of a fighting squadron." Another knock at the door stopped Singh from replying. He rolled his eyes in frustration.

"Yes?" he demanded. The door opened, and Group Captain Saltire walked in. Singh quickly stood smartly to attention. "Sorry, Sir. We weren't expecting you."

"Sit down, Mister Singh," Alastair waved his hand downwards while moving around the desk. "Mister Maxwell, Cas" he gave them both a brief nod. "Where did we get to?" he asked Singh.

"Sir?"

"I'm assuming these two officers are standing before you to explain what happened up there this morning?" The playful friendliness so often associated with his voice was noticeably absent, filling the room with a dark chill.

"Yes, Sir," Singh replied, a little surprised that the Station Commander could know what they'd been talking about.

"Good... And?"

"And Mister Oakley has accused the squadron pilots of lying in their combat reports to protect Miss Cornwall."

"Is that so?"

"It's true, Sir!" IT blustered.

275

"And what happened to your nose, Oakley?" Alastair asked

"She punched me!" He pointed at Harriet, who was doing her best to remain obedient and calm or at least appear that way.

"You're lucky she didn't shoot you out of the sky for what you just did, Oakley," Alastair said disapprovingly. Singh, Max, and Cas all raised their eyebrows in surprise. "Any decent Officer wouldn't have come back from such a comprehensive foul up. It would have cost us a Spitfire, but the price would have been worth every penny to erase some of the shame of leading five good pilots to their needless deaths."

"Sir, I protest! She..." Oakley started to bluster.

"Oh do be quiet, you thoroughly objectionable little man," Alastair said with a frown. "I've just had to sit with my operations team and listen to the entire bloody pantomime live over the airwaves. Frankly, you're an embarrassment as an officer and a failure as a gentleman. That young woman pleaded with you to let her do her job, and all you did was threaten and berate her. If you'd listened to her experience, you wouldn't have wiped out almost half a squadron in two minutes, you incompetent oaf, and don't even get me started on your feeble and pathetic attempts to lay the blame on her! Instead of being a man and owning your mistakes!" IT shook as he searched for words to defend himself, but there was no defending the indefensible. He'd got people killed and blamed it on somebody else, and there were witnesses. There was no coming back from that. "You're lucky she only broke your nose. In her place, I'd have taken you out back and shot you. Put you out of all our misery," Alastair continued, while Max bit his tongue to stop himself laughing, and Harriet frowned and opened her eyes wide in surprise as she listened to the Group Captain's words.

"What would you have me do with Mister Oakley, Sir?" Singh asked.

"I'm assuming you've got no reasonable defence for his actions, Squadron
Leader?"

"Absolutely none, Sir."

"Do you want to keep him?"

"Absolutely not, Sir."

"Good. Me neither." He turned back to Oakley, "I'm demoting you to the rank of Flying Officer, Mister Oakley, effective immediately."

"But Sir!" IT protested.

"Oh I wouldn't, Mister Oakley, not yet," Alastair warned with a smile as cold as ice. "I'm suspending you from all flying duties, effective immediately, and I'm placing you under Mess Arrest, effective immediately. You'll remain in your room pending transfer to the coldest, darkest, most miserable shit hole these isles possess; where you'll work in non flying duties awaiting your courts martial for dereliction of duties occasioning the loss of half a squadron of Spitfires, and you'll think yourself lucky. Once the AOC finds out what happened, you'll be lucky to avoid the firing squad! We're having a hard enough time keeping pace with Jerry trying to kill off our already scarce pilots, without fools like you getting in on the act. Now get out of my sight!" Oakley left the room, head bowed and nose still bleeding from Harriet's punch. "Now what to do with you, young lady?" Alastair barked, equally as gruffly and making her spine straighten with tension.

"I'm sorry, Sir, I know I behaved improperly, and my only excuse is that the situation got the better of me. I acted without thinking, and I won't do it again."

"Raj, do you mind if I make an observation?" Alastair asked, a hint of playful warmth returning to his voice.

"Not at all, Sir."

"Well it would appear that I've left you short of a Flight Commander, not long after you'd lost old Archie, who I believe is still in the hospital and not going anywhere soon?"

"That's right, Sir."

"Miss Cornwall. Are you prepared to accept my handling of this incident, and the subsequent recommendations, regardless of how onerous and objectionable?"

"Yes, Sir."

"Good. In that case, unless Squadron Leader Singh objects sufficiently, I'm promoting you to Flight Lieutenant." He looked at Singh with a mischievous smile, awaiting a response.

"I can't think of anyone better," Singh replied with a big smile. "If you can square it with the Air Ministry, I'd much rather have her than another unknown posted in. We've got some rebuilding to do, and a stranger may make that difficult."

"That's it settled, then. Don't worry about the Air Ministry. I'll talk to a friend of mine over there and make it all happen with ease. I'll have a word with the boss, too, I doubt he'll have a problem with it. Having talked with him about her several times I think he's quite a Harry fan anyway," Alastair turned back to Harriet. "Happy with that, Harry?"

"Sir?" she asked with a questioning frown.

"Don't look so disappointed old man. I'm certainly not giving you another bloody gong; you've got enough of those already, and it's starting to embarrass some of us." He gave her a wink and a healthy slap on the shoulder, which jarred her a little. "Right, I need to get back to Ops, we've got a battle to win. Raj, I'm standing your chaps down for an hour to pull yourselves together after this morning's charade, then you're back on standby. Group can't afford to have you sitting around licking your wounds. Gentlemen, Ma'am," he smiled as the room came to attention

278

as he opened the door. "Oh, Harry?" He turned and looked back in the office.

"Sir?"

"I think the drinks are on you tonight. Good show!" He winked and left, closing the door behind him

"Well that's that," Singh said. "Max, you're my senior Flight Commander. I want you to take A Flight. Harry, you'll look after B Flight. I'll get on the phone and see if Spanners can release any of the aeroplanes in for repair or maintenance, but for now, we'll go with what we've got. Pick your best three pilots for your flights for now. In the meantime, Cas will brief everyone on what's happening while I try and find out about our missing pilots. Any questions?"

"What am I supposed to do?" Harriet asked.

"Be a leader" Singh replied. "Put your aeroplanes in the right place at the right time, look after your pilots, and keep shooting down Germans. It's simple, really. Oh, and don't be afraid to be in charge, the pilots need you to lead them, they need to trust in you. Not that I think that'll be a problem. Cas will teach you the rest, with a little help from Max." He walked around the desk and offered his hand. "Congratulations, Harry. I think you've had the fastest promotion in the history of the RAF, but I wouldn't have agreed, and Groupie wouldn't have even suggested it, if we didn't think you could handle the job" She smiled nervously as they shook hands. Cas gave her a wink, and Max put his hand on her shoulder.

"Welcome to the dizzy heights of Flight Commander," he said as he walked her from the room, leaving Singh and Cas alone to discuss the morning's events for a moment.

"It doesn't feel like I should be congratulated," she said quietly, feeling quite conflicted at the almost dismissive nature of the senior officers towards their losses.

279

"That's one of the privileges of command, Harry. You get to bear the burden of loss in private. We've got a war to fight, and we're gonna lose a lot of close friends, I don't need to tell you that, but outwards we've got to keep it together. If we don't, we'll join them."

"It makes sense, I suppose."

"It's one of the only things that does right now. Don't let anything in that slows you down as a pilot or clouds your judgement as a leader. Save that for the right time."

"When's the right time?"

"When it's all over," he said firmly as they stepped outside into the sunshine, where the other pilots were drinking tea and talking amongst themselves. Harriet picked up the bacon sandwich she'd started before being scrambled and took a bite. It tasted surprisingly good; Archie was right about cold bacon.

"Good flying up there today, boss," Kiwi said as he joined Harriet and Max.

"Me?" Harriet replied. "You're the one who kept them off me, and your attack on that 109 was almost textbook, you couldn't have done it any better."

"Thanks, Harry, I appreciate that."

"Who did we lose?" Max asked.

"Sergeants Jones and Rudstone, along with Bryn North, Jonny Isaac, and Grumpy." Harriet's heart sank as she heard the last two names. Jones and Rudstone had joined the squadron when it returned from France and were popular and talented pilots, and Bryn North was a new Pilot Officer fresh from training who had arrived only a few days earlier. Grumpy and Jonny were hard to accept, though. When she'd first met

280

Jonny, she'd thought him a bit of a fool, but she'd warmed to him and realised what a genuinely nice person he was, something evidenced by the way he'd stood up to IT in the bar the previous evening. She thought of how he'd talked about his mother bringing him up properly, and how she'd be furious if she thought he was a womaniser, and she thought of how heartbreaking it was going to be when she got Cas' letter telling her that her gentle giant of a son was dead. Then there was Grumpy. A former soldier and Policeman, and other than Cas, by far the oldest member of the squadron, he'd earned his name Grumpy by being short and blunt with almost everyone he talked to, even his friends. He wasn't actually a miserable man, he just sounded it, but it had become something he enjoyed and being grumpy became part of his identity. He'd been kind to Harriet since they'd met in France when as a Sergeant he was the top pilot with the most kills in the whole squadron. He gave advice and tips and always kept an eye on Harriet even when she wasn't expecting him to. She'd miss them both. Her thoughts were disturbed by Cas, who gathered the squadron together and announced Harriet's promotion, something which was so well received that she found herself blushing when the pilots threw her in the air with rounds and rounds of cheers and singing. When the celebrations dulled, Singh rearranged the squadron, they had seven aeroplanes available and nine pilots, and Max and Harriet decided who they'd take. Harriet asked for Kiwi to fly as her number two, something both Kiwi and Max were very obliging with, and she managed to pick up Dolph while Murph went with Max. Pops, the Pole who'd been with the squadron since France, was asked to be Singh's number two. While flattered by the recognition, he was slightly irritated too. He'd always liked the idea of being a lone wolf, chasing Germans around the sky without worrying about anything else, but Singh needed him to learn to be a team player. Harriet also took Sergeant Newton, a quiet young man who'd been in the squadron since after France, and Max had taken Hugo, the French ace.

The rest of the day, the squadron went up four more times. Sometimes they came back to a bombed airfield as it was still unprotected while they flew, and it was taking damage which threatened to put it out of action altogether. This, of course, was precisely what the Luftwaffe wanted. If they launched their invasion while the RAF was still in the fight, their ships would be sunk before they made shore by both the bomber force and the Navy. If they could put air stations out of action, destroy the fighters, and push the rest of the RAF north of London, there would be no protection for the Royal Navy. The Luftwaffe could bomb them out of existence, and the invasion fleet could sail across the Channel with virtually no opposition. Despite the morning's disaster, the squadron fared better for the rest of the day, with only one damaged Spitfire for two kills and three probables. It didn't make the losses of the morning any easier to take, but it made them feel better that they didn't lose any more. The squadron was close to being ineffective as it was, and despite being exhausted, none of the pilots wanted to be withdrawn. Something that had happened to a nearby Hurricane squadron that had been totally clobbered and lost half its number in one action. It was so severely mauled that it was put out of the battle and sent north to regroup.

"I hear celebrations are in order," Daisy said with a smile when she greeted Harriet at the door to her room.

"I don't think I've got the energy," Harriet replied as she walked in, dropped her kit in a pile, then collapsed on her bed. "I'd rather just sleep."

"Don't be silly. Promotion to Flight Lieutenant and appointed Flight Commander? That don't happen often, so it'll be a wild one tonight."

"Oh God..."

"I've run you a bath. Why don't you get in and have a soak, and I'll get your things ready? You've got a few hours so no need to rush."

"What would I do without you?" Harriet groaned as she dragged herself up and pulled off her clothes.

"You couldn't do without me."

"Just leave my things, I'll pick them up after my bath."

"Of course I won't," Daisy replied. Harriet rolled her eyes and stepped into the bathroom, then climbed into the luxuriously hot bath and promptly fell asleep. "What are you doing? You're due in the bar!" Daisy said as she entered the bathroom.

"What?" Harriet mumbled as she sat up. In her mind, she'd only just closed her eyes, but she soon realised the water was cold and her neck was stiff. Daisy handed her a towel and left her underwear on the shelf. When she'd towelled off and pulled on her underwear, she went through to her room. Hanging on the locker door was her tunic, cleaned and with new rank braid sewn onto her sleeve. "How did you do that?" she asked.

"Cas gave me some braid and asked me to sew it on for you. Can't have you going to the party incorrectly dressed, you'll get punishment drinks as a fine."

"I'm not sure I like this aspect of RAF life," Harriet frowned as she dressed.

"Rather be shot at by Germans, would you?"

"Much."

"I bet. I heard about what you did to that arse IT today."

"He deserved it. Besides, I only bloodied his nose. I'd have done more if Max hadn't stopped me."

"You did more than that. Simon checked him over, and he's got a broken nose and fractured cheek like he'd been hit in the face with a shovel."

"That actually makes me feel better," Harriet said with a smile. Daisy helped straighten her tie and tidy her hair, then she left and headed down to the bar where things rapidly got out of control with drinking, singing, and rough games of Mess rugby.

"Where the hell have you been?" Cas demanded loudly during a lull in the chaos, and the entire bar turned to look at the door.

"Learning to swim..." Grumpy said as he walked in, still dripping wet, and carrying his wet parachute under his arm. "Brandy please, Dickie, and make it a large one!" The barman presented him with a large brandy as requested, which he savoured for a moment, smelled, then downed in one before tapping it on the bar. "Fill her up again."

"Did you get one?" Max asked.

"All I got was a belly full of English Channel," came the reply. "Hence, the need for good brandy." The bar erupted in cheers and Grumpy was dragged into the party.

The following days continued in the same vein, though one of them was a washout due to weather, which meant the squadron didn't fly at all and were stood down early. Such an occurrence would usually result in a party, but the pilots were so exhausted they agreed on a rare night off the booze. Harriet herself indulged in a long bath before crawling into bed and sleeping through. Time and again the squadron was called up, either by flights or full squadron scrambles and each time they went up, it felt like they were hitting stronger and stronger opposition. If it wasn't out over Dover and the Channel, they were out over the south coast as the Luftwaffe tried to bypass the squadrons based inland and sneak around to attack Southampton and other targets, including the Supermarine factory. Through it, all the squadron's tally climbed steadily, and Harriet became a trusted and respected leader, and all the time they didn't lose one more aeroplane. They were still tired, but they were confident. The engineering team worked hard to get aeroplanes back online, and Group Captain Saltire did his best to make sure replacements were requested, and arrived. By the last days of August the squadron was functioning at full strength again, though many of the pilots still didn't have the experience needed to make the Squadron fully effective.

Chapter 12

Silk

As summer faded into autumn, the Squadron found themselves in the centre of increasingly heavy fighting, which saw ever larger formations of a hundred or more German bombers and fighters attacking RAF airfields from London to the south coast. Hitting most of them at least once, and pushing some so close to being unusable that their squadrons had to fly from satellite fields until repairs had been done and they could return home. Harriet was now operating on autopilot as far as her morning routine was concerned. Daisy would come in before first light, and Harriet would sit up, drink her coffee, wash in cold water, then dress before heading to the squadron dispersal on her Harley. She'd be briefed, she'd brief her flight, check her aeroplane, make sure all of her pilots had what they needed, then slump in her deckchair and sleep until they were called up to patrol or to intercept, or breakfast came. When she was stood down, she'd spend time with Cas, learning and studying everything there was to know about the RAF and leadership.

During one of the many early morning patrols across the south coast, the Squadron ran into a small bomber raid of just a handful of Stukas escorted by a swarm of over a hundred fighters, but Silver Control diverted the Squadron back home to land and refuel instead of sending them in a head to head battle with overwhelming numbers of German fighters, especially when it was bombers they needed to stop. It was frustrating for the pilots. They wanted to get up and get in the fight, but despite being called up three times before lunch, they were still to get any action. The heat was rising, as was the humidity, and by mid afternoon the skies were clear, except for a haze out over the Channel, and up the Thames estuary.

"Have you got a minute?" AP asked as she stood over Harriet's deckchair. "Hey, wake up!" She kicked the leg and Harriet jumped. She was startled and quickly looked around, expecting to see pilots running for their Spitfires, having been dragged from a dream about sitting in her chair and missing a scramble call.

"What do you want?" she asked with a frown, reversing the roles of their first meeting in France several months earlier, when she'd taken AP some Champagne and chocolate and offered to help her fix a Merlin engine.

"You, if you've got a couple of minutes to spare from your busy life of sleeping?" Harriet nodded, and AP pulled her from her chair.

"What's up?" Harriet asked as she tried to shake the tiredness from her brain while they walked.

"My orders have arrived."

"What do you mean?"

"I'm finally leaving for flight training."

"What? That's great! When do you leave?"

"Today, the orders just came through. I'm on a train this afternoon to get there tonight and start tomorrow."

"Today? That's not fair..."

"I know..."

"I was hoping we'd be able to have a party."

"Is that all?"

"No... I was hoping to say goodbye properly. I'm going to miss you. You're one of the oldest friends I've got."

"We've only known each other a few months..."

286

"I know. That's what makes it even harder."

"I'll write."

"I hope you do. I will miss you a lot. The Squadron treat me like family, but you're different."

"If it helps to know, I'm terrified."

"What can you possibly have to be terrified of?"

"Being able to actually do it, now I'm here. I've wanted it for so long that I don't want to mess it up. You've set a pretty high bar for us girls, you know?"

"You'll do it, and you'll do it better than me or anyone else. You're the most focused person I know. You can't fail."

"Thanks..."

"You're welcome. Here." Harriet reached down and pulled the holster containing the German Major's Walther pistol from the top of her flying boot. She'd carried it on every operational flight since the Germans had overrun the airfield in France, worried about what she'd face if she was shot down, and desperate to have a way of defending herself. She handed it to AP "Look after it for me."

"I can't!" AP protested.

"You can. You have to. You can look at it if you ever doubt yourself, and remember that I shot down a German ace on my first Hurricane flight to get it, and you've got to do better..." AP shoved her, and they both laughed.

"But it's yours…"

287

"If I need it to defend myself while flying over England, things have got worse than anyone dare imagine." AP smiled and looked at the pistol. "You're going to be an awesome pilot. You'll be the best in the RAF, you'll see. Have you told your parents yet?"

"Not yet," AP shook her head as she put the pistol away. "I didn't dare, in case the RAF changed their minds."

"They won't. Take a photo as soon as you're there and send it to them. They'll love it."

"Actually, I was hoping we could have a photo together before I left. I borrowed a camera from The Spy?" She held up a black and silver camera. Harriet nodded, and they grabbed one of the passing fitters to take a photo of them together, with the Squadron's Spitfires scattered behind them in the near distance.

"You'll send me a copy?"

"If you want one?"

"Of course I want one!"

"Squadron scramble!" a voice yelled from dispersal. Harriet's heart fluttered, and her stomach squeezed. The bell rang, and Harriet pulled herself away.

"Go get 'em!" AP shouted. Harriet waved her hand as she ran, feeling herself smile as she approached her Spitfire and bounced up the wing. Lanky had leapt out just seconds before after starting the engine, having volunteered to do the job as there was no way Corporal Holland was getting himself out of the cockpit quick enough. Four hands reached in and strapped her in.

"Clear!" Harriet shouted, and Lanky and Holland jumped from the wings while she looked around, gave her flight the nod, then opened the throttle and started taxiing. They were soon in the air and formed up to the right of Singh.

"Goose Squadron, Silver Control, make angels one five and vector Dungeness."

"Roger, Silver Control," Singh replied.

"Look out for Hurricanes joining you."

"Understood. Goose Squadron, climb to angels one five and keep your eyes open." The Squadron climbed hard and soon arrived at fifteen thousand feet. As they levelled off, Harriet found herself scanning the horizon and above for signs of the enemy, while encouraging her Flight to do the same as they approached the hazy coast around Dungeness.

"Hurricanes low, port and starboard," Grumpy called. Harriet looked around to see a squadron of Hurricanes each side of them about five thousand feet lower. She smiled. Usually, they were sent up in squadron strength at the most, and only a handful of times had they met with another squadron, but never more. Three Squadrons going together was something unheard of, she counted thirty eight fighters in all. It was going to be a nasty surprise for the German raid they were heading to intercept.

"Eyes forward, Goose Squadron, there they are," Singh called. The sky ahead was full. Over one hundred bombers of different types, escorted by a similar number of fighters approaching in layers, a squadron every couple of thousand feet stacked high to twenty five thousand feet. There'd be no avoiding the fighters this time. No matter what they did there'd be at least one more Squadron of German fighters able to come down from above, so Singh made the only decision he could. "Line abreast, Goose Squadron." The fighters stretched out in their pairs. "Let's hit them head on, and see if we can break up the attack and give the Hurricanes something to do. On my mark, get through the gate and keep up. Three, two, one, mark!" Harriet pushed her throttle forward and through the wire gate to get the maximum boost from the roaring Merlin engine.

"A Flight, pick a target and hit it hard, then over the top and hit the next wave," Harriet instructed. "Watch for the fighters, they'll drop on us in no time, and don't stay among the bombers or they'll cut you to pieces." She lined up on her chosen bomber and kept an eye on it while intermittently checking on the German fighters, which hadn't yet started their dive. The bomber closed quickly and soon filled her sights, and Harriet pushed the fire button at the same time as the rest of the Squadron. Twelve Spitfires with eight machine guns each, and all were firing at the same time. A bridge of ninety six streams of white smoke spanned the sky between the fighters and bombers in a beautifully deadly display of death. The cockpit of Harriet's target flashed as her incendiary and armour piercing bullets ripped through the metal fittings, sparking and ricocheting, and cutting the crew to ribbons. The nose immediately dipped, and Harriet pulled back on the stick to hop over the tail and avoid a head on collision. Immediately she set her sights on the following bomber in the next wave, opening fire from a distance and raking its right wing with explosive bullets, which wrecked the engine and made it splutter black smoke. The first fighters were diving, given away by the stream of tracer that passed along her left side. The bomber formation splintered in different directions as a 110 fighter shot down in front of Harriet. She flipped her Spitfire on its back, pulled back on the stick and dropped into a sharp dive which narrowly avoided another bomber and followed the 110. A stream of bullets flew from the tail gunner and more tracer came down from the next wave of bombers, forcing her to push her stick over hard and roll to avoid being shot out of the sky. Leaving the 110, which was now far out of reach, she centred her stick and pulled it back into her stomach, only just steadying herself and getting her vision straight when the bottom of a bomber passed overhead. She pushed her fire button and watched as her bullets scraped along the fuselage as she pulled away to avoid it, and the 110 coming the other way. She broke through the remains of the scattering bomber formation and then realised the seriousness of her position. The sky above was black with 110s and 109s, all diving down on the battle, and she knew if she continued her climb, she'd be knocked down in seconds, but if she turned

290

and dived, they'd be on her tail, and she'd be a sitting duck. A quick glance around and she locked her eyes on a bomber rapidly banking hard to turn home as it trailed black smoke from its port engine. She pulled out of her climb and aimed for it, not to shoot it, but to use its hull to shield herself from the diving fighters. The rear gunner fired and left a line of bullet holes along her left wing, but she stayed on course and tucked in underneath the bomber, as close as she dared, as it continued its wide turn, making sure the diving fighters would have to shoot it down to get to her, or level out and change direction, which would give her a better chance to escape. To her relief, the fighters flew past in a wave while she held her position. The airwaves were noisy with warnings and shouts as the pilots fought their way through an increasingly chaotic battle. A quick spin of her head showed a 109 turning in to get on Harriet's tail, she dipped away from the bomber then pulled into a turn, shallow at first to bring the 109 closer, then tightening and tightening, knowing a Spitfire could out turn a 109. Once she'd reeled him in, she flew so tight her eyesight dimmed to a tiny cone of light, but she had him within a couple of turns and put a stream of bullets into him. The 109 immediately started trailing white smoke and dived, leaving Harriet breathing hard and dripping with sweat as she climbed steeply and scanned the sky. The battle was raging across many miles. Some of the more committed German bomber pilots were approaching the coast around Dungeness, only to face what looked like a third squadron of Hurricanes charging up to greet them. Behind them was a trail of chaos stretching back almost as far as the French coast. Bombers were twisting, turning, and running for home, while others smashed into the sea and raised huge plumes of white spray hundreds of feet into the air. 109s and 110s were all around them, dancing with Hurricanes and Spitfires, all of which were scrapping to knock the bombers down and stop them getting inland to smash the RAF stations. A pair of Spitfires were out to the east in the middle of a whole mess of 109s, twisting and turning, desperately trying to escape. Harriet checked behind her, then opened her throttle and headed down, ignoring the many raging battles taking place all around as aeroplanes of both sides fought, ran, and died around her. She dipped under a Hurricane in pursuit of a bomber and fixed her sights on the tail of the rearmost 109 chasing her squadron mates. As she got closer she realised from their identification letters it was Max and Murph who were under attack. Max's Spitfire was already trailing a thin smudge of dark smoke, and the longer he twisted and turned to avoid the fighters, the less chance he had of getting back over land before his engine either burst into flames or seized. Harriet got close and let the nearest 109 have a blast, shattering parts off the fuselage and making it peel away from the battle. She carried on and put more bullets into the next, hitting the fuel tanks and exploding it into a fiery ball, which shook his comrades enough to break their attack on Max and Murph and splinter in every direction. Just a pair remained, committed to chasing tight on their tail. "Max, it's Harry, on my mark you and Murph pull hard right. Three, two, one, now!" Max did as he was told and pulled the 109s right across Harriet's nose. She put a stream of bullets into the first, making him break away to the left, followed by his comrade, leaving Max and Murph clear. Max's engine was spluttering smoke, and he was running slow when he straightened out. Murph wasn't much better, the left tip of his wing had been cut off, and half of his tail was missing. She lined up beside them briefly.

"Thanks, Harry! My engine has almost had it; I'm flying at half power and don't know how long I have left," Max said.

"Get back over land, head home."

"I don't have a choice."

"Good. Murph, sit on his wing and get him back through that mess, and keep the Huns off him! I'll give you both a head start." She pulled back on her stick and into a loop after seeing the 109s start to reform, ready to come back for another go at the two badly mauled Spitfires.

"Got it, Harry," Murph replied.

"Harry, no!" Max shouted.

"Go!" she yelled in reply. "I'll be right behind you, now go!" Executing the perfect Immelmann turn, she rolled off the top of her loop and was facing the group of five 109s starting to give chase in a loose pair of pairs with one out in front. Her mouth was as dry as sand, as was her throat, and she licked at the sweat running down her face to try and get the smallest amount of moisture to stop her throat closing altogether. The only way she could think of that would split them up and stop them flying after Max and Murph, was to go straight at them, but she knew that if she did, they'd simply knock her out of the sky. In a moment of madness, she found herself smiling as she pushed the throttle through the gate once more and took her engine to maximum power, then as she closed to within firing range she pushed her fire button. She pulled her stick hard over, starting a tight, fast, dizzying, blinding, spinning roll towards the 109s. Her bullets spun a cone of glowing tracer and white trails which crisscrossed as she rolled and sent bullets in the direction of the centre three 109s. The Germans must have thought she was insane. Her bullets hit the leader on the nose and sent him straight down, while the other four split left and right in two pairs, climbing hard and turning out of danger. Harriet stopped firing, slowed the spin, and pulled the stick into her stomach to put her into a hard climb that made her stomach feel like it was going to come out of her mouth. The 109s quickly converged on her and followed behind in the climb, filling the air around her with tracer. She spun onwards to avoid the bullets until she felt her speed scrubbing off fast. She prepared herself as a stream of bullets rattled off her engine cowling and sparked off the exhaust stubs. The familiar shake of an approaching stall shook the cockpit, and she closed the throttle and timed her kick of the rudder bar for the second the stall dropped the wing. In her trademark move, she stall turned and flipped the tail over her head and found herself staring at four angry 109s, the lead of which was firing, and his bullets rattled into her engine. She fired, pushing the button hard and watching as her last one second of ammunition was spent returning the favour, and wrecking the German's engine. She rolled through them and clattered one with her wing, taking the tip off hers in the process. Her engine seized, and she fell like a rock, there was no recovering, no turning, and no forced landing, not in the sea with half a wing and no engine. There was nothing for it, she was going to have to jump, but she couldn't even pull the Spitfire level so she could roll and drop, the stick was dead and she was going straight down. She took a deep breath, pulled off her helmet and mask, then ripped open her canopy, unfastened her harness, and nothing. She was hoping the air

293

would simply pull her out, but it didn't. She grabbed hold of the frame close to the mirror and pulled, then flew out like a cork, flying directly backwards and tumbling past where the tail of her Spitfire used to be. Now it was no more than a stump, shot away, mercifully, and saving her from killing herself in a collision with it as many on both sides had done when escaping. She didn't escape entirely unscathed; her left cheek connected with the remains of the tail and whipped her head back while her shoulder crashed against the rear stabiliser and sent her spinning and twisting through the air. She flipped and spun until finally finding the D ring of her ripcord under her armpit and tugging on it hard. To her horror, nothing happened. It felt like she was destined to die, and for a few short seconds, she just closed her eyes and waited for the inevitable to happen. In a moment of calm and clarity remembered Cas' words. 'If it doesn't open, wrap the rope around your wrist and pull it again!' She opened her eyes and did it. The parachute flew from its pack, and she was jerked up roughly and violently as she was slowed, then suddenly she was surrounded by peace and quiet as she floated down on the warm breeze. A 109 circled her from a distance. The pilot saluted before turning and heading east. She planned to give Max and Murph a head start, and she was quite confident she'd done that, something confirmed by the 109 circling her and not chasing them west. She hadn't let them down, and that's all that was important to her. She was left with the nagging thought that she hadn't seen much else of the squadron, and certainly none of her own flight. How many of them had got through, and how many had she failed to look after? Her thoughts were driven out of her fuddled mind as she hit the sea with a heavy splash before disappearing under the tranquil surface. Her lungs filled with saltwater as she yelled, then struggled madly as the parachute came down on top of her, making it almost impossible to surface properly. The riser lines from the parachute entangled her limbs, and she started to panic. She grabbed at the inflation toggle of her Mae West and pulled hard. It quickly inflated and pulled her up to the surface where the wet parachute pulled tight around her head and forced her mouth open, stretching it wide and allowing a trickle of salt water to seep in, forcing her to close her throat and try to cough it out to stop herself from drowning slowly. She struggled to move her hands to her face, but the more she struggled, the tighter the parachute lines became around her arms and legs until she was hardly able to move at all, and facing the terrifying prospect of slowly drowning. Her mind spun. From nowhere, she faced memories, visions, very clear and vivid pictures of floating in the sea having been torpedoed. She remembered the face of the sailor who'd saved her, and the sound of his voice as he talked to her and sang songs; while desperately trying to keep her engaged and stop her dying. The last of the air in her lungs was bursting to get out, and her mouth was almost full of seawater, she held as long as she could before coughing the water out. More water immediately ran into her throat, and this time there was no air holding it out. Drowning had always been Harriet's biggest fear, and after all that she'd been through in the air and on the land, it was being trapped under her own parachute in the English Channel which was going to do for her; and it made her angry. One last struggle to break free and the water seeped into her lungs. The anger was quickly overwhelmed by her fear as she convulsed, then a glimmer of hope crept in as a shadow loomed over the white parachute. The silk and her hair were grabbed tight together, and her head was lifted above the surface, while simultaneously the parachute silk covering her mouth ripped. With another tug, it was pulled from her face, and she was looking into the piercing blue eyes of a dark haired and lightly tanned German pilot sitting in a yellow life raft and holding a large knife above her. She stared at him and waited for the blade to be pushed down into her chest or run across her throat. She struggled again, but her arms and chest were so tight they'd hardly move.

"Stay still, English, or you'll drown. Ja?" he barked. She nodded and watched as he cut the ropes from around her neck and shoulders, which instantly reduced the tightness in her arms. As the German worked his knife through the ropes, she reached under the strangely green water and pulled her bindings away until finally she could reach the harness and release it. He grabbed her by the collar, turned her, then pulled her into his small life raft. She let out a gasp and clutched at her shoulder, which felt like a hot knife had been pushed in underneath the muscle, then she laid back beside him and gasped for air while coughing water from her lungs, as her boots trailed in the Channel.

"Why is the water green?" she asked as she looked around, asking the first question that came to her mind. She frowned and bit her lip at the pain in her shoulder, which was now throbbing in waves of burning heat.

"Emergency dye," he replied, as he pushed his knife back into the scabbard in his boot. "So our rescue aeroplanes can find us."

"Thank you," she said as she calmed her breathing. "For rescuing me, I mean."

"I wanted to see the face of the pilot who shot me out of the sky."

"Sorry..." Harriet replied meekly. She grabbed at her shoulder again as she talked. Now she was no longer drowning she was aware it was bothering her more and more as a result of the collision with the rear of her Spitfire, and she was finding it difficult to clench a fist or even move her arm. Her bruised cheek was a long way down the list of concerns.

"You're as sorry as I am for shooting you down," he laughed as he sat back in the small dinghy beside Harriet, hanging his feet in the water as they shared the narrow space. "You're a good pilot. Though a little crazy, I think. Stall turning onto chasing fighters isn't something intelligent people do."

"It was either that, or let you shoot me down."

"Desperation, yes?"

"I suppose... You speak good English."

"Thank you. I lived for two years in England. Do you speak German?"

"Only French, sorry." She put a handful of cold water to her face, especially her sore left cheek.

"Maybe you'll now have time to learn?"

"Maybe..."

"You're a good pilot. Why didn't you turn and run with your friends when you had the chance?"

"They were both damaged, and you wouldn't have let them get back to England."

"This is true. It is not good for us to let pilots go, only to have to fight them again tomorrow. It was still a very noble thing you did, sacrificing your own return."

"I didn't sacrifice myself."

"Then what would you call it?"

"Giving them a head start."

"You can't tell me that you expected to hold off five of us, and still hope to escape?"

"I actually expected to shoot a few of you down before escaping," she replied with a forced smile of resignation.

"Ha! I like you!" he laughed, then reached inside his jacket and pulled out a metal tin, from which he pulled a small cigar and storm lighter. "Would you like one?" He offered the tin. Harriet shook her head and smiled politely. He lit the cigar and put his tin away safe before relaxing back into his raft. Harriet held her shoulder and thought through her actions. Should she have run? Could she have out turned them and ran them around before escaping? "That's an interesting scarf you're wearing, Miss?"

"Cornwall," Harriet replied, turning and half smiling, still with resignation at her position. "Flight Lieutenant Harry Cornwall." She kept it simple, remembering Cas' instructions on what was and wasn't OK to tell the enemy, should she ever be unfortunate enough to fall into their hands, and that's something she'd done almost literally.

"Major Dieter Beck. It's a pleasure to meet you at last, Harry." Harriet's stomach squeezed, and a chill went up her spine as she looked him in the eyes. "Oh, don't be so surprised, there's nothing sinister. One of my Flight Commanders made you famous in our Squadron. Apparently, you and he shared a French prison cell for a short while earlier this year after you'd shot him down; something you seem to have a habit of doing to pilots from my Squadron." She frowned as she thought back, then remembered her escapade with the French General. A slight smile crept onto her face.

"How is he?"

"He's doing well."

"How did you know it was me? There are lots of pilots in the RAF."

"Not many that are girls who wear the silk Bavarian neck scarf that was hand made for a very good friend of mine, who I'm told you also shot down?"

"Sorry..." She smiled.

"Though I thought you were English, not Norwegian," he pointed his cigar at her shoulder flash. "I doubt that you are sorry, though, I wouldn't be. How are your face and arm?" He pointed to her, again with his cigar.

"They're OK," she replied. "Thank you again for helping me. I thought I was going to drown."

"Me too. You were unlucky to be caught in your parachute when you landed. The smart thing to do is release your harness a metre or two from the water. It reduces the chances of drowning."

298

"Thank you. I'll try and remember that for next time."

"It surprises me you don't have a life raft like mine."

"Me too..." She frowned. "And I've no idea why I don't."

"Maybe you'd have been better joining the Luftwaffe when you left Norway, instead of the RAF. You'd have been safer!" he laughed again. "You should ask for a transfer."

"What happens now?" Harriet asked, ignoring his teasing and laughing.

"You see over there?" He pointed to the land a few miles to their right.

"Yes?"

"That's the French coast, it's five kilometres away, maybe a little less. My comrades noted our position and a rescue aeroplane will be here soon to collect us, and then we'll go to my airfield which is just a few hundred metres inland." Harriet slumped, resigned to her capture. She thought of jumping off the raft for a moment and trying to swim back to England, but her shoulder was so sore she knew that she wouldn't get far. "Don't be so despondent, at least you're alive," he continued. She nodded and shrugged. It was better than drowning.

The two talked for over an hour. The Major talked about his home in the Bavarian mountains, and how thoroughly irritated he was that the Nazi party leadership had moved into the area. He was a proud German, and believed in his fight, but not in his government. He and Willie, the last Major Harriet had shot down, had climbed mountains and hunted together when they were young, and he was happy to know his friend was safe, though a prisoner somewhere in England. Eventually, just as Beck had said, a distant buzzing heralded the arrival of a white seaplane with red crosses on the wings. It circled for a while, before landing on the calm sea and coming to a steady halt beside them. The hatch opened, and Beck grabbed the float, then pulled them to the ladder below the hatch. A crewman looked down on them with a smile and shouted for them to hurry aboard.

"Quickly," Beck said. "Your pilots have been known to shoot down our rescue aeroplanes, despite them being painted white with red crosses, and protected by the Geneva convention."

"I don't think we'd do that," Harriet argued.

"Think all you like, if we wait and find out you may get to see what it's like to have a Spitfire shoot at you. Now hurry, climb the ladder," he barked, and she shook her head defiantly.

"I'll stay with the boat and take my chances if you don't mind," she said. Swimming home would be impossible, but she could use a paddle, and if she worked hard she might be home by morning.

"The wind is from the west," Beck replied. "By nightfall, you'll be blown onto the beach defences on the French coast, and picked up by the army, if you don't hit a mine. Trust me; you'd be better being my prisoner than theirs. You'll be treated properly, I promise." Harriet looked at the coast, then with resignation, she held the ladder and steadied herself to climb. It was awkward thanks to her shoulder pain, which meant she could only use one arm, but with Beck's instructions, the crewman helped her inside the cabin and into one of the seats. Next came Beck, who sat facing her. The crewman closed up and gave the signal to the pilot. Seconds later, the seaplane was bouncing along the waves ready for a take off, which eventually launched them into the air and had them heading to France and captivity. Harriet couldn't control her disappointment and felt tears running down her cheeks. The crewman handed her a tin cup with a healthy splash of rum, which she drank with a grateful yet forced smile, before slumping back into her seat and trying not to think of what would come next.

Chapter 13

Unwanted Guests

The seaplane ran slowly into the harbour; and after thanking the crew, Beck and Harriet were shown up the walkway to the car waiting on the dockside. The pilot had radioed ahead, and Beck's squadron had sent a driver to bring him home, along with his guest. Another officer had come to greet them, and he and Beck talked noisily in German as the car sped to the airfield. Ever the gentleman, Beck had introduced them.

"Andreas is my Adjutant," he said as he took the glasses of Calvados from the smiling officer, who'd somehow managed to pour them without spilling a drop. "He's young but well trained," he smirked as he handed Harriet a glass. "Andreas, meet Hel," he laughed. "She got a few of us today."

"Even you?" Andreas asked.

"Even me. Maybe I'm getting slow in my old age."

"It's a pleasure," Andreas said to Harriet politely. "Your reputation precedes you." Harriet smiled nervously. "Many of us thought you were a myth, but it seems you're as real as our humble leader here."

"More real," Beck blustered. "The crazy woman dived at me headfirst and shot my engine dead."

"Maybe you are getting old," Andreas smiled. Beck laughed, and they went back to talking in German, while Harriet focused on sipping her Calvados, hoping it would dull the ache in her shoulder. After a short ride they arrived at the airfield, a grass strip where 109s were lined up neatly and being worked on by ground crews, and drove down a track to where a grand looking farmhouse sat on the cliffs overlooking the sea. Harriet was escorted out.

"Come on, Hel, let's get you settled," Beck said as he guided her into the house and into a large room packed with pilots, all of whom were enjoying a drink. Andreas shouted something Harriet struggled to understand as they entered, and the gathering cheered loudly and started singing and stamping their feet. A young pilot brought large glasses of Calvados for both Beck and Harriet. Then, after calling a hush, Beck gave a rousing speech which Harriet struggled to follow, other than the word Hel, over and over, and finally her name, 'Flight Lieutenant Harry.' They then toasted her, before the officers went back to their conversations. Beck called one of them over. "Hel, this is our doctor, Ferdie. Ferdie, our guest here hurt her shoulder when stepping out of her Spitfire. Have a look at it, would you? We'll have dinner outside tonight, I think, maybe in a couple of hours?"

"Of course," Ferdie smiled politely and gave a small bow, then led Harriet to his clinic where she was surprised to be met by a female nurse. "This is Erika, my nurse and assistant," he said as he took off his jacket. Harriet was surprised by the English language skills of almost every German pilot she'd met so far. Erika started to unfasten the belt on Harriet's tunic, which made her stand back instinctively. "It's quite OK, Hel, she's going to help you remove your tunic so I can examine your shoulder. She'll stay throughout the examination, as a chaperone to ease your mind." Harriet nodded and let Erika ease the tunic from her torso, being careful not to inflict too much pain on Harriet, who was now feeling very nauseous as she looked at the bulge of her shoulder pushed forward out of place. "A dislocation, I think..." Ferdie said as he looked at the displaced shoulder. "Have a seat, and I'll put it back for you, please remove your blouse so I can inspect you." He gave Erika a nod as Harriet sat, and her blouse was unbuttoned halfway and pulled down over her left shoulder. Ferdie examined it carefully, making her jump when he touched the swollen joint. "You should drink that Calvados," he said as he moved to her side. She looked at him nervously, and he gave her a fatherly nod. She raised the glass and started to drink, then unexpectedly he grabbed her shoulder firmly and forced it back into place. Harriet coughed on the Calvados then let out a deafening scream as the tendons twanged and the bone went back to place with a sickening thud. "Drink!" he said. Erika guided the glass and Harriet gulped it all down before gasping for breath. "Play the piano?" he said with a frown.

"Yes..."

"Show me."

"How? You don't have a piano!" she said with irritation.

"Your fingers," he pointed to her left hand. "Play the piano!" Harriet frowned, then the penny finally dropped, and she wiggled her fingers as though she was playing. "Good," he said. "No nerves are trapped. You'll live." He turned to Erika and gave her instructions.

"Thank you," Harriet said as she rolled her shoulder. "I didn't know what had happened." It was still excruciating, but it moved better.

"You had pulled your arm from its socket," he explained, demonstrating by clasping his hand around his fist tightly and then pulling it away. "It'll hurt for a while as you'll have done lots of damage inside." He gave her an injection for the pain and put her arm in a clean white sling. "Erika will take you somewhere so you can recover and rest, she'll stay with you and take you to dinner this evening. She doesn't speak much English, but if you give her your uniform, she'll have it dried for you." Harriet nodded and smiled and stood from the bed.

"Thank you again."

"My bill will be in the post," he said with a wink, then clapped sharply and gestured her away. Harriet smiled to herself as Erika led her up the stairs of the farmhouse. Her hosts weren't that bad at all. She wasn't happy about what the Germans were doing, about them invading France and being in a war, but the pilots she'd met so far were all gentlemen the minute they were out of the cockpits of their aeroplanes. She was shown to a room that an older man was leaving. He said a few words to Erika and gave Harriet a polite nod. Inside was a four poster bed, and a bathtub by an open patio door overlooking the sea. Erika handed Harriet

303

a large towel then demanded her clothes, which she reluctantly handed over, undressing with her back to Erika and quickly wrapping herself in the towel.

"Bath. Sixty minutes," Erika instructed. "Bath," she gestured Harriet into the small shuttered space around the bath, then pulled the shutters closed and left Harriet alone. She looked around. The owners had picked the perfect spot. The bathtub faced the Channel, and a golden light filled the small room. She could hear the sea, and the gulls, it was almost perfect, had she not been a prisoner of war. She stood in the warmth for a while and enjoyed feeling the sun on her skin. The cold of the Channel had chilled her to the core. She looked around to make sure she couldn't be seen, then dropped her towel and enjoyed the sun all the more. The shutters behind her opened and she froze on the spot, cringing and not daring to turn and see who was there. 'Bloody timing!' she muttered to herself. "Drink. Bath," Erika said with the faintest hint of a smile as she handed Harriet a large glass of Champagne. Harriet smiled painfully and nodded, then waited for her to leave and close the shutters again, before quickly climbing into the large copper bathtub and slipping beneath the surface of the rose scented milky water before anyone else came in. She sipped the Champagne before putting the glass on the small bath side table, then dunked herself and lay under the water enjoying the warmth, feeling it tingling deep in her skin and washing the sea from her hair as she ran her fingers through the knots. Finally, she surfaced and laid her head on the soft towel that had been laid over the back of the bath, then picked up her Champagne and relaxed as best she could while enjoying the view. Despite her luxurious surroundings, she dreamed of being elsewhere, of being back England and sitting in a cold bath run by Daisy. England was going through hell. Rations, bombing, and the ever present fear of invasion; and she'd been exhausted after a run of early morning scrambles and patrols. Day after day was combat and food, and snatching sleep between action, the same as the rest of the pilots living in Kent, or Hell's Corner as it was becoming known due to the severity of the fighting in the air. It was a world away from a deep copper bathtub filled with rose scented water, overlooking the Channel on a beautiful summer's day. It was a world away from the Channel she'd been drowning in a couple of hours earlier. Her head struggled to make sense of it all, but she was also struggling to stay awake. She'd been through a traumatic incident. She'd almost died, and now all her body wanted to do was sleep. As she finished her large glass of Champagne, she stopped fighting and let her eyes close. She drifted back to Claude's old airfield long before Sully and his Hurricane had arrived and turned their lives upside down, she was lying beside Nicole and enjoying the sun on her skin while enjoying the sweet smell of late spring. "Hey!" Erika barked, dragging Harriet from her slumber and startling her back to the present.

"What is it?" Harriet asked, as she rubbed her eyes with the now lukewarm water and looked around at the eye rolling nurse who stood tapping on her watch. Harriet picked up the watch Cas had given her from the bath side table. Over an hour had passed in an instant. She felt like she'd only just closed her eyes.

"Eat," Erika said, tapping her watch before leaving the shuttered balcony. Harriet ducked herself and rinsed her hair, then climbed from the bath and wrapped herself in the long towel in one smooth move which spared her from any more unforeseen embarrassing situations. She followed Erika into the bedroom where her uniform was hanging in pristine condition from the wardrobe door. Her eyes widened as she looked closer. The tunic was as smart as the day Cas had bought it for her, which immediately reminded her that she still hadn't repaid him for his kindness, buying her a perfect handmade uniform from the most exclusive tailor in London. She'd wanted to find a way to thank him for that, and for everything else. The many hours that he'd spent teaching her the workings of the RAF, and doing his best to give her everything he knew to help her be the officer the AOC was expecting. As soon as she got a couple of days off, she'd planned to go into London to find him a gift. Though that was now looking significantly less likely to happen. She looked at her uniform as she took it from the hanger. The stubborn sweat stains from the armpits of her blouse were gone without a trace; something Daisy had struggled with thanks to the repeated drenching the blouses were taking in daily scrambles and combat. Even the oil stain had gone from her flying trousers, and her boots were smartly polished with even the sheepskin lining fluffed and brushed.

"Thank you," Harriet said to Erika, who simply shrugged then headed to the balcony, where she closed the door behind her to give Harriet the privacy to dress, while at the same time keeping an eye on her, so she didn't try and escape. She was a prisoner, after all. She quickly dressed in her smartly pressed and cleaned, and very dry uniform, even noting how clean and sweet smelling her underwear was, which was a little embarrassing, she then fixed her hair in a tight ponytail. "Ready when you are," she called to Erika, who, whether she understood or not, came through to the bedroom and looked Harriet up and down before smiling slightly and giving a nod of approval, then led her back through the house to the pilot's Mess.

"There she is! You look smart, Hel!" Beck boomed across the bar. "You'd look even smarter in one of our uniforms!" he laughed, and the other pilots laughed along with him. "Come, I have a treat for you before dinner. Andreas, let's go!" He and the smiling Adjutant walked Harriet through the house and out to the adjacent field, where their 109s were hidden away in a neat row along the tree line. Much closer to them, though, was a pristine 109 with a violet painted nose. The ground crew chief jumped down and saluted smartly, telling Beck it was ready for inspection. "My new aeroplane," Beck explained to Harriet. "A replacement for the one you filled with holes and sent to live on the bottom of the Channel," he said with a narrowing of his eyes, which soon changed into a mischievous smile. "I thought you'd like to see your nemesis up close." He climbed onto the wing and offered his hand to Harriet, obviously realising she would struggle to pull herself up with her arm in a sling. She was hauled up and invited to climb into the open cockpit, again with a helping hand from both Beck and Andreas, who'd climbed the other wing and was leaning over the cockpit. She was guided in, and her weight supported while she sat.

"It's small," she said. The cockpits of the Spitfire and Hurricane were both quite small, making it a miracle that the likes of Max could squeeze his six feet four inch tall and broad shouldered frame inside, but the 109 was smaller still, though she still fitted comfortably.

"Yes, but very manoeuvrable. Better than your Hurricanes."

306

"Faster, you mean," Harriet corrected him "The Hurricane is far superior as a gun platform, and turns tighter. I bested many of your friends in a Hurricane," she said confidently, before catching herself and remembering she was actually a prisoner of war and a guest of her enemy. "Though I think I was probably just lucky..." she added, quickly trying to appear contrite to her welcoming and unexpectedly pleasant host. "Mostly." She frowned at herself as the word left her lips, having not being able to stop herself.

"Yes, luck, of course," Beck laughed. "And it's our bad luck that the RAF decided to give you a Spitfire instead, for you to be even 'luckier' with." Harriet smiled awkwardly.

"The controls don't look too different from a Spitfire... How do you start her, though?"

"First you look over your shoulder," Beck instructed with a point of his finger. She looked and saw Andreas standing behind the cockpit with his pistol pulled and aimed straight at her, smiling as he seemed to constantly. She was instantly nervous with a knotting feeling in her stomach. "That's the device which stops young RAF pilots from flying away with my aeroplane."

"I hardly think I'll be flying anything with this," she said with a roll of her eyes as she gently lifted her slung arm an inch, far enough to feel the discomfort in her shoulder, despite the medication Ferdie had given her.

"Good. It would be a shame to shoot such a talented pilot on the ground. Though I'll ask Andreas to keep his pistol at the ready just in case, and don't let the smile fool you, he's as cold as an assassin." He winked at Andreas, who nodded slowly with a supporting shrug which suggested that while he may not necessarily enjoy it, he'd shoot Harriet without question and not lose a great deal of sleep over it. "Now, follow my instructions," Beck said as he talked her through the controls. He gave her detailed information on each, along with his thoughts on improvements that needed to be made, as well as a commentary on the flying characteristics of the 109 as a whole. He remained convinced that it was superior to the Hurricane but conceded that he could do more damage to the RAF if he had a squadron of Spitfires under his command. As he rounded up his talk, which felt like one of a boastful father introducing his pride and joy, he had Harriet switch on the battery and the magnetos, prime the fuel, and finally start the engine. She smiled as she felt the airframe vibrate and watched the air fill with blue smoke, however briefly, before being blasted away by the spinning propeller. She took hold of the control stick and felt the vibrations in her muscles and bones, and in a moment of madness, she considered releasing her arm from the sling, pushing the throttle hard, and seeing if she could unseat Beck and Andreas and get off the ground before they could react. A tap on the cockpit frame behind broke her daydreaming, and she looked back at Andreas, who was tapping the barrel of his pistol, still smiling, almost as if he could read her mind. She found herself smiling, half because she'd been caught out, and half in resignation. She shut down the engine obediently and released the stick. "You were thinking that throwing the throttle fully open you'd make us fall from the wings so you can make your escape, weren't you?" Beck asked with a knowing look.

"No. No, not at all. I was just enjoying the feel and sound; it'll probably be a while until I get to do it again."

"Of course, and if you could enjoy the feel and sound while racing back to
England with my aeroplane it would be all the sweeter, yes?"

"Maybe," she said with resignation.

"It's OK, Hel, it's OK. I'd be thinking exactly the same," he laughed. "All good pilots want to be in the air. Though your plan would have failed as you'd neglected to remove the chocks from the wheels." He winked, and her shoulders slumped. "Come, dinner is ready." He held out his hand, and after looking at it for a moment, reluctant to leave the cockpit, she took it and was helped from the aeroplane and down to the grass, where Andreas joined them again, his pistol returned to its holster. "Let us go eat," Beck said offering Harriet his arm as if going to a ball, then leading her at the head of his officers out onto the clifftop lawn, which was edged with a whitewashed decorative stone wall. A long table was adorned with candelabras, plates, cutlery, water jugs, and glasses; it all looked very formal. Beck showed Harriet to a seat beside his with a view of the Channel, while the rest of the pilots took their places. A few positions were unfilled, and in front of the empty seats, a candle was placed on a plate and lit, as waiters in smart white jackets brought glasses of Champagne. Beck said something Harriet didn't quite understand, then looked to Harriet. "Absent friends," he said. "Prost!" everyone repeated the salute and took a drink.

"Prost," Harriet said as they were all in silence, then sipped the Champagne. The pilots gave her a nod, and Beck gave his permission to sit. More drinks were quickly brought, and the gathering started chatting. Harriet looked at her Champagne, and then out over the cliffs. She wasn't sure how she felt. She knew what it was like to lose pilots, and to lose friends. She still dreamed about Nicole every night and missed her every day, but until now she'd just thought of the Germans as aeroplanes. She didn't think about the men inside, even after her run ins with them in France earlier that year. Each time she flew, she flew against an aeroplane, and each time she fired her guns, she was trying to knock an aeroplane out of the sky. She didn't consider the human being inside it, she couldn't. If she did, she'd think of Nicole, and all the others shot down and lost, and it would make her pause, and if she paused, she would be dead herself. Here, there was no hiding from the real face of her enemy. Men her age and older, all of whom had treated her with nothing but respect, as had their leader, Beck, who was every inch the gentleman.

"It's OK," Beck said as he sat back in his chair and sipped on his Champagne. "We only see Spitfires and Hurricanes when we're fighting. If we saw the people inside, we'd never fight." He gave her a wink like he knew exactly what she was thinking. She nodded and forced a smile, then took a long drink of Champagne before her glass was refilled. "Bollinger," Beck said. "The French kindly left us a few bottles when they left."

"Very civil of them." Harriet smiled.

"You like Champagne?"

"I like Bollinger."

"You have good taste." They clinked glasses and drank.

"What will happen to me?" Harriet asked. "I'd imagine I won't be staying here?"

"Sadly not," Beck said with a frown. "Andreas and I were talking about that very subject while old Joachim was working his magic on your uniform."

"Oh?"

"Yes... Prisoners are usually handed over to the military police, but we agreed that may not be in your best interest. So, tonight you'll be our guest; and tomorrow morning Andreas is going to drive you personally back to Germany, and to the Luftwaffe prisoner of war camp where you can be detained directly. Without the indignity of anything that may happen if you were to fall into the wrong hands."

"The wrong hands?"

"The Gestapo," Andreas said. "The secret police of the Nazi party. They enjoy interrogating people." Harriet's stomach started to churn uncomfortably, interrogation wasn't something she'd thought too much about, but now it was being discussed she didn't want to think about it anymore.

"Don't worry, Hel," Beck said with a smirk. "We won't let them get their hands on you." She forced a smile, again, and took another large drink of Champagne. "Tonight we celebrate being alive and being in good company," he continued. At that, the waiters appeared carrying plates, each with a thick steak and buttery mashed potatoes. Harriet stared at the meal in front of her; she'd never seen a steak so thick, in fact, she'd rarely seen a steak, and certainly not back in England where rationing had reduced every meat product she'd seen to bacon, bully beef, poor quality sausages, or sometimes chicken.

The German squadron were the perfect hosts for the evening. They ate, and they drank, and when the meal was finished, they stood in groups on the cliff tops smoking cigars and telling stories as the sun set, and the evening sky turned a beautiful mix of golds, oranges, and pinks. Many of the officers excused themselves, some going to bed, some going to play cards and drink. Soon only Beck, Harriet and a handful of others remained

"Sir..." a young pilot called nervously as he ran from the house. "Sir!"

"What is it, Franz? Where's the fire?" Beck laughed.

"Sir, it's the Gestapo!"

"What?" Beck demanded, his face switching from jolly to stern in the flick of an eye. "Where?"

"Here, coming now," Franz replied. At that, the door into the farmhouse opened, and Beck picked up Harriet and lifted her over the stone wall. The officers formed a screen in front of her to obscure her from wandering eyes.

"Sit behind the wall and keep quiet!" Beck ordered. Harriet was instantly terrified. Thirty seconds earlier her head was swimming with Champagne, and now she hid behind a wall on a narrow strip of grass between it and the cliff edge, and she was stone cold sober as she listened to the conversation.

"Major Beck, my name is Kriminalkommissar Streichen, from the local Gestapo office."

"Streichen..." Beck replied. "I didn't realise the Gestapo strayed this close to the front lines. You do realise that England is only thirty kilometres in that direction?"

"Very good, Major Beck. I'm well aware of England's location. It's curious you should mention it, considering that it's England which brings me to your headquarters."

"Oh? Looking for a ride over there so you can arrest Winston Churchill?"

"Be careful, Major, you may need a friend in the Gestapo before the night's out."

"I doubt that, Streichen. The day I need a friend in the Gestapo is the day hell freezes over. So, what are you doing on my airfield?"

"I've come for your prisoner."

"What prisoner would that be?"

"Major, please... It's my job to know what is happening on all of the Fatherland's airfields; and to know when a Valkyrie of Reims is said to have been pulled from the Channel."

"Valkyrie?"

"Don't play games with me, Major. The young female pilots fabled to have downed so many of your allegedly competent pilots when we invaded France, and reputed to be back in action over the Channel. Such celebrity is hard to hide, especially when a wet and tired looking female British flyer is seen stepping off one of our rescue aeroplanes just along the coast from here, alongside one of the Luftwaffe's most famous Majors."

"I'm afraid I don't know what you're talking about, Streichen. Perhaps your spies are incorrect this time? Maybe if they spent their time fighting

312

the English instead of imagining them on docks, we'd be in London already."

"It's a shame you want to play this game, Major. Your Reischmarshal will be disappointed to hear that one of his favourites got in the way of delivering a prize for his collection."

"Why don't you clear out, Streichen? You're not welcome here."

"How are your family back in Bavaria, Beck?"

"Excuse me?"

"Your wife and your sons, how are they? It's going to be hard on them when you're executed for treason, and all payments and benefits are withheld indefinitely."

"You wouldn't dare!"

"Then don't test me, Major. Despite your ignorant defiance, I'm prepared to overlook this incident if we stop this game now, and you hand over the prisoner!"

"And if I don't?"

"Then you and your officers will be arrested immediately and transported to Germany to face an immediate trial for harbouring the enemy, an offence punishable by death. Usually by hanging, usually with piano wire. Though the good news is that you'll all hang together, then maybe your families can all starve together, too? Keep the Squadron spirit, yes?"

"Stop!" Harriet said as she stood with one hand raised above her head, with the other still held tight in a sling. She'd heard enough, and while her German wasn't perfect, she realised exactly what was going on. Beck turned and faced her, and showed the small frame of Streichen in his long black coat and a wide brimmed hat. Either side of him were three

313

tall military police soldiers, all armed with submachine guns and looking forbidding in their helmets and chest plates, which hung around their necks on chains.

"Good evening, Fraulein," Streichen said in heavily accented English.

"They were only being gentlemen," she said nervously. Her stomach was in knots of fear, and her mouth was dry. "Major Beck told me himself that he intended to hand me over to you first thing in the morning."

"Is this so?"

"Yes. I'm sure the gentlemen were simply returning the fighter pilot's courtesy. When German pilots are shot down over England, we host them in the Mess for a meal before we hand them over to the military police. It's tradition since the last war."

"I see... Well, maybe it would have been easier for all concerned if the Major had simply said this in the first place, instead of giving me reason to believe that he and his officers are a cause for concern when it comes to security and loyalty." Harriet climbed over the wall at the gesturing of Streichen, helped by Beck and Andreas. "Unfortunately, those doubts cannot be overlooked." The military police levelled their machine guns at the small group. "You are all under arrest for harbouring the enemy, and will accompany your guest to Berlin."

"Wait," Beck said.

"Yes?"

"My officers are loyal to Germany, and they were following the orders of their commander, and they will follow the orders of any officer that may replace me..."

"Are you confessing to ordering your officers to lie, Major?"

"Yes... As their commander, I'm entirely, and solely, responsible."

314

"Very well, Major. If you'd like to hand over your pistol, we can leave your squadron under the command of your Adjutant, until your replacement can be appointed."

"Thank you."

"I told you, Major Beck. Everybody needs a friend in the Gestapo," he looked at Harriet and smiled. "It looks like you'll have company on your trip to Berlin. You can put your hand down, Valkyrie, you may fly like a demon, but you may not quite outrun machine guns on the ground. Shall we?" Beck shook hands with the others then walked beside Harriet, escorted by the military police as Streichen limped his way across the grass towards the waiting open top staff car and escort motorcycles with sidecars.

"I thought you didn't speak German?" Beck said quietly.

"I speak a little German. Enough to know he'd have shot you all." Harriet replied.

"Yes, he would. Without hesitation or remorse," Streichen said without turning as they arrived at his car. He sat in the passenger seat, and a pair of military police stood on the running boards each side of the car, while the others boarded the sidecars of the four waiting motorcycles. With a wave from Streichen, they were heading off into the darkening French country lanes.

Harriet looked at her watch, they'd been travelling for over forty five minutes and the eastern sky, towards which they were driving, was an inky dark blue as the last of the silvery daylight faded over their shoulders in the direction of home. They'd passed through small villages and army checkpoints as they made their way through the French countryside, which smelled sweet in the evening air. Harriet remembered the smells of the French countryside from her childhood, and she thought how it would almost be comforting to be home if it wasn't for the fact that she was in the hands of the Gestapo. She knew from stories back in the

315

dispersal hut that they would likely want to extract every last piece of information from her, by fair means or foul, before they finally handed what remained of her over to anybody who cared. The only thing that scared her more was what would happen to Beck and his family. They'd done nothing wrong. He was genuinely going to hand her over to spend her life in a prisoner of war camp. He was far from a traitor. They slowed as they approached yet another army checkpoint on a crossroads outside of what looked like a large town.

"Why are we slowing? Don't they know who I am?!" Streichen demanded as the soldiers at the checkpoint waved to stop the two leading motorcycles. They walked over, their distinctive coal scuttle like helmets giving a stark and chilling outline to their silhouettes against the inky blue sky. "Fools, I'm Streichen of the Gestapo, let us pass or you'll find yourselves..." He was cut short as the nearest soldier levelled their machine gun and lit up the darkness with brilliant bright flashes as it thundered into life, sending a burst of bullets into Streichen's chest and knocking him over his car door. The others fired at the same time, cutting down the motorcycle escort and guards before they even had a chance to cock their weapons. The noise was thunderous like they'd been caught in a storm, with bullets cutting through the air and German soldiers screaming as they died. The car stalled as the driver tried to throw it into reverse and escape. He was quickly riddled with bullets by a figure standing in front of the car, making his body dance in his seat. Beck had instinctively pulled Harriet down as the bullets started to fly, and she found herself pushing tight into him to try and escape as the bullets passed through the driver and into the seat she'd sat against just seconds before. Terrified and with a dry mouth, she wriggled free then stood and threw up both of her arms, screaming as she did, her left arm only raising half height due to the swelling in her shoulder and causing her a lot of pain as she tried to lift it. As the silhouettes closed on her, she called out frantically.

"Francais! Francais!" Desperately hoping that whoever was doing the shooting would hear her French voice and hold their fire. "Français! Ne pas fuer! S'il vous plaît! Francais!" The closest silhouette's hand went up to stop any further shooting and stopped everyone in their tracks. "S'il vous plaît. Je ne pas Allemande." Harriet continued.

"Your French is so poor that you may as well be German," came a reply from the darkness that stabbed into Harriet's heart like a knife. She stared at the shape walking closer to the car, she was shaking, and her head was spinning. Was she dead? Was she dreaming? Was she so scared that she was imagining things?

"Nicole?" she replied. Her heart was pounding, and her mind whirled. "Harriet?" Nicole said as she stepped up to the side of the car, and removed the German helmet that she was wearing, then pulled the scarf from her face.

"Don't call me that..." Harriet replied instinctively as she lowered her arms. Tears were streaming down her face. She'd had so many dreams where she'd met with Nicole again, and then the dreams became nightmares as she realised Nicole was dead, and every time she'd disappear from sight right at that point. "My name's Harry!"

"Harry's a boy's name," Nicole said with a smile. Harriet felt her legs go weak, and she fell, only to be caught by Beck. Nicole's machine gun instantly trained on him. "Let go of her, Boche!" Nicole demanded in a low and threatening voice.

"Wait!" Harriet said as she fought through the thousand and one thoughts circling her brain. "He's with me."

"You always did like older men, Harry, but a German? Really? I thought you had more taste." Harriet steadied herself then leaned out of the car and hugged Nicole.

"Is it really you?" she half cried, and half laughed.

"I hope so," Nicole replied. Her voice was starting to crack with emotion. "My God, Harry, I can't believe it." They hugged while Nicole's friends began looting the bodies of the dead German military police for anything

317

useful. Weapons, ammunition, maps, anything they could, even pulling the driver out of the car to search the front seats. "We must go, we can't stay here," Nicole said. "The local garrison is likely to have heard the shooting."

"Where will we go?"

"Somewhere safe, a long way from here." She opened the door and helped Harriet out of the car, and as soon as she was out of the way, Nicole levelled her machine gun at Beck, who sat back in the seat in resignation. He knew what was coming.

"No!" Harriet said as she grabbed the muzzle of the machine gun.

"Well we can't take him with us," Nicole said

"Let him go?" Harriet asked.

"He's German."

"He's a German who was being taken to Berlin to be executed for refusing to hand me over to the Gestapo."

"Is this true?" Nicole demanded of Beck.

"Yes..." he replied. "I wanted to take your friend direct to a Luftwaffe prison camp and save her the indignity of a Gestapo interrogation. However, the Gestapo got to her first, and the man you see slumped over the car door was going to have me and my senior officers shot for helping her." At that, there was a noise in the distance, and one of the others called to Nicole and told her they needed to go.

"Do you ride a motorcycle?"

"Yes, why?"

"Take one and get out of here. If anyone asks what happened, you were ambushed by British commandos. Understand?"

"I understand. Thank you." He stood then pulled Streichen's lifeless body back into the car and searched his pockets to retrieve his pistol. "It's mine," he said casually as he pushed it into his holster then jumped from the car. "I'm grateful, and I won't betray you, I swear." He turned to Harriet and held out his hand. "Does this make us even? A life for a life?" he asked with a smile.

"It does; and don't take this the wrong way, but I hope I never see you again," Harriet said as she shook his hand.

"If you take any longer to say your goodbyes, we'll all end up prisoners!" Nicole grumbled as she gestured in the direction of the distant engines. "Good luck, Hel," he said with a smile. "And thank you, from my family and I."

"Wait," Harriet said as he turned to leave.

"Oh good," Nicole protested. "More conversation, just what we need right now."

"Why do you keep calling me Hel, when you know my name is Harry?"

"Some Norwegian," he said as he tapped the country name tape on her shoulder. "Hel is the Norse Goddess of the Underworld and a notorious warrior. A she devil, if you will. Goodbye, Harry. Remember your life raft next time!" He ran and grabbed one of the motorcycles behind the car, kicked it into life, and sped off into the night.

"Come on, Norwegian," Nicole said as she pulled on Harriet's tunic, leading her off with the others as they walked quickly down the road and into the trees. "What did you do to your arm?" she asked as they walked.

"Hit it against the tail of the aeroplane..."

319

"I see that time hasn't made you a better pilot."

"If I'm dreaming all of this, I'm happy to wake up any time now."

"Shut up, both of you," one of the others said in a whispered shout. "You'll have the whole German army on us."

"Oh shut up, Pierre," Nicole replied. "We just fired several hundred bullets into a German convoy not five hundred metres away. If they didn't hear that, they're not going to hear two girls whispering in a dark forest."

"Shut up anyway. This is my unit, and you'll do as I say."

"You'd think he was British the way he gives out orders," Nicole said to Harriet. "Or German."

"Shut up!" Pierre demanded. Nicole pulled out her tongue in his general direction, and Harriet couldn't help but laugh. Nicole hadn't changed at all.

The small group walked through the woods and fields for over an hour, until finally, they came to a remote farm where everyone melted into the darkness, leaving only Harriet, Nicole, and Pierre. They headed to the farm where weapons were collected and hidden, along with German helmets, hand grenades, and any other equipment that had been taken in the ambush. Candles were lit, and wine, bread, and cheese were produced on the kitchen table, and Harriet sat with Nicole while Pierre left them to talk.

"You're not dead," Harriet said.

"I know," Nicole replied. "And you're not Norwegian."

"Shut up. You know what I mean. I saw you shot down in flames."

"I was..." Nicole shrugged, with a frown. "The dive put out most of the flames, and I managed to convince the engine to take me high enough to get out before it cut and fell to the ground. I was low, though, and I hurt my knee and ankle when I landed and knocked myself out, so I spent the night sleeping in a ditch."

"Why didn't you come to England?"

"How? I was in a ditch and not able to walk. Pierre found me three days after I crashed, he was a French soldier trying to make his way home as the defence of Dunkirk collapsed, and he'd been trapped behind German lines. I was hungry and living on ditch water, and still not able to walk. He took me to his home, at great risk to himself and his family, my uniform was buried in the garden, and I became his cousin from Reims. By the time I could walk again, the British were gone, and France had surrendered."

"I thought you were dead..."

"I knew you were alive..." Nicole shrugged. Harriet smiled and sipped on her wine. "They could never kill you, not in the sky, you're too good for a German to get you."

"They almost did. I was shot down right after you."

"No?"

"Yes... I crashed on the beach and was stuck in a burning Hurricane, not able to get out. I thought it was the end."

"How did you escape?" Nicole asked excitedly while tearing apart the bread and spreading some soft cheese onto it. "Tell me."

"I don't know. When my arm started burning, I somehow found the strength to force the cockpit open."

"But how did you get home?"

"Max..."

"Max? He's not dead?"

"No," Harriet smiled. "He'd been shot down and made his way to Dunkirk with the army. He saw my Hurricane crash and came to find me. Then I went home, and the rest is history."

"History, present, you're here again now?"

"Yes... I was shot down over the Channel. The Luftwaffe is hitting us hard in preparation for an invasion. The sky was black with them, and I got unlucky. Fortunately that German Major in the car you rescued me from saved me from drowning, the rest you know."

"Invasion?"

"Invasion. The raids are getting more intense every day; what we saw over Dunkirk was nothing. The last one, the one that got me, was maybe a hundred bombers and a hundred fighters. We had to try and stop them over the Channel so they couldn't get inland and hit the airfields. They're trying to bomb us out of existence so we can't protect the Navy from them, and then the Navy won't be able to protect us from an invasion. There's talk that they're going to try sometime in September."

"There has been a lot more activity along the coast, around the Calais area.
We can't get close enough to look, though."

"So, what are you doing here ambushing German soldiers?"

"We're the Maquis."

"The what?"

"The Maquis. The resistance. We irritate the Germans, usually by pretending to be British commandos and attacking them, but mostly we gather information or help stupid British pilots escape when they're incapable of staying in the sky. You know, we had one not so long ago who, like you, had been shot down over the Channel. He was picked up by a fishing boat after almost twenty four hours floating in the water. He was smelling of fish from his time hiding under nets on the boat, and so cold he was as blue as his uniform, but as soon as he'd gathered himself after tripping off the trawler and almost killing himself, he asked me on a date."

"He wasn't two metres tall with brown eyes and scruffy brown hair, was he?" Harriet asked with a frown and a knot of excitement in her stomach.

"That's him. That boy was hard work. Fortunately, we didn't keep him for long."

"What did you do with him?"

"What we do with them all. Pierre was allowed to return to his essential work on the trains after the French surrender, so we use the railway to get them safely to Vichy France in the south, where our contacts get them to Spain, and then Gibraltar, and England. It's a long trip, weeks or more, but it works. You'll be going the same way tomorrow." She took a drink of wine as Pierre came and joined them. Harriet found herself smiling and happy that Jonny was alive. He was very well thought of in the squadron, and his loss had been one of the more difficult for everyone to swallow. "They're asleep," Pierre said. "My wife and children," he explained to Harriet.

"Thank you for hiding me here," she replied.

"It's our pleasure. One more pilot kept out of a prison camp is one more still fighting the Germans."

"I was telling her we could put her on the train tomorrow," Nicole said.

323

"Maybe, I'll find out when I go to work in a few hours," he replied as he looked at his watch, then poured himself a glass of wine. "You know each other?"

"We flew together for the RAF," Nicole replied proudly.

"We grew up together," Harriet added.

"Wonderful. I hope you're not as much trouble as her," Pierre nodded at Nicole. "Otherwise I'll turn you in to the Germans myself. One of her is enough." He quickly drained his wine glass. "You'll stay here until we can get you a ride on the train south. Give your uniform to Nicole, and she can hide it with hers." He stood from the table. "Bed," he instructed. "We can't waste candles on reunions. I'll tidy this away. See you tomorrow." Nicole poured them more wine each and gave Pierre a wink, then led Harriet upstairs, tiptoeing so as not to wake the family, and showed her up to the loft where she had a bed. They drank the wine as they undressed and climbed in. Nicole made sure Harriet was comfortable and put a spare pillow under her left arm to ease the soreness, then snuggled close and pulled Harriet to lay against her, drawing the white sheet up around them as a cool breeze drifted through the open windows facing the bed.

"I still can't believe you're here," Nicole said.

"I still can't believe you're alive," Harriet replied.

"What's it like in the RAF in England? Is it like when we were here in France?"

"It's different. There are lots of senior people, and there's lots of planning, and the squadron is part of a much bigger group that looks after the whole south east of England. We've been on standby at first light every day since I've been with the squadron. Sometimes we go up four or five times per day. It's hard work. Then I have my studies; and the parties, of course."

"Studies? What studies?"

"The AOC, he's the officer that's in charge of all the squadrons, met me and said I could only stay if I studied and met all of the requirements of being an officer, so Cas teaches me after we've been stood down."

"Cas is still there?"

"Yes, and Singh. Archie was shot down the other day, though. He was OK, he got out, but then some soldier shot him in the behind and put him in hospital."

"A British soldier?"

"To his annoyance, yes."

"That's very funny," Nicole laughed. "I can imagine him being very angry, but very English with it."

"He was. He's in the hospital just along the coast from the airfield."

"And of course it's terrible for you spending all of that time with Cas."

"What?"

"You still like him, I bet."

"Shut up..." Harriet frowned in the darkness as Nicole laughed in her unique mischievous way. "Have you heard from Claude and Magritte?"

"Yes, I went to visit them. Pierre arranged my train tickets when I could walk again."

"Are they OK?"

"Yes, they're fine. Of course Grandpa is furious at the Germans for invading, but he's even more furious at our government for surrendering.

Naturally that's nothing compared to the anger he has for the Vichy government who are busy colluding with the Germans. He wanted to go to England and volunteer to fly for the RAF when he found out what we'd done, but Grandma wouldn't let him; she just tells him he's an old fool and better off staying out of everybody's way."

"I'm happy they're alive and OK."

"Me too, I was worried."

"Why didn't you stay with them?"

"They wanted me to, but I wanted to be with the Maquis. It feels good to be in the war still, and honestly, I couldn't do it from home, I couldn't risk being caught and them being punished for my actions. It's what the Germans do."

"Don't you worry about that here?"

"Here it's different. Here nobody knows they're my grandparents, nobody knows me, I'm just the girl from Reims whose parents died in a bombing raid. An orphan." She looked down at Harriet, who'd fallen asleep in her arms. She'd heard the tiredness in her voice and knew it was coming. She smiled; she was so happy to see her friend again.

Chapter 14

Choices

When Harriet eventually woke late the next morning, the sunlight was streaming through the windows and warming her skin. She smiled and stretched out in the soft bed, then grabbed for her shoulder as the pain reminded her of the previous day's close encounter with a dying Spitfire. It wasn't the only place that hurt either, she felt sore all over. She sat up and looked around the room, there was no sign of Nicole or her clothes, and for a moment she worried that it had all been a dream. A brief shake of her head was enough to remind her that she'd never been in the room before in her life; and if Nicole wasn't really alive, and the previous night had all been a dream, she had more to worry about. Her underwear was lying on the end of the bed, with a light blue summer dress. She smiled and put them on, then headed downstairs where Nicole greeted her.

"You're awake, at last," Nicole said

"Yes... I must have been tired. Where is everyone?" Harriet replied with a smile.

"Pierre is working, and Fleur took the children into the village to see their grandparents. Sit, I'll make you a coffee. We have none of your English tea, fortunately," she said with a smirk. Harriet sat at the kitchen table, and Nicole made her a coffee and gave her some bread and jam. The girls sat and talked over brunch, then went outside and enjoyed the sunshine, talking and reminiscing, and imagining that the war was a million miles away. They walked in the garden and lay in the grass while sipping red wine, then headed back to Pierre's farm in the early evening to have a dinner of chicken casserole with the family. Fleur and her twins, a nine year old boy and girl, were perfect hosts. The twins grilled Harriet on flying Spitfires, they'd both seen them, and both were fascinated and desperate to fly them, having spent many a long night having Nicole tell them stories of her flying exploits, and how she and her

327

best friend had flown against the Germans and won. Now that friend was in their home, they wanted her version of the stories, too. Harriet was more than happy to oblige, and despite Nicole's teasing, the twins hung on every word. They were disappointed when finally their bedtime came, and Fleur demanded they follow her upstairs, leaving Harriet, Nicole, and Pierre to talk.

"Do we go to the rail depot tonight?" Nicole asked when she was sure the children were out of earshot.

"It's impossible," Pierre replied, and Harriet's heart sank. "The Germans are searching everywhere for the British commandos who killed the local Gestapo chief last night in an ambush."

"What does that mean?" Harriet asked. "Is there another way?"

"The docks, maybe?" Nicole asked. "Maybe a trawler can take her somewhere safe?"

"Sadly not," Pierre replied with a shrug. "The Germans are there, too. All movement in or out of the area has been stopped. That's only part of the problem." He looked seriously at them. "Philippe, our friend in the gendarmerie, told me that the local German garrison is going to search all properties tonight. They're convinced that a platoon of commandos can't hide out in the open, so they must be hiding with locals, and they reason that so many commandos couldn't hide in towns or villages as they'd be seen, so they're coming to all of the farms first. They'll come at last light."

"There has to be something we can do?" Nicole pleaded.

"If there is, I don't know what it is," Pierre shrugged.

"I do," Harriet said. The pair looked at her and waited. "How far is the nearest airfield?"

"There's a small fighter airfield not far from here," Pierre said. "Maybe ten kilometres away, on the coast."

"Can you get me there?"

"Why? What are you going to do, steal an aeroplane?" he laughed.

"Yes," Harriet replied. She was looking at him in the eyes without a hint of a smile on her face.

"You're stupid!" Nicole replied. "Ignore her. Harriet, leave this to us, this is what we do."

"I'm serious," Harriet said as her heart started pounding. "Get me to the airfield, and I'll steal a 109."

"You can hardly fly British aeroplanes," Nicole scolded.

"I can fly a 109."

"How?" Pierre asked, holding his hand up to try and stop Nicole's reply.

"I've been shown, of course. It's easy, really. Not too different from a Hurricane or Spitfire. If you get me to the airfield, I can steal one."

"It wasn't your shoulder you hit when you left your Spitfire; it was your head!" Nicole said with disdain.

"Trust me, Pierre. I can do this. Besides, there's no other way out, is there? And I can't be found here, how can you help others in the future if you and your family are in a prison somewhere?"

"She makes a fair point," Pierre said. "You can both stay, of course, nobody would suspect, and I'm sure we can cover for you."

"Too risky," Harriet said. "It's decided. Get my uniform and get me to the airfield. I'll take a chance."

"And what if they catch you before you even get off the ground? Your plan is stupid!" Nicole blustered.

"Then I'll be wearing my uniform, and I'll be taken prisoner. Or I'll be shot trying to escape, in which case I won't know much about anything anyway. Besides, I can't sit around here indefinitely, or spend weeks or months going through Spain. They could invade before then, and I need to be back with the squadron if they do."

"Of course, and they could never manage without the great Harriet, could they?" Nicole rolled her eyes and let out a frustrated groan. "I'm quite sure the RAF have plenty better!"

"They don't have enough pilots, Nicole, better or worse," Harriet said softly as she put her hand on her friend's and looked her in the eyes. "They've got aeroplanes, ammunition, equipment, and ground crew, but they don't have fighter pilots. We lost too many of the best here in France, and those that are left are so exhausted that every sortie is a flip of a coin as to whether they come back. We're losing great pilots every day, and the flying schools aren't replacing them quick enough; and when we're out of pilots, we're done. Finished! If that happens the Germans have won, there's nobody else to stand against them, we can't fight them from Canada or Australia. They win, and Europe is under German rule forever. I've got to get back, you see? I've got to fight!"

"Then it's what we'll do," Pierre said with a shrug.

"You can't be serious?" Nicole blurted. "How can you even think this is remotely achievable?"

"She can fly a Messerschmitt, why wouldn't it be? It's no more dangerous than hiding on a train and hoping not to get caught by Vichy Gendarmes or Spanish soldiers. Or hoping not to be found on a fishing boat, which would get the whole crew shot. This way, she either escapes or dies trying."

"You don't have to fight anymore," Nicole said after a moment of silence and deep thought. "You can go home and live with Grandpa and Grandma, they'd love to have you, and you speak passable French, so you'd fit right in. Besides, the people in the village know you, and you'd be welcomed."

"Passable French?" Harriet asked, choosing the focus on the thinly veiled insult. Nicole simply shrugged as if she'd just stated a fact like the sky was blue or grass was green. "Will you come and live with me there, and not fight?"

"I have my duty. I'll fight the Germans until every last one of them has left
France, and we're free once again!"

"I thought as much, so you know my answer!" Harriet said forcefully. Nicole rolled her eyes at her friend's stubbornness. "You should come with me," she continued.

"Don't involve me in your death wish," Nicole responded while wagging her finger. "If you want to get yourself killed trying to steal a German aeroplane, be my guest, but don't think you'll be taking me down with you."

"You said you wanted to fight the Germans."

"Yes, fight them, not get shot stealing an aeroplane from them."

"It's not a ridiculous idea," Pierre added. "You're a pilot, and you should be fighting them in the sky, not hiding in ditches."

"She's always been an idiot," Nicole scowled. "What's your excuse?"

"Has she always been this angry?" Pierre asked Harriet, totally ignoring Nicole.

"Mostly," Harriet replied with a smile of resignation. "She gets like this when she knows she's on the wrong side of an argument."

"Shut up!" Nicole demanded as she stood from the table. "We should get your things packed. What time do we leave, Pierre?"

"You need to leave before nightfall, when the German garrison will be starting their searches. You can go to the safe place in the woods, and I'll meet you there after dark."

"I'll get ready. Are you coming?" Nicole asked. Harriet nodded and followed her up the stairs and steps to the loft space bedroom. Nicole stood in the mirror and unfastened her hair. "You know that you have the stupidest ideas," she complained as she brushed it through, before tying it into a tight braid. "You always have."

"What about my uniform?" Harriet asked.

"That's one of them!" Nicole said with a shake of her head as she sat on the side of the bed and pulled on her plimsolls. "Which idiot would wear an RAF uniform to go walking around German held land in daylight? It's a good thing you're going back to England before you get us all shot!"

"I really haven't missed you."

"Of course you have, I'm delightful. It's why Pierre and Fleur like me so much."

"I think they tolerate you."

"Well, fortunately, they won't have to tolerate you much longer, it must be terrifying for them knowing you're here with your poor language skills. Even the most ignorant German infantryman wouldn't believe you were
French."

"Nicole..."

332

"What?"

"Please come back with me."

"Don't be ridiculous."

"I mean it!" Harriet said forcefully, grabbing Nicole by the arm. "Please."

"I'm French," Nicole said softly as she stood looking into Harriet's eyes. "My place is here, in France, fighting with my people."

"Your people? What does that make me?"

"It makes you my family, my beautiful sister, the girl who I'd do anything for. Including helping you escape back to England so you can do what you do better than anyone else, shoot Germans out of the sky."

"I don't want to go without you."

"I know, and I don't want you to go, but we're in a war, and we must do what is best for everyone, not for ourselves."

"But I've only just found you again. I thought you were dead. I have nightmares, almost every night, thinking of you dead."

"Now the dreams can stop," Nicole smiled warmly. "I'm alive, and I will be for a long time, I'm quite safe here. We know the country better than the Germans, they'll never catch us, and even if they get close, we'll take the train south, we'll always be safe. I promise." A knock at the door disturbed them, and Fleur entered the room with some plimsolls for Harriet.

"I think they'll fit," she said. "They're old, but they're better than nothing."

"Thank you, Fleur. To you and your family for risking your lives, protecting me."

"It's our pleasure," she smiled.

"But it's such a risk, aren't you scared for your lives?"

"Every day... But the British are Europe's last hope. If we're to be free, and my children are to grow up with a future free of oppression and slavery, our liberation can only ever come from Britain. We attack the Germans here, of course, but we're nothing more than insects irritating an angry wolf, and our attacks are largely inconsequential. The real fight must come from the free people gathering in Britain, and the Germans know that. Sooner or later they'll have to cross the Channel or lose the war, and when they attack, the British are going to need every pilot they can get their hands on to push them back into the sea. If Britain survives, they can come back and kick the Germans out. That makes the risk and the fear worthwhile."

"Thank you," Harriet said, giving Fleur a hug and the traditional kiss on each cheek. "I promise I'll fight for you and your children, and for all of France."

"If half of what Nicole says about you is true, I believe that," Fleur said, and Harriet immediately felt herself blushing.

"Ignore her. I said nice things about you because I thought you were dead, not because they were true."

"You should be leaving," Fleur said as she turned and led the girls down to the kitchen, where Nicole hugged her tight and kissed her cheeks before joining Harriet outside in the warm evening air. "Go with God." As they walked through the sweet smelling garden, Harriet looked up and paused to wave at the children, who were watching from their bedroom on the first floor.

"It'll be dark soon," Nicole said as she joined her and stood by her side. "We should go while we can." She blew kisses to the children then took Harriet by the hand, and the pair slipped through the hedgerow and out into the fields, then to the woods, walking as quietly as possible as the orange sky turned pink and then blue. As the light finally dulled an hour later, they arrived at a small copse of old trees where they hid and waited. "This is our safe place," Nicole explained quietly. "It's got a view of the fields all around, so the Germans can't sneak up on us. There are ditches in every direction, too, so it's easy to escape."

"How many people have you helped escape?" Harriet asked as she got comfortable leaning against a tree.

"Many," Nicole replied. "Not all British. Some French pilots wanted to go to England to fight, too, we helped them, and lots of Poles and Czechs, not to mention Dutch and Belgians. Even some from Norway," she smiled. "Proper Norway, not like you."

"That's a lot of nationalities."

"Their countries are all under German occupation now. It's the only way they can keep fighting."

"I know... It's a good thing you're doing here."

"I know..." Nicole replied with a warm smile. "It feels good to do something to help the war. When I was shot down, I just wanted to try and reach England and get back into a Hurricane. Then I realised I couldn't walk, let alone fly, and accepted that maybe my story was going to be different. Pierre finding me gave me a new fight. Something I could do here." She smiled with pride. "Anyway, why don't you make me jealous and tell me what I'm missing in England?"

"Rations and bombs," Harriet said with a shrug. The pair laughed and lay beside each other. Harriet put her head on Nicole's shoulder and smiled to herself. There was something about Nicole that made her feel safe, even when she was hiding in German occupied France. She had a

335

scent about her. Not a perfume or scented water, just her natural scent which smelled sweet and fresh. A smell like candied apples, which Harriet always found so captivating. "I wish we could just stay here forever like this," Harriet said.

"Me too," Nicole replied as she played with Harriet's ponytail. "Maybe one day the Germans will be beaten, and we can spend all the time in the world together."

"I'd like that."

"Me too... We should probably stay quiet and listen for Germans now it's dark."

"I know. Thank you for rescuing me again." Nicole gave her a squeeze, which was returned, and the pair lay in the undergrowth beneath the trees. They waited patiently until the last glow of daylight was replaced by a pitch black sky littered with millions of brilliant white stars, interspersed with the occasional red and blue, and a larger than life silver white full moon. Finally, hours after they'd arrived, they were alerted to movement in one of the ditches, which made the hairs on the back of Harriet's neck stand on end. A brief whistle made her jump and freeze. Nicole replied, and Pierre entered the woods carrying a backpack and machine gun.

"Where have you been?!" Nicole demanded in a whispered shout.

"The Germans are everywhere," he replied. "They're searching every farm, village, and town, I had to make lots of diversions. They're heading in this general direction so we should probably keep moving." Nicole helped Harriet to her feet, her arm was still in the sling and her shoulder still very sore, and it was a struggle to drag herself up unaided. She stayed close behind Pierre, and Nicole followed at the rear, carrying the rifle she'd been brought. They made their way through the countryside towards the coast, until finally, they arrived at the airfield; then spent an hour skirting around the perimeter, checking for sentries and trying to find a way in. Eventually they spotted an entry point across a field away from the woods which were inhabited by a noisy German anti aircraft unit who were singing loudly around their fires. The three lay for a while and waited patiently as German soldiers clanked noisily around the woods. Patrols passed occasionally, pairs of soldiers wandering along the perimeter of the airfield talking and smoking, and generally uncaring about what could be lying in the dark. "You should get into your uniform," Pierre whispered as the noise from the artillery unit dulled. "I'm going to go and have a look around. If anything happens, you should clear out and get back home. I'll meet you there."

"Don't let anything happen," Nicole whispered in reply. He smiled and dropped his backpack by her. "Stay here and keep quiet." He lifted from the dip in the long grass where they'd been hiding, looked around, then crawled off in the direction of the airfield and the line of 109s. "Here," Nicole said as she pulled Harriet's uniform from the bag and handed it to her. Harriet struggled with her trousers and socks, pulling them on under her dress, then slipped her feet easily into her flying boots. Then came the fun part, the blouse. She lifted her arm slowly from the sling around her neck and let out a hiss between gritted teeth. Her shoulder had seized, and any hint of pain medication was long gone from her bloodstream. She pulled at the dress and dragged it over her head, then slipped the blouse awkwardly over her arm and began fiddling with the buttons, making a long slow mess of it. "My God look at you; you can hardly move your arm. How on earth do you expect to fly an aeroplane?!" Nicole muttered. She pushed Harriet's hands out of the way and fastened her blouse, before tackling the tunic. "This is ridiculous. Hold my thumb," she instructed as she sat back on her feet and knelt in front of Harriet, with her right arm outstretched and thumb pointing upwards.

"What?"

"Hold my thumb," she repeated. Harriet reached across with her right hand, and Nicole slapped it away. "Not with that hand. That hand is for the control stick. Use your left!" Harriet frowned in the moonlight then did as she was instructed, very slowly. She gasped as she extended her arm, then gently clasped Nicole's thumb.

337

"There," she said with a wince.

"Now squeeze and pull it towards you," Harriet tried, her grip was light and the only strength she could apply didn't even move Nicole's thumb. "So tell me, genius, how are you to fly with one hand?"

"Shut up," Harriet said as she pulled her hand away.

"I mean it. You have to fly over the Channel, maybe being chased. You can't fly with one hand! How do you expect to control the throttle?"

"I'll be fine," Harriet replied stubbornly.

"You'll be lucky to get off the ground!"

"I'll get off the ground, don't you worry yourself! There's a Squadron Leader back in England flying with no legs, so I'm pretty sure I'll get by with a sore shoulder. Anyway, it's not your problem."

"You have always been an idiot; I'd just forgotten how much of one!"

"Shut. Up!"

"Idiot!"

"Both of you shut up!" Pierre said as he crawled back between them. "I can here you metres away; do you want the Germans to shoot us before she even gets off the ground?"

"They may as well, it'll save us all some trouble," Nicole grumbled.

"Listen," he said, and they both moved closer. "There are four roaming sentries that I can see, two pairs opposite each other. There's a group of ground crew at the far end of the aeroplanes, repairing an engine or something, they look like they'll be there a while and they have the

338

company of what looks like a couple of pilots, so we should probably wait."

"How long?" Harriet asked.

"I don't know, as long as it takes for them to finish. If you go before that, they'll hear you and call the sentries. The pilots probably have pistols, too, they'd get you before you take off." Harriet nodded while Nicole rolled her eyes with irritation and buried her head in the grass. The three got comfortable and waited and waited. The sky was black and silver, lit by the biggest moon Harriet could remember seeing, lighting up the airfield and everything on it, including the ground crew, sentries, and pilots who came and went, bringing drinks and cigarettes, and talking loudly. The hours passed, and with them, Harriet's hope of escape diminished. She checked her watch regularly, then finally she spoke.

"I'm going to have to risk it," she said.

"What?" Pierre asked.

"No!" Nicole objected. "Ignore her. She's being an idiot again."

"Look, I have no choice," Harriet said in a firm whisper. "It's not long until first light, which means that if the Germans are anything like us, they'll be coming to standby in the next thirty to sixty minutes. Then we'll really be stuck. Sitting here in a field while they're flying about, they'll see us in no time."

"She's right," Pierre nodded to Nicole.

"No, she isn't. We should just go home now and come back another time."

"Yes, you should," Harriet replied. "I'll give you a head start. Twenty minutes should do before I start the engine. Move quickly and get out of here."

"You know you can stay?" Pierre offered, already knowing the answer.

"I know, and I can't thank you enough for all you've done for me, but I've got to get back. I've got to tell headquarters about all those boats you said are being hidden for the invasion." Pierre nodded.

"I understand. I'd do the same," he said. He offered his hand, and Harriet shook it firmly. "Good luck." He turned to Nicole "Say your goodbyes; we should leave."

"You are the most infuriating person I've ever known," Nicole whispered as she knelt in front of Harriet.

"You should look in the mirror more often," Harriet replied with a smirk.

"I mean it!"

"I'll be OK, I promise."

"You don't know that."

"I do. Honestly, I'll be fine."

"I don't like this! I hate that you came here."

"I'm happy I came here, it's the happiest thing I could have done. I found my best friend again. If nothing else, that's made me happier than I've been in a long time."

"I'm not happy."

"Take care of yourself and stay alive. I'll come back when the war's over; now I know where to find you." She hugged Nicole tight with her good arm and kissed her on the cheek. Nicole nodded and kissed Harriet. "Go," she said. "We don't have much longer. Twenty minutes and I'm gone, and the whole German Air Force will be out looking for trouble." Another hug and kiss and Pierre took Nicole by the hand and pulled her away. Harriet sat in the moonlight and watched, as her tearful friend disappeared into the undergrowth, and out of sight. She sat back and looked at her watch. So this was it. She'd found her best friend and was so happy to know she was alive that the terror of what was coming next hardly had an impact. She'd get away or she wouldn't. If she didn't it didn't matter, at least Nicole was alive. She questioned herself briefly, but something in the back of her mind said she wouldn't die in her escape attempt. Being shot and taken prisoner seemed the most realistic option, but she was in her uniform, so at least she wouldn't be shot for a spy. She kept a look out while checking her watch, then fifteen minutes after the others had left, she crawled from her hiding place and scurried as low and fast as she could to the row of 109s. At the far end she could see work was still going on by the light of the moon, as the pilots talked and joked with their mechanics. She waited a minute to check if anyone had seen her, then remembering Beck's teasing the previous night she pulled the chocks away as silently as possible and pushed them under the next aeroplane. She climbed up the wing and pushed the canopy open, cringing and shrinking against the fuselage as the hinge creaked. Her heart was pounding and almost in her throat. Another quick check for movement and she climbed into the cockpit and sunk as low as possible as the dials glowed in the moonlight. She looked around, desperately trying to remember everything Beck had told her while her head was still fuzzy from rattling it off the tail of her Spitfire. Her heart almost stopped as she glanced around and saw a face at the cockpit side, staring at her in the darkness. Every muscle tensed and a shock ran up her spine, making every hair stand on end while she choked on her own breath.

"Get out," Nicole whispered.

"What are you doing here?!" Harriet demanded almost silently, trying to spit out the words from her dry mouth and stop herself dying of heart failure on the spot.

"Stop arguing and get out!" Nicole repeated as she quickly looked around for sentries.

"No! I told you I'm going! Now bugger off before they get you!"

"If you don't get out, I can't sit underneath you and operate the throttle, can I?"

"What?"

"Well, you can't do it. Now get out, we don't have time for this." Harriet nodded, shocked and struggling to process what was happening, then let Nicole help her out of the cockpit. She crouched and waited while Nicole took her seat and strapped in, then quickly climbed in after her to the now very cramped cockpit. "This cockpit is far too small, how are you even going to fly?" Nicole complained. She was right. Harriet had flown in a Hurricane with AP, and that was tight, but this was something else.

"You do the pedals for me," Harriet said as she quickly looked around the cockpit again, desperately trying to remember Beck's instructions.

"Hurry up," Nicole said, giving Harriet a nip.

"In a minute!"

"It'll be lunchtime in a minute!"

"Shut up. I'm trying to think!"

"It's a shame you didn't try that before coming up with this stupid plan!"

"Will you be quiet while I try to remember what to do!"

"What? Remember what? You said you'd flown one before!"

"I said I'd been shown how to fly one. There's a difference!"

"Dear God, I'm trapped in an aeroplane with a lunatic."

"Here we go. Get ready," Harriet flipped the switches in turn then hit the start. The heavy Daimler Benz engine coughed into life and roared like a thousand engines had all started at once in the silence of the night. "Wrap your arm tight around my waist and hold me in. Now hit the throttle!" Nicole did as she was told. "Slowly, slowly... Left rudder..." Nicole followed the instructions meticulously. "Straighten up, right rudder, right, right, that's it, steady there." Shouts were just audible over the sound of the engine. Harriet looked out of the cockpit to see the ground crew running at them, joined by the pilots and sentries. "Now!" she shouted.

"What?" Nicole asked.

"Now! Now! Open the bloody throttle right now!" Nicole complied, and the 109 lurched forwards. "Keep the pedals level!" Harriet ducked down into the cockpit as bullets ricocheted off the framework of the canopy. Another bullet hit the glass right in front of her, leaving a white spider web of cracks around its impact point the other side of the glass from her nose. One hit the glass right in front of her, leaving a web of cracks around the impact point. Another bullet passed through the fuselage and zipped out of the cockpit, hitting the release and flipping the canopy off and sending it rattling down the runway. "Come on... Come on..." Harriet repeated.

"For God's sake, get us out of here!" Nicole screamed as they scattered the Germans like skittles, and left them firing their rifles and pistols as they passed. They gathered speed and bumped along the grass until finally, the bump they were waiting for came, and Harriet was able to pull back on the stick and coax the 109 off the ground.

"Heben..." she muttered as she looked around the cockpit. "Heben. Where are you?" The sky filled with tracer rounds as she talked, then lit up with a colossal explosion some distance above.

"Stop praying to heaven and get us out of here!" Nicole yelled.

"Heben is up in German! I'm looking for the undercarriage lever!" Harriet replied impatiently. "Got it!" She shrugged her left arm from the sling and held the stick while she operated the lever. The wheels came up with a reassuring clunk, then she pushed the nose down and dived for the rapidly approaching cliff edge, while the sky all around lit up with golden orange explosions and tracer, turning the French coast into a firework show to rival any. Harriet kept the 109 as close to the ground as she dared, reducing the angle and making a near impossible target for the anti aircraft artillery who weren't able to traverse that low, leaving just the machine gunners to wrap the fuselage in a cone of tracer light. They cliffs couldn't come fast enough, and as soon as they did Harriet dived over them and put the 109 just a few feet above the unusually calm Channel, which stretched out in the moonlight like a sea of shimmering silver. The flak was soon behind them as they raced for home. Harriet looked around and twisted in her seat while Nicole tightened her grip around her waist, then she turned a little to the left to look behind. They weren't being followed, yet, but in the eastern sky was the faintest hint of silver blue, the first signs of dawn. Harriet smiled to herself as she turned her head, looking for trouble. She'd done it. She'd really done it. She had no doubt that she could if she could get off the ground, but the getting off the ground part is what was hardest. At that, the aeroplane shuddered. The noise in the air was terrific, and she turned to look at Nicole, who shrugged and shook her head. A quick scan of the dials showed the engine temperature climbing slightly. A bullet must have hit the engine. There was no white smoke so the coolant hadn't been hit, and no black smoke so it wasn't oil burning, but something wasn't right. She was faced with a stark choice. Keep the throttle open fully and hope for the best, or climb and throttle back, and hope to get enough height to glide back to England should the engine cut. If she stayed low and the engine gave up, they'd be in the water with no life jackets or dinghies, and no chance of being found. If she climbed, they'd be picked up by the English radar, and they'd have a brace of Spitfires coming up to meet them; and in the dark, they'd simply see a 109 and knock it out of the sky without knowing or caring who was inside. She knew because she'd been scrambled to intercept at first light herself, she'd been the hunter. Another look around, and she'd made her decision. Nicole didn't have a clue what was going on, she couldn't see the dials, so continuing to race across the surface of the Channel wouldn't worry her. The theory that finally settled Harriet's mind was that the longer they went, the closer they'd get to land. If the engine started to give up, she'd climb quickly and appear on

344

the radar long enough to be spotted and have an intercept scrambled, then come back down again and ditch, and try to stay afloat long enough for the intercept Spitfires to find them and send out a launch. There was lots of wishful thinking in her plan, but it was better than drowning or being shot down in flames. She kept her eyes between the horizon and the temperature gauge, with the occasional spin of her head to check for pursuers. The engine started to run noticeably rough, and the temperature jumped again. Harriet was on edge, and she could feel her heart pounding harder and harder as each minute passed. Then it happened. She blinked and rubbed her eyes. Not a couple of miles ahead were the white cliffs of Dover, shimmering in the moonlight and merging with the silver sea. They were hard to distinguish at first, but they were there. The more she looked, the more she was certain, it was Dover. She screamed with happiness and excitement. Nicole pinched her, and she looked down at her friend's confused face. "We're home," she mouthed excitedly. "Home!" She pointed ahead, and Nicole nodded with a look on her face somewhere between a frown and relief. If the engine could just hold a bit longer... Harriet pulled back on the stick and raised the nose slowly, not wanting to upset the engine too much, and eased the 109 over the cliffs. She reached forward and throttled back, slowly reducing their speed and the strain on the engine. Harriet felt an extra hard squeeze and looked down at a furious Nicole who was gesturing at the hand Harriet had just used to control the throttle. Harriet shrugged, and winked, then turned her head forward and followed the landmarks that had been imprinted on her mind, and which she knew would take her home. The engine temperature had settled, though it was still running rough, but with every minute she became more and more confident they'd get back. Before long, she caught sight of the hangars. She lined up on a long approach. Wheels down, throttle back, glide and hold it steady. Flaps... flaps. She found them and dropped them and slowed a little more. The sky lit up in front of them, and the 109 jumped, almost throwing Harriet from the cockpit and forcing Nicole to grab tight to keep her friend from taking an unscheduled exit without a parachute. The whole world around them around them erupted and they were lit up by searchlights as they flew into a barrage of anti aircraft artillery to put the German effort to shame. The engine stuttered and, without warning, coughed, choked, and died, leaving them gliding through hell. There was nothing that Harriet could do other than switch everything off, fuel included, and get them below the gun traverse level. Any erratic movements to aid that could stall them and flip them into a fiery death, so she sat and watched the boundary hedge approach. The wheels skidded over the top of it, and quickly the 109 dropped to the ground with a bounce that sent them right back up into the air before finally settling on the grass. Vehicle headlights were lit and aimed at the 109, and silhouettes ran in all directions as she aimed at the line of Spitfires, which had been dragged out of their pits by the ground crews ready for the first light stand to. The 109 slowed and finally crept to a halt where it hissed and creaked. She sighed and leant forward, resting her head on the top of the windscreen frame. "You can let go of me now, we're home," she said as soon as she got some moisture in her mouth.

"Hande Hoch!" Cas said as he stood on the wing and aimed his revolver into the cockpit.

"Good morning, Cas," Harriet said as she looked up with a smile. "Please put your gun away. I've had enough of people shooting at me for one day. I'm starting to think the artillery here don't like me."

"My God..." he muttered as he stepped back and lowered his revolver. "Harry?" She pulled herself upwards, then lifted a boot onto the cockpit frame.

"Where on earth have you been?"

"France."

"France?"

"Yes. Don't worry. I brought you a gift."

"Your English hospitality needs refining," Nicole said as she pulled herself up behind Harriet. "I hardly think a pistol in the face is the most traditional of greetings, either. Though you're English, so it's entirely possible that's what you consider polite." Cas helped Harriet from the cockpit and held his hand to Nicole, who took it and stood, dusting herself down as though she was dressed in her most beautiful robes.

"God damn..." Max said as he joined them on the wing. "If it ain't the bad penny."

"Who is Penny?" Nicole asked as she climbed onto the wing and was guided down with the others.

"Never mind," Harriet replied. "Welcome to England."

"Welcome indeed," Cas said as he gave Nicole an unexpected hug. "The boss is going to be happy to see you."

"Boss?"

"Singh. He's been called away to group headquarters, so Max is leading the squadron today, but he'll wish he was here right now." Cas looked at them both. "France?" he asked Harriet again.

"I was shot down over the Channel and ended up being picked up by a German seaplane. I bumped into Nicole while I was there, and we borrowed the 109 to get back home. Though I don't think the Germans were so happy about it, they tried to shoot us down."

"Like your idiots here," Nicole added. "Why were they shooting at us?"

"Because you were flying over an RAF airfield in a Luftwaffe aeroplane," Cas replied. "It tends to be frowned upon these days, especially considering the lot who tried it during the night made a nuisance of themselves when they dropped their bombs all over the place."

"It's still impolite. It's not like we were shooting or anything; we even had our wheels down to land," Nicole continued. Cas couldn't help smiling. She was still as reluctant as ever to be corrected.

"Come on, let's get you both a drink." He led them to the dispersal hut.

347

"That doesn't excuse them shooting me out of the sky when I was flying a Spitfire," Harriet sighed.

"We've been over this, Harry, and the army apologised profusely. Nobody warned them to expect a pink Spitfire, that's all, it was a perfectly innocent mistake." The dispersal phone rang, and everyone stopped and looked at the dispersal hut.

"What?" Nicole asked as she looked around. Cas held a finger in the air, gesturing for her to wait a moment.

"Squadron scramble!" came the shout, followed by a bell ringing. The pilots immediately started running as their Spitfires fired into life under the control of their ground crews.

"What's happening?" Nicole asked.

"A raid is building up over France, most likely," Harriet replied. "We're about as close as you can get to the coast, and the first in line for any raids coming at the south. We try and intercept them before they get inland or hit them on their way home."

"Every day?" Nicole asked.

"Most mornings," Cas replied as the orderly brought them all a cup of tea. He nodded and smiled at the orderly before continuing. "Sometimes it's a patrol, sometimes nothing, other times it's a morning raid. Whatever it is, it usually starts at first light and doesn't stop until sundown. Then we get the night raiders, of course, and unexpected dawn visitors," he gave them a wink. "The Spy is probably going to want to talk to you."

"Good morning," The Spy said as he walked from behind the dispersal hut.

"Mention his name, and he shall appear," Cas said. "Good morning, Spy," he greeted Matthews, the intelligence officer. "I thought you'd slept in."

"Don't be ridiculous. I just prefer to start my day in a civilised way with a cup of tea in the Mess, instead of a field. Any fool can be uncomfortable, you know."

"Oh, I know."

"Speaking of fields, why's there a Messerschmitt 109 sitting on ours?"

"Ask her," he nodded at Harriet.

"Something you want to tell me, Harry?" he asked

"We borrowed it," she replied.

"We?"

"This is Nicole Delacourt. She flew with the squadron in France." Nicole lifted her face and looked down her nose at The Spy before glancing away in her usual dismissive manner and sipping on her tea.

"Yes, I've heard her name... The two of you came back in that crate?"
"Yes."

"It's a good job that you're friends. I'm not sure I'd want to get that close to a stranger. Anyway, you're going to have to give me all of the details."

"Details about sharing the cockpit of an aeroplane?" Nicole frowned. "The
English are more ridiculous than I remember."

"More about where you borrowed it from," he smirked. "It's my job to know things."

349

"Well, you don't know what I know," Nicole replied.

"Which is?"

"Which is that the Germans are lining up barges in the rivers ready for an invasion. They're hidden and camouflaged, but there's lots of them, hundreds maybe."

"You're a find! Come and show me on the map," he led her into the dispersal hut, leaving Cas and Harriet outside.

"Are you OK?" he asked her quietly. She nodded and forced a smile. "Seriously?" She nodded, and a tear ran down her cheek. She turned away and let out an irritated groan. "Hey," he said as he put his hand on her shoulder. She flinched and pulled away with a gasp. "Harry?" She turned and wiped the tear. "What is it?"

"I dislocated my shoulder when I stepped out of the office over the Channel."

"I see... Well, I think we'd better get Simon to have a look at you."

"I'm fine. A German doctor put it back in place; it just hurts a bit still."

"A German doctor? I'm not sure I want to hear this story... Anyway, how are you other than sore?" She shrugged, and he nodded. "OK... I'll leave off for now. You could probably do with some rest."

"I don't mind. Give me an hour in a chair, and I'll be ready to fly again."

"I don't think so..."

"Oh, don't be boring, Cas. I just flew a 109 across the Channel in the dark,
I'm fine."

"I'll be as boring as I like, and you'll go to your room and get some sleep.

We'll talk later."

"But..."

"No buts."

"You know, we are the same rank these days, and I don't have to do as you say."

"And you know that I'm the Adjutant, and I can have you posted to a meteorological station on the Atlantic coast of Scotland if you don't do as you're told by an officer senior to you."

"Senior? There's no need to bring your age into it."

"Is this what I'm in for now you're back? Slanderous comments relating to my age and bearing."

"I promise not to mention you being rather short, for a man at least," she said with a smile. He rolled his eyes and shook his head.

"First rate information," The Spy said as he emerged from the dispersal hut. "I'm off to HQ to make sure it gets up to Group."

"Do me a favour, would you?" Cas asked.

"What's that, old man?"

"Don't you start with the old..." Cas said with a frown, making The Spy shrugged with confusion. "Drop these two at the Mess, will you? I think they've earned a rest." He turned back to Harriet. "Go on, get some sleep, and we'll talk later. I'm happy to see you're back," he smiled warmly at her. "Though you're going to make me grey if you keep getting shot down like that. Three times is enough. I don't think I can stand a fourth."

"Shut up," she said as she felt a blush spreading across her cheeks.

"Anyway, you're grey already, old man."

"Righto," The Spy said. "Bus to the Mess, hop on." He marched off into the dark.

"Well, what are the two of you waiting for? Bed!" Cas demanded. They both walked off after The Spy.

"I haven't missed the English and their orders," Nicole complained.

"You'd prefer the Germans and theirs?"

"I'd prefer France!" She then punched Harriet in the arm, without any warning.

"What the hell are you doing!" Harriet yelped as she grabbed at her shoulder.

"That's for lying to me!"

"Lying? What on earth are you talking about now, you crazy French woman?!"

"Making me think you'd hurt your shoulder so you couldn't use the throttle, so I'd have to come with you."

"I did hurt my shoulder, you idiot!" She cradled her arm.

"Not as much as you let me believe."

"I did... It just wasn't quite as sore by the time we got to the airfield. Besides, I had to try and get you to come home, and it's the only thing I could think of. I knew you'd try and look after me, and I just let you."

"And nearly got me shot out of the sky. Twice!" The Spy held open the door to his car and let them climb into the back seat.

"Well, I have news for you."

"What's that?"

"You didn't get me to come, Fleur did."

"What?"

"You heard what she said, all of that nonsense about England being Europe's last hope. I'm a very good pilot. If I'm going to help save France,
I need to use my skills and do it from the air."

"You're very modest, too."

"I know."

"I thought as much."

The girls bickered all the way to the Mess, and up the stairs to Harriet's room. The door was thrown open by Daisy, who flung her arms around Harriet's neck as she ran out into the corridor and held on to her.

"Where the hell have you been!?" she demanded.

"To France to collect a package," Harriet replied. Daisy stepped back and put her hand over her mouth in surprise at seeing Nicole. She hadn't seen her, or anything, before she'd thrown herself at Harriet, she was so focused on knowing her friend was safe.

"Oh my God," Daisy gasped.

"Don't call me that," Nicole said as she walked into Harriet's room and looked around. "Her royal highness here in her fancy uniform will get jealous." Daisy followed her in and hugged her tight.

"I'll go and get more pyjamas," she said. "And some breakfast. I'll be back." She ran out excitedly and pulled the door closed behind her, leaving the girls looking at each other.

"Some room," Nicole said dismissively as she looked around.

"It's better than a French ditch," Harriet replied.

"Yes... Yes, it is. I like it. The bed is small, though."

"Big enough to share." They smiled and hugged, then kicked off their shoes and fell onto the bed. Both were exhausted. Nicole lay between Harriet and the wall and put her head on Harriet's right shoulder.

"I'm so tired."

"Me too."

"Thank you for coming to find me, Harry."

"I think I've been searching for you every night in my dreams."

"In mine also." She looked up at Harriet and smiled warmly, then lifted her head and kissed her before settling back onto Harriet's shoulder. "Let's not lose each other again."

"If we do, I'll find you. I promise."

"I'll hold you to that promise," Nicole laid her arm around Harriet and felt her eyes getting heavy. The sound of Merlin engines buzzed in the distance and Harriet couldn't help but smile to herself as she listened to them swooping around the distant skies. She looked down at Nicole, who was asleep already, her hazel eyes closed, and her soft lips open in a slight smile. Her golden brown hair was tousled and spread over her shoulders as they gently raised and lowered with her quiet breathing.

Chapter 15

Together Again

Both Harriet and Nicole slept through the day, and the night, and only woke in the morning of the following day when hunger and a deep thirst dragged them from their sleep. They washed and dressed, Harriet lending Nicole her spare trousers and blouse, and the shoes from her best uniform and the pair went down to the Mess for breakfast, where the duty steward put bacon and eggs with black pudding in front of them, along with toast and jam, tea, and apple juice, all without it being ordered.

"You eat like this every morning?" Nicole asked as she started on her meal.
"There's no wonder you were in a hurry to get back here!"

"Not usually..." Harriet replied with a slight frown of confusion. The pilots were always well looked after when it came to food. The powers that be had understood from the start that if the pilots were to be alert throughout the ever increasing demands of their daily work, they needed to be fed, but such large portions were unheard of. At least in Harriet's short time with the RAF. "Better make the most of it." She shrugged

"I intend to," Nicole replied with a mouth full of bacon. "The Germans requisitioned much of the food where we lived in France. One breakfast like this would feed Pierre's whole family, and me." Harriet smiled and started on her own food. It tasted good. She'd been well looked after in France, but she still felt starved after her ordeal. "What will we do today?"
Nicole asked. "Fly with the squadron?"

"Probably not," Harriet replied. "You won't, anyway. I may get a flight in later."

"Why not me?"

"It's the RAF. Nothing is easy. You'll probably have to take a flight test, among other things."

"A flight test? You're joking! I'm the best pilot here! Why should I have to take a test?"

"Everyone has to take a test. It can take the RAF up to two years to train a fighter pilot, and they don't just let people walk in off the street. Or drop out of the sky from France."

"Two years? What are they doing, teaching them to build their own aeroplanes at the same time? There's no wonder you're short of pilots!" Nicole spluttered. Harriet shrugged and continued eating. She'd been told some of what happens over the training life of a new pilot, but she hadn't actually been through it, she'd spent hours of every day learning the things she would have been taught during regular training. The only reason she'd sidestepped the system is because she was already an officer, and already recognised, however fictitiously, as a qualified Norwegian military pilot. Had that not happened, she'd have been off to a training school somewhere for anything between six and twenty four months of training.

"Harry, old man! How's breakfast?" Alastair asked as he entered the dining room.

"Good. Very good, thank you," Harriet replied as she tried to swallow a mouthful of food while standing. "Sit, sit," he gestured excitedly as he joined them. "And this young lady must be the notorious Miss Delacourt of the glorious French Armee de l'Air?" he asked as he sat at the head of the table. Nicole took a drink of apple juice to clear her throat.

"I must be," Nicole replied, eyes a little wider than usual in surprise at the sudden change to her breakfast conversation.

"This is Group Captain Saltire," Harriet said. "He's the Station Commander."

356

"It's a pleasure to meet you, I'm sure," Nicole said politely.

"Oh, the pleasure's all mine, I assure you," Alastair replied. "I heard all about your exploits with Harry when you were in France together, and Mister Salisbury told me the pair of you stole a 109 from a Luftwaffe airfield last night and brought it home for us to evaluate. Something the Air Ministry have been quite excited about. We don't get our hands on many in one piece, you see, especially not the new model like the one you borrowed. Mostly they tend to land at speed around here, having been shot out of the sky by rowdy little trouble causers like young Harry here." He gave Harriet a wink, which inexplicably made her blush. "Word is that Their Airships are most grateful and keen to meet you in the near future."

"You want me to meet an airship?" Nicole frowned. "A balloon?" she asked Harriet for confirmation.

"Oh, I like you; we're going to get on," Alastair laughed. "Balloons, wonderful. Well, it has been said they're full of hot air," he laughed again, quite amused at the misunderstanding. "Anyway, before we get to the balloons, the AOC would appreciate the pleasure of your company later this morning. You can fly her up there, Harry. Take my Tiger if you like, I won't be using it."

"Sir?" Harriet replied.

"Uxbridge, Harry. You probably want to get there a little early; it doesn't pay to keep the AOC waiting."

"I was hoping to be back with the squadron this afternoon, Sir."

"With the squadron? Operational you mean? Oh, you are a card, Harry. Operational Flying indeed. You're going on leave!"

"What? I don't want to go on leave! I want to fly! Sir..."

357

"And fly you will, to Northolt! To take young Delacourt here to her meeting at Uxbridge. Then you have a two day leave pass. I don't need the Tiger Moth for a few days, so why don't you leave it at Northolt while the two of you enjoy some time in London?"

"But..."

"No buts, Harry, not this time. You haven't had a day off since you got here, you've earned the rest."

"Yes, Sir," she said reluctantly as she slumped into her chair.

"Oh don't be like that, old man, even the best need a break every now and again. Besides, you'll need to be on your game when you get back to the squadron, we've got lots of new faces due in fresh from training, and as a Flight Commander you're going to have your work cut out whipping them into shape." He gave her a wink and watched as her smile returned. "You didn't think I was letting you off that lightly, did you? We need pilots, especially good ones." He stood and clasped his hands together excitably. "Best uniform, Harry. You too, Miss Delacourt, dress smart for the AOC, he won't abide scruffs."

"Scruffs?" Nicole asked.

"I'll have the Tiger made ready for you. Enjoy London, and Cas asked you to give him a call and let him know how you get on!" He walked off jauntily, then stopped and turned. "Oh, and if you get the time, I'd recommend the American Bar at The Savoy." He gave them a wink and left them to finish their breakfast.

"I'm not even going to ask what any of that meant," Nicole said. "He's as crazy as the rest of you English pilots."

"He means the officer in charge of all fighter pilots in the South East of England wants to see you this morning."

"Just tell me what to do; I'm too tired to think," Nicole said with a shrug.

358

"Just be polite. No arguing, at all. Understand?" Nicole shrugged again. "I mean it. The man we're going to meet can stop you ever being a fighter pilot if you annoy him enough. So do your best to bite your tongue."

Two hours later and the Tiger Moth was touching down at Northolt, and taxiing into the exact same visitor spot Lexi had used when she'd flown Harriet for her meeting. Harriet had talked Nicole through the controls before taking off, and then after swinging a long way west of London she let Nicole practise for a while before landing. They hitched up their skirts and climbed from the cockpit, attracting appreciative whistles from a couple of passing airmen, until they noted the rank and ribbons on Harriet's tunic, and quickly saluted shamefacedly. The girls straightened their clothes and headed to the duty desk, Harriet in her best uniform and Nicole in the formal outfit Aunt Mary had bought Harriet for her trip to the Air Ministry, which fortunately fit like it was made for her. Waiting in the office was the same young officer who'd greeted them last time. He looked Harriet up and down, acknowledging the rank braid and medal ribbons, and didn't hesitate to have transport provided for them immediately. Within twenty minutes of landing, they were in front of the AOC's desk.

"I'm told that thanks are in order," the AOC began. "That 109 you brought in has been remarkably helpful already. They've made a number of adjustments, and our best test pilots are flying it around the clock to try and work out the best ways of dealing with it in battle. The two of you may just have saved a few lives and given us an edge."

"We're just happy to have been able to help, Sir," Harriet replied.

"Yes, well, you've certainly done that. I also hear you've been making a name for yourself since being back with your squadron, Flight Lieutenant Cornwall, and I was happy to sign your promotion recommendation."

"Thank you, Sir."

"And this is your partner in crime... Miss Delacourt, is it?"

"It is, Sir," Nicole replied politely. "It's a pleasure to meet you at last. Your name for being a talented fighter pilot and leader is well known in my country."

"Is that so?" the AOC half smiled. "I don't mind knowing that..." He shuffled the papers in front of him almost nervously. "Anyway, I'm sure you know I didn't call you here just to make pleasantries."

"That would have been a pleasure, all the same, Sir," Nicole replied. Harriet couldn't help but look out of the corner of her eye to make sure the polite, respectful, and almost flirtatious young woman standing by her side was, in fact, her troublesome and argumentative friend.

"Yes. Wouldn't it..." he replied. "However, we have a war to fight," he added, checking himself and bringing himself back to the task. "And we need combat pilots." He opened the file and read for a moment. "It appears that you, like Cornwall, were commissioned as a Probationary Pilot Officer in the Royal Air Force Volunteer Reserve while in France?"

"Yes, Sir, an honour I was very proud to receive when I was no longer able to fly for France."

"Your record shows a number of confirmed victories in combat."

"Yes, Sir. Thirteen in all."

"You were also awarded your country's Légion d'honneur for your valour, and nominated for a Distinguished Flying Cross in recognition of your actions over France. Specifically in engaging the squadron of 109s that attacked the bomber carrying Air Vice Marshal Bristol and Mister Brompton from the Air Ministry, an honour bestowed on only the best pilots."

"I didn't know, Sir, and it is indeed a great honour."

"I'm happy to agree. Now, I have one further question to ask you."

"Yes, Sir?"

"Do you still want to fly for the RAF?"

"Yes, Sir, without question. While I'm grateful for the nomination for the medal, the greatest honour is the opportunity to fly for the RAF."

"Good. Then you won't mind having a medical and a flying assessment while you're here?"

"Not at all, Sir. I welcome the opportunity to be tested. I think it's an essential requirement that lets the RAF make sure that everyone meets, and maintains the very high standards expected of all pilots."

"It does, Miss Delacourt, you're right, and let me say it's refreshing to hear those words from a young officer." He smiled a little, then glanced back down and signed a form on his desk. "Very well. I'm making your commission in the Volunteer Reserve permanent and, subject to you passing the medical and flight examinations, I'll release you back to your squadron for local familiarisation training on the Spitfire. Once Mister Salisbury is happy with your type rating, Mister Singh can make a decision on your operational status. Any questions?"

"No, Sir," Nicole said with a smile on her face. "Thank you, Sir, I won't let you down."

"I know you won't, Miss Delacourt." He frowned a little as he paused. "Though you must remember, the same rule applies to you as does Miss Cornwall. This country isn't used to female fighter pilots, and I dare say they're not ready for you just yet, so some elements will do everything in their power to undermine you and have you removed if you give them any reason at all. Now, I know that you have a reputation for being feisty at times, Miss Delacourt, so I can only make it very clear that should you let the highest standards of the service slip, I'll have absolutely no hesitation in grounding you indefinitely. Understood?"

"Perfectly, Sir"

"Good. Now I have a war to fight if you don't mind." He handed an envelope to Nicole. "Your papers." She smiled as she took them. "Oh, and the next time I see you, you'd better make sure you're in uniform."

"Yes, Sir. Please excuse my civilian clothes."

"Not at all," he switched his gaze to Harriet. "Does the name Finn mean anything to you, Miss Cornwall?"

"The WAAF Officer, Sir?" Harriet asked as she remembered the snapdragon of a woman who'd treated her terribly when they met in France.

"That's the one... I thought you may like to know that when she returned to England from France, by your good grace, she was posted to the Manning and Records department at the Air Ministry."

"Sir..." Harriet replied.

"Apparently it was she who placed your files in the 1918 deceased section, by mistake of course."

"Of course..."

"Anyway, she's now in Scotland counting weather balloons." Harriet smiled and nodded as the AOC went back to his work while the pair left the room, walking along the corridors and out of the building, smirking.

"Are you feeling, OK?" Harriet asked.

"I'm feeling wonderful. Why?" Nicole replied with a huge smile on her face.

"You welcome the opportunity to be tested?"

"Of course I welcome testing. I'm a very good pilot, and it's important that others see that."

"Really?" Harriet rolled her eyes.

"Really," Nicole smiled. "Anyway. You told me not to argue, so I just pretended to be you." Harriet jabbed her elbow into Nicole's arm, and the girls laughed as they made their way to the hospital. It was a brief appointment. While Nicole went for testing, Harriet followed Alastair's orders and reported for a check up on her shoulder. The doctor was happy with it. It was sore and very bruised, with most of the skin across her shoulder, back, and upper arm being a pretty mix of black, blue, purple, and deep red, but she was able to move it much better after a rest, and it wasn't anywhere near as sore. He also checked her eyesight, just to make sure the hit to her head, which had resulted in some bruising to her left cheek and eye, hadn't done any damage. She was given a clean bill of health with advice to rest from flying for a few days. Nicole's medical was equally uneventful, and soon it was back to the airfield where a senior instructor was waiting to conduct her flight test, which she passed with a grade of average. Nicole was furious, inside at least. Outside she continued to be the model of a perfect lady. The instructor had actually been extremely complimentary, and an average rating from the RAF was very good anywhere else. Very few were ever rated above average. The rating didn't come as a surprise to Harriet. Nicole was far above average as a pilot, but she hadn't flown for months, and until that morning she hadn't flown a Tiger Moth, so all things considered an average rating was pretty good. Not that any amount of explaining would calm Nicole's disgust at being rated so low.

"Cas? It's Harry. She passed everything, and her commission has been made permanent," Harriet said, after the station operator had finally got her connected to the dispersal office.

"Good show! Right, you remember the tailor I took you to in Saville Row?"

"Yes."

"There's a uniform waiting for her there. Then I want you to head over to The Savoy. I've booked you both a room for the night, and dinner is at eight. Have a great time, and I'll see you both back in the Mess tomorrow evening."

"Cas, you really shouldn't have..."

"See you tomorrow, got to go." He hung up and left her hanging onto the receiver with a smile.

"Well?" Nicole asked. "What did the old man say to put a smile on your face this time?"

"You'll see," Harriet smiled as she put down the phone.

"He's sweet for you."

"If you say so."

"And you're sweet on him. Still."

"Shut up!"

"Calls during the day that leave you smiling like that, what else could it be?"

"I said shut up!"

The trip to London was as before, though the transport was obligingly supplied much quicker. After a short journey on the train and the tube the girls were back in the tailor's shop in Saville Row, and Harriet was sitting on a stool sipping sherry while Nicole was in the changing room. "Beautiful," she said as Nicole stepped out in her uniform. It was identical to Harriet's, except for the 'France' shoulder flashes, a crimson silk lining instead of turquoise blue, and fewer stripes on the cuff.

"It fits perfectly," Nicole said as she turned and looked at herself in the many mirrors. "How did this happen?" she asked. She was genuinely touched and couldn't stop looking at herself in the soft RAF blue skirt and tunic, both perfectly cut to accentuate her form.

"Mister Salisbury called yesterday and ordered it," Mister Thomas said, as he fluttered excitedly around Nicole, admiring his art. Nicole fired a look of surprise at Harriet as she took the proffered glass of sherry.

"He wanted to know when you'd passed your tests so he could send you here for your uniform. That's why I was so happy after I talked to Cas." Harriet said. Nicole simply smiled and nodded, then sipped at her sherry while continuing to gaze at her reflection from different angles, while stroking the country flash.

"If Ma'am is happy, I can pack your clothes in a bag for you to carry?"

"I'm delighted, thank you so much," Nicole replied. Mister Thomas snapped his fingers, and his assistants rushed into action around Nicole, while he and Harriet walked to his desk.

"Can I ask you something?" Harriet asked while he scribbled.

"Of course, Ma'am," he replied politely.

"Has Mister Salisbury been buying his uniforms here long?" Thomas leant back and looked over the top of his glasses with a knowing smile. "It's just that he looks after us all so well, yet I feel I hardly know him sometimes." "Yes, he can be something of an enigma at times. I know people who have called him a friend for years, yet would still swear that they don't know him."

"Do you know him?"

"A little..."

"It'll be our secret. I promise I won't tell," Harriet smiled.

"There's nothing much to tell, really, I'm sorry to say. Though I do remember the young Charles, when he came here for his first uniform after transferring to the Royal Flying Corps in the last war."

"So he's always had good taste..."

"Oh, absolutely. He knows what he likes, but he's had to work hard to be able to enjoy what he likes, too."

"That doesn't surprise me; he never seems to stop. He always seems to have a project on his mind, something, many things, occupying him all at once."

"Yes, that's him," Thomas said as he took off his glasses and looked into the distance, summoning far off memories. He was much older than she, in his late sixties, but his eyes twinkled as he glanced at Harriet. "The reason he always has a project in mind is that he's had to think that way to get ahead. Charles wasn't born to money, you see, not like many of his peers in the army back then. When he was young, he decided he wanted to better himself, so he applied for, and won, a scholarship at quite an exclusive local school. As his family weren't wealthy, and even the uniform was more than they could afford. It was a struggle, but they made it work, somehow. Anyway, he did well enough to find himself being commissioned as a subaltern in a local infantry regiment. Of course, you'd not think he was that fortunate when you consider that it got him sent to the butcher's yard of the Western Front. He first came here with a friend, a lord whose family had served in the army for generations, and were very good customers of ours. The young lord insisted on buying Charles his uniforms when he was accepted to the Royal Flying Corps. When Charles politely declined, as I've come to expect of him, the young lord found out his measurements and had his uniforms made for him anyway as a surprise," Thomas laughed to himself. "He was quite embarrassed when he came to collect them, not unlike you when you collected yours." Harriet blushed a little. "Anyway, it seems the Royal Flying Corps, and then the RAF suited him, as he did

366

quite well for himself with his flying exploits, and winning the Victoria Cross, of course. He was a Wing Commander when he asked to be put on the inactive list so he could go into business for himself, I believe."

"I didn't know any of that," Harriet said with her eyes wide.

"And you still don't," Thomas said with a wink.

"Of course," she smiled.

"Good. I don't want our mutual friend thinking I can't be trusted with his secrets. He's been buying his clothes here since that first time in the last war, and he's been a valued customer and friend, ever since. I'd hate for him to go down the road to my competition," he smiled warmly.

"Thank you for trusting me enough to tell me."

"Well, I assumed that if he trusts you so much, there's no reason I shouldn't."

"What makes you think he trusts me?"

"Charles has been shopping here for over two decades. How many of his young protégés do you imagine he's bought uniforms for?"

"I wouldn't know where to start guessing?" Harriet replied with a shrug.

"One," he tapped her with his pencil. "You!" He gave her a knowing look. "And your French friend, of course, though she is a very good friend of yours, and therefore naturally an extension of you." Harriet blushed and raised an eyebrow. "Oh, don't get me wrong. He's bought things for people and supported them when they needed it, but he's never brought them here into his world."

"I don't know what to say..." Harriet said.

"Absolutely nothing," came the reply.

"What happened to his friend? The young lord that you mentioned?"

"Shot down over the Channel, I think, though nobody can be sure as his body was never found." Harriet felt a twinge in her stomach. "They didn't have parachutes issued in those days, and from what I know, he crashed and drowned." Her mind instantly went back to how horrible she'd been to Cas when she'd met him again in England, and how awful she'd felt when AP had explained how news of her loss in the Channel had all but destroyed him. Now she was feeling a little more horrible again.

"Mister Thomas, I need a favour," she said.

"If I can," he shrugged.

"I want to buy him something, a gift as a thank you, but I wouldn't have a clue where to start. Would you have anything here?"

He thought for a moment, then stood. "I think I have just the thing! Over here." He led her to one of his display cases and took out a small wooden box and handed it to her. She took off the lid to reveal a luxurious and intricately detailed soft leather wallet, which she opened to reveal a shimmering silver cigarette case. "It's hand made from Catalonian silver pesetas from the Spanish War of Independence," he said proudly. "A small number of these were hand made in Barcelona during the Spanish Civil War as a way of hiding the silver from the fascists, and I was fortunate enough to obtain a handful of them. The inside shows the coins, while the outside was polished to look like common white metal and protect the secrets inside." He smiled warmly as he recounted the history of the rare piece. "I know our friend spent some time over there in the past, and he speaks fondly of the place when the mood takes him."

"It's beautiful," she said as she took it out of the box. She opened the case and gasped as the highly polished surface reflected light around the room. Inside, the faces of the coins were merged into each other but still

368

unique in their writing and markings, and all stamped with Barcelona 1813. "How much is it?"

"How much do you have?" he replied as he took it from her and felt its weight in his hand. "1813 was the last year of Joseph Bonaparte's reign as King of Spain. The coins used in making this particular case were some of the last minted before Wellington kicked the French out of Spain entirely. It's a rare piece…"

"Let me look." She reached inside her tunic to pull out her pocketbook. Thomas held up his hand and shook his head. "But I'd really like to buy it from you," Harriet protested.

"I'd usually sell these for twenty pounds."

"OK," Harriet said without hesitation. She was a little nervous as it was a lot of money, more than she'd ever spent on anything, but she still had the money her parents had sent Aunt Mary to keep her, and her back pay, so it would be affordable. Just not right at that moment. She pulled out a five pound note which she'd frivolously and excitedly decided to bring for her trip to London, intending to splash out and have a good time. She held it proudly in front of Thomas. "I only have this with me at the moment; but if you'd trust me, I'll bring the rest the next time I'm stood down long enough to get to London. I promise."

"No…" Thomas replied. Harriet's shoulders dropped, and she felt very embarrassed.

"I'm sorry, I shouldn't have asked. I hardly know you, and certainly not well enough to ask favours."

"If you'll allow me to finish, Miss Cornwall," he continued as she blushed a little more. "I'd normally sell them for twenty pounds, but neither you nor our friend are normal customers. "Therefore, it'll be exactly five pounds." Harriet smiled and offered the money again. "On the understanding that no payment will be made until the war is over."

"Excuse me?" Harriet asked in surprise.

"Get through the war alive, and you can settle things with me then, and only then. Agreed?" He held out his hand, and she smiled and shook it firmly. "Oh, and we've got to have won the war. You die, or we lose, and the whole deal's off."

"That doesn't exactly motivate me to win, or to stay alive for that matter."

"Nonsense. You're a decent person, Miss Cornwall. You'd never rest in your grave knowing there was a debt unpaid."

"I know..." she replied with a frown. "And please call me Harry, all of my friends do."

"Only if you call me Ralph."

"It's a pleasure to meet you, Ralph."

"And you, Harry. Now, why don't you show me what colour scarf would suit Miss Delacourt?" Harriet nodded and followed him to a rail holding a selection of beautiful silk scarves.

"That one," she said right away, pointing to the red scarf with white polka dots. "It's bright and daring, like her."

"Very well."

Nicole finally joined them, accompanied by her entourage of staff. Ralph had offered to have their bags sent to the airfield the following day, and as they only had a limited amount of space on their return flight, they happily agreed. After saying their goodbyes the girls stepped out into London, and side by side they hit the town, exploring all the West End shopping meccas that Harriet had ever heard of, including an eye opening trip to Fortnum & Mason of Piccadilly. Archie had mentioned it so many times in the past, and had always insisted they should visit 'if just

370

for the tea selection.' They bought packs of teas, teapots and cups, and a selection of expensive biscuits. The doorman held the door open for them and called them a taxi, which took them to the Savoy hotel in time to check in to the most luxurious of rooms before heading down to the American bar, where the room fell silent for their entry. Two female pilots, in uniform, in the most exclusive bar in London, and they didn't have to buy a drink all night. The place was packed with those from the upper echelons of society, and a large number of Americans, which wasn't a surprise considering the name of the bar. American military officers on attachment to the embassy plied them with drinks as they grilled them for details of their combat experience, and American businessmen talked about their products and how the RAF could do with everything they sold; as though the girls had any control over the purchasing at all. One of them even insisted on giving them an entire box of what he called 'aviators', sunglasses he told them had been designed for combat pilots, and which would be better than anything they'd ever used. His only charge was a photograph of them both wearing his wares. It was a wonderful evening, with lots of dancing to the American swing band that played live through the night.

The following day they enjoyed breakfast at the hotel before taking to the town to visit a matinee show, and visit a few more shops for Nicole to buy some toiletries and casual clothes. After lunch, they headed to the Air Ministry at Harriet's request, where she found Flight Lieutenant O'Kara processing a room full of young hopefuls. The room fell silent at the sight of two female pilots, both with their top buttons unfastened in the unofficial style of a fighter pilot, and both wearing wings and ribbons. O'Kara greeted them both like old friends, then introduced them as examples of what the crowd of young men can dream of being, should they make it through their interviews. Harriet thanked him for all he'd done for her and presented him with a small teapot, hand painted in a Japanese style, along with some tea, a gift she'd bought the previous day, and something very well received. After saying goodbye, and answering excited questions from the gathered young men about flying Spitfires and Hurricanes, an entirely different experience from Harriet's previous visit, they made their way back across London to Northolt. After loading their shopping and stowing it away, they took a low and leisurely flight back to the south coast, and touched down in time to join the rest of the squadron in the Mess for dinner. As expected, there was something of a party with Nicole, the star of the show, slipping effortlessly into the role and loving the attention of the pilots. Harriet was happy, genuinely happy, as she withdrew to the side lines and stood in the corner of the bar sipping on a sherry. At long last, she'd been reunited with her best friend; and the darkness in her heart was all of a sudden gone. Even the building stress and fatigue from the endless days of combat seemed to have gone, and for the first time since she could remember, she was truly happy. In the back of her mind she thought that if she were to be shot down the next day, she'd go with a smile, knowing that despite Britain being on its knees with the prospects of invasion, all in her own little world was as well as it could be. Nicole was alive, the squadron had become her family, and she was doing a job she loved. What more could she ask for? She looked around the room. The singing was getting boisterous, and the piano was being played almost professionally by the French Lieutenant, Hugo Romain, who for once wasn't sitting on the peripheries and sketching the pilots. Something the skilled and talented artist often did both in the Mess or around the dispersal.

"Not going to join in the party?" Cas asked as he joined her.

"Not right now."

"Why ever not?"

"It's her moment." She pointed her glass at Nicole, who was being carried around the Mess on the shoulders of singing pilots, several of whom she didn't know, and others whose names she couldn't remember. "What about you? Not joining in?"

"Me? No, it's far too energetic. Besides, I have work to do. We're not all carefree pilots with time to burn."

"You must be getting old."

"Yes..." he said with half a smile. "Yes, I am."

372

"I know. It's astounding that the RAF hasn't retired you, yet."

"They did once," he winked.

"I don't have to worry about that for a long time. One of the benefits of youth, you know?" She continued to tease, feeling a deep seated urge to keep pulling at the same thread to see if she could find a way through his armour of calm composure, and maybe get him to bite.

"I know... I remember being your age, just about."

"That's quite some memory."

"Indeed, it is. Do you know what else I remember from all those years ago?"

"It surprises me you remember anything at your age, so please do go ahead."

"Well, if you insist..."

"I do. I mean, if it's not too much effort to recall?"

"I'll try..."

"Good."

"I remember that in all the many thousands of hours I've flown, right from the early days over the trenches of the Western Front, through the dogfights and fighting the notorious Red Baron, I never once had to parachute from an aeroplane..." He winked and smirked as Harriet's face dropped and her lips pursed. He let out a slight chuckle and finished his drink. "Goodnight, Harry," he said as he put the glass down.

"That was below the belt," she complained.

373

"But true," he replied while straightening his tie in the mirror behind the bar.

"Harsh."

"Remind me, Harry. How many aeroplanes have you had shot from under you so far?"

"Can't we just be nice?" she pleaded in an overly pathetic voice, her best attempt at appearing vulnerable and avoiding further ridicule.

"You need to learn to pick your battles."

"Hilarious!" She rolled her eyes as he laughed, and she fought hard to keep the smile from her face. "Anyway, are you really leaving? It's only early." "Sadly, yes. I do genuinely have work to do. I'll see you tomorrow at dispersal. Try not to be too hungover."

"Wait," she said. Her heart was racing.

"What is it?" She waved at Dickie, and he begrudgingly handed her the small paper bag she'd had him keep behind the bar for her.

"For you," she said as she handed it to Cas.

"For me? What is it?" he asked as he opened the bag.

"Yes," she said as she snatched at the top of the bag, closing it. "You're not to open it here, though, not in front of me." He frowned. "It's just a thank you."

"A thank you? Whatever for?"

"Weren't you going somewhere?" she asked defensively. He nodded and smiled warmly, then left. She watched as he went, then finally succumbed to the calls of the others for her to join them in the party.

Chapter 16

Ascension

The next morning Harriet was dragged back to the daily routine by Daisy, who was carrying a tray of tea ever so noisily. Nicole, who was asleep next to her, was horrified by the early wakeup call and was even less thrilled than Harriet when woken by Daisy's unfalteringly chirpy morning demeanour. After a torrent of complaints, a torrent which peaked in vulgarity as Nicole was introduced to the early morning ice cold bath routine, the girls dressed and said their grudging goodbyes to Daisy before heading downstairs.

"What's this?" Nicole asked as Harriet climbed onto her Harley.

"My ride to the dispersal. Are you coming, or would you rather take the truck? It'll be here in five minutes or so."

"Since when do you have a motorcycle?" Nicole asked as she climbed on behind Harriet and held onto her hips. "Since when do you even know how to ride a motorcycle?"

"Who said I know how?" Harriet replied with a mischievous grin as she kicked the engine into life, then took off into the darkness and headed for the perimeter track which led to the dispersal hut. Harriet smiled as she felt Nicole hold tighter after the first bend. She even let the rear wheel skid out on the second, as Lexi had done to her several times, just for good measure.

"You ride a motorcycle as bad as you fly!" Nicole cursed as they parked behind the dispersal hut. Harriet couldn't help but laugh out loud as she walked around the front of the hut with Nicole in tow.

"Idiot," Nicole muttered.

"Good morning," Cas greeted. Harriet raised an eyebrow at the sight of Cas in flying boots and Mae West.

"Going somewhere?" she asked, casually.

"Miss Delacourt, welcome home," Singh said warmly.

"Thank you," Nicole replied politely. "When do we fly?"

"We fly in about thirty minutes on a dawn patrol," Singh said confidently.
"You, however, will have to wait."

"Wait? What? Why?" Nicole blustered.

"How many hours do you have flying Spitfires?"

"None, yet, but they're just an aeroplane the same as any other."

"Not quite," Singh said with a smile, quickly remembering how fiery Nicole could be if things weren't as she expected. "Mister Salisbury is our resident flying instructor as part of his duties as Adjutant, as you know, and after sunrise he'll be taking you out west and teaching you how to use your superior flying skills to make the best use of a Spitfire." He talked with sincerity as he played to Nicole's ego. "That way you'll knock even more Germans out of the sky when we make you operational, which will be good for the squadron tally."

"That makes sense, I suppose," Nicole replied, knowing when to take a well signposted get out when she saw one. "Though I'm sure I'll be back here flying in no time."

"I'm happy we agree," Singh said. "I'm looking forward to getting you back into action." The truck carrying the rest of the pilots rumbled down the track and came to a halt behind the dispersal hut. Its tailgate clanged as it was dropped, and a minute later a group of pilots filed quietly inside. "Right, come on. Let's get the morning's briefing done so we can get started." Nicole was formally introduced to the squadron, though she'd met many the previous night at the impromptu Mess party, and then Singh briefed the pilots on the plan for the day. Cas would be taking Nicole out west to put her through her paces on the Spitfire, while the rest of the squadron was due for a first light patrol. There was a suspicion at Group Headquarters that a big raid would be coming across the Channel at dawn, and they wanted the squadron to be up high and ready for an incoming raid, rather than rushing up to intercept it. The expectation was that the raid would split in two over Dover as they had the last few days, with one half heading north towards the Thames Estuary, and the other continuing along the south coast. Both groups would then splinter again and carry out smaller attacks on airfields across the South East. Every day that Harriet had been gone the format had been the same, sending fighter controllers chasing their tales trying to intercept the raids and putting the squadrons on the back foot, which led to many of the airfields being heavily bombed. Fighter command were determined to stop it happening again, so they were putting squadrons up early, ready to try and break up the raid before it even had chance to split. Joining Harriet and her fellow pilots in the elaborate trap would be five squadrons from 12 Group to the north, a mixed force of Hurricanes and Spitfires all intended to arrive at the same time in one massive, sprawling wing of fighters designed to knock the enemy down en masse. After the briefing, Harriet wished Nicole good luck, then talked with her Flight, especially the new face, Sergeant Rogers, a Canadian who'd arrived at the squadron the previous evening. Grumpy had stepped up to look after the Flight in her absence and was perfectly humble when asked to step down again on her return, a situation which could have been awkward had he not been so gracious, as he'd done an excellent job of leading the pilots in action. He agreed to stay on as second in command, though, and Kiwi was ready to take post as her number two again. She ordered Rogers to stick on Grumpy and do exactly as he was told. Once briefed, the squadron was given five minutes to make ready, and the engines rumbled into life under the confident management of their ground crews.

"Welcome back, Ma'am," Corporal Holland said from the wing of the Spitfire, having started and tested the engine, then removed himself with speed, much to Harriet's approval.

"Good morning, Dutch," she said casually, and his chest swelled with pride at her recognition and friendliness. "Anything I need to know?"

"She's one of the older kites in the squadron, but we've been working on her all night and she's running like a dream, Ma'am."

"Good show. Where's Lanky this morning?"

"Working on the new arrivals, Ma'am. A couple of new kites arrived fresh from the factory last night and need their guns setting up." He looked around to check nobody was listening, then leant into the cockpit. "I think one of them is coming your way this morning. Don't tell anyone I told you, but she's nice and a good runner, and I thought you'd like to know."

"Thanks, Dutch," Harriet said with a smile of excitement at the news she'd be getting a new Spitfire. "Best jump off." He nodded and jumped from the wing while Harriet went through her own checks, testing the magnetos and engine power, and sucking in the oxygen to make sure it worked; and dealing with what remained of her hangover. Once satisfied everything was as it should be she looked around and received nods from the pilots of her Flight, then when Singh gave the signal the squadron taxied into position and took off by Flights. Harriet smiled to herself as she bumped along the grass with her cockpit canopy open. The smell of petrol was almost intoxicating, and the comfortable vibrations that shook her muscles were welcoming like she'd come home after a long time away. There was no final bump, not like the old days in France when she clung on at high speed and hoped the final bump would lift her into the sky. Instead, after battling the aeroplane's desperate urge to yaw across the grass while on the ground, the Spitfire just lifted effortlessly and climbed gracefully. Once it was airborne it floated, the wheels came up and locked away with a secure clunk, and Harriet ran her eyes over the glowing gauges, all was fine. She closed the canopy and checked on her

Flight, then led them into place on Singh's left flank, while Max manoeuvred onto the right. They climbed hard into the darkness and watched as the distant sunlight broke a long way over France. As the altimeter wound up, Harriet increased the flow of oxygen, and every five thousand feet she felt a little brighter and a little fresher until they hit twenty five thousand feet and she was feeling ready for anything. Singh pushed a little higher, and the squadron followed, levelling at twenty seven thousand feet. A height where the 109 was known to be superior, but where the Germans likely wouldn't be expecting to see a squadron of Spitfires, having got used to seeing them desperately racing up from the ground. The sunlight was brilliant as it filtered through the atmosphere, and Harriet was thankful for the aviator sunglasses the American salesman had given her. They truly did live up to his extravagant claims, and were much more comfortable than the RAF issue type. They flew their patrol line to Dover, then circled around to Margate before returning in the direction they'd come. Radio silence was maintained, and the Spitfires flew side by side with only waves and wing waggles to communicate changes in direction, height, and speed.

"Hello, Goose Squadron, Silver here." Control had broken the silence just as the dark blue sky was starting to lighten.

"Goose Squadron receiving," Singh replied.

"I have some trade for you, Goose Squadron. Bandits, approximately one hundred plus at twenty thousand feet heading for Dover."

"Roger, Silver, understood. Goose Squadron, keep your eyes open!" Singh pointed them at Dover, which was glowing in the distance as the first rays of dawn lit up the Channel and silhouetted the menacing curtain of barrage balloons.

"Hello, Goose Squadron, Silver here. Look out for a friendly wing joining you from the north." Harriet looked around, but there was nothing to the north except the brightening darkness, there were no friendly aeroplanes she could see.

"There they are," Pops called. "Twelve o'clock on the nose!" Harriet quickly locked them in her stare, a swarm of small black crosses far below them, many more crosses than the expected one hundred. There were aeroplanes as far as she could see, filling the distant sky like a black haze. It was an incredible, yet terrifying sight, they were outnumbered at least fifteen to one. The only saving grace was that the entire show, bombers and layers of fighters, were all a long way below them for once. The plan had worked, though Harriet couldn't help thinking what damage they could have done with five times as many Spitfires, not to mention how that would help the odds a little. She looked around again for the so called 'friendly wing', but there was nothing. She consoled herself, thinking maybe they were hidden in the darkness and poised to strike.

"OK, Goose Squadron, here goes," Singh said. "Ignore the fighters, go straight through them and hit the bombers. Hopefully, we can break up the attack. We must stop them from getting through at all costs. Tally ho!" Singh started his dive as the lead bombers made landfall north of Dover, and as one the rest followed. Harriet pushed her stick forward and felt the familiar and exciting sensation in her stomach as it squeezed and flipped. Her mouth was starting to dry as she set her sights on a bomber out to the left of the formation, holding steady as her heart started to pound and her breathing quickened. The altimeter was unwinding quickly, and thousands of feet were dropping off. She held her breath as she passed through the first layer of fighters, sending them splintering in every direction to avoid a collision or being shot at by the Spitfires, which hadn't even flinched from their dive. As the next layer of fighters started to break, having seen what was happening above, a 109 passed casually along a line which, if not changed, would take him straight through Harriet's sights. She gave a burst which he flew right into, immediately sending him down with streams of white smoke in his wake. He crashed right through a bomber in the centre of the formation he was flying to protect, exploding both in a ball of blackened orange flames, and sending the bombers behind into swerves to avoid colliding. It was too late for them to break as a formation, though, the Spitfires were on them. Harriet pushed her fire button and watched as her incendiary bullets flickered across the right wing of the bomber and rattled into the engine, making it explode and blow off the entire wing.

She pulled back on her stick and put a burst into the cockpit of the following bomber, then flipped her Spitfire on its back and dived down after the falling wreckage of her previous victim, to set herself up for a climbing attack at the underbellies of the bombers. Spitfires dropped through the ceiling of bombers all around her, while the sky filled with the smoking trails of knocked down bombers, and the floating parachutes of some of their crews. As Harriet pulled up into a climb, fighting to keep her eyes open as the g forces pushed her head back tight against the rest, she could just about make out the shapes of pursuing German fighters dropping past the bombers in pursuit of the Spitfires. Remembering Singh's orders, she squirted a blast at a 109, and pulled into a turn so steep she almost blacked out, then levelled at the underside of a bomber in the tail of the formation. A gentle pull on the stick while pushing the fire button sent explosive bullets dancing across the right wing, which immediately started trailing white smoke, she'd hit the coolant tank. Not content with that, she pursued it into the turn and calculated the speed of both aircraft and the speed and drop of the ammunition, then aimed just ahead of the nose before firing and watching the bomber fly into her bullets. It was a perfect deflection shot; wreckage fell from the fuselage, and the bomber rolled onto its back before twisting into a nose down dive.

"Rogers!" she shouted as the bomber disappeared from sight to reveal her new Sergeant's Spitfire flying hard into the bomber formation, firing and blowing chunks off a bomber, and ignorant of the pair of 109s chasing to get on his tail. "Rogers, on your tail. Turn hard right, now!" he responded just as a burst of German tracer dotted a line across his wingtip, which had he not done as she'd said would have gone right through his fuselage. "Pull it tight!" she called as she turned hard left. As her vision dulled to a dim cone of light, she put a long burst ahead of the lead 109, rattling the engine fairing and forcing the pilot and his number two to break and dive to avoid her fire, clearing Rogers' tail.

More tracer rattled Harriet's right wing and forced her to reverse her turn, pushing her body against the side of the cockpit and almost making her black out as three more 109s came at her. She kept turning and turning until she saw the tail of the third 109 of the group coming closer and closer to being within her sights. Before she could fire, another burst of tracer skimmed the left side of her Spitfire, and a cannon shell blew off the canopy with a deafening bang, taking the mirror with it. She craned her neck back as she banked hard to see another two 109s on her tail. The sky was full of smoke and aeroplanes. Each time she tried to fire, she was fired upon, she was turning and twisting, but there were too many 109s, and all of them were being flown remarkably well. A long blast of the guns clipped one of the 109s, but that was as close as she got.

More bullets rattled her fuselage, forcing her to make a dizzying continuous roll before flipping the Spitfire on its back, then pulling the stick into her stomach and diving for the deck, hoping to get enough speed as she headed along the coast, dripping with sweat and breathing so hard she'd be mistaken for somebody in the middle of an Olympic sprint. The throttle was fully open, and the engine was screaming as the speed dial wound up and the altitude wound down. Having no mirror and going so fast that the entire airframe started shaking meant that there was no opportunity to look behind for followers. She physically couldn't do it because of the g forces, so she just held on and hoped while the sweat stung her already sore eyes. Thousands of feet and no more tracer, but the ground was getting very big, very fast. Harriet decided to start to level out, but faced the almost impossible task of pulling out of the dive. It took every ounce of strength to get the almost solid controls to move, but eventually the Spitfire started to respond, and she levelled out so low that she sent a group of farmers running for the ditches, and hay from the field they were working in was thrown into the air by her furious slipstream. She gasped as she twisted and looked behind, her tail was clear. Her breathing steadied as she roared over the Kent countryside, and when she'd composed herself, she looked up for signs of the bombers, but everything had gone. Just a few minutes before the sky had been so full of aeroplanes that not crashing into one was a miracle, but now there was nothing except a mesh of fading crossed smoke trails. Doing a quick calculation, Harriet worked out that her ammunition must be almost spent, so made the decision to head home and be reloaded, ready for whatever was to come next. She pulled up a few thousand feet to get her bearings, and after working out her position, she set a course back to her airfield. She could see Spitfires were already on the ground

383

when she arrived home, and for once, the gunners weren't trying to shoot her out of the sky. She felt safe to assume the Germans hadn't been visiting, so with a quick search of the sky she lined up, dropped her flaps, then wheels, then lowered to the ground where she glided lightly across the grass before rolling to a halt near the dispersal hut, swinging the nose, and cutting the engine. She sat for a moment and got her breath while removing her helmet and hanging it on what remained of the stem that used to hold the mirror in place. She looked up, half hoping to see AP there to greet her, then with a disappointed sigh she unfastened her own harness and pulled herself up to stand on her seat.

"Bloody hell, Ma'am. Are you OK?" Holland asked as he climbed up the wing to greet her. Harriet nodded as she clambered onto the wing.

"I've had better mornings. It'll need a new mirror, and a canopy hood if you've got one lying around. I can go up without one, though, if needs be. Get her refuelled and rearmed. It's looking set to be a busy day up there so be quick."

"I don't think so, Ma'am," he said as he followed her off the bullet holed wing.

"Excuse me?" She fired him a stern look

"She's gonna need more than some petrol and a few bullets. I've seen Swiss cheese with less holes." He nodded at the Spitfire, and Harriet turned to look. The fuselage was indeed full of holes, and the engine cowling was leaking a stream of oil. Her shoulders slumped with disappointment. "You're going to have to take that one instead." He pointed over to the spotless new Spitfire sitting back from the others. Harriet's face broke into a big smile as she noticed the large H painted on the fuselage following the squadron code.

"That's mine?" she asked.

"Yes, Ma'am. H for Harry, just as Mister Salisbury ordered." Her smile stretched from ear to ear, so big she felt her jaw aching. "I'll move your

384

parachute and helmet over, Ma'am and get her ready to go. You get over to the squadron, I reckon you're needed."

"Thanks, Dutch." Harriet smiled as she walked over to the gathering of pilots outside the dispersal hut.

"Good to see you back," The Spy said as he pushed a cup of tea into her hand. "Did you get one?" He asked Grumpy as he walked over, the look on his face betraying him.

"Two bombers and a fighter. I think. What's happened?" she asked urgently, not caring about her tally, just needing to hear the news.

"It's the skipper," The Spy replied. "Murphy saw him going down in smoke after knocking down a bomber."

"A 109 got him," Grumpy added. Harriet felt sick in her stomach and she quickly took a sip of tea as her mouth dried. "They got young Harper, too. Dolph saw him going in just north of Dover."

"That's not all," The Spy added. "Max hasn't come back, either; and nobody saw a thing of him after the battle started. We were worried we'd lost you, too. It was a big relief when you landed, I can tell you!" Harriet nodded and drank more of her tea, partly because her mouth was so dry with fear for Singh and Max, partly to help try and settle the sick feeling in the pit of her stomach, and partly because she didn't have a clue what to say, or how to say it. The smile had been knocked from her face in a few short minutes. "That makes you the senior officer in the squadron. You'd better call Groupie and let him know what's going on; unless you'd rather I did the deed?" Harriet shook her head and drained the tea before handing him the cup.

"Thanks, Spy. I'll do it." She forced a half smile and headed to the dispersal hut while unfastening her Mae West. "Get Group Captain Saltire on Mister Singh's phone, would you?" she asked Corporal Clarke, the duty orderly.

385

"Ma'am," he replied with a subdued air, clearly as shocked as everyone else at the squadron's loss. She slumped in Singh's chair behind his desk while Clarke picked up the phone. "Hello? Yes, 508 Squadron here. Flight Lieutenant Cornwall for Group Captain Saltire. OK," he handed the phone to Harriet then stepped out of the office quietly and closed the door after himself.

"Harry, old man! How the devil are you?" Alastair said in his usual jovial manner.

"I'm OK, Sir."

"Good, good. What the hell happened up there? Did the big wing turn up at all?"

"No, Sir. It was just us."

"Bloody hell! You wait until Group hear about this!" he barked. "The bastards promised us they'd link up! My God, you must have been outnumbered twenty to one?" His joviality turned to burning irritation.

"Something like that, Sir. Look, Sir, I need to report something," she jumped in before he could continue.

"Oh? What is it, Harry? Are you OK?"

"I am, Sir, but it's Mister Singh."

"Go on..."

"He was seen going down in smoke somewhere north of Dover."

"My God."

"Yes, Sir. Max hasn't come back, either. We also lost one of the new Pilot Officers, Harper." She felt a single tear roll down her cheek and quickly wiped it away then nipped her thigh to distract herself. "Sir?" she asked as the silence continued for what felt like a lifetime.

"Sorry, Harry, I'm here."

"Yes, Sir."

"Now listen, Harry, I have to ask you something very important, but before you say anything I want you to know that there's absolutely no wrong answer, and there's no judgement no matter what you say."

"OK..." Harriet replied nervously.

"You're now the senior officer flying. Would you be confident looking after the squadron for me, at least until I can get somebody over there to help you out? And don't feel pressured at all. If you don't feel ready, and God alone knows why you would be for somebody so young and with such little service, I'll stand the squadron down until we can get things back on an even keel."

"No! I mean, I'll keep them flying, Sir. It's OK, don't stand us down."

"If you're sure?"

"Positive, Sir." Her heart was pounding as a fear similar to that she felt when climbing up to battle took control and brought her out in a cold sweat.

"Harry, you're something special. Thank you. Now, as acting Squadron Commander, I want your squadron on standby as soon as you're refuelled and rearmed. I suspect that raid you intercepted will be coming back this way in the not too distant future, and we'll want to have another go at them. Remember, every bomber we knock down is one less to come back again." "Yes, Sir. You can rely on us!"

"I know I can, Harry. Good luck." She put the phone down and leant back in the chair to take stock of what was happening, then immediately jumped to her feet, determined not to overthink anything and put doubts in her own mind. Right now she needed to focus on the job, and that was defending England. She walked around the desk and looked in the small mirror hanging on the back of Singh's door.

"Well, Harry," she said as she looked at herself. Her hair, which was usually tied in a smart and tight ponytail was a little ruffled, and her face was streaked with sweat and smoke. "You couldn't buy life insurance now if you owned all the tea in China." She tidied her hair, then took a deep breath, and after one last check in the mirror she pulled the door open and headed to the dispersal. The gathered pilots were talking until Grumpy saw her watching them, spending a moment looking at each pilot, then glancing up to the cloudless sky above.

"OK, listen up," Grumpy shouted. The pilots hushed and joined him in looking at Harriet. "Ma'am?" Grumpy asked, inviting her to talk.

"I'm going to be leading the squadron for the time being," she said confidently and firmly. "And Group Captain Saltire wants us ready for wheels up as soon as we're refuelled and rearmed." The assembled pilots nodded compliantly. "Mister MacDonald will look after A Flight for the time being, with Bevan as Section leader, and Lieutenant Romain will take over B Flight with Van Darne as his deputy. Sergeant Rogers, you'll be my number two. When we get up, I want us in line abreast, A Flight on my left, B Flight, right. Any questions?"

"You forgot about me?" Pops asked. He was frowning, and his Polish accented voice sounded irritated at being left out.

"No, I haven't," Harriet replied.

"Then what do I do?"

"Exactly as you like, when you like," Harriet replied with half a smirk. Pops widened his eyes, then smiled, standing tall and proud. "Experience tells me that you tend to disappear off on your own as soon as the fighting starts anyway, so I want you to fly behind us and keep the

Germans from sneaking around on our tails, then when we engage, you can go and do what you do best. If you don't mind, of course?"

"She'll make a good boss," he said to Romain with a nudge and wink, getting a laugh from the pilots and breaking some of the tension.

"OK, that'll do," Harriet said, quietening the pilots again. "Remember that it's the bombers we're after, so don't go getting into anything with the fighters if you can avoid it. Right, finish your drinks and get to your aeroplanes. We need to be ready to go." The pilots drained their cups and quickly headed off, leaving Harriet to step out of the hut and stand beside The Spy.

"Well done," The Spy said quietly.

"Thank you," she replied while wiggling her fingers and letting them shake and release the tension that had been bursting to get out of her.

"Just remember that you're a uniquely talented and popular pilot and an outstanding leader. Do what you always do up there, and you'll be absolutely fine." He gave her a wink and a slap on the back. She nodded and smiled, and hid a blush by walking away quickly towards her Spitfire.

"Do me a favour?" she shouted back

"What?"

"Get in touch with Cas if you can. I could do with him back here."

"Will do. Good luck." A million thoughts swirled through her mind as she walked, among them her recent attack on IT for his poor job leading the squadron. Now it was her turn, would she do any better? Had she been too arrogant? Too quick to judge? It was one thing asking questions from the back, but how difficult would it be to lead from the front, and make the hard decisions on the spot?

"She's ready for you," Lanky said as she stepped up to meet Harriet.

"Thanks... Thanks for all your work getting her ready, too. I heard you've been at it all night."

"You're welcome," Lanky said with a warm smile. "I heard you're the new skipper?"

"Acting."

"Doesn't matter. They wouldn't have asked you to do it if they didn't think you capable. There are lots of good pilots in the squadron, like Grumpy or Kiwi, they could have asked any of them and sidelined you. I've seen the
RAF do it, but they asked you."

"Thanks," Harriet grinned. She felt her confidence growing.

"AP would be proud. She'd roll her eyes and pretend to be disgusted, but she'd be proud," Lanky said with a laugh. Harriet nodded then climbed up onto the wing and into the cockpit and Lanky helped strap her into her new aeroplane.

"Why Trinity?" Harriet asked.

"What's that?"

"The word Trinity is written in bold on the nose of the aeroplane?"

"It's a gift from the Spitfire Fund. The public have been making donations to buy us fighters, and if they raise seven thousand pounds, they get to name one. This one came from a maritime guild on the Yorkshire coast, apparently. They wanted to buy a Spitfire as a thank you to the squadron who protected shipping in the Humber Estuary earlier this year."

"Nice of the Navy to buy us an aeroplane," Harriet laughed.

"That's the Navy for you," Lanky smiled. Harriet looked around and gave the signal for the squadron to start their engines, which they did one at a time, then she started her own mighty Merlin engine and felt it rumble into life and fill the air with blue smoke as fire spat from the exhaust stubs. A blast of the propeller and the smoke cleared, and her engine joined the roar. "Good luck," Lanky said before jumping down and leaving Harriet to run through her pre flight checks. Her mind went back to the expectations of her. They were going up to the certainty of battle. No patrols, no maybes, just guaranteed combat.

What if she got it wrong? What if pilots died because she made a poor decision? Her stomach started flipping and beads of sweat started to form on her brow. She thought hard to distract herself, and remembered Cas' words 'If you're faced with a momentous challenge, ask yourself what's the worst that can happen? Once you know that, you can accept it, and focus on the task ahead.' It seemed logical, so she gave it a try, and immediately imagined the entire Squadron being wiped out except for her. That was the worst, and it wasn't a pleasant thought. She immediately cursed herself for thinking it and cursed Cas for his advice, which she was filing under 'ridiculous' while also questioning everything else he'd ever said to her. Then, as if that wasn't enough, she got irritated at him for swanning off to teach Nicole to fly Spitfires when he was needed in the squadron, when he was needed by her! What the hell was he doing leaving the squadron during a battle anyway? The cycle of anger at everything Cas had ever done, including breathing, was broken by a green flare being launched. The sign for take off.

"OK, let's go," she said into her microphone, then pushed her throttle forward and felt all of her thoughts and distractions melt away. The Spitfire eased into life and started to roll. A little more pressure and it was bouncing, a little more and a push forward on the stick and the tail came up into the airstream, and she lifted gracefully into the air. Undercarriage up and locked, a quick check of the instruments, a look around and quick headcount, everyone was there, and Rogers was in position on her wing.

"Hello Silver, Goose Squadron airborne," she said over the radio.

"Hello, Goose Squadron. Silver, here. Vector one eight zero and make angels one five, as fast as you can."

"Wilco, Silver." Harriet turned the squadron to the Channel and pushed them into a hard climb.

"Come around to three six zero," Silver instructed after reaching their height, bringing them back towards land. "Bandits should be crossing your nose from west to east." Harriet looked around and searched the sky. There they were, twenty or so Heinkels a few thousand feet below in a loose formation. She searched above and behind but couldn't see their fighter escort.

"OK, Silver, we've got them: Goose Squadron, bombers at ten o'clock low. Turn starboard on my mark. Three, two, one, mark." The squadron turned as one to line up with the bomber formation below. "Pick your targets but keep your eyes open for fighters," she ordered. "Tally ho!" She opened her throttle full and pushed the stick forward, dropping the nose and leading the squadron into a screaming dive. She took her aim ahead of her chosen target, then as she closed to two hundred feet, she fired. The incendiary bullets shattered into the cockpit and exploded along the fuselage, making the bomber dip its nose and immediately go into a dive. The rear gunner got in a wide burst as she passed and overtook the bomber, then pulled back on her stick and headed back up, watching as Rogers followed a bomber, rattling it with gunfire. "Well done, Rogers, keep on him and knock him down, and I'll watch your tail," she instructed as she pulled the Spitfire into a tight split turn, which put her behind Rogers by some distance so she could cover him. "Get closer," she ordered. He did as she instructed and put a burst into the right wing which immediately coughed out a shock of orange flame followed by streams of black and white smoke which entwined and braided themselves together. "OK. You got him. Back off and see him down." Rogers did as he was told and seconds later three crew took to their parachutes. "Back up and do another. Fast as you can," she ordered. Rogers pulled up and opened his throttle, and Harriet pulled onto his wing. He looked over with a huge smile and waved. Harriet nodded and pointed up to the bomber above. "Hit his engines, if you can. Get in as close as you dare but watch for erratic moves." Rogers complied, and let a stream of bullets go into the bomber's engine. It immediately exploded and blew off the wing, making both Rogers and Harriet take hard evasive action as they banked and climbed up above the burning and twisting bomber. "Good show, well done! Now let's get some height and take stock." She looked around as they climbed. The sky was crisscrossed with black smoke trails as the squadron took the bomber formation apart. A group of bombers were off into the far distance with a few Spitfires giving chase and biting at their tails. A search of the horizon showed no more bombers following behind, or fighters, the sky was clear except for smoke. "Hello Silver, Goose Leader here. Do you have any more trade for us?" she called.

"Stand by, Goose Leader," came the reply. "Goose Leader, this is Silver. Head to Dover. We have something showing up ten miles off the coast and heading this way, could be a fighter sweep so look sharp. Angels five."

"Wilco, Silver. Rogers, stick to my wing. Let's see if we can get you a third," she said confidently. She started a dive and opened her throttle. The pair dived out over the Dover barrage balloons and headed for France.

"There, one o'clock low, skimming the waves," Rogers said.

"OK, follow me," Harriet dived in for the attack, but on closing she saw a white flying boat with red crosses on the wings. It was a German rescue aeroplane, the type that had rescued her, and it was quickly skimming away from a pool of green dye in the turquoise sea. "Hold it," Harriet instructed. "Go up top and keep an eye out for fighters," Rogers pulled away, and she slowed her throttle back then dropped to the seaplane's side. The pilot looked over nervously. She could see the fear on his face at the sight of a Spitfire pulling alongside. She unfastened her mask, then saluted and gave a waggle of her wings. The German pilot stared in amazement, then returned the salute and opened his throttle full. Harriet waved, then pulled up and away to leave the flying boat alone so it could

393

take its likely scared and injured cargo to safety. There was no honour in shooting down an unarmed rescue aeroplane. She joined Rogers, and they watched as the small white aeroplane raced to France. "Let's get back to the airfield." She led them down and circled, then dropped and landed to join the others that had landed ahead of them. Engine off, and she let out a sigh of relief while hanging her helmet on the mirror.

"All OK?" Lanky asked as she reached in and unfastened Harriet's harness.

"Yeah..." She smiled and took Lanky's hand as she pulled her up and out of the cockpit. She shook her head and tidied her hair. "I think I got her back without a scratch, but better check just to be sure. I didn't see or feel anything."

"Will do, Ma'am," Lanky said with a mischievous smile. Harriet winked and jumped from the wing, unfastening her Mae West and letting out some of the heat.

"Rogers, well done up there!" she said as the young Sergeant joined her. "They call you Buck, don't they?"

"Yes, Ma'am, they do, and thank you for the training session. I feel much better about taking on Jerry now."

"You're welcome. You're a good pilot, just remember to get in close and only fire when you're guaranteed to hit something, and if you can, try and hit the engine."

"Got it."

"How'd it go?" The Spy asked, appearing as always like a vulture ready to devour the news of somebody's end.

"Put Buck here down for two Heinkels," Harriet replied.

"But you got in on him first," Rogers protested.

394

"Nonsense, I just scared him. You're the one that got him."

"There you go, Sergeant, combat report as quickly as you can!" The Spy handed Rogers a form and pencil.

"Any news from Cas?"

"Not yet. I've put word out, though."

"OK..." She carried on towards the hut.

"I'm told you're the skipper," Spanners, the engineering officer, said as he stepped out of the hut.

"Acting," Harriet replied, as she grabbed a tin cup and poured some tea from the loaded folding table that had been refreshed in their brief absence. "That may be, but either way I suppose it's you who'll want to know our serviceability status?"

"Yes please." She went into Singh's office and put her mug on the table.

"The one you flew this morning is going back to the factory for repair. It's beyond what we can do here to fix it. There's another in the hangar that we've been fighting with, but in all honesty, that'll have to go back, too. There's far too much metal damage for us to simply patch it and hope for the best."

"OK, so what do we have?"

"Well, with the three we lost this morning, four including yours, and as long as everyone behaves, I think I can get you twelve. But that's everything we've got. No reserves, and we'll be working double time tonight to get two through their mandatory hundred hour checks." The phone rang and stopped him mid sentence.

"508 Squadron dispersal," Harriet said as she answered. "OK. OK, thank you for letting me know. Tell him to sit tight, and we'll send somebody." She put the phone down and looked at Spanners with a sigh. "Make that eleven. Van Darne has put down on a golf course outside Folkstone. You'd better get somebody over there to have a look. Send Van Darne back by road if you can't fix it quickly."

"Eleven it is..." Spanners said. "I'll get a crew over there. Toodle pip." He left the office and Harriet followed.

"Is everyone back? Except for Van Darne?" she asked the gathered pilots.

"All accounted for except him," The Spy called back. "Seven bombers destroyed, two probables, and nine damaged, Ma'am. For the record." She nodded and went back in and called control.

"508 Squadron will be ready to stand by in twenty minutes." She sat at the desk and thought for a moment. She hadn't lost anyone, that was the main thing, other than Dolph's crash landing. She opened the squadron journal and documented the details of the morning's sorties so far. It wasn't even lunchtime, and they'd been up twice, claimed sixteen enemy aircraft destroyed and another seven probables, with five more damaged. In return, the Squadron had lost five aeroplanes and three pilots, including the Commanding Officer and senior Flight Commander. Nearly a four to one success rate, but the loss of such experienced pilots, and such good leaders, was a high price to pay. If the Luftwaffe was able to keep coming and the squadron kept losing at the rate they were, they would be wiped out in another couple of weeks, and if the other squadrons in the group were being hit as hard, the Germans would win. Once the RAF were wiped out, with their remnants withdrawn north, Hitler could invade at his leisure. The Luftwaffe would sink any Royal Navy ship that tried to stop them crossing the Channel, and the army was still in disarray having left most of its equipment and a significant chunk of its experienced soldiers in Dunkirk. Britain would have no choice but to surrender. It was a huge realisation for an eighteen year old girl to process, and a huge responsibility to have on her shoulders. She was now commanding a front line fighter squadron charged with the task of keeping the Germans out of England; being outnumbered ten and twenty to one, and knowing that sooner or later even the best of her pilots were going to make a mistake, probably through exhaustion, and get shot down. She sat back in her chair and put down her pencil. Of all the times her father had told her she needed to be responsible and do something worthwhile with her life, often while they were arguing about her dreams of being a pilot; and here she was leading a squadron in the battle of their lives while he was safe in Switzerland. If only he knew. If only he knew that she held the freedom of the entire world in her hands. For a few fleeting moments, anyway, until she followed Barnes and Singh, and all of the others who'd gone before her. She laughed to herself at the thought. It was quite funny, really, the way the world worked. The phone rang and disturbed her train of thoughts, immediately making her stomach knot. At the same time, the air raid siren started winding up outside and filling the air with its onerous drone. She pushed the chair back and sent it crashing to the floor and ran around the desk.

"It's a squadron scramble, Ma'am," Corporal Clarke said.

"Get to safety," she said as she ran outside. "Squadron scramble. Get them up! Get them up!" she shouted. Clarke followed and rang the bell hard, trying to make it heard above the air raid siren. The Merlin engines were already roaring when the pilots got to them. Harriet bounded up the wing and into her seat, waving Holland and Lanky off as she did. They jumped as she opened the throttle immediately and started racing across the grass. As soon as she was at speed, she lifted the tail, caught the air, and lifted, pushing the throttle open and then raising the landing gear before starting in a fast climb. "Silver, this is Goose Leader. What's happening?"

"Goose Leader, this is Silver. Bandits heading in fast and low from the south."

"Goose Squadron, form on me and keep your eyes open!" She turned south and looked out to sea as the rest of the squadron joined. "There, two thousand feet, fighters. Here we go. Tally ho!" She set her gun button to fire and opened her throttle full as the Spitfires closed with the

397

approaching 109s. The closing speed reached over seven hundred miles per hour, and the distant specks soon became larger than life and started to fill the windscreen. Harriet fired, as did the others, then shouted "break, break, break," and the Spitfires turned hard in every direction. They tried desperately to get around on the 109s which had raced under them, moving fast and turning slowly into their own breaks, too slow to get around on the Spitfires, all of which were using their superior tight turns to the best effect. Harriet pulled hard on the stick; she felt her vision go so dark she could only see pinpricks of light as she fought to stay conscious, until finally pulling out of the turn and switching her oxygen to full to try and make her brain function. As she lined up with the 109 she'd been turning to get on, he pulled straight up and opened his throttle, using his own superiority, his climb, to quickly pull away from her before she could get in an accurate shot. Harriet tried to give chase, but he was getting away. She looked in her mirror, and around her, and all of the 109s seemed to be making a break for France. She fired a burst, but her bullets passed over the wing of her prey, who simply rolled and dived for the ground, leaving her standing as the distance between them extended. She gave chase, following low and dodging the flak that erupted from the coastal batteries, which quickly became thick enough to suggest that the gunners were having trouble differentiating friend from foe. Instead of just holding their fire and leaving the Spitfires to their jobs, they were firing everything they had. The air became thick and heavy with exploding flak when Harriet got a call. "Goose Squadron! Silver! We are under attack, I repeat, we are under attack!"

"Understood. On our way. Goose Squadron, break off and set up top cover at home." Harriet pulled up hard out of the flak and climbed, pointing her nose straight up before pulling back further into a loop and rolling out at the top. As she did, she saw the pall of black smoke in the distance rising from the direction of the airfield. She arrived and circled at five thousand feet, there was no sign of any bombers, and other Spitfires soon joined her. "Silver, this is Goose Leader on station directly above." She waited. "Silver, Goose Leader. Anyone there?"

"Hello, Goose Leader. Sorry about that," came the reply. "Bandits now over Dungeness and heading home. Better land at the satellite, we'll let you know when it's safe to come in."

"Understood, Silver. Good luck. Goose Squadron, let's go to the satellite." She led them down the coast to the small reserve field and landed, stopping by their small control tower. Their fuel bowser came out, as did their crew truck, and soon ground crew were climbing onto the Spitfires. Harriet climbed out and jumped down. Nine aeroplanes. "Who's missing?" she asked as the pilots came together. They all looked around to check.

"Mister Wright," Buck said.

"Did anyone see what happened to him?" Heads shook. "Alright. Is everyone else OK?" The shaking heads turned to nods. "OK, I'll go talk to the duty officer. Stay close to your aeroplanes and be ready to get up if needs be. If we're hit here as well, we go to Biggin. Grumpy, Hugo, brief your Flights." She headed for the officer standing in the doorway of the control tower.

"Morning," he greeted. "I hear you had something of a ding dong over at your place."

"Something like that."

"Hey, you're that girl pilot people are talking about."

"Wonderful observation skills, well done. Do you have a phone I can use?"

"Sorry I spoke, I'm sure. Yes, this way."

"And can you get some drinks for my pilots?"

"Delighted to, old girl. Anything else?" She fired him a look as she picked up the phone, daring him to say something else. He put up his hands in mock surrender and bowed his head. She spoke with Alastair then left the office and joined the pilots.

"What's the news?" Grumpy asked.

"It was a trap, by the sounds of it," Harriet replied. "They used the fighters to lure us away, then as soon as we were out of the way a squadron of Stukas hiding high up above came down and flattened the place."

"I wondered why the 109s didn't want to play."

"Yeah. Did anyone get anything?"

"A cannon shell through the wing," Kiwi replied.

"Anyone else get anything more useful?" Everyone shook their heads. "OK, well done anyway. We were caught out, and there's no way we could have done much." A van brought them tea and biscuits from the Mess, and the pilots sat around in a group, making the most of the sun, smoking, talking, and in some cases sleeping while they could. Harriet walked around impatiently, not able to rest. She wanted to know what was happening, and standing around at a satellite airfield waiting to be attacked made her feel uneasy. She kept looking up and scanning the sky, looking for raiders and remembering France when Stukas attacked them. The phone rang several times while they waited. Each time everyone looked, and each time nothing happened. Finally, the duty officer made an appearance.

"That was your station. Apparently, lunch is ready, if you fancy nipping back."

"Thank you," Harriet said. "Come on, you lot. Let's go home."

"You're welcome..." the duty officer shouted after them. Fifteen minutes later, and they were landing on their still smoking airfield and parking by the dispersal.

"Who are you?" Harriet asked the three pilots sitting outside the dispersal hut.

"Lieutenant Catt, Royal Navy Fleet Air Arm," The one in the almost black uniform of the Royal Navy with gold braid on the cuffs said. "Ma'am. Otherwise known as Ships."

"Ships?"

"Ship's Cat. Some of my colleagues appear to think they have a sense of humour. Anyway, I was told by your Group Captain to report to you. Apparently, you're in need of Spitfire pilots, and I'm one."

"I see. Nice to meet you. Who are your friends?"

"Pilot Officer Jones, Ma'am."

"Pilot Officer Smythe, Ma'am."

"How many hours on Spits, Ships?" Harriet asked.

"Oh, a dozen or so. Got a few hundred in Hurricanes, though, so I'm not as green as the sea."

"You two?"

"Five, Ma'am" Jones replied.

"Nine, Ma'am" Smythe added.

"Anything else?"

"They're fresh out of the box," Cas said as he stepped out of the dispersal hut. "Ma'am..." Harriet couldn't help but smile as she saw him. His presence made things instantly calmer, both around the dispersal and inside her body, where her heart was pounding and stomach spinning with everything that had happened that morning. "Apart from our friend from the Navy, of course. Anyone that can land an aeroplane on the only solid surface bobbing around in the sea can't be half bad, as pilots go. Besides, it's nice of the Navy to volunteer to help out, don't you think?"

"I do," Harriet replied through her grin "A volunteer? It's good to have you," she said to Ships, offering her hand which he shook politely. "Make yourself at home."

"Thank you. I will. Mister Salisbury has shown us to our aeroplanes and briefed us on what's going on."

"Has he...?" She looked at Cas and smiled.

"I've put Ships and Jones in A Flight with Grumpy, and Smythe in B Flight. It should plug a few gaps."
"How are the gaps, Cas?"

"Wright's engine failed halfway along the airfield. A Stuka got him and the ground crew who'd gone out to tow him back in. We've only just got it all cleared away and filled the holes. An infantry battalion from down the road offered their help, and they've done a fantastic job."

"I'm sorry to hear about Wright," Harriet said. Another loss, this time without even a chance to fight back. The day was becoming expensive.

"Yes... Unfortunately, Van Darne is out, too."

"What? How? I thought he got down OK?"

"He did, but not before he'd managed to get a Jerry bullet in the arm. He won't be flying any time soon."

"Damn it. How long?"

"He's at the local hospital. I expect we'll get a report from Simon this afternoon."

"Where's Nicole?" she asked with a frown, appearing to detach herself from the conversation and focus instead on the notable absence.

"The bathroom, I think."

"How's her flying?"

"A little rusty, but we got four hours in."

"Four hours isn't a lot."

"A lot for what?" Nicole asked as she emerged from behind the dispersal hut.

"For you to be flying."

"Nonsense. The Spitfire is even easier than the Hurricane, and I'm more than competent."

"Cas says you're still a bit rusty."

"Does he?" If looks could kill, Cas would have been walking with a very severe limp, at best. "Maybe it's him that's rusty, with age. That 109 almost got him, after all…"

"What 109?" Harriet asked with a frown.

"Oh, nothing to worry about," Cas smiled. "We ran into a gaggle of trouble causers looking for a scrap out west, so we gave them a tickle while we were there."

"A tickle?"

"I shot one down, of course!" Nicole said confidently. "The one sitting on the old man's tail…" She stared at Cas. "So much for rusty."

"Quite… Anyway, she's yours whenever you're ready for her," Cas said.

"What about aeroplanes?" Harriet asked Cas, again moving on.

"Well, we brought two more back with us. They're old recycles, but they've been well serviced, Spanners is getting them ready now and should have them to us in no time. They'll replace the two we've lost this morning. With the others that arrived yesterday, and the ground crew's hard work, I think we can stretch to thirteen all told. Though we're at our limit on that."

"OK…" Harriet turned to Nicole. "You fly as my number two." Nicole smiled a little, desperately trying to contain herself, being both excited to be allowed to fly while struggling not to complain about being anybody's number two, let alone Harriet's. The phone rang, and everyone stared at the door in silence.

"Lunch is going to be late, Ma'am," Corporal Clarke said as he stood in the doorway. Smythe, one of the new pilots, walked away quietly, disappearing behind the hut. The sound of him vomiting was the only noise from anyone. He wasn't the first and wouldn't be the last. The sound of a telephone ringing got to most in one way or another, Harriet herself felt a cold sweat and the hair on the back of her neck stand on end every time, and at one point she'd sworn never to own a telephone in her life. She took a deep breath and clenched her fists to stop any nervous shaking. At that, the Station Commander's car pulled around and stopped on the grass in front of the dispersal hut, followed by another large black car. Jenny jumped from the driver's seat and quickly ran around to open the door closest to them. Harriet frowned in confusion. Jenny was Alastair's driver and had been since the squadron had arrived at the station, but she very rarely drove him to the dispersal unless it was a formal inspection. Even then he'd never dream of having her open the car door for him. It wasn't his style.

"Bloody hell…" Cas whispered under his breath as Alastair stepped out, followed by a tall officer with a moustache. He wasn't too dissimilar from the AOC, but older, with more medals and rank braid "It's the CinC! Best behaviour," he looked at Nicole.

"Don't be rude," she replied with a frown of deep hurt. "Anyway, who is he? The King or something?" she laughed.

"No, He's the Commander in Chief of Fighter Command. That even taller gentleman they're greeting at the other car is the King. The King of Norway to be precise."

"Oh God," Harriet whispered.

"Do you actually know any Norwegian?" Cas asked as the group of officers walked slowly towards them, talking away amongst themselves.

"Not a word," Harriet replied.

"Well, this could be interesting... Stand to attention. You're not wearing your service hat, so I'll salute for you. Here we go, and call him Your Grace." He looked around at the gathered pilots who were already standing smartly, then looked forward and saluted the King, who elegantly returned the salute.

"Flight Lieutenants Cornwall and Salisbury, Pilot Officer Delacourt, may I introduce His Royal Highness, the King of Norway, and our Commander in Chief," Alastair said

"Cornwall is a strange name for a Norwegian," the King said as he stepped forward and looked Harriet in the eyes sternly, then glanced at the 'Norway' country flash on her shoulder.

"Yes, Your Grace," she replied politely. He then said something to her in Norwegian, which had Harriet raising an eyebrow. "I'm sorry, Your Grace. My heritage is through my grandfather's family, and my Norwegian is a little rusty." His eyes narrowed, while the gathered officers and the King's entourage looked instantly nervous as one, then a smile broke onto his stern face, and he patted her on the shoulder.

"I'm sorry, Flight Lieutenant, I'm teasing you," he laughed. "Of course I know your heritage, the ambassador has told me all about you."

"That's OK, Sir," Harriet replied as politely as possible, while her insides spun and she found herself wishing she was fifteen thousand feet higher and surrounded by 109s, preferring the fear of that to facing the King of Norway.

"I'm told that you're doing our country proud in this war, Miss Cornwall. I do have your name right, don't I? Harriet Cornwall?"

"Yes, Your Grace, you do. Harry to my friends." She smiled politely and instantly cursed herself for adding the 'Harry' part. Out of the corner of her eye, she could see Nicole rolling her eyes in despair.

"Group Captain Saltire tells me you're the leading ace under his command. Is that right, Group Captain?" he asked, turning to look at Alastair.

"Absolutely, Sir. In fact, as of this morning Flight Lieutenant Cornwall has also been acting as Squadron Commander. Under her stewardship, the squadron has destroyed ten enemy bombers confirmed and damaged many more."

"Very good, Harry. Very good!" The King beamed with pleasure. "Perhaps what this war needs is more Norwegian Spitfire pilots, Yes?"

"I'd take good pilots of every nationality, Your Grace," she replied politely. "In addition to the many talented and hardworking British pilots we have on the squadron, we have Poles, New Zealanders, South Africans, Indians, Americans, and of course French," she said as she gestured at Nicole, who the King smiled at politely before returning his stare to Harriet.

"I stand corrected," he said with a warm smile. "Though a few more Norwegians wouldn't hurt, I think?"

"Absolutely, Your Grace," Harriet replied with a smile, happily taking the way out of a difficult situation offered by an intelligent and kindly monarch, who'd just been openly corrected by a junior officer.

"Perhaps it's more female pilots we need, Your Grace?" the CinC added with the slightest chuckle. "After all, between them, Miss Cornwall and Miss Delacourt have destroyed more German aeroplanes than some entire squadrons in other areas."

"Perhaps you're right," the King agreed enthusiastically.

"No offence intended towards the gentlemen among us, of course," the CinC said to Cas.

"None taken, Sir. As a matter of fact, I couldn't agree with you more."

"Flight Lieutenant Salisbury was a notorious fighter ace himself in the last war," the CinC introduced Cas to the King.

"You're very kind, Sir," Cas replied before the King shook his hand firmly. "Though maybe a little overstated, my talents were distinctly average when compared to those whose company I'm honoured to share today." The King nodded and smiled enthusiastically.

"Though you didn't have female pilots in the last war, I don't think?" the King said mischievously.

"Much to our detriment, Your Grace."

"He's not so average that he wasn't able to shoot down three German bombers headed for a convoy this morning," Nicole said casually, "and damage a fighter, which I doubt will get as far as home." Cas sighed and frowned, uncomfortable at what had been said.

"Is this true, Cas?" the CinC asked as Harriet stood with her eyes wide open in surprise.

"Pure luck, Sir, I assure you.' Cas replied. "Miss Delacourt and I were on a training flight when we saw a raid sneaking up on a convoy at low level. It wasn't anything to write home about, not my part at least. We had the height, so I dropped in and broke them up a little, that's all. It's Miss Delacourt's actions that are truly worthy of mention. She hasn't been in combat since May, and has only had a couple of hours in the air since returning from her exile in France, yet she still knocked down a fighter that had got on my tail and flew rings around his friends, enough to scare them and send them packing."

"Still got it, I see?" the CinC said with a laugh. "Make sure they go on the
Squadron's tally for the day, Group Captain Saltire."

"Oh, I'll certainly do that," Alastair replied.

"I hope you don't mind our visiting today?" the King continued to address Harriet, having given Cas and Nicole a warm smile of congratulations. "The CinC finally bowed to my demands to meet my famous Norwegian pilot, the one I've been hearing so much about, and he agreed it would be proper for me to present you with the Distinguished Flying Cross you've been awarded."

"Not at all, Your Grace, it's an honour." Harriet fought the familiar blush she knew was heading to her cheeks.

"Very well. I hope you don't mind, but we invited a photographer along?" Harriet shook her head with a nervous smile. "Perhaps with the Spitfires in the background?" he asked the photographer, who quickly agreed and went about moving Harriet and the King into the perfect position. His aide handed the King the medal, and the photographer took a photo of him shaking Harriet's hand with the Spitfires lined neatly behind. "I'm not sure where I should pin it?" the King said quietly to Harriet. She looked down and realised she was still wearing her Mae West, which was covering her tunic. At that moment the phone rang.

Harriet turned to look, the cold sweat and hair on end returning immediately.

"Squadron scramble!" Clarke yelled as he rang the scramble bell. Harriet took off in a sprint towards her Spitfire, which was already rumbling into life. Lanky jumped from the cockpit as Harriet leapt in, and quickly followed after her to fasten the harness before jumping from the wing with a 'good luck.' Minutes later Harriet was climbing hard, with the squadron forming around her. She looked to her left to check on Nicole, who was quickly racing up from the ground.

"Hello, Goose Squadron, this is Silver. Make angels two zero and vector zero one zero; there's a large amount of trade heading up the Thames Estuary."

"Wilco, Silver." She looked around and checked her pilots were in place. "Close up, Goose two," she ordered Nicole, who immediately did as she was told before the squadron was wheeled onto the heading while still climbing hard. They hadn't even had lunch, and they were charging towards their fourth combat of the day.

"There they are," Pops called. "Two o'clock. Fighters stacked above them." Harriet looked at the hazy black mass of aeroplanes. It was another giant raid. How many aeroplanes did the Germans have? They just kept coming in bigger and bigger raids, no matter how many the RAF knocked down.

"Hurricanes below us," Grumpy called. "A squadron of them heading right at the bombers, nose on."

"OK, Goose Squadron. Let's try and keep the fighters off the Hurricanes, A Flight, go after those 110s right in front of us, B Flight go after the 109s below them. Keep in your pairs and fight together. Goose two stick to me like glue, we'll go in with A Flight. Tally ho!" Harriet pushed her throttle wide open, and the full squadron raced into action. The 110s saw the attack coming and tried to form into a defensive circle, their favourite formation for defending against Spitfires, but they were too late and too slow, and A Flight were soon among them. Harriet focused on the last 110 in line. "Goose two, he's all yours. Watch his rear gunner, and I'll watch your tail."

"Understood, Goose Leader," Nicole replied. She pulled ahead and chased onto the 110's tail, coming in from the starboard quarter, just out of the gunner's field of fire, and letting him have a stream of bullets which ripped the tail off and immediately sent the 110 spiralling downwards.

"Good shooting!" Harriet called. "Look out, Goose Squadron, more fighters coming down. Break, break, break!" The squadron scattered, winding in their pairs, most chasing a fighter, and soon the sky was full. A stream of tracer cut between Harriet and Nicole, startling Harriet and making Nicole flip and dive away while Harriet cut her throttle and pulled up, turning her Spitfire into a giant air brake and letting the pursuing pair of 109s dive underneath and follow Nicole down. Nicole was twisting and rolling to avoid the chasing tracer. "You can't out dive them!" Harriet shouted, "you've got to out turn them."

"I can't!" Nicole replied. "If I pull out now, he'll get me!"

"He'll get you if you don't! On my mark I want you to pull up and right, then turn tight."

"OK."

"Three, two, one, mark!" Nicole pulled up and right, and dragged the chasing 109 right across Harriet's sights as she held her thumb on the fire button, watching as her rounds riddled the 109 with holes. A split second later it burst into flames and dived away, forcing the second 109 to pull up and left to avoid the wreckage and leave Nicole's tail. Harriet banked left and gave the second 109 a burst into his wing. He pulled hard left to escape, and as if by design came nose to nose with Nicole's tight turning Spitfire. She fired and the 109 burst into flames before spinning down, then eased out of her turn and took her place on Harriet's wing.

"Where did everybody go?" Nicole asked. In the minutes they'd been fighting they'd lost over ten thousand feet, and the battle was long gone.

"It's over, let's head home," Harriet said

"Should we go back up and try to find the others?"

"No, we need to rearm and get ready for the next raid. Come on, and keep your eyes open for stray fighters." She led Nicole down low and back to the airfield, where they landed in perfect synchronisation and rolled back towards the dispersal and the waiting dignitaries. Harriet shut down, pulled off her helmet and unfastened her harness while wondering where Lanky was. She took a breath, then stood and was immediately blinded by the flash of a camera. Something that continued as she climbed out onto her wing.

"Did you get one?" the King asked excitedly.

"Yes..." Harriet wiped the sweat from her eyes. "Your Grace."

"Excellent!" he replied. He shook her by the hand as she stepped down from the wing. "Excellent! Well done, my girl! You're a hero to us all!" Harriet felt herself blushing. She didn't feel very heroic. The battle was a total blur and over in minutes. It took longer to get to the battle than it did to fight it.

"My friend, Nicole Delacourt…" she said as Nicole joined her. "She shot down two Messerschmitt 109s just now. As Mister Salisbury said before we left, today is her first combat since May this year, when she was shot down protecting the beaches at Dunkirk. She's the hero."

"Very well done," the King said as he shook Nicole's hand. "France must be as proud of you as I am, and if they're not, you're welcome in Norway any day!"

"You're very kind, Your Grace," Nicole said with a slight curtsy. The photographer did his thing, and then they walked back towards the

411

dispersal, where the CinC was talking with Cas and the pilots that had returned already.

"Three between them!" the King announced, making Harriet feel a little embarrassed in the process, while Nicole walked as elegantly as a princess, taking in the moment.

"We should probably leave them to it, Your Grace," The CinC said, noting the fatigue on Harriet's face. "I dare say it's been a busy day already, with more of the same to come. Besides, lunch is here, and we shouldn't get in the way of that." Harriet smiled gratefully, and the CinC gave her a wink.

"Yes. Yes, of course. Though before I leave, I think it only proper to formally invite Miss Cornwall, and her friend, of course, to dinner one evening. If you'd be so gracious as to accept?"

"I'd love to, thank you," Harriet replied. He shook her hand again, and Nicole's, and Cas', then wished all of the returned pilots good luck before leaving with his entourage.

"Well done," The CinC said as he stood in front of Harriet and Nicole. "You've just done more for equality than you can ever imagine, not to mention the war effort. Well done, indeed." He shook their hands, then moved on to Cas. "I see you're still disobeying orders and insisting on wearing those outdated Royal Flying Corps wings on your tunic?"

"Oh, these?" Cas said after briefly glancing down at the pilot's wings on his chest. "This is my old tunic, the other's at the cleaners."

"Of course… You're sure I can't tempt you back to the Priory, Cas? Substantive Group Captain rank, you'd do a fantastic job up there running things for me?"

"Thank you, Sir," Cas replied. "I'm truly honoured that you should think of me, but I think my place is here with the squadron, for now at least." The CinC smiled and saluted, then left with a grinning Alastair in tow.

"Well, there's a turn up for the books," Cas said as he watched the cars leave. "Not every day you get to meet royalty. Or correct them," he raised an eyebrow at Harriet.

"Well it needed to be said," Harriet replied. "Anyway, did everyone make it back?"

"The boy, Smythe, he hasn't come back yet."

"Everyone else?"

"A few bullet holes here and there, but nothing that can't be buffed out by the ground crews. Nothing to keep us out of the war at least. Why don't you both grab some lunch? I'll make a few phone calls and see if Smythe has turned up somewhere." Harriet and Nicole nodded and went over to the table. The pilots were excitable following their exploits, and all tucked into their corned beef sandwiches and tea. Harriet enjoyed listening to them and listening to how Nicole quickly joined in and became part of the squadron, picking up where she'd left off with those she'd known from France, and quickly getting to know the new pilots. She thought of Smythe for a moment. He was quiet, but pleasant enough, and hadn't been with the squadron long enough to learn the names of the pilots he was flying with. She quickly pushed the thought out of her mind before it took hold.

If she thought too much about everyone they'd lost she'd go mad. She was already painfully aware that the day was taking its toll. Four engagements, five pilots lost with their aeroplanes, three of those still unaccounted for, and it was only the early afternoon. The squadron was giving a good account of itself, but if things continued the same way, there'd only be Cas and the ground crew left by evening. The phone rang, and the chill returned.

"Stand down to thirty minutes notice," Clarke announced. A visible relief could be seen on the faces of the pilots.

"If I could have your attention for a moment," Cas said as he stood in the doorway. "I have some news you all may find pleasing, after a tough morning in harm's way."

"The CinC is sending us on a month's leave effective immediately?" Murph replied to the sniggers of the others.

"I do hope so; I'm missing my ship. Things are a bit dangerous around here," Ships added.

"Not quite," Cas replied. "Squadron Leader Singh has been found." The group fell silent "He's in a bad way after being shot down and forcing a wheel up landing on the beach out near Dungeness, but he's alive, talking, and being looked after in hospital." A cheer went up, and Harriet felt a wave of relief pass through her. The squadron was standing down in readiness and Singh was alive. "Anyway, the truck is leaving for the Messes in a couple of minutes. Get yourselves down there and get freshened up. Don't leave, though, we're on thirty minutes notice and need you back here as soon as possible if we get the call, if that's OK, Ma'am?" Harriet nodded and smiled, and the pilots pulled each other up before quickly making their exit.

"Not going with them?" Harriet asked Nicole.

"I think perhaps I'll stay here and enjoy the sun for a while," came the reply. "You should do the same. You're as pale as ever."

"Thanks..." Harriet rolled her eyes, she was happy to have Nicole back, and her teasing.

"No sunbathing for you!" Cas said to Harriet. "The less glamorous side of commanding a squadron awaits…"

"There's a side less glamorous than being soaked in sweat and filthy with smoke while being shot at by Germans?" she sighed.

414

"Well, that depends on how glamorous you think paperwork is, I suppose?"

"Suddenly sweat and smoke seems appealing."

"Doesn't it?" he smirked. "Come on. I'll show you the ropes. We can have it done by evening if we get cracking."

"Have fun…" Nicole smiled as she eased back in her chair.

Harriet took her seat behind Singh's desk as Cas guided her through the paperwork, and showed her the things that needed to be done while she was commanding the squadron. It was an endless and thankless task, though he couldn't help doing much of the work for her while she watched and signed. He also wrote the letters for the families of the missing and injured pilots, which Harriet had to steel herself to read through and sign. The duty orderly brought them tea at Cas' request when they were ready for a break from the routine of administration, which Harriet was secretly enjoying, despite rolling her eyes and sighing enough to suggest otherwise.

"It seems like a chore, I know," Cas said as he relaxed in his chair, "but it's all vitally important." Harriet pulled a face of disbelief in reply. "You don't agree?"

"I can think of better things for a pilot to do than sit around writing reports!"

"Reports which request the spares, ammunition, and fuel we need to keep the squadron flying. Reports which document the missing and injured. Reports which recommend medals for brave pilots. Reports which promote young ladies and assign them as pilots on a fighter squadron…" She blushed a little and sighed as his point hit home. "It's every bit as essential as the fighting. Without the administration, there wouldn't be a squadron to fly."

"Point made…"

415

"Good. You're going to need to know every aspect of managing a squadron if you're going to lead it effectively."

"Temporarily."

"You don't know that."

"I do, Alastair will have a replacement in no time."

"Think good Squadron Commanders grow on trees, do you?

"I'm quite sure there are lots better than me, with lots more experience."

"In that case, we'd better get on with the remaining reports, so they have something of a squadron to take over from you," he winked.

"Though while I am in charge of the squadron, there is one thing I'd like you to teach me…" she asked with a mischievous smile.

"Oh, what's that?'

"I need to write a recommendation, so I can show somebody I know that no good deed goes unpunished…"

"I think I can help you with that," he laughed. "Reports first, though." He tapped his pencil on the papers in front of her, and she let out an exaggerated sigh before picking up her pen and continuing with the arduous task. The rest of the afternoon was quiet, apart from a section needed to patrol the coast; which Harriet chose to do with Nicole instead of sending for others from the Mess. As the afternoon turned into evening, the call came through standing the squadron down. That was it. Harriet, Cas, and Nicole stood outside and looked at the row of Spitfires in the early evening glow; they were a magnificent sight. A drone filled the air unexpectedly, and they looked up to see a Tiger Moth circling and descending, before landing and bouncing its way over to the dispersal. A tall figure in pilot's clothing climbed from the front seat, shook the pilot's hand, then jumped down and watched as the Tiger Moth taxied away. The disembarked pilot waved, then turned and walked over, parachute under his arm.

"Some reception committee," Max said as he stood before them. "You'd think you'd seen a ghost looking at your faces."

"Wouldn't you just?" Cas said as a smile spread over his face. He stepped forward and shook Max's hand. "What the hell happened? I've been calling everywhere I could think of."

"A pair of 109s plugged me. I had to jump, then spent most of the day hanging from a tree not far from Canterbury. Hell, I thought I was going to die there until some kids found me and fetched their Mom. It took some fighting, but she got me down, eventually."

"Haven't you heard of a phone?" Harriet asked.

"Sure I have, but the local exchange had been taken out in a raid, so I made my way to the nearest airfield and hitched a ride. Anyway, enough about me. How's the squadron getting on?"

"Better, now you're back," Harriet replied.

"Oh, I doubt that," Max laughed.

"We lost Singh at the same time as you went down. He's in a bad way, but he'll live."

"God damn."

"Yeah. We lost another two as well, Wright and Smythe."

"Smythe? Do I know him?"

"No, he arrived this morning."

"Damn."

"And Dolph took a bullet in his arm before crash landing."

"That's quite a day. Who's been running the squadron?" Harriet just looked at him and smiled. "They couldn't have asked for better," he said warmly as he patted her on the shoulder.

"Well they're getting better," Harriet replied. "It's all yours!"

"Now just wait a minute..."

"Seniority," Harriet said.

"Well, damn."

"I'll let the Group Captain know you're home," Cas said. "I'll catch you in the Mess later, do you want a ride?"

"Sure."

"What about you, Nicole? Want a ride? Or are you going to take your life in your hands one last time today, on the back of that damned motorcycle?"

"I'll take my chances," Nicole said as she put her arm in Harriet's. "She hasn't killed me so far."

"Well done today, champ," Max said with a playful tap to her arm.

Chapter 17

Thanks...

The following day Max was confirmed as acting Squadron Leader, and Harriet stepped back down to her Flight Commander role, while Grumpy looked after B Flight. The morning weather was miserable. Grey and wet, with thick cloud almost down to the ground, making it impossible to do much other than sit in the dispersal hut and wait, while the rain battered against the window. Even when it finally started to clear in the evening, there was nothing to do other than listen to the radio and play cards. The Germans had obviously decided to take the day off when they saw the morning weather, and nobody could really blame them. Most of the pilots slept the day away, Harriet included, catching up on the sleep they needed after weeks of combat, and when the phone finally rang to stand them down, they were so exhausted that every one of them went straight back to the Mess and climbed into bed.

Harriet was woken the next morning by Daisy being her usual cheery self, though despite having a day off flying she felt more tired than ever before, and it took a lot of badgering from Daisy to get her ready and out of the door. The motorcycle ride with Nicole to the dispersal helped wake her a little, as did the oxygen from her Spitfire while she went through her morning checks, giving her clarity enough to prepare herself for the day ahead; which the cloud free sky suggested would be a busy one. Max put them through their briefing before they took to their deckchairs and rested, waiting for breakfast while expecting the phone to ring and send them skywards first. Breakfast came, as did sunrise, and still the phone hadn't rung. It made Harriet feel uneasy, and she wasn't the only one. Those that could sleep did, but every waking moment was spent checking the skies and wondering what the Germans were up to. The restless inaction continued into the late morning, allowing even the twitchiest of the pilots to slip into an uncomfortable sleep, which finally broken by the phone just after eleven. Everyone sat up in their chairs and watched.

"Squadron scramble!" The orderly shouted as he rang the bell, and the groggy pilots were dragged into life. Harriet felt her head spinning as she ran, trying to focus on what it was she was supposed to be doing, her brain still back in a deep sleep. She climbed in the cockpit, and for the first time realised how much her body ached. Lanky strapped her in, and she was off, following the others down the grass strip. Less than two minutes after the scramble call, they were lifting off the grass and climbing into the hazy blue sky.

"Silver, this is Goose Squadron" Max called, "Where are we heading?"

"Silver here. Make angels one five and vector London."

"Confirm vector London?" Max asked. It was the first time they'd ever received that instruction. Usually it was the coast, or Channel, even up around Biggin Hill sometimes, but never London.

"Confirmed, Goose Squadron. Make haste."

"Wilco, Silver. Goose Squadron, we're heading for London. Buckle up and watch out for bandits." He wheeled the squadron in a climbing turn, then set course for the dark haze of smoke climbing from the London docks. "What're we looking for, Silver?" he asked.

"Three hundred plus bandits in three waves," came the reply. As they closed on London, the sky filled with small black clouds of flak all along the Thames, right into the heart of the city. "Head north west, Goose Squadron, bandits should be below you."

"There they are," Max said. Harriet tipped her wing and looked down at the stream of bombers. They were lined in rows of five that stretched into the distance, with swarms of fighters all around. "Goose Squadron, follow me. We're gonna turn and dive, and take them head on. See if we can't break this little party up." He banked, and the squadron followed as he lined them into the best position to attack, right on the nose. As they closed, the air filled with tracer and long white streams of smoke

420

stretching out from both lines of aeroplanes, and Harriet's mind wandered back to Dunkirk.

"Stay on my wing, Red Two!" she instructed Nicole, as she looked over.

"Look forward and pay attention," Nicole replied. Harriet did just that, and her windscreen filled with the greenhouse nose of the Heinkel bomber. She pushed her gun button and fired, and watched the incendiary bullets explode around the cockpit, as the armour piercing rounds riddled the pilot. The bomber banked left and down in a steep spiralling dive. Harriet flew into the gap it had left and fired at the next, then felt the thud of bullets hitting the back of her armoured seat as she passed the front wave and made herself a nice target for their gunners, one of whom managed to get more hits on her, this time on the engine, making it run rough and smoke a little. She flipped and pulled on the stick, diving, then rolling and pulling up and firing a burst into the next bomber in the stream. "Fighters!" Nicole called, as 109s appeared under the bomber stream. "There's one behind me, no two, now three, we need to turn!"

"OK, go for it, I'll try and catch one of them!" Harriet replied. Nicole pulled hard left into a tight turn, and two of the fighters went with her. Harriet counted to three, then turned hard herself and got in a quick shot at the second 109 chasing Nicole in her ever tightening circle. The third 109 had another shot at Harriet, then exploded and spiralled away as another Spitfire came through and gave it a long squirt. By the time Harriet had corrected herself, Nicole had out turned the 109 chasing her and was now on its tail, blasting away and knocking chunks off it. Harriet chased the fighter she'd already damaged and fired again, hitting home and doing enough to watch him turn tail, dive, and run for home. The sky was a mess of aeroplanes, and crisscrossed with black and white smoke as bombers and fighters fought high above London. Harriet lined her sights on a bomber and gave it a squirt of bullets to the engine. It stuttered and coughed smoke, then started a shallow dive. Harriet followed, then swung out wide before turning back in and getting shots on its nose and making it sparkle all around the cockpit. The bomber kept diving and turning, and rolling violently to escape her guns, then after another burst to the engine it started streaming white smoke; she'd hit the coolant, and there was no way it was getting all the way home. As she pulled away to leave the bomber to its fate, she noticed another far below her, flying hard and fast just above the London rooftops. She instinctively pulled her Spitfire around and gave chase. The temperature gauge had started to climb as her engine shuddered more and more in the chase. The cockpit was getting unbearably hot, making her look around nervously as flames started licking from the bottom of the engine and lapping against the wing root. She throttled back a little and pulled the cockpit hood back to let out some of the heat, then put her focus back on the bomber and closed in. The rear gunner fired wildly, then quickly found his mark and rattled her wing with bullets, making her twist and turn to avoid his fire while trying to get into position for an accurate shot. Just as she was about to fire, the bomber did the unexpected and dropped down, then flew along the street while the gunners started firing into the people below. Harriet dropped in behind and below him, slipping snugly and dangerously between the buildings where she fired into the rear gunner, silencing him, then pulled back a little. For the briefest of moments, the surroundings passed by in slow motion. She was in Piccadilly in the heart of London, and flying below the roofs of the towering buildings. In the most surreal moment of her life, the doorman from Fortnum & Mason waved his top hat at her, ever so formally as she passed. She snapped out of her amazement and fired, hitting the bomber again and again, but still he carried on, until he lifted over Green Park and aimed at Buckingham Palace. The flames were starting to lick up the side of her cockpit, and the temperature needle was climbing again; she didn't have long. She took aim and pushed the fire button. Nothing happened. Was she out of ammunition already? There was no time to think, or to be logical, so she opened the throttle full and watched as her propeller cut through the bomber's tail, slicing and shredding it, and sending debris flying into the air. The Spitfire shook violently, and the engine revs quickly elevated. She pulled up and right while shutting off the throttle and switches, and watched as the bomber shot upwards and stood on what remained of its tail, then hit a tree and toppled nose first into the ground. It exploded and sent a fireball rolling across The Mall and into St James' Park, filling the air with smoke, debris, and rough turbulence which stretched up and threw Harriet's Spitfire around as she fought to take control. Her propeller was shattered to stubs, and her engine shut down, she was flying a dead stick and dropping fast. She fought to keep the wings level as the tarmac of The Mall came up to meet her. There was no response from the undercarriage, so she pulled back on the stick and kept the Spitfire flat, then hit the ground at speed. On impact, she flew forward and hit her cheek on the gunsight, before being thrown back into her armoured seat as sparks sprayed the cockpit. The fuselage scraped noisily, until finally she came to a standstill with Buckingham Palace almost within reach. Harriet tried to lift herself up from her seat but was pinned, and she immediately started to panic as she caught the smell of petrol in the cockpit, and remembered the Hurricane at Dunkirk. She pulled at the harness release and let out a groan of frustration as the taste of blood filled her mouth while her eyes kept going out of focus. She couldn't move; she was trapped. She slumped back in her seat and put her hands to her eyes for a moment while she tried to focus and calm her breathing. When she looked out again, soldiers were running towards her.

"Alright, chum, we'll get you out," one of them said as he looked down into the cockpit. He fiddled with the harness release but couldn't move it, so took a bayonet from one of his friends and cut through the harnesses, while another soldier joined in and did the same from the other side. Finally, the tension which was holding Harriet tight in place was released, and hands reached in and pulled her out. She took off her helmet as she was lifted, and let it fall into the cockpit before she was carried over to the grass and laid down. "Bloody hell, it's her!" the soldier said as he knelt and looked down at her.

"Who?" one of the sea of faces staring down at her asked.

"That Norwegian fighter ace from the newspaper, the girl. Look at her shoulder flashes." He pointed down while Harriet stared up, still trying to focus and catch her breath.

"Does she speak English then?" another asked.

423

"Of course she bloody does. Don't any of you clowns actually read the papers?"

"I just look at the pictures," another replied. "She's the one, though, and she's even prettier in real life."

"Ere, love, are you alright?" the soldier who'd carried her from the Spitfire asked.

"I thi..." she tried to reply, but quickly choked on the blood in her mouth. She coughed and rolled onto her side, lifting onto her elbow so she could cough the blood onto the ground. A water canteen was pushed to her lips and she sipped, rinsed, spat, and then took a drink as she sat up. "Yes." she finally replied. "Yes, I think so. Thank you for helping me out of my Spitfire. I was a bit stuck."

"Alright, you men. Make way." The soldiers parted as their Captain stepped forward.

"It's that lady fighter ace, Sir," the soldier said.

"I see that. Give her some air, come on, move back. Better get a cordon around that Spitfire before anyone gets too close, it could go up any minute; and get a section over to that Jerry bomber." The soldiers moved away and left Harriet to look up at the officer kneeling in front of her. "That was quite some move," he said quietly. Harriet just nodded and pulled off her gloves, then raised her hand to the side of her face. It was throbbing from the hairline to just below her jaw. She flinched as she felt her face. "Careful," the Captain said as he lowered her hand. "It looks like you've taken a beating." He pulled out a white handkerchief and handed it to her. She wiped around the soreness and looked at the handkerchief, which was now smeared black and red. She suddenly felt faint and dizzy, and laid back on the grass.

"My gosh, it's her," a very well spoken woman said. Harriet didn't have the strength to open her eyes for another discussion on whether she could speak English, so instead just focused on breathing deep and trying not to throw up all over herself. "Is she OK?"

"Ma'am..." the Captain said in a surprised tone. "She's feeling a bit off, not surprising really. It looks like she rattled her head all over the inside of her plane when it came down."

"Aeroplane," Harriet muttered.

"What's that?" the woman asked. "What did you say? I missed it, I'm afraid."

"It's an aeroplane," Harriet repeated as she opened her eyes. "A plane is used for shaving doors..." Her vision came into focus as she raised herself onto her elbows and looked at the young woman kneeling before her in an army uniform. She stared for a moment. Her eyes were piercing blue, and her dark hair looked so soft.

"I like her!" the young woman said with the slightest giggle. "You men, bring that stretcher. Captain, have this young pilot brought into the house, the surgeon is visiting so he can look at her right away." Boots crunched on the ground as the soldiers ran.

"It's OK..." Harriet protested. "Just help me up, and I'll be able to walk."

"Don't be ridiculous," the young woman replied firmly. "You've just fallen out of the sky and knocked your head. You can be carried like anyone sensible."

"Please..." Harriet asked. "I'll feel better if I walk it off."

"Argumentative, too. OK, come on fighter pilot, let's get you upright. Take her other hand Captain, would you?"

"Ma'am." Between them, they helped Harriet to her feet. Once up and steady, she dusted herself down and walked over to her Spitfire.

425

"Where on earth do you think you're going?" the young woman demanded.

"Just to look..." Harriet said as the soldiers moved away to keep the gathering crowd at a safe distance. "It was brand new a couple of days ago." she sighed as she surveyed the smoking and creaking wreck laid out before them.

"Well, we'd better hope they don't take it out of your pay."

"That would be awkward."

"Why's that?"

"I haven't finished paying off the last one I crashed. Or the one before that, for that matter." Harriet said with a smile.

"I'll have to see if I can put in a good word for you with the Air Ministry. Maybe they can let you off with this one, you stopped that German from bombing my house, after all."

"Over here, Miss," a man shouted from behind. The pair turned, and their photo was taken.

"OK, that's enough!" a Police Constable shouted as he walked over. The young woman waved her arm casually to ward off the Constable from getting too excited.

"Any words for the Gazette, Ma'am?"

"Yes," came the woman's reply. "Tell the country that the Germans won't dare invade as long as our brave RAF pilots still have Spitfires to fly."

"Alright, you've got your story. Off you go." The Constable guided the reporter away, and Harriet started to walk, but felt instantly unsteady

426

and dropped to one knee, as the young woman grabbed her arm and helped stop her falling completely.

"Maybe that stretcher isn't a bad idea after all," Harriet said as she fought to stay conscious. The young woman waved the soldiers over, and Harriet was put on the stretcher and carried quickly, but carefully, along The Mall. "Where are we going?" Harriet asked in confusion, as she lifted her head and looked at the gates she was passing through. She worried for a moment that she'd died and been collected by an angel, who was now taking her through the pearly gates. Cas had always joked about 'getting his harp' one day, and maybe she was getting hers.

"My house!" the young woman said with a smile. Harriet laid back and closed her eyes. Even thinking was hurting, and she didn't really care if it was the end, as long as it released her from the headache.

Five days later, when the Royal Surgeon and the young princess were satisfied that Harriet was suitably rested, she was escorted to a waiting Rolls Royce which was instructed to return her to her home airfield. She'd lived like a princess for the best part of a week, sleeping in a luxurious four poster bed and living in a room almost as big as the entire dispersal hut, with footmen bringing food and a lady in waiting making sure her every need was catered for. Before leaving she was invited to take breakfast with the family, which was the most unbelievable experience Harriet could ever have imagined, something that once again made her think of her father's rants about doing something with her life. The family were charming and engaging, and asked all about Harriet's life and career, and all were warmly grateful for Harriet's intervention in stopping the bomber from hitting the palace. The King and the young princess had watched the battle from the balcony, and they were convinced that they'd have been killed had the bomber got through to them. After breakfast, they walked in the garden, again as a family, and Harriet was given a very old and very expensive looking sword as a token of appreciation for her bravery. The young princess hugged her before she climbed into the car, which took Harriet by surprise and made her blush terribly. She couldn't help but look over her shoulder and wave as the car pulled out of the palace courtyard. Finally, she turned and looked around her at the crates stacked in the car, all from Fortnum & Mason. A card said simply 'With our gratitude to the pilots of 508 Squadron. G.R.' Harriet smiled and sat back in the leather seat and watched London go by, still as busy and thriving as ever, despite the bomb damage and rubble, and the many wrecked buildings.

"Would you look at this," Max said as the royal Rolls Royce pulled into the dispersal. He opened the door smartly and saluted as Harriet stepped out. "Your highness..."

"Oh, stop it!" Harriet said with a blush. The rest of the pilots crowded around her, Nicole at the front. "I thought I told you to stay on my wing!" Harriet said firmly.

"You should learn to fly better, then maybe I would," Nicole replied with her trademark Gallic shrug.

"Your loss," Harriet said with a smile, before hugging her friend. "There are some things in the car for everyone." She handed Max the card. "Squadron Leader," she said with a smile as she saw the braid on his cuff.

"The old man put in a good word, and it was made official yesterday. You missed the party," Max replied.

"It's well deserved."

"Well, I'm told I'm no match for the person who had the job before me, but I'll do for now." The dispersal phone rang, and Harriet instantly felt her stomach clench and the hair on her neck stand on end.

"A Flight, scramble!" the orderly shouted, then rang the bell. Harriet started to run, but felt a hand grab her shoulder and hold her back.

"Hey, Tiger, where's the fire?" Max asked.

"He said A Flight..." she said with eyes wide open, her hand pointing in the direction of the Spitfires, which were already roaring into life.

"Yeah, and they'll go look after it. Y'know, we've done OK while you've been living it up at the palace," he smiled warmly as Harriet frowned.

"But..."

"But nothing, let's go talk." She nodded, and followed him towards the dispersal hut and stepped inside. Simon was waiting in Max's office, and he greeted her fondly.

"It's good to see you back," Simon said. "How are you feeling?"

"I don't know..." Harriet replied as Max closed the door behind her, then sat on the corner of his desk. "What's going on, Max?" she asked.

"You're going home," he said with a smile. "Well, back to your aunt's place up in Yorkshire, anyway."

"What? I don't understand?"

"This," Simon said as he pulled a letter from his tunic pocket.

"What is it?"

"A letter from the Royal Surgeon."

"So what? I'm fine."

"Yes you are, mostly. Though it's the Royal Surgeon's professional medical opinion that as you've broken your cheekbone, you shouldn't be allowed to fly until it's healed."

"What?! That's ridiculous! There's nothing wrong with me!"

"Harry..." Max said calmly. "It's just a few weeks rest, that's all. As soon as you're OK, we can get back to it. I talked with the old man, and he agreed I could keep you on strength until you're ready, and Hugo can look after things with A Flight until you're back to it. OK?"

"No! No, it's not OK!" She threw the ceremonial sword the King had given her on Max's desk in frustration. "I don't want to go home; I want to fly!"

"Harry..." Simon interrupted. "It's for your own good. The pressure in your head, and against your cheekbone, will be incredible above ten thousand feet; and it'll be agony. You won't be able to concentrate, let alone be awake enough to fight."

"Then I'll fly below ten thousand feet. Send me up under the squadron. I'll fly reconnaissance, whatever, just let me fly!"

"I'm afraid I can't," Simon said with regret.

"You can overrule him," she said to Max. "Let me fly."

"Simon's a good doctor, Harry, and I'd be a fool to go against his advice, especially when that advice is backed up by the King's own surgeon. I'm afraid the order stands, you're grounded until recovered."

"I can't believe I'm hearing this!" She shook with fury. "Where's Cas?"

"What's that got to do anything?"

"Where is he?"

"He's up at headquarters, why?"

"Get him back here."

"Look, Harry, I know you're upset..."

"Get him back here right now! He'll know how to fix this; he'll find a way for me to fly. Get him!" She picked up the phone and handed it to Max. "Get Cas here!" She was shaking and using every last ounce of self control to stop the tears flowing down her cheek. Max took the phone and put it down.

"Harry, we've been friends for a long time, and we've been through a lot together. Let's not lock horns on this. I get that you're upset, I really do. Maybe sleep it over, and we can talk things through tomorrow when you're rested."

"I'm not bloody tired!" she yelled. "And I'm not bloody broken! I had a crash, and I'm over it, now get me back up in the bloody air!"

"I'm sorry..." Max said.

"For God's sake!" Harriet cursed, then grabbed her sword and turned for the door.

"Harry, where are you going?"

"To join the bloody Navy! Maybe they don't have their heads so far up their air force blue arses that they can see I'm supposed to be flying!" She grabbed the handle and ripped the door open and went to march out, but stopped in her tracks as Group Captain Saltire filled the doorway, with Cas standing behind.

"Harry, old man, I heard you were back!" Alastair said in his usual jovial tones. "Shall we?" He stepped into Max's office, and Cas followed, closing the door behind him. "How are you feeling?" He looked at the scars and bruises down the side of Harriet's face. "Better, I hope?"

"Yes..." Harriet replied. "As I was trying to explain to these two."

"Oh?" Alastair replied.

431

"Yes! Sir, they want to ground me just because I had a crash. I'm absolutely fine. You believe me. Don't you?"

"Of course I believe you, old man. Unfortunately, orders are orders, and there's not a great deal any of us can do," he shrugged. She rolled her eyes, then looked pleadingly at Cas. He held his finger to his mouth and shook his head. "Sometimes we can bend the rules, other rules we can break altogether," Alastair continued. "They are, after all, for the obedience of fools and guidance of wise men. However, when the King himself calls me and tells me that you're going on rest leave, who am I to argue?"

"The King?" Harriet sighed.

"Yes, he called just this morning. We had a lovely chat, he's quite a fan of yours, and he's recommended you personally for the DSO! Which means it's practically pinned on, of course. Well done for that, by the way."

"I don't want a DSO, whatever that is, I just want to fly!"

"Distinguished Service Order. Another gong for your collection," Alastair gave her a wink. "Anyway, when the King says jump, the likes of you and I simply ask, 'how high?' We wear his crown on our hats, so I suppose it's only right we do as he says."

"But Sir..." Harriet pleaded.

"However, no matter how much we discuss it, it's all a moot point. You're going home, and the squadron is going with you."

"Sir?" Max asked in surprise. Cas smiled, unable to contain himself anymore.

"Group is in agreement that your squadron has punched well above its weight for the duration of the battle, and you're being sent north to regroup."

432

"Where?"

"Leconfield. It's in East Yorkshire somewhere. It's pretty quiet up that way at the moment, compared to here at least; so you'll have time to get all those new faces in your Squadron trained and get your aeroplanes up to strength, so when you come back down here you can continue to fight the good fight. As soon as A Flight are back from their sortie, you can start packing."

"Yes, Sir!" Max said with a smile of relief.

"You're stood down as of now. Well done, Max, your scrappers have the highest rate of confirmed victories in the air, not to mention probables and damaged, and you've all earned a rest." He shook Max's hand. "I'll buy them all a drink in the Mess tonight by way of thanks for the hard work."

"It'll be appreciated, Sir, though I know I speak for us all when I say we'll feel like we're letting the team down by leaving now."

"Nonsense! You'll be back before you know it, and you'll be thankful for the rest." He smiled and turned to Harriet. "Your family are from up that way, aren't they? East Yorkshire, I mean?"

"My aunt lives there," Harriet replied.

"Good. So it all works out then. You all get to go north together. You can have some leave, and I'm sure a few of your friends are due some, too, then you can all get back to some hard training. Assuming Simon says that cheek's OK."

"Yes, Sir," Harriet said. She was blushing a little, already feeling guilty for her rant at Max.

"That's it agreed, then. Oh, and that naughty little recommendation you put in when you were commanding the squadron has been approved, with my pleasure. We haven't said anything, as I'm quite sure you'd like to break the news yourself." Harriet frowned as she thought back to what she'd done, then smiled as she remembered. "When you're back from the wilds of the north you can tell me what it's like living in the palace." He gave her a wink, then breezed out of the door. "I'll let you tell your chaps, Max." Cas closed the door quietly behind him.

"Sorry..." Harriet said to Max, and then Simon.

"Don't be silly," Simon said. "I've had pilots throw full bedpans at me before now when I've said they couldn't fly. I was expecting worse." He gave her a warm smile, then turned to Max. "If that's all?" Max nodded, and Simon left.

"Anything else we need to talk about?" Max asked Harriet. She shook her head.

"It's good to have you back, Harry," he said affectionately. "And if I'm honest, I'd have been as angry as you at being stood down, though you scared me for a minute when you picked up that sword."

"I think Nicole is owed some leave," Cas said. "She was with the resistance the whole time she was in France."

"I think you're right. How about we send them both north ahead of us to get started on their leave?"

"Sounds like a good idea. I'll have the rail warrants ready."

"There you go. Party in the Mess tonight, and you can take the train home in the morning. Why don't you head to the Mess now and share the news? I'm pretty sure Cas won't mind giving you a ride." Harriet nodded, then followed Cas from the room and around to his Aston, picking up her bag from the palace and a box of Fortnum treats. She climbed in and relaxed into the soft leather seat.

"It's good to have you back," Cas said as he started the engine.

434

"Thank you... I was so frustrated while being laid up, I missed..." She stopped herself and smiled at him as they started the short journey to the Mess. He gave her a wink and a knowing smile.

"Nicole was beside herself when you went down. I haven't seen her like that..."

"I know the feeling." Harriet forced a smile as she looked out of the car.

"Dunkirk?"

"Yes... It was hard thinking she was dead."

"Yes, it was. It doesn't get any easier, you know. You reach a point where you stop making friends with the new pilots, because you know they likely won't last the week and you'll have another name to remember and face to miss. You create this ridiculous rule that if you don't acknowledge them, they don't exist, so it won't really matter all that much when they don't come back."

"Does it work?

"Of course not... If it did, I wouldn't have been such a bloody mess when
I thought we'd lost you over there."

"Oh... You didn't say..." Harriet blushed as he talked.

"Not a word to a soul, or I'll have you posted to the desert. Regardless of how many kings you count as personal friends these days."

"I promise." She smiled warmly. "I'm happy we don't stop making friends."

"Me too. Though it makes it more difficult knowing that you're in combat four or five times per day, and that they could get you at any time."

"It works both ways, you know?"

"Oh?"

"Yes. It wasn't long ago that you and Nicole were taking on what turned out to be slightly more than the small raid you claimed. Fifteen bombers and over thirty fighters, Alastair said. It makes me worry knowing they could have got you."

"I didn't realise… Though we were quite safe, I've been around long enough to know what I can get away with." He smiled as he pulled up outside the Mess.

"The German that Nicole shot down had got on your tail."

"He got lucky."

"Or maybe you're getting old and slow."

"Harsh!"

"Maybe stay on the ground where you're safe."

"It's easy to go off people, you know!" he said with a frown as she climbed from the car.

"Will you be coming north with us?"

"I expect so. Why?"

"Good. Thanks for the ride. I'll see you in the Mess later."

"You will…" He revved his engine and pulled away with a wave, leaving her standing on the pavement and smiling at herself, and him. Part amused at her teasing, and part with warmth at their conversation about caring, and knowing that the fears of loss were mutual. She turned and headed into the Mess, where Daisy was waiting for her by the door of her room, as usual. Not once had she been absent when Harriet arrived, it was uncanny.

"Welcome back, Ma'am," Daisy said with a big smile. She'd been as worried as everyone else when she'd heard that Harriet had gone down, and continued to be worried even when she knew she was safe and in good hands.

"Wilson, we need to talk," Harriet said firmly as she walked into her room, showing no hint of emotion on her face.

"Ma'am?" Daisy asked nervously as she followed Harriet.

"Close the door! Come on, I don't have all day!" Harriet barked, making Daisy frowned as she obediently closed the door.

"Harry, are you OK?"

"I believe it's convention for a Corporal to refer to an officer as Ma'am; and stand to attention when I address you!"

"Ma'am… Please… What did I do?" Daisy was now trembling, and the first tears were starting to form in her eyes.

"What did you do?" Harriet asked firmly, as she stood in front of Daisy with her hands on her hips. "You've done plenty of things, Wilson, and I had hoped for at least some change while I'd been gone, but no! It looks like it falls on me to deal with you, when even now you dare stand before me incorrectly dressed!"

"Ma'am?" Daisy repeated. She looked herself over, desperately searching for some part of her always impeccable uniform that was out of place. "I don't understand?"

"I may still be relatively new to the RAF, Wilson, but even I know that Sergeants wear three stripes on their uniform!"

"Ma'am... Wait. What?"

"Congratulations on your promotion, Sergeant Wilson," Harriet finally let out a smile as she pulled out the Sergeant's stripes that Alastair had handed her after giving her the news. "I couldn't think of anyone more deserving."

"Ma'am..."

"Harry."

"I'm so confused."

"I'm sorry, I couldn't help myself." Harriet laughed. "I was channelling my very best impression of Section Officer Finn."

"Channelling? It was like old Sharkey was back in the bloody room! You nearly gave me a bloody heart attack!" Daisy smiled and took the Sergeant's stripes. "You're serious, though. I'm being promoted?"

"Absolutely. Groupie just confirmed it."

"I can't believe it!" Daisy giggled. "Me, a Sergeant? Who'd have thought?"

"There's only one thing..."

"What's that?"

"The promotion comes with a posting."

"A posting? What?" Daisy frowned.

"Yes. It's part of the package, I'm afraid. We can get away with having a Corporal as a batman, but not a Sergeant."

"Well, I'm not sure I want the promotion in that case." She looked at the stripes for a moment, then handed them back to Harriet.

"Don't be ridiculous."

"I'm not. My place is here, with you, and if being promoted means that I'm being sent away, I don't want it. I didn't want to be a Sergeant anyway, I'm more than happy as a Corporal."

"Well you can stay here if you want, but I'm going north, to Yorkshire."

"Where?"

"Oh come on, Daisy. I know that you're a Londoner, but you've heard of Yorkshire!"

"Oi, cheeky! Of course I know where Yorkshire is, I just meant which station, and why?"

"Leconfield, in the east. The Squadron is being stood down and withdrawn north to rest refit."

"Thank God!"

"Yes, quite. Anyway, you can stay here, or you can pack your bags and come with us."

"I don't understand. I thought you said I was being posted?"

"You are. Though before you go to the Central Flying School for assessment to see if you'll make it as a pilot, Max has agreed that Cas is going to give you a few weeks of flying lessons to increase your chances."

"Don't tease me."

"Still want me to take those stripes back?" Harriet smirked.

439

"I'm going to be a pilot?" Daisy gasped.

"No, you're going to be assessed to see whether you can be trained to be a pilot. It's not easy! You need to be mentally very sharp, good at engineering and maths, and have an aptitude for aviation. If you get through the assessment, you're looking at over a year of training. If you get through all that, then you'll be a pilot."

"But how?" Tears were now flowing freely down Daisy's cheeks.

"Well, it takes a recommendation from the Station and Group Commanders for a Sergeant to be considered for pilot training, which only happens when the Station Commander receives a recommendation from the Sergeant's Squadron Commander." Daisy's eyes narrowed as she worked out what had happened, then she threw herself at Harriet and hugged her tight.

"I don't know how to thank you."

"You don't need to. This is my thanks for all you've done to help me. You've been so kind to me since the day we met in that tent back in France.
Do you remember? You told me you'd never even been in an aeroplane, as much as you'd like to, and never expected you would." Daisy nodded and smiled as she stepped back and stared at the Sergeant's stripes.

"I don't have the words."

"You don't need them. Not yet, anyway. We're having a bit of a bash in the Mess tonight to celebrate the squadron moving north, and Groupie has given the OK to invite you in for a drink to celebrate your promotion." Daisy nodded and smiled while her tears were in freefall. "So you'd better go and get those stripes sewn on, so you're not incorrectly dressed. We can sneak a Sergeant into the Mess, but not a Corporal."

"Thank you," Daisy whispered as she stepped forward and kissed Harriet softly on the cheek, making her blush fiercely. Harriet nodded in reply, and Daisy left the room in silence.

Two weeks later and Harriet and Nicole were back with the squadron in the north, having spent their leave with Aunt Mary, and both were feeling refreshed. Harriet had accepted once she was home just how exhausted she was. She slept lots, almost all of the time, and she came to terms with the fear she'd been living with every day since being back with the squadron. Being killed was part of the job, she accepted it as a reality every time she flew, but this didn't make it any easier each time somebody didn't come back. She'd known that sooner or later it was going to be her turn, but as long as it didn't involve burning to death or drowning, she made her peace with it. The more difficult fear to handle was that of letting people down. Letting her squadron down. Letting her friends down. It's why she kept going and kept pushing so hard, and why she fell apart when she was told she'd been grounded. Secretly, she was relieved to be escaping the exhaustion of continually facing certain death. When the full squadron was stood down, it was a relief because she could rest without letting anyone down. Harriet still wasn't allowed to fly for a couple of weeks when she returned to the squadron, but being in the north with only the occasional scramble to investigate a report of a stray German made it easier to keep herself busy with ground duties. Mostly she helped Cas by picking up some of his duties, while he spent as much time as he could getting Daisy flying; something which resulted in him rating her skill and competence very highly before she departed for her assessment and training. Finally, Simon allowed her to fly. Despite it being weeks since her crash there was still some discomfort in her cheek when at altitude, but she didn't mention it to anyone. She wasn't prepared to spend the rest of the war on the ground. Then, as the cold, wet, and miserable glory of autumn took hold, the squadron was finally moved back south to their home on the coast, where they spent their time either weathered in or on patrol. The days of constant scrambles were gone, to be replaced by hours of nothing except cold and rain. It was miserable.

In only a few days, the routine became almost unbearable. The Germans had moved most of their bombing raids to night time, so they could hide in the darkness and avoid the fighters, having sustained debilitating losses in August and September. Occasionally a fighter sweep would come in high and fast, drop a scattering of light bombs, then leave before the defending fighters stood a chance of getting anywhere close to them. In a departure from the daily extremes of violence and loss that defined the summer, in the squadron's first week back in Hell's Corner they had lost only one pilot to engine failure, and claimed only two victories. Rumours did the rounds, as they always did, but this time they were saying that Hitler had postponed the invasion, and that nothing much would be happening until the next spring at the earliest. Harriet found herself pacing for much of the days, full of nervous energy that she didn't know how to release.

Day after day of grey and miserable weather kept the squadron on the ground, and the boredom and tension threatened to push Harriet over the edge. It was almost a relief when the dispersal phone rang as a spot of blue sky peeked from behind a wall of thick black clouds. Her heart raced, but gone were the cold sweats and hair standing on end, she just wanted something to do, and her wish was granted. Two Spitfires were needed to go and look around Dover, where a reconnaissance bomber had been spotted nosing around in and out of the cloud base. Harriet volunteered and decided to take Nicole with her, and the pair quickly got their Spitfires into the air and headed south. Harriet felt the familiar excitement as she led Nicole through the patchy clouds, scanning the horizon for the bomber, and turning her head to look for phantom fighters; which were known to hang around in the clouds, just waiting to spring their trap when an unwitting fighter pilot dived in to attack a lone bomber. No fighters came down on them, but they did find the reconnaissance bomber skimming the base of the cloud, almost invisible as a shadow against the greyness.

"See him?" Harriet asked.

"I do..." Nicole replied. "But I don't see anyone else. Do you think he's alone?"

"I think so… Hello, Silver, this is Goose one. We have your target, and we're going to engage."

"Understood, Goose one. Happy hunting."

"Do you want him?" Harriet asked Nicole.

"Of course."

"OK, try and get his right engine and knock out his coolant and the hydraulic gear for his wheels. That way if he escapes into the clouds, he's still unlikely to get home."

"I'm not a child. I know where to hit an 88."

"Then you'd better get on with it. I'll watch your tail, just in case the fighters turn up."

"That's very kind of you."

"I know. Now get on with it, before he gets bored of waiting for you to shoot him down and buggers off." Harriet dropped behind Nicole and pulled up a little high, then watched as she stalked her prey until she was in the perfect spot. Silver grey streaks of smoke shot out from Nicole's wings, and small golden explosions danced all over the starboard engine, immediately making it stream white smoke. Another burst and the wing started to burn, and the bomber dipped its wing slightly and started a wide arcing turn, losing height and heading inland, away from the choppy and grey looking Channel. Nicole pulled in a little closer, ready to finish him off, when his wheels suddenly dropped. "Hold your fire!" Harriet shouted. "He's surrendering, I think..." She'd remembered one of Cas' lectures on the rules of combat, and how an enemy aeroplane dropping its wheels in combat was considered a sign of surrender, and how shooting down a surrendering pilot is considered very uncivilised. "Stay on him and cover me."

443

"What? What are you talking about?" Nicole demanded.

"Just do as I say!" Harriet pulled ahead and came level with the German bomber. She looked at the pilot, who pointed down to the ground before giving her a thumbs up, nodding eagerly as he did, and looking very nervous. She nodded and waved at him to follow her, and he nodded enthusiastically in reply while giving her another thumbs up. Harriet opened her throttle a little and pulled in front of the bomber, feeling her heart pound as she hoped her hunch, and Cas' teaching, were right; otherwise, she'd just put herself in harm's way and deserved to be shot down.

"What the hell are you doing?" Nicole yelled.

"Leading him down," Harriet replied. "Stay behind him, and shoot him down if he does anything stupid."

"What about you? Can I shoot you down for doing something stupid?"

"You can try, but you're not that good. Silver, this is Goose one. Tell the army to hold their fire, and have an armed guard meet us at dispersal."

"Will do, Goose one. What are you up to?"

"We're bringing a present home," Harriet replied with a smile. She guided the damaged bomber to the airfield and watched it land, where a reception committee of soldiers met it; then she and Nicole followed it in and went over to meet the pilots. The German crew were very grateful for her benevolence. Nicole's attack had severely damaged their reconnaissance bomber, and they knew they wouldn't get any further than halfway across the Channel, which was cold and very turbulent, not the place they fancied ending their days. They were taken off by the military police while The Spy pawed excitedly over the reconnaissance bomber, leaving the girls with Cas, who'd met them when they came down.

444

"I suppose it's sometimes important to know when not to shoot in a battle," he said.

"It didn't seem right to flatten them for no reason, not when they were already finished," Harriet replied.

"I couldn't agree more. We're killers in this business, not murderers, and what you've just done today reassures us all that we're still on the right side of that line. Well done."

"I still deserve to claim it as a kill," Nicole said.

"I'm sure we can manage that," Cas said with a laugh. "Anyway, come on the both of you, the new AOC's CoS arrived while you were gone. He's been talking to some of the pilots, and wanted to see you when you landed."

"The what?" Nicole asked.

"CoS. Chief of Staff."

"Can you English not just give people normal names?" She rolled her eyes in disappointment.

"What on earth does he want?" Harriet asked, smirking at Nicole's response.

"I've no idea, he hasn't been here that long," Cas shrugged as he led them to the dispersal hut, where they put their jackets and Mae Wests on their chairs before following Cas into Max's office. The Chief of Staff, an Air Commodore who'd only recently taken office under the newly appointed AOC, was taking a seat behind Max's desk and making himself comfortable, while Alastair stood at his side.

"Harry, Nicole, there you are," Alastair said warmly. "Come in, the AOC's new CoS would like to talk to you both." Cas closed the door behind them, as they stood smartly to attention in front of the Air Commodore.

"I've heard a lot about you both," the CoS said bluntly. "And I think you've earned the right for me to be straight with you." He looked at them both in turn. "The truth is, ladies, that while your contribution to your squadron's performance over the summer is undeniable, I just don't see a place for female pilots on a fighter squadron," he said tersely. "The fact is that women are highly emotional, irrational at times, and in my experience they're dangerous to morale and unit cohesion. An opinion shared by many; I should add." Harriet's stomach knotted as though the scramble bell had just been rung. "So, with that in mind, the decision has been made to have you posted out immediately."

"Sir..." Harriet replied. Her head was spinning faster than it ever did in any aerial combat.

"Yes?" he asked, clearly irritated at being interrupted.

"I don't understand. How can we be bad for morale just because we're female?"

"It is what it is, Cornwall," he replied. "And the decision's been made. You'll retain your commissions in the Volunteer Reserve, though I don't mind admitting that's against my better judgement; but you're suspended from flying duties effectively immediately, pending your posting to Balloon Command, in Edinburgh."

"You're firing us for being girls?" Nicole asked.

"Frankly, yes," the CoS replied. "It's well known that the male instinct is to protect females. In a battle, your presence will bring a significant and unavoidable risk to your male colleagues. They'll instinctively try and protect you instead of focusing on their mission and fighting the Germans; not to mention the challenges that are introduced by the female propensity to be emotionally driven at times. Ultimately, your presence will get good pilots killed, it's that simple; and while the

446

previous AOC was prepared to take that risk, and practically encourage it at times, it's not something we're content to entertain. We have a war to fight, and I need effective squadrons." Harriet was stunned, and she wasn't the only one, Alastair, Max, and Cas were equally aghast. She felt a tear on her cheek, and there was absolutely nothing she could do to stop it.

"This is what your country is?" Nicole asked angrily, filling the silence with a thunderous storm. "You let us fight, and you give us medals, and badges, and then you tell us we're no longer welcome?"

"Be careful, Miss Delacourt. You're still an officer in the Royal Air Force, for now, and I can still have you charged and arrested."

"Charge me? With what? Being a woman? You and your kind make me sick!"

"Miss Delacourt! I'm warning you!" the CoS blustered, as he stood and slammed his hands on the desk. Nicole opened her breast pocket and pulled out the Distinguished Flying Cross she'd been awarded for her flying in France, then threw it on the desk. "How dare you!" he hissed.

"Stick it up your arse, and stick your war up your arse," she replied angrily. "If I'd known what I was risking my life for, I'd have stayed home and joined up with the Germans!" she yelled with rage.

"Well?" he said as he looked at Harriet. "Going to prove my point and behave as irrationally as your friend?"

"No..." Harriet said calmly. "If she's upset, it's because she saw the Germans march across her country while she was helpless to stop them. She joined the RAF to fight back, which she did with the type of tenacity and bravery you can only imagine; and when she was shot down while trying to help the British Army, our army, escape the hell of Dunkirk, she joined the resistance and saved a stream of airmen, helping them back to England so they could fight on. I brought her here because our country needed pilots, we needed her; and she fought as bravely as any man, all

447

while her friends and family live and die under the boot of German occupation. If she's upset, it's because you've just thrown all of that in her face. Not because she's not good enough, not because she's incompetent, but because she's a woman; and for that, you should be ashamed." Harriet stepped forward and picked up Nicole's medal. "She was so proud of receiving this from the CinC himself that she carried it around in the pocket next to her heart; in every battle, every day. She earned it with her blood and sweat…" She paused for a moment and looked him in the eyes. "You can charge us, and kick us out of your squadrons, and you can throw us out of your air force, but you can't take this away from her, you sad and pathetic little man." Harriet shook her head in heartbreaking disappointment.

"Sir, if I may?" Cas spoke, finally breaking the incredibly awkward silence.

"What is it, Salisbury?"

"Well, Sir, with the greatest respect, I'm not sure what you've been told about female pilots, or by whom, but I can assure you that you've been woefully misadvised." The CoS scowled at him in reply. "In their short time with the service these young ladies have accounted for many enemy aircraft destroyed between them, more than most. In fact, I'd go as far as to say that these young ladies are, in my experience, two of the best pilots I've ever had the privilege to serve with, in this war or the last."

"That's your opinion," the CoS muttered.

"One shared by many," Cas replied.

"Be that as it may, the decision is made!" The CoS paused for a moment, then sat back in the chair and smiled warmly. "Look, Salisbury, I'm doing this for their own good, and the good of the squadron. It may seem a little rough now, especially after a tough battle; but it's over, we won the Battle of Britain! The days of desperation are behind us, and we're ready to go on the offensive. Times have changed, and we need the best pilots we've got to take the fight to the enemy. You've been in the service long enough to know how it is."

"I've been in the service long enough to know the difference between right and wrong, Sir, and what's being done here today couldn't be more wrong. That said, I won't be part of it," Cas declared calmly, as the CoS's face turned to thunder.

"Be very careful, Mister Salisbury, I have a great deal of respect for you and your reputation from the last war, but I won't stand for insubordination, not like this, not in front of other officers."

"Then let me relieve that particular predicament for you, Sir. In line with my rights as an officer, I hereby formally resign my commission."

"Excuse me?"

"You heard. I resign my commission, and as such you don't need to worry about insubordination when I call you a contemptuous, arrogant, and most ignorant officer."

"You can't just resign!"

"I can, and I have."

"We're at war! If you resign now, I'll have you arrested for cowardice in the face of the enemy!"

"I'm happy to face those charges in a court martial, Sir. I believe I have more than enough to say in my defence."

"This is preposterous! All this over two bloody silly little girls!"

"All this over two courageous young pilots who've earned the right to have somebody stand up for them, when they're faced with erroneous, unfounded, and frankly ridiculous charges."

449

"Fine!" the CoS said dismissively, trying his best to control his rage. "If you want to throw away your career, who am I to stop you? I accept your resignation. You can pack your bags and remove yourself from my station immediately. We can always find another adjutant."

"Then you'd better find yourself another squadron commander at the same time, Sir," Max said as he threw his hat on the desk.

"Don't be so bloody stupid, Maxwell!" the CoS blustered. "I've had enough of this nonsense already, without you getting involved!"

"I was involved the second you insulted my pilots, and kicked them off my squadron."

"It's not your squadron, Mister Maxwell! This squadron belongs to me!"

"Well, you'd better get busy commanding it, Sir. I resign my commission effective immediately."

"You, I can throw to the wolves, Maxwell."

"Be my guest. Last I checked I was an American citizen, and I'm sure as hell you're not allowed to force foreign nationals into your war. The isolationists back home would love to hear all about that, and we'll see how quickly your support across the Atlantic dries up."

"This is nothing short of mutiny!" the CoS said quietly as he stood. "I never thought I'd see the day... Rest assured, gentlemen, your actions will have far reaching repercussions. Ladies, your postings are retracted, forget what I said about Balloon Command." Harriet felt a glimmer of hope in her heart. "Your services are no longer required, and I hereby dismiss you from the RAF. Your commissions will be transferred to the ATA, and you can be somebody else's problem." He glared at the girls, then Cas and Max. "How's that for solidarity?" He picked up his hat and turned to Alastair. "Group Captain Saltire, I'll not stand for mutiny in one of my squadrons, I'm therefore standing this squadron down forthwith, pending a move out of the Group. You can see that these four former officers are escorted from the station immediately." He glared around the room angrily for a moment. "If we erase their names, we may be able to erase the shame; and if we're lucky we can put a stop to this nonsense about female pilots once and for all!"

Harriet felt herself choking. Her chest was tight, and she couldn't breathe. She'd given everything she had and more, and it was over, ending as quickly as it had started all those months ago. Not with the rattle of a German machine gun, or with the choking heat of a burning cockpit, as many of her friends had met their end. Not even with the mandatory retirement of advancing years. Just inglorious humiliation delivered in a dark office on a grey autumn morning; with the expectation of acceptance, and a duty to melt away into the shadows, quietly and meekly, as any obedient and subservient woman of the twentieth century should.

The End

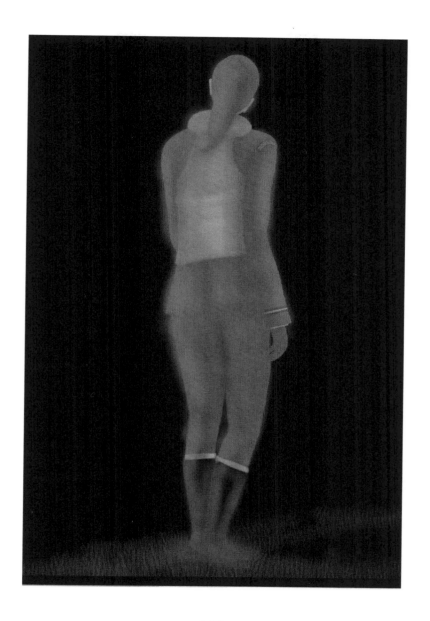

453

454

455

456

Printed in Poland
by Amazon Fulfillment
Poland Sp. z o.o., Wrocław

60475951R00270